HUGO WOOLLEY was born in West Sussex.
grown-up children. His mother was an eccentric
a farmer and lawyer. As a dyslexic, he went to a
because, in those days, dyslexia had hardly been i
was known as 'word-blindness' and dyslectics wer
below intelligence. How wrong they were!

Hugo is a caterer by training, ran various bars and restaurants in London before starting his own sandwich shops in the City of London in 1984 with his youngest brother, Oliver. In 1993 he opened designer sausage shops in Kent and Sussex, well before sausages became a fad. Unfortunately, after just over a year of trading, he was badly injured in a car accident and was airlifted to hospital, where Hugo remained for eight months being glued back together. Whilst in hospital he started writing, mainly about his experience during 'my crippledom' – as he called it.

In 2002, when Hugo was mainly recovered, he moved to Cornwall. After over twenty years running a boutique small hotel just outside of Padstow, with his wife, Hugo has retired and has moved to a quiet village on the edges of Bodmin Moor, where he continues writing.

BOOK TWO IN THE CHARLOTTE'S WAR TRILOGY

CHARLOTTE'S WAR

HUGO WOOLLEY

Published in 2023 by SilverWood Books

SilverWood Books Ltd
14 Small Street, Bristol, BS1 1DE, United Kingdom
www.silverwoodbooks.co.uk

ISBN 978-1-80042-259-9 (paperback)

British Library Cataloguing in Publication Data
A CIP catalogue record for this book is available from the British Library

Page design and typesetting by SilverWood Books

To my father

1

Le Palais, 19 Avenue Foch, Paris 1940

"You've what?" Theodora shouted angrily, when Charlotte bounced into their private sitting room in the servants' quarters at the top of the house. Juliet and Agatha were still in nightwear and nursing bowls of black coffee. They all looked at Charlotte, who was glowing with pleasure. Her long golden hair was in disarray, she wore no make-up, and she was still in her evening dress of shimmering light gold, with its bare back and plunging neckline.

"A night of bliss with my wonderful, handsome SS captain, Jost Krupp!" She looked at Theodora's stern face. "I'm sorry, Theodora, but—"

"You'd better come to my room." Theodora took Charlotte by the arm and led her down the corridor. She opened the door, virtually threw Charlotte through it, and shut the door quietly behind her. Charlotte was surprised Theodora didn't slam it – she must have been conscious of all the important sleeping guests below.

"What have you done?" Theodora looked at her with dread at what she was about to hear.

"Jost made wonderful love to me, nearly all night." Charlotte hugged herself. She did not meet Theodora's eyes, knowing she would be cross. "He was gentle. I said that I didn't want him on top of me, so we lay together, side by side, or me on top and—"

"Stop, stop, stop! You are only sixteen!" Theodora hissed. "He is twenty-six and was a fixture in my club in Berlin for years. He is not going to be a man that you will end up marrying."

"I know," Charlotte said, and slumped on the bed, all her happiness draining away as reality seeped in. "But it was so lovely. He is going to take me on a picnic in the summer … he wants to take me to Fontainebleau to look at the gardens. He thinks I need a cultural education."

"Stop! He thinks you are" – Theodora stuck up her thumb – "one, nineteen years old; two" – she waved her thumb and forefinger in Charlotte's face – "nothing but a lowly daughter of servants; and three, Swedish. If he ever hears or finds out you are, in fact, only just sixteen, the rich owner of this very mansion – this house we are virtually prisoners of – *and* you are, technically, British!" She lowered her voice. "And that your real name isn't Freya, but Charlotte … not only will he drop you like a stone, but also send you off to a camp as a prison whore." Charlotte looked at Theodora, shocked. Theodora was pacing the room. "It's too late now. You are just going to have to hope he doesn't find out before the war ends – and God knows when that will happen. Didn't that big oaf captain put you off men? He nearly raped you last night!" Theodora's Turkish accent was getting more pronounced.

"Well, he didn't, and he wouldn't have raped me in the drawing room. Jost stepped in just in time. I was about to—"

"Jost saved you as he wanted you for himself. I doubt he was jealous." Theodora continued to pace up and down. She was elegantly dressed in a long crimson silk dressing gown, her black hair tied up into a rough bun. "Give me a cigarette. I need a cigarette," she demanded.

"Theodora, I don't smoke." Charlotte was dejected. Theodora had become such a good friend, almost like a sister.

"Did he look angry to you?" Theodora asked.

"Who?"

"Jost! When he was pummelling that army captain with a fire iron who was about to molest you in the drawing room last night."

Charlotte thought for a while. "No, he was very calm, not really any emotion that I could see." She began to feel worried.

"I warned you about him, Freya." Theodora sat heavily on the bed beside Charlotte and draped an arm around her. "I don't know what to do. You are going to have to be very, very careful."

Charlotte licked her lips and said guiltily, "He is also taking me to the Drancy prison."

Theodora slumped forward, her shoulders drooped, her hands covering her face.

"Why on earth is he taking you there?"

"I asked him," Charlotte said with a slight wince of shame. She anticipated a tirade of questions. Theodora sighed and dropped back onto the bed. She seemed so miserable, it surprised Charlotte.

"I suppose you think you will see your servants there – your pretend Swedish parents," Theodora said.

"Well … yes." Charlotte was astonished. How did Theodora come to that conclusion?

"I will have to come too."

"What? I am going to be with Jost, have some time with him. Get out of this place with a man!" Charlotte shouted. Theodora took hold of her hand. Charlotte was confused. She had no idea what Theodora was trying to tell her. "He is not going to lock me up or anything," she said quietly. "He wants to introduce me to his colleagues. Show me off, possibly."

"Yes, but darling, it is not a place for you – or me, come to that. You will never see Bo and Christina. There are too many people."

"Have you been to this prison?"

"No, but I know about it. I must insist that I go with you. Just to keep you out of trouble. I will not get in the way … promise."

"Jost may not invite you."

"Yes, he will," Theodora said emphatically. "Remember, I have known him for many years, unlike you, darling!"

She was not sure why Theodora was being so protective. Charlotte was confident she could handle most situations now. Or was she being too naive? Getting close to SS Captain Jost Krupp would be a level of defence if something went wrong. He had a lot more influence than Theodora. But then Theodora was her good friend, her only friend in war-torn Paris. And, from what Theodora said, Jost would be little help to her if she was found to be Charlotte de Tournet, not Freya Jorgensen. He would clap her in irons!

*

As Theodora predicted, she was invited to go with Charlotte to the Drancy internment prison in northern Paris. They drove in Jost Krupp's car. It was a cold morning in early December, and the streets were empty, grey and cold. Hardly any people were around, no shops were open as far as Charlotte could see. They sat either side of Jost on the back seat of the car, swathed in coats and scarves. Two glamorous women, one dark, one fair. Theodora had a fur hat and matching hand muffler. Charlotte was not so ostentatiously dressed; she wore a thick cloak and a beret and a bright-green wool scarf.

Krupp was being charming and funny, distracting the women from the dull, dirty cityscape rolling past them.

"We took over the Drancy entirely yesterday, so it is an opportune time for you to come," Krupp said with pride.

"Who was running it until yesterday?" Charlotte asked.

"The French, or rather the French police, and us. They rounded up over four thousand Jews last summer for us."

Charlotte could not hide her disapproval and confusion. "Why, what had they done?" she asked.

"They were mostly stateless – no country. They will be there only temporarily. Here we are," Krupp said as a massive building loomed up before them. It was ugly. Modern. An immense concrete mass, dark grey and foreboding. Each of the four floors had terraces covered in coils of barbed wire all around the outside. At the main gate in the centre of the building were car-size concrete blocks and more endless tubes of barbed wire, looking like steel waves on a rolling sea.

A red-and-white striped pole barrier rose up as the Mercedes approached, opened by a Waffen SS soldier armed with a sub-machine gun. Charlotte had hardly ever seen an armed German combat soldier, only the more ceremonial guards back at Le Palais. It brought it home to her that they were in a war.

The black car sailed in under a plain archway. High wire double gates were opened, leading into a yard. The gates were shut behind the car by two more Waffen SS soldiers.

After walking up eight flights of concrete stairs, dully lit, accompanied by a sour, acidic smell, they came to a door.

"Freya, my dear, Madame Theodora, my office," Krupp announced with pride, throwing open a light-brown painted door with *Directeur* in cream lettering. The women walked into the office. They took little notice of any of the fine art on the wall, the antique French desk or the vast picture window. They both went over to the open fire to warm their hands, then fell into the sumptuous, ornate sofa, exhausted. The furniture was more suited to an art gallery than a prison.

"What was that quite extraordinary smell, Jost, darling?" Theodora asked. She had placed a handkerchief over her nose.

"It is the smell of a jail, madame. What did you expect, jasmine-scented stairwells?"

Charlotte noticed the wide window that took up an entire wall and strolled over to it. She took in the scene beyond, her mouth wide open in astonishment. The view was a concrete quadrangle, the size of half a football pitch. The building rose up on all three sides, four storeys of dark, oppressive windows. In the courtyard, hundreds of people purposelessly ambled around, trying to keep warm, in mostly tatty black clothes. Nearly all in the throng had a big yellow star on their breast pocket and a yellow armband.

A low discernible moaning could be heard through the glass. People's breath could be seen in the cold as they stamped their feet or flapped their arms to keep warm. In the centre of the concrete quadrangle was an enclosure portioned off by high wire fencing. It was full of women and children, mostly sitting or clustered around an oil barrel that was burning something that produced swirls of black smoke.

There was an enclosure just below where Charlotte stood. It was empty of people and only three sides were fenced. A tall concrete wall riddled with pockmarks stood behind six posts, which had shackles attached to them and were covered with dark blotches. She involuntarily shivered at the thought of what might happen at these posts.

Krupp came up to Charlotte. "Do you like our prison, Freya?"

"No, Jost, to be honest," she said, looking up at his handsome face with a half-hearted smile. "Why are they not all inside, in the warm?"

"They spend most of the day in the courtyard in the summer, and the mornings in the winter. They start plotting if they are cooped up." Jost put his arm around Charlotte's waist. "But isn't it a splendid prison! Modern, serviceable, easy to clean out. What is there not to like?"

"It is a bit grim," said Charlotte. "And who are all these people? They look like ordinary Parisians to me, but in scruffy clothes." On a little plinth in the centre of the window was a pair of powerful binoculars. She picked them up and scanned the crowds of people in the courtyard, hoping not to see Bo and Christina Jorgensen, her old governess and her chauffeur, amongst the miserable throng. But if she did see them, how was she going to get them out?

The Jorgensens disappeared when the Germans took over Nineteen Avenue Foch – or Le Palais as it was called now. Charlotte thought they may have been taken prisoner rather than repatriated back to Sweden as should have happened. Maybe they had been imprisoned because they lied about Charlotte being their daughter – she had adopted the name Freya and added three years to her age – and someone found out.

She was shocked when she saw these prisoners up close. She was surprised to see not only ragged men in the compounds but also equally shabby women and children.

"Jost, there are women and children. They must be freezing out there." She continued to scan the prisoners with the binoculars. "Who are all these people?" she asked again with a note of anger.

"Jews, my dear, all Jews."

"But what have they done?"

"Freya, darling." Theodora came over to the window. "Leave it. Don't get involved. They are all in here for one reason or another." She flashed a warning in her eyes when it was clear Krupp could not see.

Charlotte thought for a while.

"It is a lovely prison, Jost," she said quietly. "It looks very well organised … very busy."

"It is well organised," Krupp said, surveying his domain, "now *we* have taken it over. The French police did a terrible job of running it. Unsegregated prisoners, women and children mixed up with men. Old and young all together and Jews mixed with others."

"Where do you keep the 'others', Jost?"

"They were all shot last month or moved to other camps," Krupp said without feeling. Charlotte slowly lowered the binoculars and sat down.

The door to the office suddenly flew open and a short SS captain marched through the door, reading a document in a brown folder. He didn't see them until the last moment.

"Captain Brunner," Jost boomed, "may I introduce you to my friends?"

"Oh!" On seeing the women, the little man took off his cap and stuffed it under his arm, revealing a virtually bald head. He looked a little flustered. "How delightful. We have never had visitors before."

"*SS-Hauptsturmführer* Alois Brunner, may I present Madame Theodora and Mademoiselle Freya Jorgensen."

"Enchanted!" the neat little man said, and clicked his heels and bowed slightly to each lady. He had dark sunken eyes and a handsome face that looked sad even when he was smiling. "Well, you have come at a good time. We are about to execute some terrorists," Brunner said with glee. "And Krupp, we are executing that woman." He winked at Jost.

"Oh!" Charlotte said, unsure whether she wanted to witness an execution.

"We will watch up here, Captain," Jost said. "The ladies are not used to this kind of spectacle."

"I see," Brunner said, not concealing his disappointment. "It was a delight to meet you both, if briefly. I trust Krupp will bring you here another day, for dinner perhaps. We have a very good kitchen. Good day." With that he placed the file on the only desk in the room, picked up a list of names from a records tray, and left, cramming his cap back onto his head.

"Who was that strange little man?" Theodora asked.

"Captain Brunner – he runs the place," Jost said, looking at the file Brunner had left on the desk, "along with Captain Theodor Dannecker. He's the *Judenberater* – the Jewish advisor. And me, I liaise between Avenue Foch and here."

Charlotte sat quietly in the chair.

"Jost, darling, I don't think Freya, or I, want to see the execution."

"Well I do, I'm afraid," Jost said firmly. "It will not take long, you don't have to watch. I thought you would enjoy seeing Jews being executed."

Charlotte was astonished. She could not understand the man standing before her, the man she felt so much love for. He was completely different. He plainly thought Charlotte was a different kind of woman, one who would enjoy seeing people killed. Charlotte was so confused. Had she missed something in life? Was it common to execute people? Why were they imprisoning Jews? She quite liked Jews. She had Jewish friends. Nevertheless, it seemed that nobody else liked Jews, especially the Germans. She would ask Theodora when they returned to Le Palais.

The execution happened quickly. Two sets of thunderous volleys, then total silence. Neither Charlotte nor Theodora could bear to watch. Charlotte was shocked and disappointed to see Jost watching with glee, hands behind his back, rising onto the balls of his feet and then bouncing back on his heels each time there was a volley of shots, and proudly shouting "*Ausgezeichnet* – Excellent."

Charlotte stood and went over to Jost by the window overlooking the execution wall. She took his arm and quickly looked down at the scene. There was a pile of nine androgenous bodies being loaded onto a cart by two dishevelled people, possibly men, with yellow stars on their tatty black jackets. A rank of riflemen in SS uniforms were marching off, with Captain Brunner giving orders. Brunner went over to the bodies, unholstered his pistol, cocked it and fired at the top body, which twitched. He then fired at the head of another body. Blood and matter sprayed everywhere.

"What is that man doing?" Charlotte asked in alarm.

"Making sure they are dead," Krupp said. "You see, if we pile the bodies up, he need only use one bullet. We tried to execute them the same way, but the prisoners would never stay still! Nazi efficiency, see?"

Charlotte's eyes were drawn to the one remaining body that was tethered to a post. The woman's chest had two small bloody holes. She hung to one side, limp and thin, only a dirty floral cotton dress to shield her last few moments against the terrible cold. Her arms were bound by metal shackles, preventing her from sliding down. Her long dark greasy hair hung like seaweed over her face, a face that was pretty, even in death. Her feet were turned inward as though she had been punched in the stomach.

The two men with yellow stars went over to her, and with gentleness, as though she was sleeping, undid the shackles, carried her corpse to the cart and threw her on top of the other bodies. She must have weighed nothing – a collection of sinews being held together by her skin and her clothes. Brunner shot a bullet into her head.

"That" – Jost pointed proudly at the dead woman – "was Violette Szabo. She was a British spy. She killed a guard whilst trying to escape from a transport to Ravensbrück. She murdered many Germans before we caught her. A dangerous—" Jost stopped when he saw Charlotte looking pale. Tears were rolling down her cheeks.

"Jost, I would like to go back now," Charlotte said shakily. "This was probably a mistake. I had no idea you killed people, women as well."

"They are criminals, Freya. They were sentenced to be executed. Some of these people started a riot."

"Oh, I see," Charlotte said softly.

"I am sorry, Jost, darling. Freya obviously had some romantic idea about Drancy. I can take her back in a taxi."

"No lunch?" Jost was disappointed, but it was obvious that Charlotte was not enjoying herself.

"Thank you, Jost, but I don't really feel like eating."

"I will take you back," he said, putting his arms around her. "Come on. I will just tell Brunner." At the same moment Brunner appeared at the office door, a huge smile across his face. "Did you enjoy that?" he said with glee.

"I am sorry, Captain, but it is not really my—" Charlotte broke off when she saw specks of blood and bits of flesh all over Brunner's boots. She was worried that she was about to be sick on the captain but just managed to swallow hard, holding her hand tight over her mouth. She suddenly felt faint and fell into Krupp's arms.

2

Paris was being stripped of its art. The Germans wanted to transport everything that Paris, and France, was famous for, to Germany and Austria: fashion, food, art and society. Hitler demanded the best from the countries he occupied to ensure that Germany would profit and the empire would become powerful – even more powerful than America and Japan, culturally and in strength of arms.

Le Palais was becoming the centre for corporate entertainment. The *Allgemeine SS* – the political branch of the SS – had found that Paris offered many attractions to ease business negotiations through more smoothly. Le Palais operated as a place for men to relax and conduct business without the drabness of war, the worries of rationing and austerity, or even the anxiety of being killed. Only the most important men, and some women, got invited to Le Palais.

However, in Paris the Gaullist and Communist *Résistance* had tried to upset the smooth running of Le Palais. Consequently, the guarding of the houses in Avenue Foch was extremely strict, and the restrictions Theodora and Charlotte had to endure were most tiresome. The servants who worked at the house were exhaustively vetted. They were scrupulously searched when entering or leaving. Staff stayed in the house for three months and worked continuously, without a break. But they were very well paid.

Every now and then, usually early in the morning, searches were conducted throughout the servant's quarters, which included the rooms on the top floor. Except, that was, for Charlotte and Theodora's bedrooms. They were not touched, and Captain Wil would make sure they were never disturbed.

The standard of living for those who ran and visited the house was by far the best in Paris, possibly in France. Rationing did not seem to exist there – shortages were never mentioned. The near complete absence of rationing and austerity at Le Palais was the main reason Jost Krupp was there all through Christmas and up to the start of 1941. Krupp seemed a little cold for the first two meetings with Charlotte; he was well-mannered but distant. He was disappointed, Charlotte thought, in Freya's reaction to the executions.

"He may also be worried," Theodora said when Charlotte voiced her concerns about Krupp's coolness, "that you may have some empathy for the Jews."

"Well, I am not sure that I fully understand Jost's hatred of Jewish people."

"Freya, it is not just Jost, it is all Germans … well, most of them. They are trying to rid Europe of the Jewish race. I am not sure how. This feeling is something you must never even hint at to anybody! It is death to anyone who may have sympathies for the Jews."

Charlotte looked unhappily at Theodora. "OK, I will not say anything about the Jews. But will Jost forgive me, or just forget me, do you think?" she said woefully.

"Use your charms. Enchant him. He will come around. But don't mention Drancy if I were you. It's always better to have Jost as a friend than an enemy."

The first Christmas under Nazi occupation was a lavish affair. Germans loved Christmas and the food at Le Palais was bountiful. General von Ardle dressed as Odin, in a long green coat edged with brown fur, sporting a thick grey beard and a green, fur-edged bobble cap. He carried a sack full of gifts of soap and chocolate for the ladies, and tobacco and cigars for the men. Charlotte and Theodora were presented with wooden music boxes that looked like Tirolian cottages, which chimed Christmas carols "Stille Nacht" and "O Tannenbaum".

Roast goose, potato pancakes and red cabbage were lavishly served at Christmas Eve dinner. Captain Wil proudly produced a superior French red wine that was, he proclaimed, one of the best Bordeauxs. Charlotte was amused to see that virtually all the table chose to drink hot glühwein, much to Captain Wil's disappointment. Only she, Theodora and Captain Wil drank the delicious Château Palmer. Charlotte had a wonderful time, but Theodora gave her a maternal look of warning not to drink too much.

When a huge Christstollen was brought to the table with great ceremony, Charlotte tried to refuse a generous slice of the sweet-looking cake, saying she was too full. Her refusal was disregarded.

"What is this nectar?" Charlotte asked, holding up a small glass of amber liquid.

"It is Trockenbeerenauslese, a rare wine from Schloss Johannisberg," Captain Will said, sounding like a history teacher.

"My finest wine," the general slurred. "I have saved it for this, the best Christmas in Paris. You will enjoy it. Prost!"

"Prost!" the table echoed. Charlotte cast her eyes towards Jost. She was delighted to see him wink at her and raise his glass.

Charlotte got Krupp on his own that Christmas Eve evening and enchanted him. Drancy was never mentioned again. They slept together in Charlotte's old room – the room she had before she became Freya. They rose late Christmas morning, like newlyweds.

Charlotte knew Theodora was not at all happy about this relationship and hoped Krupp was not just using her.

When Jost woke up that Christmas morning, Charlotte stood before him, naked except for a large red and green ribbon bow clipped to her hair.

"I have not been able to buy you a Christmas present, Jost, so your present is ..." She performed a balletic gesture with her arms above her head, then sweeping down over her body.

He sighed deeply, his eyes wandering over her. Then he sat up in the bed, and slowly a smile appeared on his face. "Ah, how wonderful. I have always wanted a red and green ribbon."

"The present is me, you oaf!" Charlotte fell on the bed on top of him, where they remained for another hour.

*

The year 1941 was an uneventful one for Charlotte and Le Palais. She and Theodora went out when possible. Charlotte would insist on driving past a gallery in the Opéra district whenever they could, to see if it was open. She had seen a lovely portrait in the window the year before. The painting looked like her mother, who died when Charlotte was only a few days old. The portrait was still there, in the window behind the metal bars.

When summer came at last, it was a hot one again, but not peaceful for the residents of Paris. In August, there was a lot of unrest in the city, and dissention was mounting. But none of this seemed to filter into the established world of Le Palais. Charlotte sometimes heard of incidents that were going on in the war, or in Paris, but would be told there was nothing to worry about. If she asked about the war and what was happening, she would be told only the basic facts and that the Reich was winning. She rarely saw a newspaper and the guests did not ever want to talk about war.

Krupp visited once, sometimes twice a month. They would be together throughout the weekend, and Charlotte would entertain in the evenings while

Krupp would act as the host. Charlotte loved him more and more. He was kind, gentle, undemanding – he was so handsome. She pampered and stroked him, loving him.

She longed to go on holiday with Jost, to escape Le Palais, virtually her prison. But every time she suggested it, he said it was not safe, or that fighting was still going on. The only safe place was Le Palais. The picnic at Fontainebleau never happened, and she was beginning to feel extremely shut in.

Charlotte spent a lot of time in the garden that summer, anything to get out of the confines of the house. It was a large garden with an ugly high wire mesh fence and barbed wire coils along the top – like a prison camp, except it was to stop people getting in.

One day, Charlotte was sitting on an old sofa in what used to be a stable area, in the big shed at the bottom of the garden, a book on her lap, taking shelter from a summer shower. But she was distracted and couldn't concentrate on reading, wondering what had become of her. Was she safe? Was she doing the right thing with Jost Krupp? Should she try to escape to England? She had never been to England, and she didn't know anybody there, apart from her rather creepy uncle, Sir Jason Barrett. However, she wanted to remain "missing". Start her life over again. She loved being Freya Jorgensen and being four years older. But then, what would happen to her house, Le Palais, and the Barrett Collection – the wonderful, priceless art that had been taken by, she thought, SS Lieutenant-Colonel Franz-Joseph Deller? She might have to come back to life when the war was over.

Charlotte's thoughts drifted to her mother, Alice, the mother she could not remember as she had died when Charlotte was only a week old, according to her stepmother, Aunt Stella de Tournet. The tragic circumstances of her death had only recently been spoken about when Charlotte had asked her stepmother. She remembered the shock when she was told Alice died due to a terrible catastrophe – she had fallen off a cliff and crashed onto rocks during a storm. It was thought Charlotte's father was responsible. He had killed her. No one seemed to know who her father was, or else they would not tell her. She was grateful for Theodora, her only real friend and the only person in the world who knew her true identity.

Would it be so bad for her to return to being Charlotte again when peace came? It depended on whether the house would still be occupied by the SS after the war, she supposed. Would her uncle Jason take over the house? Would her other uncle and stepfather, Jean de Tournet … Charlotte suddenly felt a wave of nausea at the thought of her uncle Jean. She had blocked him out of her mind for the past year or so. The painful recollection of being raped by him when she was twelve, here in Le Palais, was the principal reason why she enjoyed being Freya. She tried to banish the memory of those traumatic nights when he visited her in her room when her Aunt Stella was away. She punched the sofa she was sitting on and a cloud of dust flew up and into her face. She coughed, and realised tears were dripping from her cheeks. She wiped them away, furious that this man had resurfaced in her mind.

She heard someone come into the shed, hoping it might be Jost looking for her. She stood up and looked over the low wooden stable wall, only to see Lieutenant-Colonel Franz-Joseph Deller standing in the middle of the floor, looking around with a huge smile.

"Hello, Colonel Deller. We haven't seen you for a while."

Deller was startled by the greeting and looked around in an erratic way. He seemed unsure he had actually heard anything. His eyes eventually rested on Charlotte, who was beaming at him over the low wall. He appeared stunned and surprised. His jacket and belt were undone.

"Are you all right, Colonel? Did I frighten you?" Charlotte asked.

"N-No … no, my dear." Maybe he was slightly drunk, she wasn't sure; it was only ten thirty in the morning. "I was just exploring," he said weakly, with a look of confusion. He stared at Charlotte for a long while, then scanned the big shed, and then his eyes settled back on Charlotte again. He frowned.

"It's Freya, Colonel."

"Is it?" He seemed unconvinced. He did up his jacket, clipped his black belt around his waist and attached the holster strap. He swept back his unruly curly hair and straightened his tie as he walked towards the stable. Charlotte felt uneasy. She opened her mouth to say something but he put up his hand to stop her.

"You are a goddess, the goddess Freya." Deller walked over to Charlotte, then hesitated, keeping his narrow, bloodshot eyes on her. He took her hands in his. "You are looking beautiful, mademoiselle."

"Thank you, Colonel. Are you all right? Do you want to sit down?"

"Thank you, no. Just to look at you, if you don't mind."

"Well … fine." Charlotte tried to keep a steady gaze on him as he stared at her. She felt a little embarrassed. "Tell me, Colonel, do you know what has happened to the Barrett Collection? The paintings that belong to Charlotte

Barrett?" It felt very strange using her real name. This shook Deller out of his stupor, a spell was broken. He scowled.

"What did you say?" He did not wait for a reply. "They are not Charlotte's paintings, they belong to Sir Jason Barrett. Anyway, what is it to you? These are not things for you to worry about, my dear. You are a painting, mademoiselle, a work of art. Statuesque and poised. Stunning!"

He peered into her eyes, which widened in fascination. She was trying to conceal a smile of amusement. She half-wondered what he had in mind. She was not alarmed or worried, just amused by his condition.

He stepped up to her and drew her close to him, wrapping his arms around her. He clasped his hand onto one of her buttocks and pulled their bodies together while plunging his lips onto hers, their teeth clashing lightly.

After a few moments they stopped kissing and his embrace relaxed. With his eyes still closed and a beatific smile on his face, he looked quite comical. Charlotte had to suppress a giggle. His breath had the sweet, acrid smell of alcohol.

Deller opened his eyes and gently lowered Charlotte onto the old sofa. Charlotte was about to protest, but as soon as she opened her mouth to speak, he went down on her lips and kissed her more fervently. He lay nearly on top of her. It was not like being assaulted by her uncle, or that awful Wehrmacht captain, Moltke. She was not as alarmed as she thought she should be, just uncomfortable, in every sense of the word – the sofa was lumpy, and Deller's hands were hurting her shoulders.

Was it because he was so drunk, and somewhat absurd, that she found him unthreatening? He was not a violent man, just a rather sad inebriate. She was allowing his behaviour only because she hoped he would be more forthcoming about where the collection was. He must know. But Charlotte was beginning to think she may have let the situation go too far.

As they kissed, Deller delicately drew up Charlotte's dress, his hand slowly moving between her legs to the tops of her stockings. His hands were cold and soft. He was gentle, like Jost, but she decided to put an end to it before he got too passionate. She pushed him away with both of her hands on his shoulders. His eyes were shut, as though in a dream.

"Colonel Deller," she said loudly, "will you stop this at once!"

Deller came to his senses, a look of alarm on his face.

"I am very sorry, fräulein!" He scrambled off her, stood up and brushed himself down. He held his forehead, staggering slightly with the speed of standing. He tried to pull down her skirt, which was up over her knees, but Charlotte smacked his hand away. "I am so very, very sorry. I got carried away. You are so much like someone I loved."

"I do not think that is an excuse, Colonel Deller." Charlotte could see he was contrite. He was standing before her, miserable, looking as though he was going to cry. She was surprised. He apologised once more, swept his hair back with both hands, and with a click of his heels and a short bow of his head, he left quickly, walking as though on the deck of a rolling ship.

Charlotte patted down her ruffled clothing and wiped her mouth. Her heart was beating fast. Deller was clearly a disturbed man but harmless. Who was this love of his life? And what was the comment about the pictures being her uncle Jason's collection? She desperately wanted to know more about that comment. How would Deller know Jason? The Barrett Collection was left to Charlotte's mother, when Charlotte's grandmother died, and everything that was left to her mother came to Charlotte when she was only ten. The bequest included the house, the contents of the library, and the collection of priceless works of art that mysteriously disappeared when the Germans took over the house. And Deller, in Charlotte's view, had something to do with the artworks vanishing.

Lieutenant-Colonel Deller hardly ever returned to Le Palais after that. If he did, he managed to avoid her. Charlotte thought he must be in love with her, or else hated the thought of Krupp being so close to her. Charlotte wanted to get to know the sober Deller a little more, so she could find out about the collection: if it was secure, and when it would be restored to the house. Her mother also left a lovely painting by Gustav Klimt, *The Girl on a Golden Pillow*. Charlotte had removed it from her mother's old room. The painting was now out of its frame and rolled up, locked in the trunk in her bedroom in the attic.

3

The summer of 1941 turned into winter, and in December, the whole of Le Palais was talking about Japan entering the war – and, more worryingly for Germany, the Americans. The house took on a different feel. Normally, Charlotte had no idea what was going on in the war, but plainly the Germans were concerned. There were often celebrations for a battle won, but Charlotte had no idea where these battles were. There were hardly any parties at Le Palais by the end of 1941, and the house became more of an elite hotel for high-ranking German officers and businessmen having meetings.

Charlotte's second Christmas at Le Palais was without Jost Krupp, as the winter of 1942 was the coldest winter in living memory. Le Palais had to be closed in February – the house became too cold. Supplies of coal could not get through the snow, and the ice was treacherous. It got down to minus eighteen degrees centigrade, and the only way Charlotte, Theodora and the other two girls, Juliet and Agatha, could keep warm was to huddle around the log fire in their attic sitting room. Captain Wil and General von Ardle, who ran Le Palais, stayed mainly in the study around the fire. The guards had fires in barrels around the outside, and a stove in the servant's parlour managed to keep the servants warm when they were not working. The kitchen was the warmest room in the house, with gas cookers and grills nearly permanently on. Detlev, the butler, and his wife stayed away from the house, presumably not able to get transport back from wherever they were after January.

Electricity was cut off and only came on intermittently. But it was cosy, huddled around the fire, candles providing light to read. Theodora, Agatha and Juliet would share anecdotes of their life in Germany, whilst Charlotte kept quiet and listened.

The wood for the fires was running low by the end of February. All the coal had gone. The large garden shed was chopped up and used for fuel. The smell of the wood as it burned was terrible. Some of the trees in the avenue were chopped down for fuel, but it took a long time to get the wood to burn; the trunks were not only frozen into ice, but the green sap, when the trunk melted, would hiss and spit and put the fire out.

Food was getting short. The household had to survive on vats of watery soup and no meat or fish. One day, Captain Wil – who spent most of his time scrounging food and fuel around Paris and Le Havre – returned after being away for a week, with a huge case of tinned German sausages. Le Palais had no guests. There were only thirteen people huddling from the cold in the large house: two guards, two kitchen and two cleaning staff, Captain Wil, General von Ardle, SS Sergeant Hildegard Ritter and the four women – Theodora, Charlotte, Juliet and Agatha. They all had their own "sausage party". It felt like a celebration somehow.

On 26 February 1942, a two-day ice storm brought most of Northern France and Paris to a complete halt. The electricity was still cut off.

To stave off boredom, Agatha showed Theodora and Juliet how to knit, and they produced lots of clothes to wear to keep out the cold. They had a huge supply of wool of all colours that Captain Wil managed to find somewhere. Charlotte was told it was as a result of a raid on a haberdasher that belonged to Jewish people, so she would not take any part in the knitting classes.

She hated this oppression of Jews and had no idea why all the Germans – including Juliet and Agatha – had this discrimination against the Jewish community. Theodora tried to explain it to Charlotte, but she still found it barbaric and was annoyed that her friend was not concerned one way or the other about Jewish people. This was the only serious flaw in their friendship. After what she had seen at Drancy prison, and the thought that at least another four thousand people were still in there, in this cold, filled Charlotte with dread for their lives. She truly hoped Bo and Christina were safely back in Sweden.

Charlotte read books from the library. She was not sure if they were valuable, but there were some wonderful old books there, first editions, in both French and English. The English books had at one time, in 1940, been removed and stacked up in a corner of the library in boxes, but nothing was done about them. Charlotte, dressed in layer upon layer of warm, newly knitted clothing, started putting them back on the shelves. Some she would read, the English books she would read in private. At one stage Captain Wil took some of the books to burn on the study fire, but the general would not allow it, to Charlotte's huge relief.

The bodies of the head butler, Detlev, and his wife Bertha, were discovered on the fourth of March, when a slight thaw started. They were only a few metres from Nineteen Avenue Foch. They must have died, presumably, whilst walking to Le Palais on the first morning of the ice storm. There was a rumour they were killed by the Resistance, but no marks could be found on them.

*

In early April 1942, the weather at last became springlike. Easter Sunday was on the fifth of April and Le Palais was once again becoming the centre of the social whirl for German businessmen and the SS. The evenings were full of chatter and life. Everything had almost gone back to usual.

Charlotte had not seen Jost Krupp for over five months. He had promised he would be with her for Easter. Theodora hoped he had given up Charlotte and moved on to another woman, or women. By Good Friday, Krupp had not turned up and Theodora could see Charlotte was getting very worried.

"What if he is dead?" she asked Theodora late in the evening of Good Friday.

"He's not dead, Freya," Theodora assured her disdainfully. "He is not in the 'getting killed' bit of the war. He is safely in an office somewhere – probably in Berlin, or running a prison camp."

"Remember his Iron Cross. He was certainly in the thick of it there."

"I know," Theodora said. Theodora had never believed that Jost's Iron Cross was actually awarded for great derring-do, but she could never tell Charlotte. She would confront Krupp one day and find out how he managed it.

Easter came and went, with no sign of Jost Krupp. As spring took hold, Theodora could see Charlotte was getting fed up with the war, the entertaining, the men demanding her attention as though she was a piece of equipment to be switched on, to do as she was told, at their command. She had changed a little, growing disdainful of the men that visited Le Palais.

"They are arrogant, rude and some are just very odd. The businessmen think I am some kind of waitress," Charlotte confided to Theodora. "Major Kieffer, for instance: I know he is head of the Gestapo and the SD in Paris, and very dangerous, but can he not lighten up a bit? He's so dull!"

The women were feeling stifled and as the days got longer and hotter, they were getting restless, unable to leave the confines of the house and grounds. Theodora tried to help Charlotte as best she could, but Charlotte was young and intelligent and needed more to stimulate her mind. Charlotte read most of the time during the day, in the library – when it was not being used as a theatre – or in the garden.

One particularly balmy spring day, Charlotte was in the garden reading a tome about the French Revolution when Theodora came running from the drawing room. "Freya, we are all going to a matinée at the opera."

"To see what?" Charlotte asked, not looking up from her book.

"I can't remember – but we are going to an opening of a gallery afterwards, and as far as I can gather ..." Theodora smiled knowingly.

Charlotte sprung up. "Is it *the* gallery in Rue Ste Anne? The gallery where I saw my mother's portrait in the window?" Her excitement waned. "Is Captain Wil or the general coming?"

"No." Theodora looked around to make sure they could not be overheard. "Just us girls."

"You mean Juliet and Agatha as well?"

"No. They are staying to entertain Major Kieffer and two of his Gestapo friends."

"This is excellent news. How did you hear about it? Who organised the tickets?"

"Not really sure. The general asked if we would like to go to the opera and the art exhibition. Apparently, Colonel Deller suggested you and I go and meet the proprietor of the gallery – a baron, would you believe!" she whispered.

"But this is wonderful, Theodora. What have you got there?" Charlotte had spotted the letter in Theodora's hand.

"Oh, I forgot! You have a letter from Jost."

"Give it to me, give it to me!" She nearly snatched it out of Theodora's hand and carelessly tore it open.

"*My dear Freya,*" Charlotte read. The letter heading stated he was writing from Reich Headquarters in Bordeaux.

"I am sorry not to have been with you for a while, my darling. I have been serving with the general staff and have had little time to come and see you. I cannot tell you too much in this letter, but I have been transferred out of Paris, to take over a region of France. This has meant a promotion. I am proud to say I am now an SS-Sturmbannführer – a major – one of the youngest in the SS. I am very honoured.

"I hope to see you in the summer.

"I will see you very soon, my queen.

"Jost"

"Short and sweet," Charlotte said, a little despondently. "So brief, and typically about himself, not a thought about me. I'm disappointed that he is being posted away from Paris. Does this mean I will see even less of him?" She looked up from her letter to find she was talking to herself.

*

They went in the general's car. The opera was an unmemorable Wagner and went on forever. Charlotte was dying for it to end so that she could go to the gallery. She was anxious that it would be the gallery where she had seen her mother's portrait hanging in the window. What if it was not? There couldn't be many art galleries in Rue Ste Anne.

The last time Charlotte and Theodora had been allowed out of Le Palais was over a year and a half before. She recalled crossing the road for a closer look in the gallery window, only to realise she was looking at a portrait of her mother, Alice Barrett. The only reason she knew it to be her mother was that it looked the spitting image of the photograph of her mother hidden in her bedroom back at Le Palais.

The opera finished, and the curtain came down. Germans, businessmen, SS and army uniforms, some with their spouses – and some plainly not with their wives – made up the vast proportion of the audience. As they left, Charlotte and Theodora were stopped along with everyone else as an important person was ushered out of the door. There were murmurs of it being General Carl-Heinrich von Stülpnagel, the new military commander of France.

Charlotte was delighted to see it was *the* gallery when they arrived. It was called the Galerie Bayser. The window that had displayed her mother's portrait now had an abstract painting of vividly coloured triangular shapes, in the centre of which a herd of deer appeared to be camouflaged in a forest of colourful triangular trees.

They drove through an arch into a courtyard busy with other cars dropping people off. In front of the main doorway, immensely long Nazi red flags were draped from the guttering all the way down either side of the entrance. The flags were a jarring sight against the buttery sandstone walls.

With a click of his heels, the young driver who drove the general's car whisked open the back doors for the ladies to get out.

The gallery was busy with more German army officers, high-powered German businessmen, and ladies of every age. There were plenty of men there that Charlotte and Theodora recognised, and many of them came over to reacquaint themselves with the Le Palais celebrities.

A man in a long black leather coat hovered nearby.

"Bloody Gestapo!" Theodora hissed. "Won't leave us alone."

A well-built, blond and handsome SS captain came up to Charlotte and Theodora. He clicked his heels with a sharp bow of the head. He was a relatively regular visitor to Le Palais and was delighted to see the women at the gallery.

"Madame Theodora, Fräulein Freya, how lovely to see you here. Welcome to our gallery. Glass of champagne?"

"How delicious!" Charlotte said.

"Captain Fuhrman, we are astonished by this. Is this why we have not seen you for a while?" admonished Theodora.

"I am just the high command representative. Baron Olivier Ferdinand Saumures is *le directeur.*"

The captain was in his late thirties, with smiling steel-blue eyes. He was a shy man who obviously had trouble talking to women. Charlotte thought he had a thing for Theodora. Ulrich Fuhrman was not like all the other confident, self-assured SS officers, and he clearly knew Theodora quite well – an old lover perhaps? Charlotte smiled inwardly. And now here he was, in this gallery. She looked at the young SS captain in a new light. She seldom took any notice of him at Le Palais; he was not as assertive or interesting, but he was nearly as handsome as Jost Krupp.

The first painting on display once through the main entrance was a striking life-size portrait of a *Hitler Jugend* – Hitler Youth. A boy of no more than twelve: blond – of course – good-looking, pleased to be wearing his shirt of burnt sienna bedecked with Nazi badges, powerful and proud. The "Youth" looked at his viewers intently, challenging them to become a member of the Hitler Youth, like him. There were also modern, colourful paintings, and portraits of Hitler in various masterly poses.

The gallery was substantial. The walls were covered in jingoistic art and images of the German Reich. Gallery rooms lined the square, with more large canvases of German battleships at sea and German soldiers fighting in trenches. Charlotte ambled around whilst Theodora talked to Captain Fuhrman. At each doorway into the different gallery rooms stood an attendant. Each attendant smiled and bowed. One winked at Charlotte as she went through. He must be a Frenchman or Italian, she thought. You would never get a German to be so presumptuous towards a lady!

She wandered into an end room beyond a half-drawn curtain, which she calculated to be the room nearest to the window at the front of the gallery. This room had visibly not been finished and there was nobody around, not even an attendant. A single bare light bulb on a standard lamp was lit. The window onto the street was blocked in with white board; the painting of the deer in the forest of triangles was hung on the other side. Charlotte recognised this as the room opposite the café, where she first saw the portrait of her mother hanging in the window. The portrait no longer being displayed.

Stacked on the floor like books were a few unhung pictures, and at the front of one row was the portrait she had been looking for. She held it at arm's length by its simple black frame to have a better look. It was surprisingly heavy.

Behind the painting of her mother was another interesting portrait, possibly by the same artist: a portrait of a young man in summer clothes, sitting on a deckchair. It was the spitting image of a younger version of someone she knew, but she could not put a name to him. Who could it be? And why was it with the portrait of her mother?

4

Admiral Wilhelm Canaris, the head of *Abwehr* – the German military intelligence service – arrived at the convent in a taxi driven by Ferdi. The arrangement was that Canaris, with no staff, would be picked up by a taxi in front of the Hôtel Majestic, the German headquarters in Paris. A pleasant-looking middle-aged man, short in stature, with close-set eyes and grey hair, he exuded calm, intelligence and wisdom. He was not in naval uniform but a grey suit, heavy overcoat and a black homburg hat, a little cluster of feathers on the left-hand side.

"I am sorry about the venue being so cold and gloomy, Admiral," Ferdi said as they stepped into the dreary and deserted convent courtyard, hidden in the back streets of Paris.

"We needed to keep this very quiet, Baron," Canaris said. "This fits the conditions commendably."

A squat unshaven man stood at the chipped dark-green door. He eyed both men as they approached him. "What business have you here, gentlemen?" he asked in French.

"Jade Amicol," was all Ferdi said. The man raised his arms, gesturing to the men to do the same so they could be searched. Ferdi noticed he had a pistol tucked into the belt of his trousers.

Ferdi undid his fawn overcoat and raised his arms. The squat man patted down his body and the bottoms of both of his legs, and similarly patted down the admiral, all done in stony silence. He grunted approval and opened the door.

They entered a cavernous, sparse room. "Where are we? A monastery?" Canaris looked around the cold, bland room. A row of small windows was set high in one of the grey stone walls. A large crucifix hung at one end of the room and a faded painting depicting the Virgin Mary holding a baby Jesus at the other. In the middle of the room stood a table with four chairs, a jug of water and a stack of four glasses in the centre.

Canaris turned to Ferdi. "Just to make sure we are secure, tell me again about yourself, and who we are meeting." Ferdi felt a pang of excitement. He had only met the admiral once before.

"You know me as 'Baron', Admiral. You recruited me in 1938."

"Yes, and how did I recruit you, Baron?" He was abrupt; possibly, Ferdi thought, as he had never been searched for arms before.

"Through your cousin's son, Ulrich Fuhrman. I have been helping you with information about various Nazis that you felt should be accountable for their actions during this war."

"Yes, sir," the admiral said, slightly more pleasantly. "Baron, why are you involved in this meeting?"

"Because of my connections with the British Secret Service."

"Very important to us, this channel of communication," Canaris said. The admiral sat, keeping his heavy dark-blue coat on. "Well, let us get on with it, Baron! Who are we waiting for?"

"We are waiting for the head of Franco-British Intelligence, sir. You know him as 'Colonel Arnould'."

Just then, a bald man, probably in his late fifties, came into the room. He looked serious, more like a businessman or a politician than the co-leader of a resistance group called the Jade Amicol network. He saw the admiral and smiled broadly.

"Admiral, my name is Arnould. Thank you for getting in touch."

"How did I contact you?" Canaris said simply. Again, Ferdi thought, just checking Arnould's provenance.

"You sent word via the consulate in Zürich," Arnould said. "We replied via your agent in Gibraltar. Your message, sir, said you wanted to discuss the terms that would draw this war to a conclusion."

Colonel Arnould sat down opposite Canaris at the table, and Ferdi took an end seat. There was a tension in the air. Ferdi took out a cigarette case and offered a cigarette to Canaris, who refused, and then to Arnould, who accepted. The colonel looked at Ferdi and said, "You are Baron?"

"Yes, sir, *Abwehr*, Paris."

"Herr Arnould, to get to the point," Canaris said, "I wanted to ask Mr Churchill his views of surrender, if we were to neutralise Herr Hitler and his senior cabinet."

Ferdi caught Arnould's eye. Both were stunned.

"I doubt Mr Churchill would agree to a *surrender*, sir," said the colonel, "even if you imprisoned Herr Hitler and his senior advisors. He would consider an Axis surrender, of course."

"When I say neutralise, Herr Arnould, I mean assassinate." Admiral Canaris looked steadily into the man's face. Arnould could not conceal his shock.

"The only thing I would say is that you would be as bad as Hitler and Röhm in 1934. The purge was a disgusting—"

"Herr Arnould, I do not seek leadership, I seek peace between our nations. These hostilities are only serving to damage the economy of Europe and invite the USSR to extend its communist power, which none of us want."

"Admiral, if you are not going to take over the leadership of Germany, who will?"

"I leave that to the politicians."

"Who?" Arnould asked incredulously. "Most of Hitler's ex-adversaries have been killed or jailed."

"There are plenty of candidates, sir." The admiral sighed impatiently.

"Admiral, I cannot take a message to Mr Churchill or the Allies about surrendering to the Reich. Perhaps an armistice, to be followed by a German withdrawal of all invaded territories." Arnould eyed the admiral. "The atrocities committed by the Nazis so far are terrible. The treatment of Jews, gypsies and coloured people has been horrendous. Has this … this *idea* got any support in Germany, or is it just you and a couple of other German traitors?"

"I think that is unfair, Colonel Arnould," said Ferdi. "Admiral Canaris is a loyal German. His only thought is for the German people and—"

"There is a lot of support for the cessation of hostilities in Germany," Canaris said. "There is widespread dissatisfaction with the leadership in the Reich. The war is damaging our economies and allowing Soviet Russia to gain power in Europe." He sighed. "I would be grateful if you could just take this message to the British government and Mr Churchill." He stood – the meeting was over. "I look forward to your reply through the usual channels as soon as possible. This conversation is very sensitive as you will appreciate." Canaris frowned at both men. "Baron, please take me back."

"Yes, of course, sir." Ferdi stood and looked at Arnould, who remained seated. "Do you have anything more, Colonel Arnould?"

"I do not." Rising to his feet, Arnould extended his hand to Admiral Canaris. As they shook hands, he said, "I will convey your message, sir.

However, I cannot see any kind of consensus within the British government. I am willing to be surprised, though. I admire your courage, sir. This cannot have been easy for you to undertake." Arnould then turned to Ferdi, and shook his hand. "Your servant, Herr Baron."

5

It was nearly a year before Charlotte could return to the gallery. General von Ardle told her that Paris was being bombed by the Allied forces. Charlotte was surprised by this news; she normally never heard about the war. She also had not heard any bombing. Why would the British bomb Paris in any case? General von Ardle insisted it could be quite dangerous to go outside of the safety of Le Palais. So, she and Theodora were virtually prisoners at Le Palais – again. Charlotte wondered why.

It was not until one Saturday in late summer, the end of September in 1943, that Charlotte was able to get a pass to go into Paris to buy some clothes. Theodora was not allowed to accompany her, so she had to go on her own. She was driven by a young SS private in the car that Bo, her Swedish chauffeur, used to drive her to and from school.

They drove down the Boulevard St Martin, turned under the arch at Porte St Denis, to Lucien Lelong, couturiers in Rue St Denis. As she was driven through the ghostly, empty streets of Paris, she thought of her friends and surrogate parents, Bo and Christina. What had happened to them? This was the route Bo would have taken to see the museums at the end of the Boulevard St Martin when she was a young girl.

It was a sunny afternoon, not hot but a pleasant heat. The air that streamed in through the car window smelt of acrid smoke and sewage, not the usual heady mix of exhaust fumes, coffee and cooking. The pavements were filled with men in various German uniforms swaggering in tight groups, smoking and laughing, some with worried-looking women. Civilians scurried furtively in the shadows with bags of vegetables or precious baguettes, trying not to be noticed by uniformed soldiers. There were no children anywhere to be seen. Paris was looking very sad, Charlotte thought. The only other motor vehicles were military – big black German staff cars with large silver headlamps, decorated in swastikas and military badges. A taxi was a rare sight. Sometimes a horse and cart loaded with sacks or sullen French passengers would trot by on their way to or from work.

Every now and again, officious soldiers at checkpoints would stop Charlotte's car to check credentials. They were always delighted to see the beautiful young woman sitting in the back, her proud chin tipped up, returning no acknowledgement to their entreaties, letting her young driver do all the talking. He would brandish names like General von Ardle and General von Stülpnagel – the Paris military commander – who had co-signed the papers.

The dressmaker, a painfully thin woman with dyed black hair, was sombre, greeting Charlotte with clipped politeness. Everybody else in the couturiers scowled at Charlotte, only smiling, ingenuously when she looked directly at any one of the drab, thin French women that attended and dressed her. The whole experience depressed Charlotte. She felt hated and despised. Though her French was impeccable, with a Parisian, metropolitan accent, she still never felt accepted as being French. She believed, somehow, everybody knew she was working at Le Palais for the Germans.

On the way back, Charlotte persuaded the young driver to just turn off at the Opéra, to Rue Ste Anne, to look at the gallery. She wanted to buy a portrait, she said. He was very unsure but succumbed.

When they drove into the gallery courtyard, she went straight to the room where she had found her mother's portrait. The portraits – not surprisingly – had gone. She asked an attendant where they were, she wanted to buy two of them. She asked to see Captain Fuhrman, but he was not at the gallery that day.

"I will ask Baron Saumures. One moment," the elderly French attendant said. Charlotte became worried whilst waiting. What if the artist put two and two together and realised who she was?

"Mademoiselle, Baron Saumures will see you in his office. This way."

"Thank you." Charlotte felt like bolting, but that would be even more suspicious.

Just be Freya, she told herself. You have her story, her papers.

They climbed some stairs to the first floor, then passed through a large room with four unoccupied desks, and on to an office at the end. It had a clear glass-panelled door with thick brown tape stuck across it in the shape of a cross so it would not shatter too much if a bomb exploded nearby.

"Come in, mademoiselle," a man said.

There he was – the portrait painter, tall and suave.

"Baron Saumures, I presume," she said as haughtily as she could.

He stood up from his desk and came over, offering his hand with a charming smile.

"Yes, let me close the door. Take a seat here."

The office was bathed in light from the large windows, all with brown tape crosses. The wood-panelled wall behind the man's desk was covered in posters of past exhibitions.

Charlotte was offered a deep leather sofa.

"Monsieur …" Charlotte started but the man put up his hand for her to wait a moment. He checked that there were no people around by looking out of the office door. He then sat close beside her, which she found a little disconcerting. He perched on the edge of the sofa, his knees together, with a straight back, like a prim schoolteacher. He offered her a cigarette, which she refused. He put a cigarette into a holder, lit it and took in a long draw whilst scrutinising Charlotte's face.

"I'm going to take a big chance here, mademoiselle," he said quietly. "I'm about to ask a question, and I would like you to answer as truthfully as possible. Don't be frightened. I can assure you I am a friend."

"All right," Charlotte said slowly and cautiously. The man was immaculately styled in a grey pinstripe suit, a dark-blue puff of a silk handkerchief sticking out of his top pocket and a dark-blue silk tie with a pearl tiepin. His black shoes were shined to a heavy gloss, as was his hair with hair oil. His handsome brown eyes looked into her eyes thoughtfully. She noticed that he had removed his thin moustache. He was nothing like an artist in the traditional sense.

"Are you Charlotte Joy Barrett, posing as Freya Jorgensen, the Swedish daughter of Bo and Christina Jorgensen?" he asked abruptly.

After a long silence, Charlotte asked, "Who are you … apart from being Monsieur or Baron Saumures?"

"As I said, a friend. I understand this may be a strange question, but before I answer, can you affirm who you are?"

Another long pause. Charlotte could not work out how to answer. He was not French, and his accent was not German. He could be English, not American; that would be very dangerous for him, but he did not seem the type to be dangerous. He was not a soldier-type and yet he was athletic, strong, in good shape. The danger of answering was that he could be the Gestapo, and she would be imprisoned and shot. However, he was not the Gestapo – she knew the Gestapo-type; she had met enough of them, all self-absorbed, arrogant, unattractive, strutting around with superiority and self-importance.

He knew that she was, technically, Charlotte Barrett, not de Tournet, and that her middle name was Joy – very few people knew that. In addition, he claimed to have known her mother.

"Monsieur, you said you painted a portrait of Alice Barrett. Do you know what her two brothers were called, and what do they do?"

He looked momentarily confused. "She had only one brother, Sir Jason Barrett, and he was the chargé d'affaires in the British Embassy in Paris when I knew your … Alice. And she had an older sister called Stella, married to Jean de Tournet and stepmother to Charlotte."

Charlotte studied the man before her and smiled. "Yes, I am Charlotte. Who are you?"

"Thank you, I will keep calling you Freya, just in case." He edged a little closer to her on the sofa. "I am Baron Olivier Ferdinand Saumures. My friends call me Ferdi."

"How do you do," she said formally. "Tell me what you know about Colonel Deller."

He paused and took a deep breath. "Franz-Joseph Deller is your father."

Charlotte was shocked and remained speechless as Ferdi gently told her about her mother. "Your mother had, I believe unwisely, decided to have a baby. *Her* mother, Lady Joy, was to leave her house in Avenue Foch to Alice. Your mother did not want to get married only for the house to go to her husband. She wanted her child to get the house." Ferdi eyed Charlotte warily. "Are you okay with this?"

"Please go on. I'm fine … I think," Charlotte said.

"Alice …" Ferdi hesitated for a few seconds. "Alice chose Joseph to … have a child with. They went to a place in Brittany during her final five months of pregnancy, where I did the sketches for the portraits. They were quite happy."

"Did she love him, do you know?"

"I think she was very fond of him. I am not sure. He certainly loved her."

"Then why did he kill her?"

"I think it was a tragic accident. I don't think he murdered her. There was a hell of a gale—"

"He didn't push her?"

"No. I believe it was just a terrible mishap."

"I see." Charlotte felt a mixture of sadness and anger. "Why didn't the police get involved? How is it that he is strolling around, an SS colonel, stealing paintings?"

"His parents were very close to Hitler. I believe he went back to Austria and then Germany just after the accident and joined his parents."

"You are calling it an accident, are you? When everybody else in the family said he killed my mother!" Charlotte scrutinised the baron closely. She saw no prevarication or guilt. "How do you know all this, Baron?"

"Ferdi, please. My name here is just Ferdi." He composed himself. "I got to know Franz-Joseph in Berlin and Paris when I was studying art. He had tried a degree in theology in England and got bored, and then started studying art in Berlin, where we met. We both moved to Paris. He was not getting much help from his father, so he did some gardening. One of his gardens was at your grandmother's house, where you are now."

"Was he a drinker then?" she asked.

"No, he only started really drinking when they moved to Brittany to have you."

Charlotte got up from the sofa. She saw the portrait of her mother propped up behind Ferdi's desk. The painting alongside it had to be a portrait of Deller as a young man. That's why she somehow knew who it was the first time she saw it. She felt uneasiness and disgust at the thought of Deller being her father. It was taking a long time to sink in. She could hardly accept it.

She turned back to her mother's portrait. She could see there was a merest suggestion of pregnancy. "She looked lovely, my mother. I have seen photos of her, but somehow, this is more personal … intimate."

"She was lovely. But very set in her ways. She was quite quiet and not very gregarious … shy, I suppose you could say." Charlotte gazed upon the portrait of her mother with longing. She would have loved to have got to know her.

"Where was the portrait done?"

"I sketched it at Alston House in Val-André. Finished them here, in Paris."

"Where she died … Alston House."

"Yes," Ferdi said quietly. "I did Franz-Joseph's portrait at the same time."

Charlotte turned to Deller's portrait. A sense of anger grew inside her.

"Why should I trust you? Your friend is a colonel in the SS!"

"He is, I know, but he is a friend that I have not talked to for well over three years." Ferdi sighed. "I suppose we will be friends again after the war."

"I see." Charlotte was not convinced.

"Freya, could you sit here? I have something rather sensitive to talk to you about." Saumures composed himself. Charlotte could see he was trying to work out the best way to ask her something, and she was beginning to feel a sense of foreboding.

"What I am about to tell you will be enough to ensure my death if you are not who you say you are." He spoke a little too melodramatically for Charlotte.

"But how do you know that I am telling the truth?" she asked.

"Because you look like your mother," he said slightly tersely, but then glanced up into Charlotte's face and gave a quick apologetic grimace. "I work with the British Secret Service," he said steadily. "I work in MI6 in a special department that gathers information on the Germans in France – mostly the Nazis in Paris."

"What?" Charlotte said, with a little incredulity which she hoped was not conveyed.

"I am part of Department Six, an arm of the British Secret Service that—"

"Yes, yes, yes, I understand. But why on God's earth are you telling me? Aren't you a German baron?"

"No, I am a Luxembourg baron with an English mother."

"Oh, I see."

"I am telling you, mademoiselle, because I need information about Le Palais."

"But are you sure I am the kind of person who can be trusted?"

"You are just the kind of person we could have faith in. You are young and eager and, after all, half British and half Austrian."

"Austrian?"

"Franz-Joseph is Austrian."

"Oh! Really?" Charlotte had not considered that she could be half Austrian. Nobody had told her the nationality of her father. Just that he killed her mother.

"The reason I think you will do well is that the Germans seem to trust you." Ferdi carried on selling the concept.

"No, they don't. They think I am feeding Charlotte de Tournet information or at least hiding her somewhere. However, I think they have given up that theory."

"Why do they think that?"

"A rather nasty Gestapo man, called Karl Hueber, was going to cart me off somewhere to ask questions a couple of years ago, and I've been followed ever since, mainly because my aunt and uncle asked about my whereabouts from Spain."

“Ah … Well, you were not followed today.”

“How do you know?”

“Ulrich checked.”

“Who’s Ulrich? You mean Ulrich Fuhrman?”

“Yes, he runs my gallery on behalf of the German high command, but he is also run by me.”

“We’ve met him before,” she said, “at Le Palais.”

“I know,” Ferdi answered with a sardonic smile. “That is why I know about you. It was I who asked if you and Theodora could come to the gallery opening.”

Charlotte sat with her mouth open, amazed. “You know Theodora?”

There was a short pause, then Ferdi said, “Ulrich does.”

“This is all so quick. I wish you had done this more slowly.”

“I do not have much time. The war is taking quite a few turns, with the Americans. We are possibly going to win the war.”

“I don’t know much of what has happened,” Charlotte said quietly, feeling a little ashamed. This could be an opportunity for her to find out what was going on in the war. She did not feel particularly loyal to one side or the other. She was mostly British yet loved France, and she enjoyed her time – with some exceptions – with the Germans. Then there was Jost, her love, a German SS officer. “Ferdi, I am not sure I am the right person. I have an SS officer as my … how shall I say, romantic interest, at the moment. He is called Jost Krupp.”

Ferdi leapt up from the sofa. “Ah yes, we know about him.” He went over to his desk and picked up a fawn-coloured file. He read out loud: “‘*Jost Krupp: born Aschersleben, tenth February 1913, parents General Helmut Krupp*’ and a question mark for his mother – no mothers name, ‘*studied law in Munich, member of the Nazi Party from 1933. He has been a member of the SS since 1934, made an* Unterscharführer (a junior squad leader) *after Operation Hummingbird. There was a rumour that he was responsible for the execution of three top members of the government in 1934: Ernst Röhm*’ … etc, etc. The list of people he is said to have executed is impressive.” He peeked over the top of the file at Charlotte. “Have you heard of the ‘Night of the Long Knives’ or Operation Hummingbird, Freya?” clearly waiting for some sign of recognition from her. She shrugged her shoulders. “You know, when the Nazis spent three days and nights on a purge to execute all politicians who stood against Hitler and the Nazi Party?”

"I was nine, living in America! What would I know about German politics?"

"Anyway," he went on. "'*He was part of the execution party and was made a junior SS officer in 1934. He was awarded the Blutorden, or Blood Order, for his actions*'. A rare distinction." Ferdi nearly talked in admiration.

"He can't have done all that – he is a poet. He could not execute people!" Charlotte then thought of Drancy and hesitated, remembering his delight at the executions. She stood up and looked over Ferdi's shoulder at the file. "Where did you get all this information?"

"I would rather not say."

"So why are you reading out this secret file to me?"

"Mainly to show you that Krupp is not a person you should be acquainted with … so closely." Charlotte was appalled. "Will it be difficult to detach yourself from Krupp?"

"I don't want to. I love him!"

"I see."

"Why have you got a file on Jost?"

"I have details on virtually all SS officers, especially the ones serving in the Hôtel Majestic – the Paris high command headquarters – and at Eighty-Four Avenue Foch. Also a few Gestapo officers."

Ferdi sat back down on the sofa and Charlotte sat down beside him. As she sat, her dress got caught on the arm of the sofa and rode up to her thighs, revealing the tops of her stockings. She flashed a look at Ferdi to see if he had seen. To her surprise, he not only noticed but he seemed to not take any pleasure or embarrassment in her mistake.

"Sorry about that," she said with a nervous smile, pulling down the hem to her knees.

"Doesn't worry me. Very nice legs," he said plainly and carried on referring to the file. "According to this file, he is also the official poet to the SS … well I never! Has he offered any poetry to you?"

"No." Charlotte's stomach was churning. He had always said he would dedicate a poem to her beauty. He had said some beautiful things to her, but no poetry as yet.

"'*He has been an SS first lieutenant since 1939*'," Ferdi carried on, seemingly insensitive to Charlotte's disquiet about hearing this. "'*He joined the SD when he arrived in Paris and oversees the interrogation of captive French underground at Eighty-Four Avenue Foch, and was in charge of Drancy prison.*'"

"What is it about Eighty-Four Avenue Foch?" Charlotte asked.

Ferdi sighed sadly. "Eighty-Four Avenue Foch is where they interrogate enemies of the Reich: secret agents, French underground, Allied subversives, et cetera. They use appalling cruelty, psychological torture as well as physical." Charlotte was shocked. "If they have not killed them in interrogation, these poor people – men and women – go off to Drancy or to prison camps." Ferdi went back to the file. "'*He was made a captain in April 1942*'. The last entry concerns him being awarded the Iron Cross for leading an attack on prisoners and Jews who had taken over part of the Drancy prison in northern Paris. '*He oversaw the massacre of nearly eighty people. He personally executed the ringleaders: David Shulman and Bo Jor-gen-sen …*'" As he said "Jorgensen" his voice cracked. "I am sorry, Freya, I should have thought."

Charlotte stood up, red with fury, tears coursing down her cheeks. "That bastard, that absolute bloody bastard!"

"Freya, be careful. As soon as he knows you know, you will go the same way."

Charlotte fell back onto the sofa, devastated. She didn't know whether to cry or grieve. She hugged her stomach to stop it hurting. "Oh, don't worry about that. I haven't seen him for nearly a year," she said miserably.

"No, I believe he has left Paris and gone back to Germany, or possibly somewhere else in France—" He stopped when he saw Charlotte hide her face in her hands, pressing her fingers into her eyes, trying to stop herself from crying. The very first love of her life appeared to be a serial murderer. Her beautiful, handsome SS officer, who she thought loved her, who was gentle and kind, was in fact a brutal executioner and an indiscriminate killer.

"Freya, who else knows your real identity?" asked Ferdi, a worried expression on his face.

"My great friend, Theodora. She is a … she works at Le Palais," she said with a sniff, wiping tears away from her eyes.

"Theodora who?" he asked gently.

"I don't know her other name, she is just known as 'Madame Theodora'. Her father was Turkish and moved to Berlin. Her mother was French."

"She sounds like a good friend."

"Yes, she is."

"I will tell you more the next time we meet. In the meantime, I need a rough plan of the upper and lower floors of Nineteen Avenue Foch."

"Why?"

"Ulrich has only ever had access to the main ground floor."

"Yes, but why do you need a plan of the rest of the house?"

Ferdi looked deep in thought, which made Charlotte nervous. "I just need to gather as much information about the places the Nazis have taken over. There are no public plans of Nineteen Avenue Foch. It's an old house."

"I see." Charlotte was not convinced. "I will see what I can do. I will give something to Ulrich the next time he is at Le Palais." She decided it could not do any harm.

"I would be very grateful if you said nothing about this to Theodora."

"But she knows about the portraits."

"Well … just keep it at that."

"She is a very important person to me!" Charlotte warned. "She has saved me more than once, and she is the only person I trust in Paris. Ulrich Fuhrman knows her, you can ask him. I hope you will not put her in any danger."

"No, of course not," Ferdi said.

After a short silence, Charlotte asked, "Where do you come from, Ferdi?"

"I'm from Luxembourg, but my mother was English. Why?"

"Oh, yes … you said. You need to work on your French. I wondered what the accent was."

"I thought I had an eastern European accent." He laughed.

"You do, but with a hint of something else." She gave Ferdi a brave grin; her eyes felt sore and her nose was still blocked. "We are all mongrels, you, me and Theodora," Charlotte said. Ferdi just smiled. "I'd better get going. There is a soldier in a car waiting for me outside. He will get fed up and report me."

"No he won't. He is being entertained by Brigitte, our cleaning girl."

"Does the whole gallery work for you?"

"Yes," he said matter-of-factly. "I think you should go as well. Here is my card, my telephone number for emergencies. My code name is 'Baron' – should you want to talk to me privately, if Deller appears, which he shouldn't. If there is anything untoward, just say you want to talk to Baron as opposed to Ferdi Saumures. I hope you can trust me. When can you come again?"

"I am not sure – it has taken nearly a year to get here since my last visit!"

"You could say you want to buy a painting and you are negotiating for it."

"I don't have any money." Charlotte walked over to the picture of her mother. "But I would love to buy that. Is it a good likeness?" she said, pointing at Alice's portrait.

"I think so," said Ferdi. "It is yours anyway. Your mother bought it." Charlotte's eyes filled with tears again.

"I am sorry. You must think I'm a complete wet blanket."

"I have cried more for your mother than anybody else," Ferdi said wistfully, "and I didn't know her that well." He went across to Charlotte and took her hands. Their eyes met. "You are very beautiful, Charlotte." To hear her real name being spoken was a bit of a shock. "You are even more beautiful than your mother and your aunt Stella put together." He was being terribly serious. Charlotte felt uncomfortable. He was so handsome, but he seldom smiled. Not a hair out of place, well dressed ... if he tried, he could charm any woman easily into his arms.

"Are you making love to me?" she asked.

"No!" Ferdi chortled dismissively. "I am just remembering your mother, and how proud she would be of you." Charlotte wiped away a tear.

As Ferdi and Charlotte went down the stairs, she thanked him, although she was not sure what for. Captain Ulrich Fuhrman came up to meet them. He clicked his heels and bobbed his head to Charlotte and announced his name in clipped German. Charlotte saw the young soldier scamper to the car from somewhere, jamming on his hat and waving at someone through the window surreptitiously.

"We look forward to seeing you again soon, Fräulein Jorgensen," Ferdi said as he opened the rear car door.

All the way back to Le Palais, Charlotte could not stop thinking about Jost Krupp and his execution of Bo. Why weren't Bo and Christina back in Sweden? What had happened to Christina? And what was she going to do about Jost? She wanted to kill him. He had now become her enemy. As had Franz-Joseph Deller ... her father.

6

"I met the artist who painted my mother's portrait," Charlotte confided to Theodora on her return to Le Palais. "He is very nice, from Luxembourg. Quite handsome."

"How lovely. Did he charm you?" Theodora grinned in a knowing way.

"No, he didn't. I am probably not his type."

"Not his type? Don't be silly. You are every man's type. Or he may be a … how do you say … a homosexual, I suppose."

"Oh, surely not." But as she said it, she wondered. She had never met a homosexual or knowingly met one. In fact she had little knowledge of homosexuality. Theodora's experience of life would doubtless have come across all spheres of sexuality.

"Ferdi told me Colonel Deller is my father."

"No! That is impossible. How would he know that?" Theodora was visibly shocked.

"And, he found out that Jost executed Bo in Drancy Prison."

"But how would he know this? Freya, you must not trust this man. He is after something from you. I don't know what."

"He says he's …" Charlotte paused, remembering Ferdi preferring to keep everything confidential. "Ferdi's a baron, from Luxembourg. And Ulrich Fuhrman works for him." Theodora looked away. "Are you all right, Theodora?"

"Yes, fine, darling. There has been a lot more bombing in the south of Paris today. Did you have to go to the shelters?"

"No. Why?"

"I just wondered why you were out so long. Captain Wil was asking after you. We have a lot of guests coming tonight."

Charlotte wanted to tell Theodora everything but thought it unwise. Was Ferdi Saumures to be entirely trusted? Was all that information about Jost and Deller made up? She knew Jost a lot better than the baron. And Ferdi's friend was an SS colonel. The war had made her question: who could she trust? Theodora had been a rock and become a true friend – her only trusted friend at

Le Palais; her only trusted friend anywhere, come to that. A feeling of loneliness began to set in, something she hadn't felt since the day her stepfather forced his attention on her, just before she went to school in Paris. She had nobody she could tell. If Theodora turned out to be like Jost, she would be utterly alone.

"Oh, I wish I could confide in Theodora," Charlotte said aloud in her room, now that Theodora had left. She looked at the trunk where the Klimt painting lay rolled up inside. Her mother's painting by the Austrian painter, *Girl on a Golden Pillow*, was now hidden away, away from Lieutenant-Colonel Deller ... her father. She flopped back onto her bed. She was exhausted with all the emotion coursing through her, all the new information that was crowding into her brain. The last thing she wanted to do that night was to chat aimlessly, to be ingratiating to a bunch of narcissistic men. What would she do if Jost Krupp appeared, though, or even Franz-Joseph Deller?

*

Charlotte dressed in her new gown, an ocean blue-green silk strapless dress with a long and full-flowing skirt. The figure-hugging, intricately patterned bodice was revealing and enticing. Her golden waves flowed, full and lustrous. Apart from her mother's opal ring, her only other jewellery was the innocent-looking large silver cross that Theodora had given her, which hid a deadly ejecting stiletto blade.

Theodora was in black satin, complementing her dark complexion. Her hair was in a French bun, showing off an elegant neck, and she sparkled with a diamond necklace and earrings.

As Charlotte descended the golden-carpeted stairs with Theodora, she was reminded of how she always enjoyed the attention they got from the gentlemen as they glided down.

Many businessmen had come to be entertained, wined and dined. An all-women brass band from Berlin was playing in the library, and the house was crowded with new staff. There seemed to be a lot more guards. Perhaps Himmler was coming again, or even Hitler.

As they got to the bottom step, a group of men in black dinner suits were taking off their coats and chatting animatedly to each other. One in particular caught Charlotte's attention. He was tall and well-built with broad shoulders, and had thinning blond hair. He stood side-on to Charlotte, and as she looked at him, he seemed somehow familiar. He was puffing on a cigar and laughing, speaking German with a French accent.

Charlotte's heart froze as she recognised him. She felt a wave of nausea come over her. She darted off and scurried through the brown baize-covered servant's door under the stairs. Theodora hurried along behind her.

"What have you seen, Freya?" she hissed.

Charlotte looked through the little window in the baize door out into the hall. There he was, walking towards the drawing room: Jean de Tournet, her stepfather.

My God, what a day!

*

Charlotte feigned a headache and excused herself from the evening, much to Captain Wil's dissatisfaction.

"The general has many important guests here," Wil blustered at the bottom of the stairs as Charlotte was going up, holding the back of her hand to her forehead. "You must come and help with them."

"I am sorry, Captain Wil. You will have to forgive me; my head is splitting. This must be the first time I have done this, isn't it?" She came back down the stairs, wincing at every step, and put her hand on his. This bold manoeuvre worked. He smiled a consensual smile and Charlotte resumed climbing the stairs. She turned on the half landing, knowing Wil would be watching her bare back.

"Captain Wil, would that tall gentleman with blond hair and moustache be Monsieur Jean de Tournet?"

"Yes, it is … aha!" He pointed his finger at Charlotte. "You want to avoid your old employer. This is what all the headache business is about."

"No, I hardly know him." Charlotte realised her mistake. "He was never around. That man just looked like Monsieur de Tournet. What is he doing here?"

"I don't think that is any of your business, Freya. Perhaps you should come down and ask him." He shoved his thick round glasses back up his nose briskly and strode off back to the drawing room.

Isn't it any of my business, Captain Wil? Charlotte thought. She was in two minds whether to go back down and face Jean de Tournet, but decided it was too dangerous. She wanted to talk to someone, but Theodora was already in the drawing room.

Charlotte decided that she would call the baron. He was the only other person who knew her situation. Perhaps she would have to trust him now.

She could hear Agatha playing the piano as she crept down the stairs and went towards the library. The Berlin ladies' band, clad in corsets and stockings, were setting up in the library while a large fat woman in a floral dressing gown shouted at them to be quicker. Charlotte crept past to the study door. She checked that the sergeant was not at his desk in the outer office and quickly went through to the general's office. Not wanting anyone to find her there, she locked the door just in case.

Charlotte took the baron's card out of her little handbag and picked up the phone handset.

"*Ja*, Herr General?" Charlotte had not counted on a switchboard. In her best German she said, "Put me through to the Bayser gallery, in the Rue Sainte Anne."

"*Ja*, madame, *bitte haben Sie einen Moment Geduld*." There was a short delay. "Do you have the number, madame?"

Charlotte decided she would get him to do some work. "No – you find it for me," she barked, in the way an SS officer would.

"*Ja, madame*." The switchboard operator sighed.

"*Und beeilen Sie sich!*" Charlotte shouted for him to hurry up. There were a few clicks and she could hear the burr of a ringtone. After the third ring the phone was answered. Thank God someone was still there.

"Galerie Bayser."

"I would like to speak with the baron," Charlotte said in German, just in case the operator was listening.

"Who is this, please?"

"I am calling on behalf of General von Ardle at Le Palais."

"One moment, madame." Charlotte thought that the man on the phone was Ulrich Fuhrman. There was a click, followed by another. "This is Saumures," Ferdi said in German with a heavy French accent.

"This is Fräulein Jorgensen. I would like to discuss the portrait with you urgently. Are you able to talk over the phone?"

"One moment, please, fräulein." There was a short buzz and a click. "I have put on a scrambler," Ferdi said in French, his voice now very tinny. "You can talk freely, if you can. Keep it in French, and no names just in case."

"Something strange has happened," she said. "We have a party of businessmen here, one of which is my stepfather." There was silence on the other end of the phone. Charlotte's heart beat faster.

At last Ferdi spoke. "Are you sure? Sorry … a stupid question. I don't know what to say. Has he seen you?"

"No, but I think he will be told that I am here because Captain Wi … sorry, the captain in charge, believes that I am the daughter of *his* chauffeur." As she spoke, her heart ached as she remembered that Bo was now dead, killed by Krupp. "Is he part of your organisation … in your business?" she asked hopefully.

"No! He is not. He must be doing some kind of deal with the Germans for steel." Ferdi sounded thoughtful and then said, "I am sorry, I think you are going to have to meet him, if only to somehow stop him identifying you as the other person, if you see what I mean."

"Oh … Christ, I don't know if I can." Get a grip on yourself, Charlotte, she thought. "OK, I will go and meet him. Can your captain come to Le Palais tonight? Just for moral support?"

"He's not been invited. I will try and think of something. Be very careful." Charlotte wondered what he meant by "being careful". How much danger was she in? "Are you still there?"

"Yes," she said, swallowing nervously.

"I will talk to my captain, see if he can get in tonight. If he can't, then it's up to you."

"OK. I will be in touch if I need you to help."

"Goodbye," Ferdi said in a slightly impersonal way.

She wished she had not spoken to Ferdi Saumures. The whole situation was getting out of hand. She decided to go into the drawing room and confront de Tournet, try and get him on his own to tell him to keep quiet. But she had nothing to bargain with. She had no idea what to do, other than convince de Tournet that she was as loyal to the Reich as he seemed to be. But what if he was part of British or French intelligence? Ferdi said he wasn't, but what if Ferdi wasn't what *he* claimed to be? What a muddle.

Charlotte sat in the general's chair behind the desk. She heard the band of ladies strike up in the library next door and imagined her grandmother turning in her grave. If she was caught in the general's office, she would be in even more trouble, so she straightened the telephone, switched off the desk lamp and went out into the outer office. She unlocked the door into the service passage, intending to go up the back stairs. But as she unlocked the door, she saw the knob turn. She dived behind the door as it opened and kept her back to the wall. The lights came on. She could hear the general talking to someone.

"We will find out more about her. There will be a file in my study," the general was saying.

"It is just that I cannot remember meeting a daughter of theirs." It was de Tournet. "I could be wrong, I didn't spend much time in this awful house. I hated it and everybody in it."

"How could you hate this house, Herr de Tournet? It is so lovely."

"After the war, I will sell it to you, General. It is mine now, after all."

Charlotte's heart beat faster. She could not believe what she was hearing. Their voices faded as they went into the study. She quickly stepped out from behind the door and slipped through into the passage on tiptoe so her shoes would not clatter on the wood floor. She hovered at the threshold, hoping to hear more. If they came out of the office, she could quickly go up the servant's stairs to the first floor and then come down the main stairs. Or slip out the back door and hide in the garden, or even escape if the guards were not around. She quickly discounted the escape idea; given the dress she was wearing she would not get very far.

She heard the general unlocking and opening a filing drawer.

"I am not sure where Captain Wil has put the files on the girls. I might have to ask him."

"Don't worry, General. I am not staying the night here, I am at my old apartment. I will be back tomorrow and I can talk to her then. If it is their daughter, we will have to think about what to do with her. She must not tell anybody I am here."

"That is not likely, Herr de Tournet. She is a very loyal girl – to the Fatherland, that is."

"If the Allies or the Americans know I am here selling steel to the Reich, I will be a marked man for life, even in peacetime."

That voice, that man … that bastard! A vision filled Charlotte's mind of him bearing down on her when she was barely twelve, and many times after during the following three years. Hurting her, his breath of stale champagne and cigars drowning her lungs like a noxious gas. She shivered at the thought.

The general spoke. "Yes – well, let us enjoy the evening, Herr de Tournet. You've a busy day tomorrow."

Charlotte had two things in mind: to somehow find Theodora and warn her of what had happened, and to get out of her dress so they, or she, could escape somehow. She went up the back stairs to her little room on the top floor. She sat on her bed, her head in her hands, trying to think of a plan.

The door opened and Theodora rushed in.

"Freya, you are still in your dress!"

"Theodora, thank God. De Tournet knows a girl called Freya is here. I heard the general and my uncle in the study trying to find a file on me."

"What? Well you have to go, and go now!"

"I can't go, Theodora. Ferdi told me to confront de Tournet. I just think I need to meet him."

"Freya, you're mad. The man's awful, a complete ball sack. I have been talking to him this evening." Theodora looked thoughtful. "Funny, he never mentioned you … Freya, that is. He would have done, wouldn't you think?"

"I don't think I am that important to him. I will confront him tomorrow. He is not staying here tonight, thank God," Charlotte said, looking up in a kind of prayer.

7

The next day, Charlotte was up and ready to confront de Tournet. She went down the stairs and into the breakfast room. There was General von Ardle and Captain Wil.

"Good morning, Freya," the general said in a loud and unfriendly way. He was polishing his monocle. Captain Wil just carried on reading a newspaper and drinking coffee. None of them stood as they usually did when she or Theodora entered. Agatha was helping herself to toast at the sideboard, a sad, condescending smile on her face. Charlotte wondered why; they had no fondness for each other.

"I hear Monsieur de Tournet was here last night?" Charlotte said innocently as she poured herself a cup of chocolate, which was only just being served again after months of no chocolate to be had anywhere. Helmut the waiter pulled out a chair for her and she sat, waiting for an answer. Theodora then came into the dining room. As Charlotte's and her eyes met, Theodora gave a little wink.

"Well, Freya, he can't remember meeting you, he says," the general said. She could not read what the general was thinking. It did not seem as though Captain Wil was about to suddenly clap her in irons – he was peacefully reading a week-old German newspaper, not taking any notice of what was going on. Charlotte decided to play it down.

"Is he here?" she asked, taking a delicious sip of chocolate.

"No, he is at meetings. But he will be back tonight. And Freya" – the general rose from the table and scowled at her as he went to the drawing room door – "you will be in attendance tonight with or without a headache, or there will be trouble," he thundered. "I cannot have my prettiest girl being cooped up in the attic and not helping me with the guests!"

"Thank you, General," Charlotte responded with a modest and relieved smile. Theodora was looking at the general with her mouth open.

He stopped at the door and turned contritely to Theodora and Agatha. "That is to say, you are all my most beautiful assets. And by the way, we have a very senior officer coming tonight, so be pretty." With that, he left.

"Any ideas who is coming tonight, Captain Wil?" Theodora asked lightly.

"None of your business," he replied. He pushed his round tortoiseshell glasses back up his nose. "You will not be allowed to leave the building today, any of you. Agatha, tell Juliet." He stood, brushed down his jacket, looked at the women with a furrowed brow, and left the room.

"Oh, Theodora," cried Charlotte, "this has been an upsetting couple of days. I am sure the general, and especially Captain Wil, are not happy with me."

"You are going to have to be very careful, Freya," Agatha said. Charlotte thought she was suppressing a smile. "They will turn on you if you don't behave, no matter how pretty you are."

"That's enough, Agatha," Theodora said. "Leave her alone. You have stayed in bed a few times and we had to cover for you."

"I was ill!"

"So was Freya. Now go and get Juliet; take your toast with you." Agatha got up and walked sullenly to the door.

"There is no Captain Krupp to protect you now, Freya." Agatha swept out the door before Charlotte could answer. She felt like she had been punched in the stomach.

"Take no notice of that cow. She is just jealous of your beauty," Theodora said.

"I doubt it, Theodora. I am going to read and have a think."

"Do you believe your stepfather knows what you are doing here?"

"I have absolutely no idea. We will know later today, won't we?" She felt depressed. So much had changed so quickly. Her somewhat routine and steady life at Le Palais was up in the air.

"Fräulein Freya?" Sergeant Hildegard Becker clicked her heels from the door of the breakfast room.

"Yes, Sergeant Hildegard?"

"An SS officer wishes to see you. You are to go to the general's office immediately – alone!" she barked in an army way while looking at Theodora.

"Oh … right. Thank you. Who—?" The sergeant turned on her heels and left before Charlotte could ask anything.

Theodora caught Charlotte's eye but said nothing. Charlotte shrugged and Theodora just stroked Charlotte's hair in comfort and support.

*

"This is *Hauptmann* Ulrich Fuhrman from the Galerie Bayser – I believe you know each other," the general said from his desk, remaining seated when Charlotte entered the office. Ulrich Fuhrman stood, plainly happy to see her. "He has news of the portrait you admired in the gallery and that you asked to be presented here in my office." The general was looking impatient.

"Yes, we have met. Good morning, Captain Fuhrman." Charlotte was genuinely delighted. Was this some kind of help coming from the baron?

"Fräulein, the baron sent me here with the portrait you organised for Le Palais." Fuhrman walked over to a large flat parcel leaning against the desk, and presented the picture wrapped in brown paper to Charlotte.

"Oh, how lovely. For us? How very kind," Charlotte gushed, not quite sure what was being presented or to whom. General von Ardle became suddenly curious.

"Perhaps the general would be kind enough to unwrap it?" Fuhrman suggested.

"Yes, of course." Charlotte played along, wondering who the portrait was of.

"Well, yes." The general stood, now intrigued, and started to gently rip off the brown paper after cutting the string that surrounded the frame.

An oil portrait of Adolf Hitler, of superior quality, emerged as the paper was torn away. The Führer was sitting on the corner of his desk, looking slightly to the left, his gloves in his hand and his peaked hat on the desk beside him. His long dark-brown leather coat was slung over his shoulders, his right hand on his hip drawing the coat open to reveal his deep-brown crossbelt and his Iron Cross, Golden Party Badge and Wound Badge on his ochre uniform jacket. The portrait was in a modern, plain, dark wood frame.

"But this is superb!" the general shouted in delight.

"It was Fräulein Jorgensen's wish that Le Palais should have this portrait of the Führer for your office. She noticed you only have this black and white image here." Fuhrman gestured at the cheaply framed photo that every office had of Adolf Hitler.

"Freya … I am speechless … Who is the baron?"

"He is the artist, sir," said Fuhrman. Charlotte's mind was racing. She just stood there looking modest, hoping Ulrich Fuhrman was going to guide her through the lie or the plan. "Fräulein Jorgensen and her friend saw this portrait at the opening of the exhibition last year and loved it, and thought it perfect for your office, sir. However, they did not have the means to buy it, sir."

"No," Charlotte chipped in, now seeing where this was going. "So I pleaded with the artist, Baron Saumures, to let us borrow it to hang at our house. He refused to start with."

"And then you appeared yesterday" – Fuhrman turned to Charlotte – "and the baron happened to be there at the same time. He succumbed to fräulein's charming request. And he is giving it to you and Le Palais as a gift."

"How very kind of him," said Charlotte.

"But this is so very generous of him." The general was delighted, gazing at his leader with adoration. "The baron must come to Le Palais. I shall send a personal invitation" – he checked himself – "but I am afraid not tonight."

"That would be very kind of you, sir. The baron has asked for only one favour, however, as payment." The general looked at Fuhrman dubiously. "He wishes to capture Fräulein Jorgensen's beauty on canvas."

The general brightened. "But of course. You must come too, captain. Tomorrow evening?"

"Thank you, sir. I will see if the baron can come, but I am not sure he is free."

"Freya, will you see the captain out? And thank you again, captain." The general turned to Charlotte with a huge grin. "And thank you so much, Freya." He was flushed with joy, nearly in tears!

*

"Was that one of Ferdi's portraits?" Charlotte hissed as they entered the library from the outer office door.

"Yes. He can paint portraits of Hitler in his sleep, but he took some time on this one."

"But why?"

"You were followed the other day. We saw a Gestapo man emerge from a little café just across the road. He has been keeping an eye on the gallery ever since your first visit."

"He's been there since last year?"

"Just about, we assume. He looks like the man you described – Hueber?"

"Yes, Hueber. Nasty little man." Charlotte shook at the thought of him. "I have not been able to draw out plans for the house. I haven't had time."

"Don't worry about plans. Take this book on art." The captain handed Charlotte a book, in German, on French art. "Inside the spine are instructions." Fuhrman kept looking around the library, making sure they were alone. "We have plans for tomorrow. You will be leaving to go to Spain."

"What?"

"Shhh! It is too dangerous for you here, and we are going to leave with a bang!"

"I can't leave. What about my paintings – the collection? And what about Theodora?"

"She will be coming too. The others will have to take their chances."

"What others?" Charlotte was beginning to feel dread mount up in her chest.

"Listen, Freya, you are about to be discovered – your stepfather is here at Le Palais. He is selling American steel via Canada to Sweden and then on to Germany."

"My God!"

"You must get out by tomorrow morning."

"But how?"

"Just read the instructions." The library door opened and a group of SS officers strolled through. Fuhrman sprang away from Charlotte as though caught in a private assignation, causing winks and smirks from the officers. One young lieutenant clicked his heels in salute to his superior officer.

"Good morning, my dear Freya." Fuhrman saluted Charlotte and strolled out of the library.

8

Charlotte sat on the edge of her bed in her little attic bedroom. Sitting opposite was Theodora, looking at her in anticipation, no doubt wondering why she had been summoned to Charlotte's room in such a covert way.

Charlotte pulled out the rice-paper message from the spine of the book.

"*Goddess,*" it read in English. "*The morning of the ninth of September 1943, at 04.00 hours, Allied bombers will be bombing the western suburbs of Paris. At the same time, your house will be bombed. Your instructions are for you and your friend to escape whilst the bombing is happening.*

"A detachment of the Free French and Allied agents are going to attack an adjacent target. An agent will be with you at the back-garden door – the western side of the house – to help you escape. You must be at the garden door, beside the study, by 03.55 – no later – and you should be taken out of the house by 04:00. You will dress accordingly and have minimum luggage. The house will be destroyed by grenades as you leave, so you must keep low and do exactly what the agent in charge says." Charlotte's hand went to her mouth as she gasped. "*Make your way to Rue de Dragon, St Germain, house number: your real age. Go to the side door, then the second floor. On no account show this paper to anybody else. Baron.*"

Charlotte read the final part again. Destroy her house? She was aghast. But why? She was going to have to stop this.

Charlotte stood, handed the paper to Theodora, and went to her wardrobe to find a suitable dress. "Are you 'Goddess'?" Theodora asked with a little smile, not able to read the message, her English being limited.

Charlotte grabbed the paper back and translated it into French. Theodora looked in astonishment.

"Why 'Goddess'?"

"No idea," Charlotte said shortly. She was furious.

"I presume I am 'your friend'?"

"Yes, I don't have any others here." Charlotte went to the mirror and checked her make-up. "I am going to see the general to see if I can go to the gallery. I want to know what is going on. I don't want my house destroyed!"

"Quiet, Freya, someone will hear."

"I really don't care!" Charlotte stormed towards the door, smoothing her dress down over her hips. Theodora got hold of Charlotte's shoulders before she reached the door and turned her round to face her.

"What exactly are you going to say?" Theodora looked angry, something Charlotte had seldom seen. "Just be careful. You are on dangerous ground."

"I will not say anything about the note," Charlotte said, contrite and wary that she had somehow offended Theodora. She took the note and shoved it into her mouth. It melted away with a strange sweet and metallic taste.

"Just you be very careful, Freya. You must not jeopardise anything the Allies have planned."

Charlotte pried herself out of Theodora's hold, and stood and eyed her friend in some bewilderment. Just who was this woman? Theodora's anger turned to concern.

"I worry about you, Freya. This is just a building that can be rebuilt. I cannot rebuild you back to life if you are killed by these bastards." Theodora turned and looked out the window.

*

"General!" Charlotte was at her most charming. "I have a huge request to ask you."

"Anything, my dear. Anything in my power, that is." He was jovial. The Hitler portrait had been hung and he was admiring it from his chair.

"I really want to go to the Galerie Bayser and thank the baron for the portrait of our Führer. He is going away for a while, to Berlin apparently, and he will only be at the gallery today."

"Oh, I see." The general looked unsettled.

"I know we are not allowed to leave the house today, but if Captain Wil or the sergeant could come with me, or even Theodora—"

"No, no, that is out of the question." The general thought some more. He looked at the portrait.

"Is he not coming tomorrow night?"

"According to his captain, no. He is attending something at Reich Chancellery, I think the captain said."

"I thought he said he would ask the baron."

"He remembered just as he was leaving and asked me to convey his apologies. But the captain says he can come." Charlotte finished brightly as though Captain Fuhrman was as good a catch as the baron.

"Well, Freya. That is a shame." The general still looked hesitant. Charlotte walked over to him and placed both her hands on his arm. The general was one of the few men taller than her.

"It won't take long if I borrow your car and driver. I could try to get him to come tomorrow, before he goes away. It seemed to work with the portrait."

"Very well, my dear." The general melted. "As long as you are back before midday. Sergeant!" he barked into a telephone. The sergeant in the outer office did not need to answer the phone; he must have heard the general through the wall and came scampering into the study.

"*Ja*, Herr General."

"*Mein Auto und ein Reiseausweis für* Fräulein Freya."

A car and a travel pass were produced for Charlotte. The general also gave her a terracotta bottle from his private stock of Grassl schnapps to give to the baron as thanks for the portrait. "I would give him a box of my best cigars, but stocks are running low and I have important guests tonight."

As Charlotte left the office, the general called her back. "Tell me, Freya. Monsieur de Tournet was asking after you last night." Charlotte's stomach turned with dread; she desperately hoped she managed to keep her feelings of alarm off her face. "He could not recall the chauffeur and housekeeper having a daughter. Why is that, do you suppose?"

"I have no idea, General. He had so many staff and so many houses, I suppose he just forgot."

"Perhaps … perhaps," the general said, now distracted by the portrait of Hitler on the wall. Charlotte slipped out of the office as the general sat in his chair, gazing admiringly at the painting of his beloved leader.

*

As soon as the door of Ferdi's office was closed, Charlotte said, "Are you completely out of your senses? You are not, I repeat *not* going to destroy my house!"

"I am sorry, Freya, it is unavoidable, and not up to me. A man called Heinrich Müller is going to stay the night, along with a few other notable SS and senior Gestapo figures, and we want them dead before they torture and kill any more of our men and women. Hundreds of agents have been captured and tortured, and it is thought that one of our agents talked."

"But that is terrible, Ferdi. Why would they talk?"

"They probably had no choice. The head of the SD, Josef Kieffer, along with Müller, probably tortured it out of them."

"What is the SD?"

"The intelligence arm of the SS. Krupp is part of the SD."

Charlotte was silent. She was about to launch into a tirade she had rehearsed in the car on the way to the gallery when Ferdi continued. "Freya, we plan to do huge damage tonight. It will destroy the tyranny that is happening in Avenue Foch."

"What tyranny?" Charlotte said, still angry.

"Plainly you have no idea what happens in Eighty-Four Avenue Foch or the prisons just outside Paris, including the Drancy internment camp."

"Well, yes, I have seen—"

"Last year, your friend Jost Krupp, with the help of another horrid and contemptible Nazi, Colonel Hans-Jürgen Stoltz, rounded up and sent for slaughter over twelve thousand Jews. Stoltz is a *Judenberater* – a Jew expert. We think Stoltz will also be at Le Palais tonight."

Charlotte shook her head. "I thought it was some kind of police station, where the Gestapo take people to question them."

"I regret it cannot be further from the truth," he said, his head bowed in thought. After a while, he sighed. "Freya, I told you Eighty-Four Avenue Foch is basically a torture chamber. Hundreds of people, mainly French underground agents and a few British, have been dragged into that place and tortured to give the Gestapo and the SD details about spies and military information." Charlotte listened, feeling a little sick. "We know of at least thirty highly trained agents that have been tortured to death there. These torturers then enjoy themselves as guests at Nineteen Avenue Foch … Le Palais."

"I had no idea it was as bad as that," Charlotte said meekly. "But how can you be sure of this?"

"We have files on all these people – eighty-eight top Nazis, Gestapo and SS officers so far – and we get information on a new one each day, just about."

"How do you get this information?"

"I cannot say, I'm afraid. Except" – he hesitated – "your friend Theodora is part of my team in the British Secret Intelligence Service."

"Theodora is?" Charlotte gasped. "But she cannot be! She hardly speaks any English."

"No, she does not. Not many of our recruits do. She is not able to tell anybody, even you, that she is SIS. Especially if there is a chance she may be overheard in a place like Le Palais, or if you were captured and tortured."

"I would never give up Theodora!"

"You may not have the luxury of a choice," the baron said sadly.

Charlotte thought about what Ferdi had said. "But this is wonderful, Theodora working for the Allies. No wonder she was so kind and helpful to me," Charlotte said quietly. "And she kept warning me about these men, the SS men."

"That is strictly confidential. I would not have told you were it not for the fact that we need to get her out of Le Palais as well as you, tonight. SIS have not heard from her since the winter of 1942. But I saw her last year, when you saw your mother's portrait in the window."

"That was you who Theodora saw skulking in the shadows?"

"Yes, but I was not skulking in the shadows. I waved at her, hoping she would come to me."

"Doesn't she know what you look like?"

"No. Ulrich Fuhrman is her contact. I was asked by London to find out about Theodora after my report about you."

"They know about me, Charlotte Barrett?"

"No, I thought you wanted that secret. I told them about you, Freya Jorgensen."

"Are you the only person, other than Theodora, who knows my real identity?"

"Well ... yes. But I am surprised you told Theodora."

"I'm not a trained agent, am I?" Charlotte said angrily.

"No, I suppose not. Sorry." Ferdi sounded apologetic but did not look it. The whole purpose of her visit to the gallery was to prevent her beloved house from being blown up. What Theodora said came back to her: bricks can be rebuilt, but people cannot be brought back from death.

"How did you get out of the house?" Ferdi asked, suddenly looking worried.

"I have come to officially thank the baron for the portrait," Charlotte said with a triumphant smile, and handed over the bottle of the general's schnapps. "From General von Ardle."

"That is a relief. I thought you may have sneaked out and would find it difficult to sneak back in again."

"I'd better go," she said. "See you tomorrow morning?"

"You will see Ulrich just before four o'clock. Try and get to the cloakroom by three o'clock with Theodora and wait there. You must be at the back door at five minutes to four in the morning. No earlier, and certainly no later."

"Does she know?"

"What?" asked Ferdi.

"About your plans for tonight?"

"I presumed you would have told her," he said. Charlotte felt embarrassed.

"By the way" – Charlotte turned at the door – "was it your idea to give me the code name 'Goddess'?"

"No, it was Ulrich's idea, after the goddess Freya." Charlotte suddenly had a recollection of her last meeting with Colonel Deller, when he had called her the goddess Freya. "I was going to use 'Duchess' – which would you prefer?"

"Oh, Goddess, absolutely!" Charlotte chuckled. She went through the door out to the car.

As she left the gallery, she saw a familiar figure leaning against the general's car, the driver sitting nervously inside.

"Miss Jorgensen," Hueber said, pushing himself off the car and walking over towards her, hands in his pockets, in a kind of swagger. "You cannot keep away from this place."

"And what business is it of yours?" Charlotte's heart was in her throat. She coughed lightly, but she held herself together.

"Very much Gestapo business, actually. We are about to search these premises – we suspect you are keeping Charlotte de Tournet here, or some kind of contact."

Charlotte sighed dramatically. "And why do you think that? This is the third time I have been to this gallery in as many years."

"Not quite. Once last year and twice in the past three days. Papers, please." Hueber held out his hand.

Charlotte produced her documents from her handbag, when a low voice from behind her asked, "Can I help you, sir?" Ulrich Fuhrman had come out of the gallery, in full SS captain's uniform and with two SS soldiers. He had his hand on his Luger pistol in its holster like an American western gunslinger about to draw.

Hueber went to his inside pocket and produced an identity card. "*Kriminalkommissar* Karl Hueber, Gestapo, Captain Fuhrman. This lady is thought to be taking information to the enemy via an agent in this building."

"Really, Herr Hueber? And what evidence have you of this?" Ulrich laughed, making Hueber agitated.

"This is not a matter for you, sir. We are about to search these premises to see for ourselves if this is the case."

"Are you?" Ulrich said, unperturbed. Charlotte thought of all the files they had on the eighty-eight Gestapo and SS officers. "Follow me, Hueber. Fräulein Jorgensen, you had better get back to Le Palais."

"She stays here!" said the little rat-like man, his cigarette stuck permanently in his thin lips. Ulrich Fuhrman drew himself up to his full height. He strolled over to Hueber and bore down on him. "I am going to have to insist that Fräulein Jorgensen is allowed to go back to Le Palais. She is under orders from General von Ardle." Charlotte waved the pass in Hueber's face. Ulrich was calm but very firm. He placed his large hand on Hueber's shoulder in what was outwardly a friendly gesture, but Charlotte could see the firm grip he had on Hueber was the opposite of friendly.

"Take your hands off me, Fuhrman. Do you realise who I am, who I represent?"

"You are a minor official in the secret police who enjoys bullying young ladies."

"I am the assistant to Major Heinrich Müller, head of Gestapo, in Paris. Hardly minor."

"I have only your word for that. You and I will go into my office in the gallery and arrange the search. You can call whoever you like – try old Heinrich if you care to. But Fräulein Jorgensen must be back at Le Palais. Am I understood?"

"You are, captain. But you have made a big mistake."

As Captain Fuhrman put his hand on Hueber's shoulder, Charlotte noticed four men emerge from the archway into the gallery courtyard, all with pistols drawn. She watched as Ulrich and his two soldiers drew out their pistols. Ulrich pointed his Luger at Hueber's crotch as the other men approached. The clasp on Hueber's right shoulder got even tighter and the end of the captain's pistol nestled into Hueber's groin. Hueber winced.

"What is this, Hueber? Germans pointing weapons at Germans? You Gestapo are a disgrace." He looked up at the approaching men and shouted, "Holster your weapons, or I put a round in this man's scrotum!" Hueber looked alarmed.

"Do as he says!" shouted Hueber, his voice going nearly falsetto.

All this time Charlotte was standing in the middle of the courtyard, watching everything, wondering how she could help. She felt uncomfortable and slightly scared, but the excitement of Ulrich Fuhrman taking command of the situation, and the sight of the horrid little Gestapo man being humiliated, was most enjoyable.

"Fräulein Jorgensen, I think you should take to your car and get back to Le Palais. I will phone the general and explain why you were held up."

"Thank you, Captain Fuhrman. Good day to you."

"But ..." Hueber protested.

"You will accompany me into the gallery, and we will talk to your superiors at Eighty-Four. Good day, fräulein."

Charlotte watched Ulrich march Hueber into the gallery from the rear window of the general's car as she sped away, Hueber's colleagues all following behind.

*

Charlotte walked over to the door of their private sitting room, on the attic floor, and looked out into the corridor to check nobody was around. She closed the door, wound up the small gramophone and put on some music – not too loud.

"This is the plan, Theodora. It still grieves me the house has to suffer." Charlotte told her everything that had happened at the gallery. Theodora watched her with interest, especially when she said, "I gather from the baron that you are a British secret agent."

Theodora looked uncomfortable. "Yes, I am, of sorts."

"What do you mean, 'of sorts'?"

"Well, my task was to report back on general staff movements in Germany. I would get in radio contact with London, informing the British of what I gathered from the club in Berlin where I worked: Das Katzenclubhaus. I also passed information that came in on to Baron."

"Was that not dangerous? Could anyone detect the radio or listen to your transmission?"

"Freya, why do you want to know?"

"I'm just fascinated." Charlotte sat closely to Theodora on the sofa.

"All I will say is that I transmitted in a kind of Turkish: Kurdish. There are very few people who speak it."

"And nobody knew it was coming from the club?"

"No, but I was moved here and could not easily move the radio transmitter too. I had organised for another radio to be sent to me here somehow. It arrived in my trunk of clothes two years ago and I had it set up in the garden shed." Theodora sighed. "Until the day I saw Deller going into the shed, I thought it was safe. Then, that awful winter when the shed was destroyed for firewood … I was anxious they would discover the radio, but they obviously did not dig up the floor."

"So the radio is still there?" Charlotte asked, riveted.

"Yes, but it will have got damp. In any case, if I pulled it out of the hole, I would be seen from the house. Did the baron tell you about me?"

"Yes, because he was instructed by London to get you out of Le Palais before they bomb it. London had not realised I – Charlotte de Tournet – was also here."

"Does anybody know Charlotte is in Paris?"

"No, I told Ferdi that I was dead, I didn't want anybody to know I was still alive. Especially now my bloody stepfather has turned traitor!" Charlotte raged. "What will happen to Agatha and Juliet?"

"I don't know. In any case, they are both good Nazis."

"And what about little Helmut the waiter and the old general? They are not mass murderers."

"They are still the enemy, Freya. The general is not that innocent. He was responsible for the setting up of the death camps and concentration camps in Poland. He became a general because of his contribution to the extermination of the Jews in Europe, along with a man called Stoltz – Colonel Hans-Jürgen Stoltz."

"Him again! He's a friend of Jost's, according to Ferdi."

"I did warn you right at the beginning. Most SS men seek acknowledgement from their peers as well as promotion. They are mostly ruthless criminals and cannot be trusted."

"I know," Charlotte said wistfully. "I've met so many nice, charming gentlemen at Le Palais. Now it seems they are all terrible, torturers and murderers. And then there is Captain Fuhrman: tall, strong, handsome—"

"Yes, but he is not a Nazi."

"You should have seen him with Hueber, Theodora. He was wonderful. I could quite easily …"

"We will have to be careful not to give ourselves away this evening." Theodora had changed, Charlotte thought. She had become more business-like, serious – not the licentious, free-spirited person she normally was. A side of Theodora she had only seen tiny glimpses of in the past few years.

Charlotte was dreading the evening. She wondered how she was going to get through it without being maudlin about seeing the house as it was for the last time. How would she feel about seeing de Tournet again? What would he say? Would he recognise her after three, nearly four years? She was a woman now, elegant, sophisticated, nothing like the little girl he knew in 1940. Perhaps she would have to sit with Heinrich Müller and not de Tournet. Müller did seem to be more important.

"Will you stay close to me tonight, Theodora? Kick me if I start to look unhappy?" Both of them laughed nervously as they hugged each other for courage.

Charlotte went to her room to prepare. She took out her mother's rolled-up Klimt painting, *Girl on a Golden Pillow*, and put it into a canvas bag. This would be all she would have left of the Barrett art collection. Her house was about to be destroyed, and her life was about to be altered dramatically, again. The only man she had ever loved had turned out to be no less than a mass murderer, and worse still, had killed Bo and possibly Christina as well. Her father, it seemed, was not only a drunk but also an art thief, an SS officer, *and* he murdered Charlotte's mother, and possibly numerous Jews and God knows how many other people.

Then there was the man she hated most of all, who was here, in her house. Charlotte fingered the crucifix under her dress as she thought of Jean de Tournet.

9

The evening started like most important evenings. Charlotte, Theodora, Agatha and Juliet, with the other senior house staff, stood at the front door, awaiting the arrival of the guest of honour. Two heavily armed SS guards stood at ease either side of the front door. Also there, waiting in anticipation but only when important visitors were arriving, was General von Ardle, along with Captain Wil, both in their finest formal mess uniforms. With them was Herr Wagner, who was something to do with the German finance department. A bespectacled man with chubby cheeks and thin black hair, the sides clipped severely to about ten centimetres above his ears, he stood nervously, perspiring. Herr Wagner, a civilian, was said to be a relative of Hitler's favourite composer, Richard Wagner. Charlotte could see the sweaty little man being related to a man who composed such dreary music.

The guests started to arrive. Heinrich "Gestapo" Müller turned up with a small entourage of his officers, which included, to Charlotte's horror, Karl Hueber. Hueber glanced at her as he took off his coat and hat and gave them to Sergeant Becker. He strolled over to her and being shorter, bounced up on his toes as he said with a smirk, "Glad we could clear up that little mess this morning." He then strolled off, smiling to himself. He looked scruffy and dirty, even in his best evening suit with black bow tie.

Charlotte had no idea what Hueber meant by "clear up". Had he arrested Ulrich Fuhrman? She looked across at Theodora who was being presented to Heinrich Müller. He was kissing her hand. Müller was a handsome, dark-haired man. He looked more like a matinée idol than a high-powered Gestapo officer. As he and Theodora went into the drawing room, Charlotte kept a close eye on Hueber.

"How do you do?" a man said beside Charlotte. She felt her hand being gathered up, and a tall man with fair hair bent down, about to kiss it. He raised his head and clicked his heels, and in German, but with a heavy French accent, he continued to speak. "My name is Jean de Tournet, and I am here" – he stopped and looked at Charlotte quizzically – "here, at the invitation of Herr Wagner … Have we met before?"

Charlotte was stunned, speechless.

"Are you all right, mademoiselle?"

She was not "all right". She felt her face go cold and pale.

On seeing his guest arrive, Wagner came over from the library door.

"Monsieur de Tournet," he said, dabbing sweat from his forehead with a white handkerchief, "I am delighted to have this opportunity to meet you at last. May I present Mademoiselle …?" Wagner looked at Charlotte as though he required her to finish the introduction. Charlotte looked at both the men, still unsure what to say. "Your name, mademoiselle?" Wagner prompted.

"I am sorry, gentlemen," she stuttered in German. "I am Freya Jorgensen. I once met Monsieur de Tournet when I was a little girl, so it was a surprise to see him again after all these years."

"I see," said Wagner indifferently. "Shall we go into the drawing room?" De Tournet was still observing Charlotte closely as they walked through to the large room where all the other guests were gathering.

"You know this lovely creature, Herr de Tournet?" Wagner had put on some wire-rimmed spectacles to take a better look at her.

"Yes, Herr Wagner. I used to have a Swedish couple work for me. They looked after my step—" He looked at Charlotte closely, smiling like a cat about to consume a captured mouse. "Yes, as I was saying, they looked after my stepdaughter. I must say, I did not know they had such a beautiful daughter. You are enchanting, my dear." He kissed her hand again. Charlotte felt as though ice had formed around her sternum. He has recognised me, she thought, and if he says something to Hueber, God knows what will happen to me.

"Freya, darling, you look like you are about to faint," Theodora said quietly at Charlotte's shoulder. "Monsieur de Tournet, I am Madame Theodora. We met not so long ago." She winked at de Tournet and he beamed.

"We did indeed meet, madame." He took her hand in both of his and he kissed it with enthusiasm.

"Would you excuse me?" Charlotte said and raced off, out of the hall and into the cloakroom. Theodora also made her excuses, saying she would see if she could help Freya.

Charlotte was slumped over the basin in the large marble-decked cloakroom. She felt like she was about to vomit. Theodora came in and locked the door behind her.

"Freya, you are going to have to bear up a little better than this. I credited you with more mettle." Theodora was being stern.

"I know, I thought I could deal with meeting that bastard, but he suddenly appeared – I was taken off guard and I found it difficult to recover. I will get myself together and come back in. After a glass of champagne, I will be fine. Just don't let me be left alone with him for too long!"

"I don't think I can guarantee that. You may be left on your own with him. If you are, just ask him why he is here – a Frenchman selling steel to the enemy?"

"Yes, I should, I suppose. I'm OK," she said, her colour coming back. "I will have a think about what to say and be there in in a minute. You go ahead, Theodora."

After five minutes in the cloakroom, reapplying her make-up and pulling up the bodice of her silk dress so less of her chest was exposed, Charlotte returned to the drawing room. De Tournet and Wagner were talking to General von Ardle.

"Ah, here she is," said von Ardle delightedly. "Come and join us, my dear, rescue these gentlemen from my boring company." He laughed at his own joke loudly, his monocle springing from his eye and bouncing onto his chest on its tether.

"I am sorry, gentlemen, it was either the air or seeing Monsieur de Tournet again after so many years. I just felt a little light-headed. Nothing a glass of wine will not cure."

De Tournet clicked his fingers at a waiter bearing a tray of champagne saucers. When the tray arrived, he whisked off two glasses and handed one to Charlotte, who graciously accepted and swallowed the contents in one gulp. De Tournet had anticipated this and swapped the empty glass with a second full one. He plucked a full one for himself and raised it up for a toast. "To a resolution to hostilities between our nations, so that we can defeat the Russians and the communist rabble."

"Well said, Herr de Tournet!" Heinrich Müller agreed as he wandered over, Hueber by his side. The whole room raised their glasses and drank to the toast.

"A bit early for toasts," von Ardle said, "but we should toast de Tournet for bravely coming to help Germany, his natural enemy." The general raised his glass to de Tournet, who bowed graciously to acknowledge the salute.

The evening continued smoothly. At dinner, Charlotte found herself sitting in between de Tournet and Müller. Müller was a charming man, the complete opposite to how she imagined the head of the Gestapo would be. She saw de Tournet was drinking heavily, and worried that he might blurt out something in a drunken moment that could put her at risk. She decided that if she was extremely charming towards him, even flirtatious, it might avoid any outbursts.

Hueber had taken a liking to Agatha, and they played a duet on the piano after dinner. At the beginning of the evening, Agatha found his attentions decidedly distasteful, but he did not seem to notice, or care, that she was not enjoying his company. Hueber was also getting more and more drunk, which alleviated Charlotte's concerns. Charlotte wondered if Hueber was staying the night at Le Palais. Hopefully he would be a victim of Ferdi's invasion plans later that evening.

Charlotte felt nervous about the raid. She had forgotten about the plan for part of the evening, her mind taken up with worrying about her stepfather. What was going to happen to everyone else in the house? Should they warn Agatha and Juliet? How much of the house was going to be damaged? She looked about her, at the wonderful painted ceiling in the dining room, the huge chandeliers in the drawing room and the halls. The marble floors, the books in the library.

All her paintings had gone, disappeared. With any luck, she would find the collection intact after the war. She had worked out that of the eighteen major works of art in the collection (according to the insurance documents she found in the study a few years ago), there were fifteen paintings missing, unaccounted for, taken by Franz-Joseph Deller, for what he called "safe storage". She had her mother's Gustav Klimt, and there were two Félix Vallotton paintings being restored in London when the war started.

As the evening came to a close, Charlotte approached Theodora and whispered in her ear, "When can we slip away this evening?"

"I thought midnight," Theodora said sharply.

"What about Agatha and Juliet?"

"We cannot warn them, I'm afraid. We certainly mustn't tell Agatha, she is Nazi through and through."

Agatha was now giggling with Hueber. She had plainly drunk herself to a state where even Hueber was attractive! Or did she already know him?

Charlotte was never very keen on Agatha and she was now suspicious of her apparent friendship with Hueber.

Charlotte looked over at Juliet. Juliet was one of the stupidest people she had ever met, but she was a kind young woman and looked up to Charlotte.

"And Juliet, should we not tell her something?" Juliet was in the middle of a group of junior SS officers, having a wonderful time. Her pretty little face was a picture of delight, laughing at everything the men were telling her.

"Well, I have asked her to do us a favour."

"What?"

"You will see later!" Theodora gave a little wink.

As Charlotte watched Juliet, she felt sad that this was possibly her last night in this world. She looked so happy, surrounded by adoring men.

Just then, de Tournet, Müller and Wagner emerged from the general's study where they had been drinking brandy and smoking cigars. Two other senior SS officers accompanied them. They were part of Heinrich Müller's party and looked like typical SS officers, with short, clipped hair. One was thin with a Hitler-style moustache and huge eyebrows – he looked more like Charlie Chaplin than the Führer. The other was also thin and had large bags under his hooded eyes. He looked as though he was half asleep. They all came over to Charlotte and Theodora.

"Goodnight, sweet Freya, goddess of love," said de Tournet to Charlotte, placing a kiss on her cheek. Charlotte tried her best not to cringe.

"And to you, *chère* Madame Theodora." He kissed Theodora full on the lips. She lightly returned the kiss. Charlotte had always admired how Theodora managed to keep up the pretence of lovemaking with the men who came to Le Palais. The officer with bags under his eyes clicked his heels and said he was going to the library to read as he never slept well. The Charlie Chaplin officer threw up his hand in a Nazi salute and shouted, "Heil Hitler!" taking everybody by surprise. All the remaining men in the room leapt to their feet and answered the salute. Jean de Tournet also stood proud, his right arm thrust out in front of him.

Charlotte bade goodnight to everybody in the room and went to her top-floor bedroom. She hoped Theodora was not required to entertain any of the gentlemen for the night.

*

Charlotte could not sleep. She was relieved that she no longer needed to worry about de Tournet. He had not once approached her that evening to get her on her own. Perhaps he did not recognise her, or was that just wishful thinking? She kept seeing him looking at her, but that was usual when men were bantering with other men.

She placed the canvas bag containing a few personal items, including the Klimt, under her bed. It was just after twelve thirty. She would never sleep; it was only three hours before she would have to go down to the garden door to meet Ulrich Fuhrman. She had arranged that Theodora would come to her bedroom first.

Charlotte got undressed and put on a slip over her head. She hung her lovely dress up in the cupboard, knowing that it would probably be destroyed. A shame, she thought, such a waste. She was about to take out her clothes for the escape when she heard her door open. She did not have time to put on her dressing gown over her slip. As the door opened, the last person she expected edged into the room, his large body filling the doorway. De Tournet's eyes slowly took in Charlotte's half-dressed figure, his delighted smile turned to a leer.

"Are you lost, monsieur?"

"No, Charlotte. I know exactly where I am going in my own house."

Charlotte took in a long, trembling, deep breath. She hurriedly put on her dressing gown and sat slowly onto the bed, trying to ensure her legs were covered, her slip being quite short.

"It was a surprise to see my dead stepdaughter still alive and apparently well," he said with a sneering smile, his eyes cruising over her, from her golden hair slowly down over her body, her stockinged legs to her toes. He stood over her, filling the room. His face turned serious. "Have you nothing to say to your uncle?"

"No, uncle," Charlotte said, her eyes cast down to the floor.

"Oh!" He strolled up to the little window and looked out at the darkness. "Perhaps you can tell me what you have been doing for the last three or four years?"

"Trying to stay alive, uncle." Charlotte was very quiet, her mind racing. What should she do? If she made a fuss, he would expose her. If she made a dash to escape, all Ferdi's plans would be at risk. It was unlikely he would just leave her in peace after a short chat. She knew what was going to happen. "How is Aunt Stella?"

"She has gone insane," he said bluntly. "Ever since she was told you were dead."

"Who told her I was dead?"

"Your uncle Jason."

"What?" Charlotte stood in alarm and then sat again, wrapping her gown around her. Her aunt had always been pretty fragile, dealing with her husband, his indiscretions. His cruelty towards Stella was unforgivable in Charlotte's opinion. But her stepfather would not care a jot what his stepdaughter thought.

"She had what is called a nervous breakdown when we got back to England," he said simply. "The journey from Spain to Gibraltar and the flight back to England was very nerve-racking and she never really got over it." He spoke in a matter-of-fact way, no feeling about his poor wife. "She is happy, in an asylum near Brighton, by the sea ... quite content." He looked out the little window, hands behind his back.

There was an uncomfortable silence.

Charlotte spoke first. "Uncle, will you leave, please? I want to go to bed. I am very tired."

De Tournet turned and gazed at Charlotte, a Cheshire-cat smile on his face. He came over from the window and sat heavily next to Charlotte on the bed, putting his arm around her waist. Charlotte gave a little squeak of shock and stood up. De Tournet took hold of her hips and pulled her down onto his knees. An arm encircled her waist, a hand rested on her knee, gently stroking. Her robe gaped and de Tournet's eyes were drawn to her chest beneath the slip, and the large cross on a thin chain. He reeked of cigars and brandy, normally an aroma Charlotte enjoyed on a man, but mixed with his pungent cologne it brought back bad memories.

"Charlotte, do you remember what we used to get up to in this house?"

"Yes, uncle, I do." Charlotte felt a dread creep over her like a cold, wet fog. As she held her dressing gown together, she realised she was going to have to endure her uncle's lust again. It was never a pleasure, always a painful ordeal.

"I remember how you enjoyed our trysts."

"Really, uncle?" How could he possibly imagine she enjoyed his loathsome attentions? Even when she objected, when she was twelve, he did not hear her protestations. She decided, however, that it would be the last time this was going to happen. "Would you like me again?" Charlotte said and somehow mustered a shy smile. She stood, and started to take off her dressing gown.

De Tournet's face lit up with delight and total disbelief. "Charlotte!" he exclaimed, standing, and ripping off his jacket. His face was red with anticipation. He sat again, his hands holding Charlotte's waist and then wandering over her thighs and bottom. "You have grown into a beautiful woman, Charlotte. You really have become a lovely girl and—"

"Uncle, slow down. Let me unbutton your shirt, loosen your collar, take off your tie," she said easily with a crack in her voice, trying not to let her nerves show. "Lie down on the bed, let me pamper you. This is, after all what they – the Nazis – have trained me to do." She pushed her uncle onto his back on her narrow bed. The springs creaked. He swung his legs up onto the bed, his shoes hanging over the end. His blond hair was ruffled, and he looked tense in expectancy, breathing heavily. He licked his lips then swiped the bottom of his blond moustache with the back of his forefinger, like the evil landlord in a Chaplin film.

Charlotte sat beside him on the edge of the bed, her face demure, her eyes looking down to her task, an enigmatic smile on her lips. She pulled at his bow tie, unbuttoned his collar stud and then his shirt to the top of his trousers. De Tournet stroked her bare thigh, his hand under her slip. He did not notice Charlotte's hands shaking as she unbuttoned him. He was about to speak but Charlotte placed a finger on his lips and said, "Shhh, no need to say anything. Just relax."

He was captivated, bewildered by Charlotte's cooperation. Once his shirt was unbuttoned, she took off his cummerbund and unclasped the top of his trousers. She felt sick, but persevered. She stood, took a deep breath for courage, and slowly pulled her slip over her head.

"Oh Charlotte, you are—"

"Shhh!" she commanded. Between her breasts hung the cross on a long chain. She was naked except for her underwear, stockings … and the silver cross.

Charlotte took off the chain and the cross and lay down on top and to one side of her uncle. He moaned with pleasure. She felt revulsion rise up in her throat.

"Lie back onto the pillow," she instructed as coolly as possible. "Close your eyes."

She lay her head just below his chin, her trembling hand stroking the tight blond curls on his chest. She could hear his breathing was getting heavier and more rapid. She shifted her weight to allow her to pull out her crucifix. As she moved, de Tournet inhaled deeply and then sighed. She could feel her stomach turn again. She had to get this over and done with quickly.

"This is bliss. I can smell your perf—" He stopped as Charlotte placed the end of the crucifix just to the left of his sternum. "What is—?"

There was a sharp click as she pressed the button on the back of the crucifix, and she quickly straddled his chest. His left hand grabbed her thigh. With a sharp tug, Charlotte pulled out the stiletto. He looked confused, his mouth hung open. Noticing the time on de Tournet's wristwatch, she reloaded the spring action on the blade and plunged the cross into his right ear. As he was about to exclaim, she covered his mouth with her other hand and pressed the little button that launched the blade out from the bottom of the cross. She visualised it penetrating through his eardrum into his brain. He tried to move his right arm, but it was trapped underneath her body. He started to shake. She reset the blade and sank the crucifix into his left ear. Red flecks formed in the whites of his eyes. His back suddenly arched, and Charlotte felt a rush of air come out of his mouth under her hand. His eyes looked blindly up at her, wide in panic. His body then relaxed, his left hand falling away from her thigh. She bent down to his ear.

"Why are you here, you rapist filth? You will roast in hell!" She hoped he could still hear her.

She wiped the thin blade on his trousers. A small drip of blood seeped out of the wound on his chest.

Charlotte stood, tears of rage washing down her flushed face. She was shaking as if she was agonisingly cold, except she was hot with fury. She had thought of killing her uncle for many years but did not ever think it would come about. She never imagined it would be so easy.

De Tournet lay on her bed, his eyes still wide open in terror, his mouth gaping. She was unable to move. She could not stop staring at her victim. She was proud of her work but appalled at the same time.

Charlotte heard someone at the door. Slowly, it began to open.

10

Theodora entered the bedroom. She saw the corpse of de Tournet, and her hand went to her mouth to stifle a scream. Charlotte was standing in the centre of the room, near naked, breathing heavily and still shuddering with the rush of adrenaline. Theodora gathered Charlotte up in her arms and turned her away from the sight of her uncle's tortured face. She found her robe on the floor and slung it over her shoulders. She opened the window; the muggy bedroom was hot and stuffy, the smell of death hanging in the air.

"Stay there, Freya. Do not turn around. I will deal with this."

Quietly, Theodora pulled the bed out from the wall. She then rolled the body over the back edge of the bed and allowed it to silently slide onto the floor. She pushed de Tournet's feet in and pulled the bed up against the wall, leaving the body hidden underneath. She then pulled Charlotte onto the bed to sit down.

"I'm all right, Theodora." Charlotte's bubbling temper had subsided.

"Are you?"

"Yes. It was just a bit of a shock. It was all so quick." Charlotte realised the bed was clear of a body. "Where is he?"

"Under the bed, don't worry."

"Oh my God." Charlotte reached under but was relieved to find her bag and the Klimt painting were still there.

"Get dressed, we need to get going. We must make sure the coast is clear."

Theodora was wearing a grey-brown wool skirt, a thin black sweater with a short black jacket, and walking shoes. Charlotte had never seen Theodora dressed so … functionally before. She always looked glamorous in silks, cashmere and high heels.

"I suppose I will have to find something that will do for tonight's exercise," Charlotte said quietly, looking at Theodora's outfit.

"Where is all your jewellery, Freya?"

"Should I bring it with me? There isn't much. Stella took a lot of it to England before the war, after my grandmother died."

"We could use it for currency, you see. I don't think Reichsmarks are going to help us."

"I see. Well, I have some of Granny's that I never liked, but I must keep my mother's ring." Her mother had an opal ring surrounded by diamonds and set in platinum, which Charlotte wore in the evenings.

"Put it on the chain with the cross," Theodora instructed.

The cross, Charlotte thought. The crucifix that had just murdered a man. She looked at the cross. Ironic that such a holy symbol could be so violent. She shivered a little and then decided to get dressed. She put all the jewellery, along with some Reichsmarks she had left over from the dress shopping the day before, into a flat leather pouch that she put in the canvas bag, along with her Charlotte de Tournet French passport containing a photograph of a thirteen-year-old Charlotte.

Charlotte dressed in a sturdy, thick dark-blue pleated skirt she had not worn for about three years, a dark-blue blouse and a blazer. She packed a thin mackintosh and a blue wool jumper – it could be useful if it got cold. It was early September, still warm, but the early mornings were beginning to get chilly. She packed some underwear and a couple of blouses. She put on a pair of flat shoes – her old school shoes – and a black beret finished off the escape ensemble. Charlotte grabbed her bag and with Theodora leading, checking the corridor was clear, they slipped out of her little room for the last time.

As they descended the stairs from the attic floor, in the dark, sleeping house, the moon shone through the glass dome over the inner hall. They had to get to the far end of the corridor and through to the service-stairs door. The stairs went down to the back passageway on the ground floor, where the garden back door was, and where they were to meet Ulrich Fuhrman. But there was a guard outside Heinrich Müller's room. The guard was going to be changed at three a.m. That was the time to get to the service door.

"I have asked Juliet to distract the guard before he comes up to man his post," Theodora whispered. As it was just before three, they would have to wait for the guard to go downstairs.

However, when Theodora and Charlotte looked, the chair was there, but no guard. They searched around – he was nowhere to be seen. They bolted to the backstairs door but as they were about to open it, Theodora froze. The sound of passionate lovemaking could be heard against the other side of the door and then Juliet whispering urgently, "Slower, *liebling*, slower, or we will wake the house up."

"Good for Juliet! Well worth my nicest evening dresses," Theodora whispered. "But I think the silly girl is entertaining the wrong guard in the wrong place! She was meant to be in her room with him. Never mind, we will have to go down the main staircase."

They turned back and started down the main stairway, which was a greater risk. Guards would be everywhere. Would the relief guard be about to take his post? It was bright in the moonlight and they both edged down the stairs with their backs to the wall. No lights were on because of the blackout. They would have to somehow avoid the guards in the front hallway guarding the front door. Both guards were outside, however, smoking, and did not see Theodora and Charlotte cross the hallway. They sneaked into the cloakroom. Both exhaled with relief; they had held their breath all the way down the stairs.

The cloakroom was huge. They entered the area where the coats and hats were left and passed through to another door, which led out to the back-service entrance and the bottom of the back stairs – at the top of which Juliet was still with the guard. Theodora quietly opened the door to hear if Juliet and the guard were still enjoying themselves. There was silence.

"We should hear the bombing soon," Charlotte said, looking at her watch. It showed five minutes past three. It was deathly quiet.

The women settled down to wait. They hid in the coats, in total darkness, just in case someone came in to go to the lavatory. They were silent, full of expectation, a little excited.

Charlotte wished she could have had a proper look around the house for a final time before it was bombed, but it was too late. She thought of all the lovely times she had in this house, the tea parties with her friends from school, the huge garden in the summer, the grand evenings with her stepmother.

Her mind shifted to Jean de Tournet, his bullying of Aunt Stella, the horrid nights when he forced himself onto Charlotte. The arguments with her uncle Jason about the house. The comfort she got from Christina and Bo … What had become of Christina? Was she still alive?

She also had some good memories from when the house became Le Palais. The attention she got from the men, the evenings of levity, frivolity, and good food and wine. Agatha on the piano, Theodora charming the men and skilfully guiding their attentions from Charlotte in the late hours and towards the fun and music. Jost Krupp, who stole her heart and taught her the feelings that could be had from lovemaking. Feelings, Charlotte thought, she could only have if she were married. Was she now a whore? No money passed hands, but was that the definition of a prostitute? Was it so bad to be regarded as a prostitute? Theodora was one, and she commanded huge respect.

Jost Krupp, the man she loved – possibly still loved – who had turned out to be a murderer … Bo's murderer, if Ferdi was to be believed. Her heart ached when she thought of her handsome captain, and how she now despised him. How could she have loved a man who had such an abhorrence towards people, certain people, with no apparent shame, or emotion? She had watched him oversee the execution of ragged, defenceless men and women, with glee!

She listened to Theodora's breathing; she was sitting on the floor in the dark cloakroom, her head against some coats, her eyes closed. They had been waiting nearly half an hour. The door of the cloakroom was ajar so that they could see out into the rear passageway. The passage was dark, a little moonlight streaming in through the glass-panelled back door. The back-door guard was nowhere to be seen.

Then, from a distance, there was a rumbling, like thunder. Bombs were raining down on the suburbs of Paris. Charlotte had heard the bombs before but never so early in the morning.

Suddenly, a flash of light came, followed by the loud crump of a bomb, then another. Theodora's eyes were now open. The women moved out into the back passageway. A figure came to the outside door, not in uniform, remaining in the shadows so his face could not be seen.

Theodora crawled on all fours and reached for the deadbolt to let him in, but the bolt was already open. The man slithered in. Charlotte was about to ask who he was when she saw his hand rise up and come crashing down onto Theodora's head. She crumpled onto the floor. Charlotte saw that the man had a knife in his hand and was about to stab Theodora as she lay.

"What are you doing?" Charlotte gasped as she raced over to Theodora.

"My job, Miss Jorgensen."

The hall light was switched on, wiping out her night vision and blinding her for a moment. The voice was familiar and when her eyes became accustomed to the light she saw why. Hueber's rodent-like form came up close to her, a sickly grin on his face. He grabbed Charlotte by the hair and pulled her up onto her feet. She bunched her hand into a fist and with all her might, swung at Hueber's head, connecting with his left cheekbone. The pain that shot through Charlotte's fist and arm was excruciating, something she was unprepared for. Hueber's grasp on her hair tightened, his whole body swerved to the right, and he fell, dragging her by the hair down on top of him.

She felt Hueber let go of her hair and drag himself from under her, pushing her off him. He held onto the stair railings to lever himself up. Charlotte remained on the floor, rubbing her painful arm. Hueber now had a pistol in his left hand and raised his arm. "You bitch!" he spat, and brought the butt of his Luger down onto Charlotte's head, just above her right eye. She felt a sharp pain, bright stars flashed around in circles – and then, blackness.

*

After striking Charlotte, Hueber staggered and had to hold onto the stairs to support himself. He gazed down at her, prostrate on the floor, her thick gold hair splayed out like a sunburst. Even lying there, blood pouring out of the wound above her eye, she looked beautiful. He was transfixed. He had completely forgotten about Theodora, who was still lying unconscious at the bottom of the stairs. He thought he had killed her.

Charlotte stirred. Hueber grabbed her arm and hauled her to her feet. He half dragged, half carried her through the door into the outer office and then staggered into the general's office. He switched on the lights, threw Charlotte onto the floor and went to the desk, poured a glass of brandy from the general's decanter and swallowed it.

She tried to get up, but as soon as she moved, she cringed with pain and fell back onto the floor again.

"Where did you think you were going, Miss Jorgensen – or should I say, de Tournet?" Hueber was pleased with himself. He sat on the general's desk, the pistol in his left hand levelled at Charlotte's head. She did not answer him. She sat up on the floor, gently touched the raw area above her eye and winced. She found a handkerchief in her pocket and dabbed gently at the blood, grimacing each time she touched the wound. Hueber carried on. "I wondered who Fuhrman was helping. I was outside in the garden, watching the bombing to the west, when I saw an SS officer knife the guard. As he crept towards the door, I could see it was that traitor Fuhrman. I always knew he was a Jew-loving traitor, after his behaviour yesterday at the gallery."

"What do you mean? What have you done with him, you bastard?" Charlotte shouted.

"I put a knife into him." His eyes flicked to a bloody knife lying on the desk. "It took a while for him to die, however. He started to make a noise, so I cut his throat." He felt a satisfyingly elation; even drunk he had control.

His attention was drawn to the portrait of Hitler. He got up and tapped it with the muzzle of his pistol. "Is this what Saumures did? Nice." Charlotte started to get up from the floor. Hueber raced over to her and helped her to her feet by grabbing her throat and lifting her up.

"As for you, Fräulein de Tournet, I think you and I will have to have a chat at my office down the road. I don't believe you will see this house again."

"Why do you keep calling me Fräulein de Tournet?"

"Your uncle told me who you are, that is why. You have been, as I have suspected all along, spying. You and your Jew-friend out there."

"I have no idea what you are talking about. What do you mean, Jew-friend?" Charlotte said angrily, pushing his hand away from her throat.

"That woman has Jewish relatives. She is vermin." He was up close to Charlotte's face. "And you are a spy whore with that lot in the gallery." As he said "whore", he shoved his hand up between her legs, the pistol ramming into her groin. She gasped and let out a constricted cry. Hueber felt a wave of excitement; he was going to enjoy molesting this pretty girl. "By the end of tomorrow, Fräulein Charlotte de Tournet, the whole lot of you will be dead, hanging by your necks in Avenue Foch for all to see. You, the Jewess, that sodomite Saumures and all your filthy spy friends!" Hueber sneered.

Hueber's hand was back at her neck, choking her. He threw Charlotte into an armchair. She landed heavily. "You are a pretty thing. I think I should see what it is like to …" He did not finish the sentence. Charlotte was holding her head, dazed, seemingly unaware of what he was saying. Hueber licked his lips. Her legs were slightly apart, her blouse buttons had been pulled open, revealing her bra and a silver cross on a chain.

Hueber went down on her, his hands all over her breasts, ripping off her bra. Charlotte tried to fend him off. He stopped, pointed his pistol to her head and hissed, "I can do this whilst you are alive or dead, makes no difference to me! You will be still warm for a while." Charlotte immediately stopped thrashing at him and put her arms to her side. She looked up into his little puffy dark eyes.

"Let me stand up, then," she said breathlessly, "to make it easier for you. I don't want you to hurt me any more, and I don't want to die."

Hueber pushed himself off her. He was intrigued as to what she was going to do. He cocked the hammer on his pistol and aimed it from his hip towards her stomach. He watched her closely as she stood. She took off her jacket and unbuttoned the rest of her blouse and her bra. Hueber was entranced. He felt a little trill of elation – she was so beautiful. She was smiling … not a very convincing smile, but a smile all the same. He approached her, his unarmed right hand going straight to her breast, the pistol pointing away from her. He pulled her close, wanting to feel her body against his. His hand holding the pistol was on her buttock, drawing her tighter to him. She was taller than him, and he closed his eyes as he nestled up to her body. He was completely aroused and wished he was back in his office where he would have her tied, spread-eagled on his bed, naked.

Hueber felt a sharp prick on his chest. Before he could draw away, there was a "click" and pain shot through him. He fell back. A small stiletto blade was pulled out of his chest. He looked down to see blood from a tiny puncture seeping through his grubby white shirt. He put his hand onto his ribcage. The pain started to spread.

"What have you done, you bitch?"

"I've killed you, Herr Hueber."

"Not quite, you haven't." He breathed hoarsely and brought up his pistol. He staggered, grimacing in pain. He desperately tried to raise his pistol, but he was finding it very difficult to lift his left arm, his wavering right arm not giving any help. He was weakening, the pain in his chest spreading to his legs. Charlotte stood there, waiting to be shot.

"Hueber!" A shout came from the study door. Hueber's head turned to see Theodora crouching. In her hands was a strange tube-like weapon, like a large pistol. It emitted a loud click and a muffled thump. A bullet from Theodora's pistol went through Hueber's open mouth, through his brain and out the top of his head. He fell to the ground, the Luger firing as his hand hit the floor, the bullet driving into the skirting board beside Charlotte's ankle.

An enormous crash and explosion sounded somewhere in the house. A great draught of wind and dust burst through the study door from the outer office and the library, hurling Theodora, still crouching, backwards to the ground. Charlotte was thrown to the floor; the study door hit her in the back. The sound of smashing glass made both women cover their heads. All the lights went out, plunging the study and the passage into complete darkness. A fog of grey dust washed in like a tidal wave and enveloped the women. Breathing became suddenly very difficult.

*

Theodora climbed over Hueber's corpse and groped to see if she could find Charlotte and if she was alive.

"Freya!" Theodora shouted. Charlotte moaned a response. She was alive but perhaps semi-conscious; she could not tell. Theodora needed to get a gulp of fresh air before doing anything about rescuing Charlotte, so she went back to the dark passage, to the glass-panelled outside door, and saw the glass had been blasted out. She heard a movement behind her and looked up the service stairs. In the gloom of the moon she saw the guard standing at the top like some kind of ghostly apparition, covered in dust. He was holding his hands to his head.

"What was that?" he asked Theodora. She answered him with two shots of her silenced pistol, both to his body, and killed him. He tumbled limply down the stairs. Halfway down, his body jammed between the wall and the stair rods.

Theodora went outside the back door and steadied herself against the wall. Face down in the gravel was an SS officer, and next to him, the SS guard, both dead. She turned the officer onto his back. He had a knife gash across his throat, and blood was still pouring out onto the gravel stones. The guard also had a knife wound to the throat.

"Oh! It's Ulrich Fuhrman," Charlotte's muffled voice said just behind Theodora.

"Freya!" There was another huge explosion somewhere inside the house. Theodora swung round and grabbed Charlotte, who had made it to the back door but was about to keel over again. Blood was gradually clotting over her right eye, her face was covered in dust, her eyelashes white. Theodora tried to clean her up a bit with her hand, but there was so much dust in her hair. She wondered how she must have looked herself.

Charlotte was nearly naked, her blouse open, her bra dangling. She had her canvas bag and her beret in her hand, and her jacket in the other. Thankfully she had the presence of mind to pick them up.

Theodora sat Charlotte down on the terrace and darted back through the back door. She found her own bag and quickly returned to a dazed Charlotte.

"Come on, Freya, darling, we'd better get going." Theodora did up Charlotte's blouse as best she could and helped her up off the terrace, put on her jacket and buttoned it up. "The bomb will have distracted everybody."

"My hearing is muffled," Charlotte said loudly, tapping the side of her head. "What happened to Hueber? Did I kill him as well?" She dusted down her clothes.

"He's dead," Theodora said matter-of-factly. "Hold onto me. Let's get out of here."

"Where to? Ulrich was meant to guide us to Rue de Dragon. Where is Ferdi?" Charlotte's voice was loud, as though she was hard of hearing.

"Quiet," Theodora said abruptly. "Shut up for a bit and let me think as we go." She saw confusion on Charlotte's ashen face and said guiltily, "How are you feeling, darling?"

"My brain feels like it is made of cotton wool, and I've got a persistent high-pitched whine in my ears. My eyes are a bit sore when I blink."

"You'll be fine soon. Come on." Theodora, with Charlotte hanging onto her arm, crept down the side of the house to the front of the building and Avenue Foch. The front of the house cast a bright light from the flames, which lit up the front drive.

She leant Charlotte up against the wall once they reached the corner of the house, her pistol ready; she had five more rounds, enough to dispatch the rest of the guards but no one else.

"Where did you get that gun, Theodora?"

"I have always had it." Theodora looked at the Welrod silenced pistol with a little sadness – Ulrich Fuhrman had given it to her years ago.

As Theodora looked slowly around the corner, she could see the whole central façade of the house was ablaze – a fiery ruin. Debris littered the driveway. Half a dozen bodies, all SS guards, were strewn over the grass island in the middle of the oval driveway, their bodies incomplete, like scarecrows with an arm missing or a leg. Smoke and ash curled up into the sky, the stench of burning buildings filled the air. There were no living people around, no staff or any kind of life.

Theodora looked to see if the iron fence was intact and was thankful that the bomb had levelled most of the heavy railings to the ground. She pulled Charlotte off the wall and dragged her to the nearest gap, and went out into the darkness of Avenue Foch.

As they walked quickly down Avenue Foch, they could see the full extent of the devastation. The centre of the house, the entrance, the halls, all the way back to the *salle de séjour* – the drawing room – and Charlotte's old bedroom above, had been completely wiped out. Parts of the back wall of the salle de séjour and one of the long window frames remained but were ablaze. The garden could be seen from the road. The library and the dining room looked to have mostly survived, but the windows were hollow black gaps, glassless, like the eye sockets of a ghostly skull. The house looked dead.

As they passed the house in the shadows of what was left of the trees, they could feel the heat from the flames a hundred and fifty metres away. A few people were running through the staff gates to the right of the house. The evacuation seemed to be conducted by one of the chefs who was still in his white uniform.

"My God, Theodora, my house!"

"I know, darling, let's go." Charlotte stood and stared, tears coursing through the dust on her cheeks. Two loud explosions at the back of the house erupted, sending debris high above the house. "Ulrich must have placed time bombs somehow. It was lucky we moved when we did," Theodora whispered in awe. Charlotte could not have heard what she said as she had her hands over her ears and her eyes tightly shut. The sound of a klaxon could be heard approaching from the centre of Paris. "The fire brigade is coming – they will save what is left of your house. Come on, darling," Theodora urged. "Remember, there will be a curfew. We must not be seen!"

A massive explosion shocked them both, and debris flew up many metres in the air. The blast hit Charlotte and Theodora in the stomach and nearly knocked them over. They heard screams and shouting. The whole of the back of the house was ablaze.

"Let's get out of here!" Theodora shouted. Charlotte turned her head away from the sight of her wrecked house and ran away down the avenue. Theodora chased after her. She hoped they were running the right way. "Freya, wait!" Charlotte stopped abruptly, bent over and was sick. Theodora stroked her back. "You poor thing. You need a drink."

Charlotte stood and wiped her mouth with her sleeve.

Theodora smiled. "I know, let's find a bar!"

"What?" Charlotte was aghast. "It's either a bit early or a bit late for a bar, Theodora."

"Yes, wishful thinking," she said lightly. "We'd better get going to Rue de Dragon."

It was not cold, but not warm either. Apart from the approaching klaxon, Paris was quiet. The descending moon cast a soft blue-grey light over Avenue Foch, contrasting with the violent yellows and oranges of the blaze of Le Palais.

As they walked towards the Arc de Triomphe, Charlotte looked back for the last time at her burning house.

"Stop there!" a voice shouted. Theodora dropped to the ground, dragging Charlotte with her. She looked all around to see where the voice came from.

"Did someone say halt?" Charlotte said, and then took an intake of breath. "There are two men over there, coming our way." She pointed towards the hazy figures in the darkness. They were in trilby hats, zigzagging across the grass of the boulevard to where the women lay on the ground.

"They cannot see us," Theodora hissed. "Wait until they get closer. They may be Free French fighters."

One of the two men switched on a torch and scanned the grass in front of him. As they got closer, Theodora could hear they were talking in German.

"Stay on the ground, Freya," Theodora whispered, then stood and shouted, "Who are you?"

"Gestapo! Stay where you are." The torchlight spotted Theodora standing beside a tree, her hands behind her back.

As the other man approached, Theodora said, "Oh thank God. We have just been bombed out of our house!" She embraced him and said pathetically, "Help us, please." As soon as she had the man's partner in sight, she poked the muzzle of her pistol into his ribs and fired a silent round. He dropped, and Theodora held him up as best as she could for a shield. She fired at the second man and missed. The second man fired back, but the bullet went into his colleague. Theodora fired her pistol again and the bullet found his head. Theodora picked up his torch, patted down the Gestapo men's pockets and removed their wallets and watches.

"What are you doing?" Charlotte hissed at Theodora, clearly horrified at what she was witnessing. Theodora said nothing. She searched each man methodically and swiftly.

"Keep an eye out for any other Gestapo, Freya!"

"Yes, but should we be—"

"Just keep a look out, darling. We need cash, and ammunition."

They left the bodies of the Gestapo men in the long grass and walked wearily towards the Arc de Triomphe. A lot of military vehicles were coming up the Champs-Élysées, one or two with wailing sirens. A fire tender was noisily making its way up towards Place de l'Étoile, the road that encircled the Arc de Triomphe. Charlotte was still dazed. She walked with her arms by her side, her eyes wide open, every now and then looking back in the direction of the two Gestapo bodies.

Theodora lay on the ground and got Charlotte to lie down beside her. She took out a piece of paper and looked around. She had managed to sketch a route to Rue de Dragon from an old map in the library. She hoped it was not too out of date.

They could take the shortest route and scamper across the wide road under the massive Arc de Triomphe and then out the other side, down the Champs-Élysées to the river. But it was dangerous, especially with Charlotte in a state of shock. Although it would take longer, Theodora chose to skirt around the edge amongst the scattering of trees. It took them nearly thirty minutes to get around the circular road. The huge arch in the centre of the structure cast a shadow in the moonlight as they dodged from tree to tree.

After two and a half hours spent travelling in the darkness, Theodora virtually dragged Charlotte in the shadow of the moon down the Champs-Élysées, only getting lost once when she missed the turn onto Avenue Georges Cinq and had to double back. They hid in doorways whenever a patrol drove past.

At one point Charlotte stopped unexpectedly and pointed to a house over the road. "That is where my step-parents used to live."

At last, the women arrived at the river Seine. The bridge was expansive, wide, and exposed. There was no street lighting but plenty of moonlight.

"We are going to have to walk very quickly," said Theodora, crouching down.

"But we will still be seen," Charlotte said breathlessly.

"I cannot see anybody at the moment. Come on!" Theodora hauled Charlotte onto the wide pavement. The pillared wall to the bridge cast moonlit shadows and each time a set of car lights appeared, Theodora would duck them both behind any cover she could find. All the vehicles were going very fast and so it was plain they were not looking for curfew-dodgers.

They at last arrived at Rue de Dragon. The deserted narrow cobbled street was pitch-black. No matter how careful they were about placing their feet, their steps echoed off the walls of the tall terraced houses.

"How old are you, Freya? Your real age?"

Charlotte looked at Theodora quizzically.

"Seventeen."

"Here we are, Seventeen Rue de Dragon." They walked up the steps to the covered porch. The door was firmly closed. Nothing could be heard other than distant sirens. Both women slid down and sat, arms around each other, heads together, exhausted and with a myriad of thoughts.

11

Ferdi, along with Beatrice and Adam, had worked his way, in the dead of night, over the rooftops to an internal courtyard in Rue le Sueur. They had hidden in the Porte Maillot metro station since the curfew, for hours, before emerging at two in the morning. It was now coming up to three. All of them were dressed in black from head to toe. Beatrice led the small group. She and Adam were "Francs-Tireurs et Partisan" fighters, experts in sabotage, and dedicated communists. Beatrice was followed by Adam, who carried a haversack on his back. Ferdi brought up the rear, with a long, heavy grenade launcher slung over his shoulder. The journey over five blocks of adjoining roofs was exhausting, but it was the only way to get to the back of Nineteen Avenue Foch unobserved by the constant curfew patrols.

All three dropped down into the enclosed courtyard. Beatrice unlocked a door into the house. The group scurried through the house, through to a rear courtyard that served as a small sitting area, just off the dining room. A large pergola covered in a dead rambling rose stood at one end of the courtyard, up against the back wall. There were planted troughs of dead plants along the end wall. The only thing that still seemed to be living was green ivy, crawling up the wall and entwining itself in the roll of barbed wire that prevented entry into the garden beyond.

Ferdi and Adam, without any instruction, took the large rectangle garden table, flipped it over and placed it quietly on top of the pergola. Ferdi was given a boost up to the makeshift platform and handed a kitchen chair – brought from the house by Beatrice – followed by the rucksack and the launcher. He positioned the chair on the upended table. The pergola creaked as he moved around; he hoped it would hold him for at least thirty minutes.

He stood on the chair and found he could just see over the wall. He took a telescopic sight out of his inside pocket and fitted it to the top of the rifle-like launcher. He flipped out the three legs of the tripod and placed it on top of the wall, pushing the barrel through the barbed wire. He looked through the sight but it was obscured by ivy.

"Find me something to cut back a bit of this ivy," Ferdi whispered down to Beatrice. She was the old man's maid, and she would be best placed to know where there would be tools. Beatrice reappeared with a hoe.

Ferdi pushed the hoe through the wire and jerked it back. There was a quick, loud rustle. Nothing, Ferdi hoped, that would cause concern if heard; it could have been a bird. He looked through the sight again and got a good view of the rear windows of Le Palais. There were no lights with the blackout. The house was lit up by the moon. He panned to the right towards the back-garden door, to see if he could see Ulrich approach the door to collect Charlotte and Theodora, but a tree was in the way. He panned back to the middle of the house. He watched the guard amble past the salle de séjour, smoking a cigarette in a cupped hand.

Ferdi climbed down to the ground again with Adam's help, leaving the rifle on the wall. "It may be a bit short," Ferdi whispered. "It's about ninety metres to the house. The grenades will have to smash through a window to land in the centre of the house."

"The range of the grenade is a hundred and fifty metres," Adam said. "Surely that will be fine?"

"These grenades are high-impact and are a good fifty-six grams heavier."

"I'm sure they will carry, Baron," Adam said, looking a little uncertain, which didn't help Ferdi's worry.

"Will the bang wake up the old man?" Beatrice asked.

"Didn't you give him a sleeping draught in his brandy?" Ferdi replied.

"Yes, but he only drank half of the brandy before he locked me out this evening."

"Well, he will probably wake with the bombing. He sleeps the other side of the house in any case."

"I just don't want him to catch us. I don't want Adam to kill him." Beatrice looked concernedly at Adam.

"I won't kill him, Beatrice. I'll just give him a tap," Adam said.

"A tap will kill him," Beatrice countered.

Adam looked at Ferdi with an expression of exasperation.

"We're nearly there." Ferdi tapped his watch. It was coming up to four in the morning. As he opened his mouth, a ripple of flashing lights illuminated the sky somewhere to the west of them, followed seconds later by a long rumbling crash of bombs. "It's started. I will go up to the rifle and send in the first grenade."

Adam gave Ferdi a boost up to the pergola platform again. Ferdi took a grenade out of the haversack, pulled the launcher out of the ivy and fixed the grenade onto the end of the barrel. He looked at his watch. The luminous dial showed two minutes to four. He promised Ulrich that he would not send in the first grenade until five past four, just in case there was a hitch, and that he would make sure the first would be in the centre of the house.

Ferdi took out the pin, pushed the grenade through the ivy, angled it up by about twenty degrees, looked at his watch and then through the sight. The crosshairs in the scope landed on an upstairs window. More bombs were falling a mile away, which would drown out the report of his grenade launcher. He looked at his watch once more, and then the sight again, and squeezed the trigger.

There was a loud bang. Ferdi's ears sang for a bit. He lowered the scope, hoping to see where the grenade had fallen. He saw it smash hard through the window of the ground floor and waited for the grenade to go off. But nothing happened. "Christ!" he cursed. He quickly retracted the rifle, attached a second grenade, flipped out the pin, aimed, and fired it at the same angle. Again, nothing happened at the other end.

"Are you taking the pins out?" Adam shouted up to Ferdi.

"Yes!" Ferdi hissed back. "I don't think they are landing on the striking pin. I am going to have to launch the grenade at a steeper angle. Here we go." He put the angle up another ten degrees. A second later the third grenade crashed through the window of the ground-floor room and the whole back of the house immediately went up in a massive explosion. A ball of flames roared through the centre of the house and out the roof skylight like a volcano. The grenade must have travelled through to the central hallway.

Ferdi sent over two more grenades with delayed fuses and packed up. He climbed down. "That is very satisfactory," he said, pleased with the work he had done. He had a slight pang of conscience when he thought of Charlotte, and how upset she was with her house being destroyed, but the results would be many senior Nazis killed and injured.

As the three scurried off the way they came, they heard two more large explosions, followed fifteen minutes later, when they were two blocks away, by a third massive eruption. Ferdi looked curiously at Adam.

"The gas in the kitchens, I should think. Or a stray RAF bomb," Adam said.

No one saw them arrive or leave.

*

They had waited in a cold alcove in the Rue de Dragon until dawn for Ferdi to arrive. They'd huddled in the doorway for only thirty minutes, but it seemed like hours to Theodora. Charlotte was still semi-dazed.

Ferdi turned up looking very dirty. He was covered from head to toe in black camouflage clothes. His teeth and the whites of his eyes stood out against his blackened face. Theodora was momentarily startled by Ferdi's ghostly appearance.

"You must be Theodora," he whispered.

"Who are you?" she asked, raising her pistol.

"Call me Ferdi," Ferdi said quickly, and placed his hand onto the pistol and pushed it down. "You are safe now." Ferdi looked around, up and down the road, and ushered the women into a side door of the building, which was unlocked, much to Theodora's annoyance. They went upstairs to the apartment. Ferdi pulled down the blackout blinds after checking the street outside again, then drew the curtains and switched on a table light.

Charlotte and Theodora both looked dusty and dishevelled. Charlotte sat on the sofa, her arms stretched out in front of her, wedged between her knees. Her head flopped forward, her eyes closed. She had a huge gash above her right eye and streaks of clotting blood running down her temple and matted in her hair. Her dusty cheeks had furrows of dried tears, and her complexion was white with ash and exhaustion.

"I'm sorry," he sighed. "I hoped Ulrich would know which door to use. Where is he?"

"Hueber killed him before he got to the back door," Theodora said directly, brushing dust off herself.

"Oh God! That is awful news, terrible … terrible!" Ferdi put his hand to his forehead. His head was shaking and his mouth gaped. He looked close to tears. "But nobody knew about tonight other than you and me!" He turned away from the women and bowed his head, hunched over, the palms of his hands on his knees. Theodora was stunned to see his reaction. She thought he was going to be sick. "Christ, what a mess!" he said with anger.

"The Gestapo man, Hueber, was in the garden, watching the bombing," Theodora carried on gently. "He saw Ulrich kill the back-door guard, but Ulrich did not see Hueber. He plainly thought, being in SS uniform he would not be challenged if anybody saw him, but he was ambushed by Hueber." Theodora placed her hand on Ferdi's bent back and gently stroked him.

"Poor old Ulrich," Ferdi slurred, exhaling in a big sigh. He sniffed loudly and wiped his nose with a white handkerchief. Then he stood and eyed Charlotte with concern. She was quiet and half asleep. "Is she all right?" he said, nodding in Charlotte's direction.

"She was hit by Hueber. He was about to rape her when I regained consciousness and killed him with my pistol," Theodora said, putting her silenced pistol on a side table. "She had already skewered him with her little stiletto blade in her cross. She had also killed her uncle an hour before with it … so, she has had quite a night!"

"De Tournet's dead as well?" He turned to look at Theodora. "And you were knocked out? Are *you* feeling all right?" Ferdi looked at Theodora's head.

"Yes, I'm fine, he caught me in the temple. He thought he had killed me."

"Who did?"

"Hueber."

"Was he on his own?" Ferdi gently pulled Theodora's hair back from her face, revealing a huge bruise on the side of her head. Theodora winced when he lightly touched it.

"Yes, he was … Ow!"

"Sorry." Ferdi crouched down in front of Charlotte who was dozing. He gently pushed her back onto the sofa.

"Poor girl, she must have had a pretty traumatic night." He carefully brushed some of Charlotte's hair out of her face. She woke from her stupor and started to thrash her arms about, as if defending herself from a ghost.

"Shush, shush, darling." Theodora went to her and took hold of her hands. "It is just us, the baron and me." Charlotte calmed and went back to a doze.

Ferdi looked down at the bag. "What's in there?"

"Some of Charlotte's things. I got her to bring her jewellery. I have brought mine, for bribes."

"Good idea."

"We encountered two Gestapo in Avenue Foch – I have their wallets and watches. One had some ammunition, nine millimetre, for my Welrod pistol."

"Very good … This isn't jewellery!" Ferdi said, unrolling the Klimt. "This is gorgeous." He did a double take. "My God, it's a Klimt!"

"What are you doing with my picture?" Charlotte said groggily.

"It's lovely, Freya, simply lovely," Ferdi said. He fully unrolled it on the dining table. Charlotte staggered to her feet and went over to him.

"It is the last bit of the Barrett Collection. The rest has been stolen by the Nazis," she said with contempt, and then, in a breaking voice, "and it looks like that bastard Franz-Joseph Deller took them." She did not acknowledge that he was also her father.

"No, I don't think he stole them for the Germans," Ferdi said with conviction.

"How do you know?"

"Just a hunch."

Charlotte turned to Theodora, her mouth open in astonishment.

"Listen," Ferdi announced, "I have a few things to do, such as find Ulrich's car, and then I will collect you two in an hour or so. We must get on to Spain whilst Paris is in chaos. There is a bathroom here. No hot water, I'm afraid, but there's a kettle on the gas stove. Get cleaned up. Here are some dressings for Freya's eye." He rolled up the Klimt, found a leather painting tube to put the painting in, and handed it to Charlotte. He opened a drawer and gave Theodora a small box of dressings. "There's some brandy here, and some sugar." He tapped a decanter and a small pot. "Get some down her, it should help." Then he went out the door, hurriedly, without saying another word.

"Come on, darling, let me look at that eyebrow." Theodora poured out two very large brandies, stirred some white sugar into one of them, and added a splash of boiling water from the kettle. She gave a glass to Charlotte who sipped the whole lot down.

"That feels better," Charlotte said, and shivered as though a chill came over her. Theodora put her arm around Charlotte's shoulders, and they went into the small bathroom.

As they cleaned up, Charlotte replaced her bra and put on a new blouse. "Theodora, what is a sodomite?" Theodora turned and looked at Charlotte in some astonishment. Charlotte, seeing this confusion, went on. "It was what Hueber said. He was saying horrid things about you and—"

"What was he saying?"

"About you being a Jew."

"Oh … I'm not, of course … but a sodomite …." Theodora had to think how to answer. "I don't really know, but it could describe a homosexual, I imagine. Not a very nice thing to say."

"Why is—"

"Oh, Freya!" Theodora started impatiently, but stopped, forgetting that Charlotte was young and more innocent of life. She may have been thrust into the grittier side of living a little early and, Theodora supposed, not every element had been covered. She explained patiently: "Homosexuality is, basically, when two people of the same sex make love to each other – men having sex with men, women with women. Sometimes they love each other, but, in my experience, it is all to do with the bed."

"Theodora!" Charlotte sounded disgusted.

"You asked, Freya, you have to know these things. Hueber was referring to Ferdi; he is a homosexual man. It is illegal," Theodora said with great sadness, "which is, I believe, very cruel as they cannot help their feelings."

"I see," Charlotte said quietly. "How did you know Ferdi is a homosexual? You have only just met him, haven't you?"

"I just know. I can tell these things. And from what you said about him when you first met him" – Theodora tipped Charlotte's head up so she could look into her eyes – "I think Ferdi and Ulrich were lovers. He was distraught to hear of his death."

"They could be just good friends."

"No, I got the distinct impression they were … You must never mention this to anyone. Do you understand, Freya?" Theodora could hear Ferdi coming up the stairs. She lay her hand on the pistol.

"Yes, I understand." Charlotte suddenly remembered what Hueber had said to her just before he was going to rape her. "Theodora, we must tell Ferdi that Hueber not only knows about me, but he also knows about the gallery and what happens there!"

Ferdi came through the door. He looked purposeful: clean-faced and tidy, wearing dark trousers, a black polo-neck sweater, a dark-blue reefer jacket, topped with a black flat cap. "When did he say he knew this?" he asked.

"Last night … well, this morning, just before the bomb went off."

"He would not have reported it back, I should think. We'd better get going just in case he did!"

12

Paris was suffused in a warm dawn sunlight. There was a pervading smell of burning in the air. Ferdi drove the small black Peugeot through the back streets of Paris, threading a lengthy route to avoid any major roads. His knowledge of Paris was extraordinary. However, every now and then they came upon bombed-out streets and had to find another route.

There was no talking in the car. Ferdi drove with Charlotte in the passenger seat and Theodora in the back, ready to drop onto the floor of the car should there be any interest in them by the authorities. Charlotte had her travel documents from the day before, signed by the general. Ferdi had his work pass for the gallery, but Theodora had no travel papers.

Charlotte and Theodora had a fully loaded Welrod silenced pistol, supplied by Ferdi. When Charlotte was handed the weapon, she looked at it blankly, without any protest.

"If I say kill them, Freya, you pull back on this" – Ferdi slid back the action on the rear of the pistol's thick tubular barrel – "until it clicks. Flick this thing on the bottom – which is the safety catch – and fire it at the largest area of the closest man. We will deal with anyone else. Just keep pulling the trigger. It does not make a bang; it is quite quiet." Charlotte looked at the weapon morosely. Ferdi thought she might burst into tears. All this talk of killing … she had probably enough of that for one day. "How are you doing, Freya?"

"All right, I think," she said softly, still looking at the pistol.

Ferdi carried on, trying to not look at her. "There are only eight rounds – bullets – so don't waste them."

"But I … OK," Charlotte said meekly. She looked a little better. Apart from a plaster over her eyebrow and a rather pale face, she was as delightful as ever, thought Ferdi. He saw that Charlotte was not her normal self, and he put it down to shock. There was nothing he or Theodora could do to help her, except put a blanket over her and keep her warm.

*

Charlotte was actually feeling very frail. Her usual strength of character was at an all-time low. All she really wanted was to go to bed and sleep, but each time she dozed off, horrid images of Hueber would loom up. She had a permanent high-pitched whine inside her head and her forehead ached. The vision of de Tournet's tortured face kept flashing in front of her closed eyes as well. When she tried to banish the dead face of her stepfather from her unconscious vision, it was replaced by the fiery ruins of her lovely house.

Life was never going to be the same again. Her home, her safe place – even full of Germans – was gone. All she had left was her painting, *Girl on a Golden Pillow*.

The drive was very tense. Around every corner could be a checkpoint or a military post or, worst of all, a Gestapo barrier, manned by the Waffen SS. Luckily, they were already on the south side of the river, but there were lots of police around. Every now and then, the top of the Eiffel Tower could be seen out of Charlotte's side window to her right.

"Should we be driving towards the tower, Ferdi?" Charlotte asked. "Surely we should be driving away from it … south?"

"Yes, we should, but I need to give a wide berth to Place d'Italie to the south of here, and everything around there. It is full of military. We will turn south soon." They had to avoid the river as well, as the bridges were being heavily guarded now.

After thirty minutes of meandering through small roads, they emerged into countryside and farmland. They were free of Paris.

There were no more nervous moments as they drove along empty roads towards the town of Orsay, and then through the small towns of Dourdan, Angerville and Artenay. They circled Orléans, before driving through a forest and then over the river Loire at the little town of Gien.

It was well into the afternoon and Ferdi had been at the wheel for seven hours. He was struggling to stay awake. A dead straight road took them to the village of Aubigny-sur-Nère where they stopped to buy more petrol. There was one deserted petrol garage with a single pump and a small chalk sign saying "*L'essence ici!*" – Petrol here! It looked like it had been unused for years.

"We are not going to get to Toulouse with what we have in the tanks," Ferdi said, "and I don't think this car is going to get us another hundred metres with that tyre." He looked at the huge bulb of inner tube poking through the front tyre like a hernia.

"Do you know where we are, Ferdi?" asked Charlotte, stretching, a bit more colour in her cheeks after a fitful sleep.

"Somewhere south of Orléans, I think." Ferdi looked up at the sun like a native tracker. "What do you think, Theodora?"

"I was lost just south of the Arc de Triomphe, let alone here! I only came to France in 1940." She looked up and down the deserted street. "I cannot remember the last time I saw such desolation." The village was lifeless.

"It is well past lunchtime," said Ferdi, "so there should be some kind of life somewhere."

He rang a bell pull suspended from the petrol pump.

"*Oui*, monsieur?" an old lady shouted out of the top window above the garage, startling everybody.

"Do you have any petrol, madame?" Ferdi asked.

"Yes … a hundred francs a litre."

Ferdi gasped. "Do you take Reichsmarks?"

"Possibly, monsieur."

After much haggling, and handing over a hundred Reichsmarks – about two thousand francs – and a simple gold bracelet, they filled the little Peugeot and a twenty-litre jerrycan with petrol; enough, possibly, to get them into Spain. They decided to rest in the village, and the lady at the garage said, for another hundred Reichsmarks she would be able to let the ladies have a room. The gentleman could rest in the car, in the courtyard around the back of the garage. Ferdi did not want to leave the car anyway, in case it got stolen.

This was all fantastically expensive, nearly the last of their money, save about two hundred Reichsmarks and five thousand pre-war francs that were not really legal tender. Ferdi questioned the lady about the amount, but she just shrugged her shoulders and pouted. "Try elsewhere, monsieur. There is no place for many kilometres."

"Do you have a shower, madame?" Theodora asked.

"Yes, mademoiselle, just opposite the room. There is a little hot water, but no soap."

"Towels?" Theodora asked. The woman hesitated, plainly debating whether to charge. One look at Theodora's challenging expression and she shrugged and nodded her head.

As madame led Charlotte and Theodora up the rickety carpet-less stairs, a young lad of about fifteen, in a dirty vest, was descending. He reversed to the landing to let the women pass, swiping his long, thick hair off his forehead and back over his ears. He smiled shyly as they went past. Charlotte offered the lad a smile. His face filled with a blush and he giggled nervously.

The women both showered. Theodora had a bar of soap from Le Palais, the scent of which brought back sad memories for Charlotte. The bed was hard and not very wide. The room smelt of engine oil and had one small window that looked over the courtyard where the car was parked. They both fell into a heavy sleep as soon as their wet heads touched the pillow. They slept for three straight hours. They were in clean clothes, and the dust of Le Palais had been washed away.

*

Charlotte was the first to rise. It was seven thirty and the sun was hovering over the hills far away to the west. She looked down at the courtyard to see the back car door open and Ferdi's legs poking out.

She wandered down the stairs. She was starving. When she got to the car, Ferdi was lying on the back seat smoking a yellow cigarette.

"Hello," Charlotte said in a light voice so as not to startle him.

"Well, hello. You look better … clean! Did you sleep?"

"Like a log, but something jolted me awake. Theodora is still asleep. It was quite a small bed. I think she must have jabbed me with her elbow."

"How are you feeling?"

"A bit of a head, like I have been drinking, which I haven't, of course. I have got this continuous whine in my head. Not very loud, just annoying," she said, patting the side of her head. "I'm terribly hungry."

"Madame is making us a cassoulet. It will be ready soon."

"What is a cassoulet?" Charlotte asked, opening the front car door and getting into the passenger seat. The evening was still warm and there was no wind in the courtyard.

"A dish of the Gods, from where I used to live, near Toulouse – beans, preserved meat like duck or goose, and sausages, in a thick sauce. Except it may be just beans, maybe a little pork fat and sauce as they have not had very good supplies here during the war. Nothing like what you had at Le Palais."

"Le Palais," Charlotte mused. "That seems like a week ago and yet it was only this morning! Is that where we are going tonight, Toulouse?"

"Nearby, a place called Auch. I have contacts there and this car may not last as far as Spain, both in fuel or a lease of life."

"And from Spain?"

"I have more contacts. We will get a boat to England. From there, to my house … where you can relax."

"Really? Theodora too?" Charlotte was excited.

"Yes, Theodora too."

"Where is your house?"

"In Sussex, in the south of England," Ferdi said, stubbing out his cigarette.

"I was going to live in Sussex when I was very little, with my grandmother and Aunt Stella. Only we never went. My grandmother had a house there."

"I know, her house was in Lewes," said Ferdi. "My family house is near Petworth, the other side of Sussex and the Downs."

Charlotte was confused. "*Your* family house?"

"Yes. My mother was English, daughter of a duke, and she married my father and had me and my twin brother."

"Twins?"

"Yes, but he was killed in a boating accident in Monaco just before the war. I am an orphan, like you," he said simply. Charlotte looked sadly at Ferdi, who sat up and threw away his cigarette stub. "Are you sure you do not want your uncle Jason to know you are alive and well?"

"No, I don't want to have anything to do with him ever again. Well not until after the war, at least."

"I'm glad you feel that way about your uncle Jason. He is not a man to be trusted, I'm afraid."

"Really? Why?"

"Oh – he is involved in some shady dealings. I don't want to say much more. But you are going to have to be careful when we return to England."

Charlotte turned to look at Ferdi, fascinated. "How do you know all this?"

"Through my intelligence work."

"I know he is power-hungry. He and Uncle Jean de Tournet were as thick as thieves when I was young," she said. "Anyway, you forget, I am dead to him … literally."

"He will inherit the house in Paris."

"What's left of it."

"But the site is still valuable."

"I will write a will, then, and leave it all to Theodora. She will not mind being alive." Charlotte tittered with the thought of Theodora being mistress of Le Palais, entertaining all the great and the good of Paris society. Jason would be furious.

For the first time for a couple of days, she felt so relaxed she could have gone back to sleep – if the hunger pangs weren't there. After a few moments' silence, she asked, "Ferdi, what has happened to all the files and records that you had at the gallery?"

"I walled them up in the cellar. I hope they will never be found by the Germans. In any case, the Germans will be out of Paris soon – I hope."

"Out of Paris? How?"

"Oh, I get information from London every now and then, and it looks like there will be an offensive sometime soon. It is part of my work for the British Secret Service."

"You don't seem the type, Ferdi."

"What do you mean?" Ferdi said with a dry laugh. "Just because I'm not a rippling-muscled brute with a tattoo and a fencing scar down my cheek?"

"Nooo ..." Charlotte laughed. "You are a very talented artist, and a clever man ..."

"And a homosexual, is that what you are trying to say? I heard you talking to Theodora." Charlotte was embarrassed. She studied Ferdi's face, resting her chin on the back seat, gazing into his eyes for a long time. He looked back with a sad smile on his thin lips. His stubble was darkening around his mouth and his strong chin.

"It is not that you are a homosexual that makes you unsuitable for this secret life; you are just not a typical soldier."

"I should hope not. I could never be one of those automatons. Orders being barked at me, ugly large men telling me what to do."

"Precisely, you are too clever for all this. I wouldn't want to put my trust in anybody else's hands," she said in a quiet, sincere voice. She looked up at Theodora's window. "No movement from Theodora yet." Turning back to Ferdi, she asked, "Why is your code name 'Baron'?"

"Because I am a baron," he said simply. "Baron Olivier Ferdinand Saumures of Luxembourg, at your service."

"Oh ... I know that! But I would have thought you would make up a name that was not so obviously ... you!"

"I thought that, but it was all too late. The war had started, and everything was in motion ... so it stuck as Baron."

"And also, I don't think a baron should be called Ferdi."

"Really? What should I be called?"

"Ferdinand, or Olivier."

"It's just a bit stuffy to be called Ferdinand. My parents' generation are the only people who call me Ferdinand." He became serious. "I long for the day I will be able to call you Charlotte."

"One day, when this bloody war is over, I will get my paintings back, I will find my friends – find Christina – and I'll be happily married with lots of children, and Jason will have …" She stopped and sighed, and sat in the seat properly with her back to Ferdi. She did not want him to see the tears pool in her eyes. "Have you been in love, Ferdi?"

"Yes, I have. But he was killed by Hueber."

"Oh my God! I am so sorry." She did not turn around to face him. He lit another yellow cigarette.

"Monsieur! Cassoulet for you and mademoiselles," the woman from the garage shouted.

"Great, I'm starving," Ferdi said.

"Did someone say something about food?" shouted Theodora from the bedroom window.

"Yes! Come on … cassoulet!" Charlotte called up. An expression of "What is cassoulet?" appeared on Theodora's face, followed by her putting up a finger to indicate she would be one minute.

*

Around the table were Charlotte, Ferdi, Theodora, and the youth they'd met on the stairs – now wearing a clean vest and a scrubbed face, his hair a little less unruly. They were joined by an old man at the head of the table who grinned at the women, obviously delighted to have two such pretty guests at his table. He had no teeth and his face shrunk to a large, moist grin when Ferdi introduced everybody.

The cassoulet was good: white beans and green lentils, no sausage, but plenty of *confit de lièvre* – preserved hare, and very chewy bacon lardons, which the old man insisted on gently spooning out of his bowl and putting into either Charlotte's or Theodora's, much to their dismay. Also served was a huge bowl of lettuce – home-grown, with large holes where caterpillars had eaten the leaves – slices of fat, knobbly cucumber, and a big round loaf of bread, baked by madame. Ferdi was told the family's name but he could not understand what monsieur was saying, mostly because of an absence of teeth. The only thing he understood was that the youth was the old man and woman's grandson and was called Loup. He was hiding from National Service as he did not want to fight for the Germans.

Charlotte could not stop telling madame how much she was enjoying the cassoulet, and how delicious it and the lovely bread were. She kept asking Loup questions, but all he could do was blush, smile widely, and offer single syllable answers.

After he had eaten, Loup excused himself and left the table, constantly apologising as he made his way to the door.

Theodora was obviously not used to this kind of peasant food, as she called it snobbishly but not in earshot of the old couple. She was also asked by monsieur if she was a gipsy. This didn't make Theodora very relaxed, unlike the others.

The oil lamp above the table provided an amber glow as the old man enjoyed the company of young people. He told his repertoire of jokes about Hitler and other notable Nazis. There was a lot of laughter, even a snigger from Theodora. Charlotte's laughter illuminated the room.

The mood changed when Ferdi announced that they would have to go. He had told monsieur and madame that they had just escaped the Nazis in Paris and were on their way to Toulouse to find Ferdi's family. This made them instant heroes in the eyes of these rural people. The old man asked Ferdi if he was a gipsy, like Theodora. Ferdi said he was not a gipsy, and that Theodora was Turkish royalty and had been kidnapped by the Nazis. Charlotte had to stifle a chortle when she heard this, but the family seemed to believe all Ferdi said, and looked at Theodora with quite a different attitude. As they got into the car, Ferdi offered to pay for the supper but was waved away. Madame produced an old gingham tablecloth bound at the top with twine. It weighed quite a lot.

As they drove off into the darkness, Theodora opened the tablecloth to find two whole cheeses, the shape of a truncated pyramid. Also, a round loaf of bread that smelt divine, two labelless bottles of white wine, and dozens of apples and pears.

The petrol tank was full, and Loup had put in a new inner tube and a patch on the tyre with a hernia. The road was empty and bathed in bright moonlight.

13

The Germans were fighting a retreating war in Italy. Mussolini was rescued by Hitler as the Americans retook Rome, and Italy had surrendered to the Allies. The Italian fleet, meanwhile, surrendered at Malta and other Mediterranean ports. Greece was in turmoil with the Italians turning on their former German Allies, and the Eastern Front was crumbling. Many German reinforcements were sent to Russia as Kharkiv was recaptured by the Soviet Red army. The German army was kept busy on all fronts around most of Europe, which meant that through the centre of France, progress for the little Peugeot to Auch was unimpeded. The only people to worry about was the French police, but they had become more and more reticent in throwing their weight around and making themselves unpopular with their fellow French people, especially in the Free Zone now that the Germans weren't hovering around them any more.

*

After driving for four hours, stopping three times to consult the map, Ferdi was aware that they were getting more and more lost. They had driven for thirty minutes without a town or signpost to give a clue as to where they were. It was totally dark and Ferdi could not see any kind of landmark. There were a lot of woods. He thought, and hoped, that they were travelling to the town of La Souterraine.

"Theodora!" Ferdi shook the sleeping Theodora next to him.

"What!" Roused, she quickly picked up the pistol on her lap and looked around. "What, Ferdi?"

"I think we are lost." Once he'd parked the car, he lit a candle and unfurled a map. He pointed to a spot on the map that had been circled in pencil. "That is where we stopped for petrol, and I think we are somewhere near here." He traced his finger to La Souterraine.

"What's going on?" a sleepy Charlotte asked from the back seat.

"We're lost," Theodora said. "I think, if we keep going south, we will get to a town eventually."

Ferdi sighed. "I just worry if we run into a large town or a city, there may be police."

"I thought we were going to drive through the Free Zone?" Theodora seemed troubled. She wound down the window and looked out. "We must be in the Free Zone by now."

"I don't know, Theodora." Ferdi was apprehensive.

"Well, let's worry about that when we get there." Theodora folded up the map and blew out the candle. "Goodnight." She turned her back on Ferdi and rested her head on the window, pulling up her jacket which she used as a blanket.

"Give me the map, Ferdi," Charlotte said.

As Theodora predicted, they did, after another thirty minutes, come to a small town. They turned the car off the road, onto a forest track.

"I am just going to have a look at the town," Ferdi said. "Don't move from the car."

"I might just go for a wee," Charlotte said.

"Don't go too far."

Ferdi walked along the road, his shoes noisy in the still night. There was hardly any light; the moon was shrouded in cloud, and dawn was about three hours away. A small cottage appeared to his left, then a row of farm buildings. At the far end of the buildings was a petrol pump and a repair shop. There was nearly a full tank of fuel in the car but the jerrycan was empty. It would be useful to fill that up. He started back to the car. A road appeared to his left that he had not noticed on his way into the town. The road was signposted to Ambazac and Limoges. He made his way back to the car.

"Give me the map, I think I can work out where we are."

"Do you know where we want to go, Ferdi?" Charlotte asked.

"Yes," he said, waving a piece of paper with a list of towns.

They slept the rest of the night in the wood, each of the women taking turns to stand guard. When morning came, Ferdi walked to the petrol pump and filled up the twenty-litre jerrycan. He also bought some oil in a metal jug. Their money was now virtually wiped out.

They drove to just outside of Pierre-Buffière, south of Limoges, and hid the car in amongst some abandoned farm buildings. There they stayed until darkness.

The roads were mostly straight and deserted, as Ferdi hoped. At night, when he saw any other vehicles coming, he would switch his lights off and hide.

It took another six hours to drive from the farm buildings outside Pierre-Buffière to the small town of St Puy, deep in the south-west of France. It was here that Ferdi was going to find an Englishman called Bertrand – his Maquis name. The Maquis had been very active in and around the Midi-Pyrénées and the region of the Gers, helping escaped Allied airmen and escaping Jews to Spain. Bertrand controlled a network of agents, mostly locals, part of *le Réseau Comète* – the Comet Line. He would train them and supply some arms and money that came from the British Special Operations Executive in London, to help the steady flow of escaping Allies.

Ferdi, Theodora and Charlotte's destination proved to be difficult to find, being night time. It was meant to be three kilometres outside St Puy. It took over thirty minutes to find the end of the drive down to the little house that Ferdi had only once been to. However, when they eventually arrived at the small house nestling on one side of a wide sweeping valley, a kilometre from the road, it looked like it was abandoned. It was just past two o'clock in the morning. The front door was wide open. There were no animals or dogs to alarm the household of their arrival, only a few chickens that stirred slightly in one of the two open-sided barns.

Ferdi suggested the women stay in the car. Armed with a pistol and a torch, he went into the house, calling out Bertrand's name. After what seemed ages, there was a lot of crashing and banging coming from within the old single-storey building. Theodora leapt out of the car and put the bonnet between her and the front door of the house. She kept low, her pistol in her hands pointing at the black entrance to the house. Charlotte scrunched down in the car seat, her eyes just above the bottom of the window, nervously waiting to see what would emerge from the house.

There was another great crash and a moo. A large cow with sharp horns and a thick tethering belt around her neck careered out of the front door, bellowing loudly, and ran off to one of the barns, where she started eating grass as though nothing had happened. Ferdi was close behind, looking a little shaken.

"Well, at least we will have some milk in the morning," he said, sweeping back his hair from his brow.

"I am glad you know how to milk a cow." Theodora smiled. "I very much doubt Freya knows, and I certainly don't!"

"It can't be that hard," said Charlotte, clambering out of the car. "After all, one hears of milkmaids."

"I am not milking a cow!" Theodora was emphatic. "No one at home, I presume?"

"No," Ferdi said thoughtfully. "The door's open, window shutters all open, cold cup of coffee on the kitchen table … the place seems abandoned. It's all slightly unusual and very annoying. I don't know anybody else around here and we will certainly be treated with caution. Let's rest here and I will try and see what we can do in the morning. We will have to go into Auch and see if we can find Bertrand there; he has a priest who helps with escapers. The thing is, none of us has an Allied military uniform or identity disc, so they may not trust us to be who we say we are!"

"And," said Charlotte, "we all speak French with accents."

"That is a point," said Ferdi. "Well, we certainly must *not* speak any more German. Speak only in French."

The house, as far as could be seen in the sporadic moonlight, was old, with light-coloured stone walls and a roof made from thick serpentine terracotta tiles, which resembled waves on a perfect sea. The small windows had dark shutters, folded back. They walked towards the house and as they did, a dark cloud sailed across the moon, blocking out any light and plunging the countryside into darkness.

"I better put the car into a barn," Ferdi said. There were no closed barns, only open-sided ones with a single back and side wall. Most of the barn roofs were intact and well maintained.

The women went through the open front door, straight into a sitting room, and quickly found some full paraffin hurricane lamps – the type that were pumped up – and lit them for extra light. The interior was a terrible mess. There was no carpet, just an uneven stone floor. To the right was a door into a rudimentary kitchen with a Primus stove on a table. This, as far as they could see, was the only means of cooking. A kettle sat beside a water pump. The pump stood over a small narrow basin carved out of the stone that formed the thick sill below the window. There was a plug in the sink and it looked like the cow was drinking from it –bits of grass and saliva were floating in the water. Charlotte drained the sink and pumped some water, filling the tiny basin so they could wash their tired faces. A clean towel hung to one side, which was a surprise. Apart from the absence of electricity and a cooking range, it all seemed quite civilised.

At the back of the house, a narrow corridor led from the sitting room to a bathroom. A shower arrangement had been set up involving a canvas bag and buckets over a drain that ran out through a hole in the wall, alongside a basin again carved out of the sill below the window. A door at the end went to what smelt like the latrine. To the left of the corridor, a door led to a large bedroom, as large as the sitting room, with rugs on the floor. There was just one small bed and a pile of flat mattresses stacked up.

"No food anywhere?" said Ferdi as he caught up with the women in the bedroom.

"Can't find any," said Charlotte despondently, "but there's plenty left in the tablecloth." They were standing at the threshold, looking at the mess in the bedroom, wondering what the smells were and debating whether to sleep on the mattresses or the bed.

"We've spent too long living in luxury at Le Palais, haven't we?" Theodora said morosely. A pair of French windows at the end of the bedroom, behind a thin curtain, lit up as the moon came out from behind the cloud.

The sitting room had just three old wooden dining room chairs, a couple of crates for tables, and a large wet pile of dung from the cow. There was a hand spade beside a huge open fireplace that had fresh ash in a pile below the firedog. A small, well-stuffed sofa in pretty good condition was against the wall, beside the fireplace. A large empty solid oak wardrobe stood against the wall, a chest of drawers with some blankets beside it.

"What have you got there?" Charlotte spotted that Ferdi was carrying a small pail of milk with at least two litres sloshing around.

"The poor thing was desperate. The milk poured out as soon as I held the teats."

"Ferdi, you are a genius!" Charlotte squealed in delight. "We can warm some up on the stove."

"Oh, I don't think we should drink that," Theodora said with distaste. "It will be unhealthy, surely!"

"Theodora, you will love it. It will be creamy, and anyway, Ferdi has diced with death getting it." There was a little laughter, but Theodora was still unsure.

Hot milk was produced. Theodora had a couple of sips and agreed it was lovely – rich and creamy – not disguising her revulsion of drinking something that had just come out of an animal as opposed to a glass bottle.

They dusted off a few mattresses and lay them out on the bedroom floor. Ferdi removed the pat of dung with the spade and put a mattress in the sitting room. However, he preferred to lie on the sofa, his feet on one arm, his head resting on the other. They all bedded down for what was left of the night.

The night was cool. The French windows were open, the shutters half-closed, to let in some air. It was difficult to fall asleep. Charlotte found the stillness of the near breathless night made every sound, every hoot of an owl or a mouse rustling in the dry grass, so much louder. Her mind whirled with the memories of the past couple of days. It felt like a month ago. She still felt a mixture of excitement and trepidation, sadness for friends lost, and pleasure of enemies killed. The haunting memory of the death of Jean de Tournet would remain with her forever. The vision of his face, ugly and terrifying, frozen in death, loomed in front of her eyelids each time she closed them to go to sleep. She tried to banish the vision from her mind, which worked for a while when she thought of the cow, but then the face of Jost Krupp would appear, stealing into her heart and saddening her.

14

The dirty grey bedroom curtain was billowing in the fresh cool air when Charlotte awoke. Theodora was still asleep. That girl could sleep forever anywhere, Charlotte thought enviously.

Ferdi burst into the bedroom, a huge smile over his face.

"You have got to see this! Give Theodora a kick." Theodora mumbled an expletive and turned over. Charlotte was concerned to see Ferdi's eyes were puffy and red.

"Have you been crying, Ferdi?" she said quietly. He said nothing, just grimaced and dashed out of the room again. "Come on, outside, quick!"

Charlotte did as she was asked and told a groggy and slightly grumpy Theodora that they must follow Ferdi out of the house and be very quiet.

As they went outside, the morning sun smacked them in the face with its glare. Ferdi was at the end of the house, looking at the end wall – the kitchen wall. The whole of the front of the house was washed in bright amber morning sunlight. The barn with the tethered cow and the car parked inside stood about five metres away. It was full of hay for the cow, a very rusty ploughshare and some large oil drums.

"Look," Ferdi whispered, and pointed at the end wall. "Follow me, very slowly and very quietly." The women could not think what he wanted to show them. They walked over to the end wall, holding their coats together around their necks as it was not particularly warm, despite the sunshine.

There on the wall was a tiny rodent, a mouse of some kind. Bigger than a mouse but smaller than a rat. Charlotte gave a hushed gasp of delight. The animal was very still, clasped to the wall, watching the women with its little black-bead eyes set on either side of a little pointed, striped face, tiny ears on each side of its head. It scampered across the wall as though on the ground. It had a white stripe running down its spine, and a long tail with wisps of fur at the end that twitched with each scamper. It darted into a hole in the old yellow sandstone brick wall.

"What is it?" asked Theodora. "It is a charming little creature."

"Wait … keep very still," instructed Ferdi in a whisper. After about a minute, a little stripy head emerged from the hole and scurried out, followed by another little striped head, carrying a baby striped mouse-thing. All three creatures ran up the wall to another hole and disappeared into it. Suddenly there were other little creatures, some with babies, some just out playing in the sun. They were enchanting, all scampering around on the wall as if they were moving to a new house, from one hole to another. Whenever they met, there was a squeaky altercation and then they would pass and disappear into a hole.

Theodora turned to look at the view, leaving Charlotte enthralled by the rodents. The house was set halfway up the side of a gentle hill. Below were long, sweeping, cultivated fields, with hills and downland stretching for miles into the distance. It was a breathtaking view. She saw what looked like spiky clouds in the distance.

"What are those funny clouds, Ferdi?"

Ferdi looked at the apparition with a hand over his squinting eyes.

"They are not clouds, those are the Pyrenees mountains!"

"Really?" Theodora also put her hand up to shadow her eyes. "Didn't think we were that close to the mountains."

"We're not," Ferdi said. "We are well over two hundred kilometres away."

Theodora could not see another house in the long, expansive valley before her, only farm buildings in the distance.

A large vineyard ran up the hill behind the barns the cow was in, and all around the back of the house, in straight lines up to what might be the road, about a kilometre away.

The house had a large chimney at either end and one in the middle. At the end of the kitchen wall, where the mice were scampering, were two small sheds. One was the latrine, attached to the house. The other was a store full of well-cut wood.

"You know, there must be someone living here. It seems to have wood, a good roof, and a cow!" Theodora said.

"Well, yes, Bertrand lives here," Ferdi said. "Why?"

"I think it is very odd there is nobody around – the cow left to roam, everything seeming to be in good order."

"Perhaps they have gone to Spain for good. There is no food anywhere," Charlotte chipped in, unable to stop looking at the rodents.

"No," Ferdi said thoughtfully, "there aren't any stores, or we have missed them. Is there any bread and cheese left?"

"Tons," said Charlotte, tearing herself away from the wall of little rodents. "Aren't they sweet!" She watched the cow cautiously as she went over to the car. The cow mooed at her loudly, and aggressively pulled out a mouthful of hay from a bale. Charlotte grabbed the old tablecloth from the car to find there was still lots of cheese and bread and apples – plenty for breakfast.

"There will be some eggs somewhere," Ferdi said, going into the barn where the chickens were roosting. A chicken coop had been left open. Ferdi found some eggs, collected six large dark reddy-brown ones, and went inside the house. He discovered a cupboard that was set behind the chimney, where a stove would have been but had long since been taken out. There he found some coffee, real coffee, a bottle of Agen prunes in syrup, some solid dark-brown sugar, a jar of duck or goose fat, a corkscrew, two bottles of Armagnac – both nearly empty – and a full bottle of sweet Floc de Gascogne, a local fortified wine.

"Can you cook, Ferdi?" Charlotte asked when she brought in the gingham tablecloth full of food.

"Yes. Can't you?"

"No, never had to. It's strange that a man can cook."

"Chefs are mainly men," Ferdi countered, and broke some eggs onto a plate and beat them up with a fork.

"Yes, I suppose. What are you making?" Charlotte was intrigued by what Ferdi was doing.

"*Pain Perdu* – bread soaked in egg and fried." He put a few drops of milk in the eggs, sliced some of the bread and gently pressed the slices into the eggs, then turned the slices over and over, in a kind of daze, thinking.

"What are you doing to that bread?" Theodora asked with distaste.

"Pain Perdu," Charlotte said with some excitement. "We are going to fry the bread in some fat."

"We?" said Ferdi with a smile. "There is some real coffee there in the saucepan, Theodora."

"What is the third chimney for, at the other end of the house?" Theodora asked whilst pouring a cup of coffee and refusing milk being offered by Charlotte.

"For the sitting room fire?" Ferdi placed a frying pan on the Primus stove. He put a knob of goose fat into the pan and waited for it to sizzle.

"No, the sitting room is the middle chimney," Theodora persisted.

"Then the bedroom you slept in last night, perhaps?"

"No – there is no fireplace. I looked just in case I got cold during the night."

"There must be another room, then," Ferdi said, "but all I could find in the sitting room was a large cupboard." He switched off the Primus stove.

They all went into the sitting room to see if there was a door they had not explored yet. There was none, just a large empty wardrobe-type cupboard. Ferdi opened the cupboard doors and gave the back a push. It moved a little. He gave it a bigger push and it moved some more. He slid the panel to one side. Beyond was a dark space: a hallway. A little daylight shone through two small windows either side of a wall that may once have been the front door but had since been bricked up. Wooden steps were to the right, ascending to a trapdoor. Ferdi crept up the stairs and opened the trapdoor into an attic, quite dark and covered in broken bits of wood. A destroyed radio, some wire, and smashed wooden boxes were strewn all over the floor. A hand generator lay in bits on the floor, a small patch of oil or old blood beside it. A roof window was the only source of light, and that was shattered.

"This used to be a radio room. There is a smashed-up radio up there, and an aerial," said Ferdi, looking worried. "It must have been hidden in a cupboard, but everything has been destroyed. What is in the room below?"

They all went into a bedroom. There was an awful smell, one that was more human than bovine. To the left of the door was a single metal bed with ruffled sheets, bloodstains smeared on the pillow and the bedclothes. Thin rope was tied to the metal corner posts. A single shuttered window was at the end wall. Beside the bed, under the window, was an upturned bedside table, a military-looking canteen, an empty packet of Gauloise cigarettes, a box of matches, a ripped sheet and an unlit candle in a holder. A broom head lay on the floor beside the bed.

There was a fireplace, and an old wardrobe in the corner. A bare table stood at the other end of the room. Everything that had been on top of it – a mirror, bottle of wine, hairbrush and other things – had been swept off and was piled up, broken, on the floor. A wooden chair stood in the middle of the room.

"It's a bit smelly in here." Charlotte wrinkled up her nose. As she went to open a window, she screamed in shock.

A pistol came out from under the bed, held in a very dirty hand. A scary, fierce face of a man appeared. His face was ashen white with dark purple bruises around his jaw and streaks of oily black hair over his eyes.

"Who are you?" the man asked Charlotte croakily.

"Bertrand! It is me, Baron!" Ferdi rushed down to the man under the bed. "My God, what has happened?"

"Baron? About bloody time!" the man said in English, and slumped back, the pistol dropping onto the floor. "My bloody leg, Baron." He winced. "I thought you were the police again."

"Do I look like the police?" Charlotte was shocked.

"How long have you been here?" Theodora asked, crouching down to have a look at the leg. It was wrapped in a dirty white sheet with a broomstick down one side.

"Five–six days, I think; it may be longer, maybe less, I don't know."

Charlotte opened the shutters and the window. Light streamed in.

"Freya, get hold of that end of the bed and lift it off him." Theodora took charge. They lifted the bed up and put it down beside Bertrand. He was lying on the wood floor, looking up at them, and said, in charming English, "How do you do." He gave a slight smile and blinked away the strong light. He was terribly thin, and his dark-blue shirt and trousers were badly stained. The formerly white vest under his shirt was a filthy brown around the top.

All three of them lifted Bertrand up and placed him gently on the bed. Tears streamed from his bruised eyes with the pain, but he seemed relieved to be back on the bed.

"Everybody out!" said Theodora. "I will try and get this poor man cleaned up and comfortable."

"I need to talk to him about what has happened," Ferdi complained.

"Bugger off, Baron." A happy smile had appeared on Bertrand's face, and he now sounded stronger than he looked. "The prospect of being treated by such an attractive nurse is a lot more exciting than reminiscing with you!"

"Some water and clean rags – hot water, Freya. And my soap."

"There is some soap by the shower," Bertrand said. "This is going to be fun. Ow!" He winced in pain when Theodora started taking off his clothes.

"I am going to have to do this with a knife," Theodora said. "I will need the wine from the tablecloth, Ferdi."

"Wine in a tablecloth? Am I hearing things?"

"No, monsieur. Have you other clothes?"

"There are some clothes in the kitbag in the cupboard, Baron."

Ferdi pulled out the kitbag and found them. Hot water was produced and some cloths for wiping down Bertrand's filthy body.

"I'll sort out some breakfast, Bertrand. You must be famished."

"Bit thirsty, actually, old man. Could do with a smoke as well."

"I'll get some water," Charlotte said in English, much to her surprise. She had not spoken English for well over five years.

15

It took nearly an hour to get Bertrand looking halfway decent. Charlotte was astonished at Theodora. For a woman who was squeamish about drinking raw milk straight from a cow to then happily deal with blood and excrement was quite baffling. The leg was badly broken and, again to Charlotte's surprise, Theodora competently redressed the wounds and applied a new simple splint, with Ferdi's help, with the minimum of pain.

"The fracture has partially mended, I'm afraid," Theodora said with authority, "which means you are going to have to have it rebroken and set properly, or you will have one of your feet sticking out like Charlie Chaplin's."

"Bugger that – I think I will go for Charlie Chaplin!" said Bertrand.

They had moved Bertrand, now dressed in clean clothes, into the sitting room by placing him in a wooden chair and lifting him. He was very light, no more than eighty kilos, so it was not difficult. They laid him on a selection of mattresses with one end folded so he could sit up. He gulped down two glasses of water and then accepted a mug of coffee with gratitude.

"Is this my private stock of real coffee, Baron? I hope you have not drunk the lot!"

"No, don't worry."

"Got anything to eat? I'm starved." Bertrand looked appealingly at the women.

"Hold on, I'm cooking up something now," said Charlotte. Both Ferdi and Theodora expressed surprise. Charlotte was defensive. "Well, I learn quickly!"

"Give her a hand, Theodora," Ferdi said. Theodora followed Charlotte into the kitchen. Charlotte started frying the Pain Perdu.

Ferdi looked sadly at Bertrand's leg. "How was your leg broken, Bertrand?"

"We were raided by the police. They came storming down the track."

"The police? French police?" Ferdi was incredulous.

"Yes, French bloody police, and with some SS Nazi bloke."

"But this is Vichy all around here … the Free Zone, isn't it?" Ferdi said.

"Not for long, I gather. It didn't stop them rounding up thousands of Jews, gypsies and homosex—" Bertrand looked at Ferdi, shifted his weight and carried on. "There has been quite a lot of infiltration … treacherous stuff going on."

"What kind of treacherous stuff?"

"We had a bloke, a French-Canadian – he claimed – who came through the escape line last week – or was it two weeks ago? We think he was a Nazi infiltrator. The day after he left, along with two British airmen, I got a telegram that told us to pack up and leave quickly. We were in the middle of packing when all hell was let loose!"

Theodora and Charlotte returned with a saucepan of more coffee and a plate piled high with Pain Perdu. Charlotte gave Bertrand a bowl of hot milk, some bread soaking in it, with some chopped apple, brown sugar scattered over the top, and a slice of the eggy bread.

"This looks splendid!" Bertrand said, gulping down his breakfast hungrily.

"What happened?" Charlotte asked. "What did they do?"

"There were four of us here at Le Tuko."

"Le Tuko?" asked Charlotte.

"My house … this house," said Bertrand impatiently. "We had a chap on guard outside, halfway up the track. We were waiting for a coded message on the radio. The police have been working with the Gestapo, we'd heard. They were trying to stop us helping fugitive Allies escaping. We were about to take a whole bunch of them over the border from Saint-Girons – about a hundred and twenty-five kilometres south of Auch – then over the mountains to Esterri d'Àneu in Spain. It was a new route. All the other routes had been compromised." Bertrand lay back with his eyes squeezed shut when a bolt of pain shot up his leg. He let out a rush of breath when the pain subsided a little. "First, Alain, the guard" – Bertrand carried on in a quieter voice – "came racing down the road, saying the police were on their way down the track. I got everyone to run and hide while I smashed the radio. The police were very quick, they caught me as I was untethering Gustava, the cow."

"Why did you stop to untether the cow?" asked Ferdi.

"I don't know!" Bertrand shouted. "Something I thought I should do for her. Anyway, they dragged me into the house and hit me on the jaw with the butt of a rifle and I was out cold. They must have found the hidden bit of the house." He jerked his thumb at the fake cupboard. "When I came to, I was tied to that bed, hands and feet tethered to the frame. A tall, thin Nazi in a long black leather coat was looking down at me with a horrid smile on his face. 'Where are the escapers?' he asked. 'What escapers?' I said in my best French. He then punched me in the stomach, winding me. 'Where are the escapers?' he asked again, still smiling, and I said I didn't know what he was talking about. He produced a file, and he then said, 'You are Bertrand, code name for Major Bernard Trent, an English man, an SOE agent – Special Operations Executive – and part of the local Maquis.'" Bertrand looked at Ferdi, his hands gesticulating, angry. "Baron, how did he know all this? We must have been infiltrated somewhere along the line – and bloody high up in the chain! The Canadian was just one of dozens of the bastards!"

"Sounds like it, Bertrand. What about the Spanish girl? Could she be a mole?"

"No, she had been badly mutilated by a Nazi. She was Jewish and a Kraut had carved a Star of David onto her chest." Bertrand shivered at the thought. "She was in a bad way. She looked nothing like a Jew. Pale complexion, blonde … pretty." He was reflective. "I hope she got away. God knows what would happen if the Nazi caught up with her."

"Was the German in uniform?"

"Not really. He wore the uniform of the Gestapo, but he looked like SS to me: jackboots, sophisticated, well groomed, very short hair, you know what I mean. He told me his name – a major – it will come to me in a minute."

"Did he break your leg?" asked Charlotte.

"Yes," he said sombrely, looking at his heavily bound leg. "But he was planning to break both of them. I still did not tell him what he wanted to know after a lot of punching. He eventually took a rifle from one of the policemen and asked the question again, and when I did not answer he brought the butt down onto just above my ankle. The pain was dreadful. He was about to break the other one when a police officer came into the room and said something in his ear, and he ran out of the room saying, 'Don't go anywhere, I will be back to continue our conversation.' That was the last I saw of him."

Bertrand took a long drink of coffee and a bite of Pain Perdu. He gazed into the cup, thinking. He looked up sadly and said, "I heard shooting from quite a distance away but nothing else. I tried to get loose. I kept working at my right hand as it was slightly looser than the other one, and eventually managed to get the rope off. I untied the other ties and tried to get off the bed and crawl away. I had to get out of the house before the Nazi came back. I knew I had a pistol stashed under the bed. I managed to roll out of the bed, but the leg was too painful to do much in the way of crawling. I managed to set and brace the leg with a broom handle. I crawled under the bed and stayed there, waiting to put a bullet in the Kraut. Oh!" Bertrand suddenly remembered. "The Kraut left the file behind. It got kicked under the wardrobe, I think."

"Well done, old friend," Ferdi said, patting Bertrand on the shoulder, genuinely concerned about his friend's injury.

Charlotte stood up and rushed back to the little bedroom, groped around under the wardrobe until her hand felt the file. She brought it into the sitting room and handed it to Ferdi. He opened the dark-blue card file and took out a single sheet of paper. The heading was of the local police headquarters in Condom, and the address and location of Le Tuko. There was nothing else in the file.

"I remember who he said he was!" Bertrand suddenly sat up and snapped his fingers. "*SS-Hauptsturmführer* Jost Krupp! Told you I would remember. I thought he said, 'just crap', you see." Bertrand smiled widely, enjoying his joke, but all he saw was shocked faces. Charlotte stifled a cry by holding her hands to her mouth.

"My God, that bastard whore!" spat Theodora.

"You know this man?" Bertrand was astonished.

"Yes, we do," said Charlotte, trying not to cry with anger.

"Well," said Ferdi, "it sounds like there is a possibility he will be coming back; if not for Bertrand, for his file. We'd better get out of here pretty quickly."

"How? I've got a smashed-up leg."

"We have a car," Theodora said and started moving. "Freya ..."

"Hang on, Baron. You know I have not been officially introduced to the lovely women!"

"Oh, I am sorry. Theodora, known as 'Empress', and Freya, known as 'Goddess'."

"Very apt, Freya. I note you are not only very pretty, you also seem to be wearing the official Maquis uniform, with your little black beret. The other question is, why is there a strange smell in here?"

"What kind of smell?" Theodora asked with her hand on her hip.

"Dung."

"Gustava had made her way into the sitting room and left a deposit," Ferdi said.

"Well that explains a lot. I thought it was the police or the Germans rummaging around in here."

"Come on, Bertrand, I will give you a hand back onto the invalid chair," Ferdi said.

Charlotte was very quiet. A churn of nausea twirled in her stomach since hearing the name of Jost Krupp again after a year or so. She visualised his face close to hers, remembering his voice, his charming smile.

"Are you all right, Freya?" Theodora said as she held one of the chair legs taking Bertrand to the car. "I know you are thinking about *him*. You must forget him."

"I can't, Theodora, but I know I must. Nearly there, Bertrand." Charlotte heard Bertrand gasp with pain when they went out of step as they made their way slowly to the car.

Every minute, they imagined they could hear a car coming down the hill track towards the house. Ferdi had his pistol ready, as did Bertrand. They got into the car and packed up the food. Theodora had hard-boiled some eggs and put some milk in an old wine bottle before untethering Gustava so she could go and forage and find a nice farmer to milk her.

They drove very slowly up the hill track. There was not much petrol in the tank, the jerrycan was empty, but there should be enough, Bertrand told Ferdi, to get to Auch, and there they would find more fuel.

"What is the plan?" Charlotte asked from the back of the little Peugeot as it struggled up the hill from the house.

"If we get to the top of this hill and away from the house without half the German army or the French police stopping us, we will make a plan when, and if, we get to St Puy," said Bertrand.

"I see." Charlotte became suddenly quite nervous. The prospect of meeting up with Krupp was becoming a reality, and she dreaded it. She curled her hand around the butt of the Welrod pistol.

"If we do get stopped by someone or we see a roadblock up ahead," said Ferdi, "I will stop. You girls get out into cover as quickly as you can and somehow get to Auch, to the cathedral, where you will find a priest called *Père* Gaston Reynders."

"Father Gaston Reynders," Charlotte repeated.

"He should help," Bertrand said. "He's a good chap."

They slowly turned out of the drive, onto the top road, edging around each bend, hoping not to see any police. They were unimpeded all the way to St Puy.

"I will have a look around," Ferdi said, and got out of the car at the end of small high street. There was a couple of people about, an old lady and an old man walking back from the bakery. It was just after midday and the shops were about to close for lunch. No petrol could be found, so they slowly went on to the city of Auch.

They managed to drive the thirty kilometres to Auch without incident, meeting hardly any traffic, only the odd horse and cart driven by sullen farmers looking at the car with great suspicion. Only the Germans and police had cars.

Bertrand had slept all the way and when he was woken, he looked, even with the bruises around his eyes and jaw, much better – more colour in his slightly sunken cheeks.

The car spluttered every now and then, an indicator that they were about to run out of fuel. The car eventually stopped, dead, out of fuel in the city suburbs. Ferdi and the women pushed the car, with Bertrand steering, off the road and down a little track behind a thick hedge and beside the river. As they pushed the car, they saw the track led to an old wooden boathouse with a huge hole in the side, big enough, with the removal of a few rotten planks, for the car to be pushed into. The roof was partially intact. The old, dark boathouse smelt of rats, mud and moss. There were no boats, just a rotten slipway into the river. They rested after pushing the car; the sun was hot. It was silent apart from the river burbling past the boathouse, which produced the comforting sound of running water.

"Ladies," Bertrand said, "do you mind if I have a private word with the baron?"

"What about, Bertrand? We are all part of …" Bertrand made a gesture that Ferdi clearly understood. "Okay, sorry. Ladies, some privacy please."

"What?" Charlotte was confused. Theodora took Charlotte's arm and led her out of the boathouse. "The man needs to pee, Freya."

"Oh … sorry, had not thought."

*

Bertrand gave Ferdi instructions about finding the house where Père Reynders should be. "We must get him out as soon as possible. He cannot be safe." Bertrand looked worried. "If he cannot be found there, then there's a house with black shutters, two streets away from the cathedral. Talk to Clarice – a woman in her seventies, very much part of the Comet Line." Bertrand sounded guarded. "But as she's quite old, I have preferred not to get her involved this past year." Bertrand glanced at Charlotte thoughtfully. "I suggest this one goes with you to distract any guards or police."

"What do you mean?" Charlotte protested.

"I am sorry, mademoiselle," Bertrand said seriously. "We have to use every weapon we have at our disposal. Talking of which, you must not carry any weapons, in case you are stopped."

"What about me?" Theodora asked.

"You stay with me, my dear. I could do with the company, and you are a little conspicuous with your dark skin and, if I may say, your stunning Mediterranean looks!"

"Thank you," Theodora said staidly, with a suggestion of a smug smile.

"OK, we will try not to be too long," Ferdi said. "I wish I could have shaved. I must look a terrible scruff."

"You look fine, old chap," Bertrand said.

"Yes, fine," Theodora said, patting his arm. She winked at Charlotte with a cock of her head, indicating that they should go outside, away from the car, so that the men could have a quiet word. Just before they moved away, Charlotte heard Ferdi say, "This is not what I planned. I don't know what London is going to say when we get back."

"Theodora, what do you think Bertrand meant about using me as a weapon?"

"He suggests that you would be some kind of defence or distraction if—"

"Because I am a girl?"

"Yes, Freya. He thinks you would be just as much of an asset to Ferdi as you were to General von Ardle at Le Palais."

"So, other than being quite pretty, I am no use to Ferdi. I find this very hurtful and just a bit ..." She could not think of a word to define her frustration.

"Freya, I doubt Ferdi wants to take you – you as a friend – but Bertrand says, and Ferdi agrees, if you went with Ferdi, the mission would have a better chance, because you are pretty and blonde. Unlike me – dark and suspiciously non-European."

Charlotte kicked a twig into the river and watched it float away. "By the way, I have willed you Le Palais."

"Very funny." Realising Charlotte was not joking, Theodora said, "What do you mean?"

"Just that. You are now the proud possessor of Nineteen Avenue Foch and all therein: the Barrett Collection, library, et cetera, et cetera. I'm dead!"

"*Bok!*" Theodora swore. "What have you done?"

"I am Freya Jorgensen of Sweden now."

"Freya – Charlotte – you are going too far. You are going to have to own up at some point after the war. Remember, Jean de Tournet is dead; there is no one to hide from."

"I love my life as Freya. Apart from anything else I am three years older, and when I am getting old, I can suddenly become three years younger!" Charlotte giggled, swept her beret off her head and threw it in the air as if in celebration.

Theodora was about to say, "Until somebody Swedish tries to talk to you!" but decided this was not the time to argue. Ferdi was now coming towards them. He had a pensive expression on his handsome, stubbly face.

"Look after Bertrand, Theodora, he is a little fragile. He doesn't seem to be frail, he's doing well hiding it, but he is in a lot of pain."

"Just get some fuel, and get us out of here," Theodora said. "And look after Freya."

Charlotte punched Theodora playfully on the arm and did up her jacket, put her beret back on her loose golden hair, pulling it away from her still swollen right eyebrow. They set off for the cathedral, a good six or seven kilometres away.

16

"Will they be all right?" Theodora asked as she watched the two young people walk away towards central Auch on the river towpath.

"They make a very attractive couple, don't they?" Bertrand said.

"Yes."

"They'll be fine," he said, and winced in pain as he swivelled in the passenger seat to look round at Theodora after she climbed into the back seat.

"But she is so young," said Theodora, stroking Bertrand on the shoulder of his dark-blue canvas jacket in an attempt to comfort him.

"She's twenty-odd, isn't she?"

"No, only seventeen – a baby."

"I bet she is not a baby! She carries herself like a debutante in full sail at Ascot." Theodora was lost with the mixed metaphors. She didn't know what he was saying but gathered what he meant. "Your Freya is a very classy young lady, and if they are stopped by the police, she will charm the asses off them, you mark my words."

"How is your leg feeling, Bertrand?"

"Oh – not bad, thank you."

Theodora looked at the wiry man sitting in the front of the car. There was only a little light coming from the hole in the wall through the back window of the car, so she could not see too much detail. She could see that he was handsome, even with swollen eyes surrounded with shades of purple bruising. His eyes were grey, with a wonderful twinkle and laughter lines at the corners. His nose was a strange shape; it looked like it was broken – whether by Krupp, or in the past, Theodora could not tell. His mouth was always on the verge of a smile, even when he slept. Theodora folded her arms over the back of the seat and leant her chin on her arms, her head now level with Bertrand's. She had removed her jacket as it was quite warm in the car. She wore a cream short-sleeved blouse which left her brown arms bare.

"What is your real name?" she asked him. Bertrand was stretched out, his head resting on the seat, looking up at Theodora's face.

"Oh – it's nothing exciting. It's Bernard Trent."

"Bernarrrd?" Theodora said in the French way.

"No – 'Bernod' – don't pronounce so many *R*s. Anyway, best to keep calling me Bertrand. What is your name?"

"Theodora, of course!"

"You know what I mean. I have told you mine. What is your family name."

"It's Turkish. It's a secret."

"Why is it a secret? Are you a spy? Silly question – are you running from the police?"

"Another silly question," they both said together and then laughed. Bertrand winced, and stroked his injured leg.

"It's Güran," she replied. "I am related to a famous Turkish artist, apparently." She said this with pride.

Their eyes met.

"You look like Kay Francis," he said wistfully.

"Who?"

"She's a film star. Very beautiful."

"Oh! I should be a film star, should I?"

"You would make a wonderful film star with those eyes." He seemed smitten. "Where did you get those lovely big brown eyes from?"

She looked shocked, and said in mock surprise, "They are mine … I was born with them!" They both laughed again, but Bertrand stopped abruptly as a bolt of pain raced up his leg. He gritted his teeth, his eyes closed tightly shut, and he moaned. Theodora stroked his thin dark-blond hair.

"Phew – that was a little sharp."

"Sharp?"

"The pain, like a dagger being stuck into my leg."

"Is the pain continuous, Bertrand?"

"Yes, but I can live with it. Don't worry."

Theodora was now stroking his face, from his wide forehead, down his cheek, to his bristly chin. He was sweating a little.

"What did you do at this place in Paris?" he said lazily.

"I was a courtesan, a kind of prostitute."

"You mean a hostess, I think." He looked at Theodora with some alarm.

"No – courtesan and prostitute are accurate."

He was holding her wrist as she stroked his face. Theodora raised her head to see his expression of disbelief.

"Why are you so surprised?"

Bertrand looked momentarily embarrassed. "I'm sorry. It was just a bit of a shock. I would never have thought of you as a—"

"I am not any more! I've given up all that. I have retired. I am just going to be a spy." Bertrand laughed at that and grimaced again.

"Stop making me laugh. I like the stroking, though."

"What do you do when you are not fighting the Nazis?" Theodora asked.

"I used to own a French restaurant in London with my wife. She was French, from here in Auch. I also had a little brandy business."

"Is she here or in London?"

"Dead, I'm afraid. She bought it … died in the first bombing of London. A freak bomb landed on top of the restaurant, miles away from the other bombing."

"That is very sad. What was your restaurant called?"

"It was called *La Renarde*."

"Oh!" Theodora wore an expression of fake shock. "Why did you call it The Vixen?"

"There was a pub opposite, called The Fox. This was in South London, in Chelsea. The restaurant was totally destroyed, bombed out. And my wife, who did all the cooking, was killed."

"What a terrible blow. But how do you know this area?"

"I used to export Armagnac, which is the local brandy around here, but it was not very successful. I bought Le Tuko—"

"Oh, that is your house."

"Yes, I bought Le Tuko and the vineyards around it, but the cooperative that distilled our Armagnac lost the main distiller and the workers to the army. They are all very patriotic down here. I bought it from Celeste's father just before he died. That is where I met Celeste, my wife."

"You don't seem to be having much luck, *mon cher* Bernarrrd."

Theodora sat up and found the tablecloth with an apple, cheese and bread still inside. She unstoppered a bottle of water and handed it to Bertrand. "You must drink lots of water."

"Wine would be better." Theodora frowned at him. "Oh, all right," he said, and drank half the bottle of water.

"Shall we eat some of this bread and cheese?"

"I'm not very hungry."

Theodora was concerned about Bertrand's health. She leant close to him, and gently held his head in her hands and placed her lips on his forehead.

"What are you doing?" he said in some alarm. When she stopped, he then said, "Whatever you were doing, do it again, I don't mind. And kiss a little lower, on my lips. That would be more beneficial for my—"

"I was testing your temperature and you are a little hot."

"It is not very hot in this car, so I can't see how."

"You have a fever. It is very warm in here." Theodora brushed his lank hair away from his prominent forehead. Bertrand smiled.

"You are lovely," he said.

"You are sick!"

"That's not very nice."

"Bertrand, you must have a doctor."

"I have you." As he said this, he gritted his teeth and inhaled a gulp of air, a sign that a shaft of pain shot up his leg. He shut his eyes and said reluctantly, "I think you're right. There's a hospital just down that path, only a kilometre or so away – this side of the river. Can you get me there?"

"Yes, of course. Will it be all right? With the doctors, I mean?"

"We will have to wing it."

"Wing it?" Theodora said in alarm.

"We will have to see. Come on, let's get going before the others get back and find us gone."

"I will leave a message in case." Theodora took out her lipstick and wrote on the car ceiling, and then put a little on her lips.

"Lovely," said Bertrand with genuine admiration.

*

Ferdi and Charlotte headed south down a dead straight path that followed the river Gers. The sun was blazing down and it was a warm September afternoon. Charlotte was feeling rather hot and sweaty. She put her beret in her coat pocket and piled her hair into a knot on top of her head with a hairpin. She took off her coat and tied the arms around her waist, and rolled up the sleeves of her dark-blue blouse.

"That's better," she said.

Ferdi had started at a fast pace, walking through parkland on the eastern side of the river. Bertrand had told him to take the footbridge across the river where the path ran out.

"This will take you to the west bank, and if you keep heading north-west," Bertrand had instructed, "through the little streets, always going uphill, you will eventually come to the cathedral square. Find Rue Espagne, and the first house on the corner, Number One. At the side of the house is a little alley called Rue Bonail. Halfway down, on the left, you will find a heavy panelled gothic door with a knocker – *don't knock*! Pull the bell pull in the small alcove to the left – if you knock, you will not be answered. If nothing happens, ring three times. If still nothing happens, get away quickly and come back here."

They walked up the hill through a labyrinth of narrow cobbled streets. It was still quite warm, but they were both getting tired and exhausted. Charlotte caused something of a stir with some French builders when they walked into the cathedral square. She smiled meekly at all the catcalls, and stuck close to Ferdi and held his hand. This took Ferdi by surprise.

Charlotte and Ferdi found the gothic metal-studded door as described. They looked up and down the alleyway. There was a good escape route straight on, into another road at the other end of the alleyway.

They rang the bell once, and waited. A bolt was slid the other side of the heavy door and the door slowly opened. They could just see a man standing behind the door in a long black cassock.

"Come in," he said sombrely from behind the door. Ferdi was uneasy and sensed something was wrong, but Charlotte walked in, so he had to follow. The door slammed behind them, and they were all plunged into near total darkness in the small entrance hall. Opposite the front door, another door swung open and the unmistakable frame of an SS officer stood, backlit by the light coming from the room behind him, his hands on his hips.

Ferdi turned quickly to the front door only to find the priest being held by a Gestapo man, a pistol pointing at the priest's head.

"Freya?" the SS officer said in disbelief. Charlotte gasped.

"Jost?" Charlotte was incredulous. She yelled in German, "You bastard! You are a damned sack of shit!" She strode over to him and pushed him in the chest, into the room. He pointed his Luger pistol at her. She stopped and stood back, looking at the Luger in disgust.

17

"And who have you brought with you, Freya?" Krupp looked delighted.

"Baron Olivier Ferdinand Saumures." Ferdi stepped forward with a pleasant smile, and held his hand out for Jost Krupp to shake. "And you are, Herr *Sturmbannführer*?"

"I am *Sturmbannführer* Jost Krupp." Krupp stood tall and elegant as usual. His hair was severely clipped above the ears, which Charlotte thought it made him look very aggressive. His cap with *Totenkopf* – the skull insignia of the SS – was tilted at a rakish angle. "Why are you here with Miss Jorgensen?"

"We are looking for the priest to marry us," Ferdi said without a second thought. Charlotte tried her best not to whisk her head around in total surprise. She blinked rapidly and cast her eyes down to the floor.

"Ah," said Krupp. He held Charlotte's chin up with his forefinger to look at her face. He was plainly displeased, and looked at Charlotte with anger, or even jealousy, Charlotte hoped. As, still holding Charlotte's chin, he eyed Ferdi, casting a critical look over him from the top of his head to his shoes, sizing him up. "You don't look dressed to get married, Baron," Krupp said with a sneer. "Let us all step into the office."

They moved through to a badly lit office that must have belonged to the priest, a crucifix on the wall and a prayer stool below. The priest looked worried. He was breathing hard, asthmatically, holding his chest, still not saying a word.

"Can your man let Father Reynders go, Jost?" Charlotte said. The Gestapo man released the priest when Krupp waved his gloves to indicate that it was safe to do so. Krupp cruised up close to Charlotte. She stepped backwards until she bumped into Ferdi's chest. She looked over her shoulder to see Ferdi with an austere expression on his face, watching Krupp's every move. She took hold of Ferdi's arm.

"You look well, Freya, apart from that gash over your eye. What happened there?"

"We were bombed. Le Palais is a pile of rubble," Charlotte said. "Ferdi kindly rescued us."

"How did you get here?"

"We came down by train." Ferdi sounded annoyed. "Listen, I don't know why you are here, Herr *Sturmbannführer*, but we just wanted to get married."

"Why all the way here, my dear baron, in Auch?" Krupp scorned.

"I used to live here."

"Why not in Paris?" Krupp was distracted by the cut over Charlotte's eye.

"It is less safe in Paris," Ferdi said.

Krupp went up to the priest. "Do you know these people, Father?"

"No, he does not know us. I am a baron and have the right to being married in the cathedral. I was given Father Reynders's name by a friend in Berlin."

"What friend in Berlin? Actually … I am not interested, Baron. I think I know who you are. I am just so surprised it is you who is escaping. And with Freya!"

"We have never met, *Sturmbannführer*. You have never been to my gallery of the Reich's art. And we are not escaping. We intend to go back to my gallery in Paris after we are married." Ferdi looked suspiciously at Krupp. "Why are *you* here, more to the point, and treating Father Reynders so badly?" Ferdi asked forcefully.

"This is the base for a French underground cell," Krupp sneered. "This is where escapers come, en route to Spain." Krupp had a pair of black leather gloves in his hand. He walked over towards the priest as he talked, then slapped the gloves hard across the priest's face. "Father Reynders here is their ringleader."

"That is rubbish, Major, I am a priest, not a combatant," Father Reynders said in a low voice.

"You will be quiet!" Krupp slashed the gloves harder across his face and the priest cried out.

"Don't, Jost." Charlotte raced over to the priest and stood in front of him, facing Krupp. "What evidence have you that the priest is part of this … this …" Charlotte looked angrily at Krupp. Krupp swaggered slowly up to Ferdi.

"An old lady called Clarice gave me all the details a few days ago." Ferdi looked more and more worried; Krupp saw his concern and smiled.

Charlotte shouted, "Well, she will tell you that Ferdi and I are—"

Charlotte stopped when Krupp went over to another door and opened it. Slumped in a bentwood chair sat an elderly woman. Charlotte moved to see if she was alive but Krupp blocked her path.

"Oh, I am afraid she succumbed to my persuasive charms," Krupp said, losing patience. "She is dead."

"My God, Jost. You killed her?"

"I believe she had a weak heart." Now angry, Krupp stormed out of the door and shouted out into the hall. "Troop!" Three armed SS soldiers appeared and clicked their heels at him.

"Take these men to headquarters," he barked. "Tell Captain Weichselberger that I will be there presently. Leave the girl with me," he said in rapid German as one of the soldiers grabbed Charlotte with glee.

Charlotte could not take her eyes off the dead woman. She saw that her hands were tied and that there was a gag in her mouth. Krupp closed the door and wrapped an arm around Charlotte's waist.

"I want to go with my fiancé, Jost."

"Be quiet, Freya," Krupp said, not looking at her. Charlotte saw that he had lost his temper. She had never seen that side of him, not even when he was protecting her from the captain who tried to rape her at Le Palais. Then, he calmly and methodically pummelled the man, with hardly an expression on his face. Why had he now lost his temper? Was it because he had been caught in Auch? Or was even jealous of Ferdi? Or that his cruelty had been exposed to her? He was no longer a friend but an enemy, and it seemed he had picked up on her feelings.

They all marched out of the house and were taken up to the other end of the alleyway, to where two Volkswagen *Kübelwagens* and a large black staff car were parked, all with drivers. The drivers leapt out of the vehicles when they saw the armed party emerge with their prisoners. The priest and Ferdi were put into one of the tinny vehicles, with the Gestapo man and the guards in the other. Charlotte was put in the back of the substantial BMW with Krupp riding beside her. The roofs of the cars were all down so as they went through the deserted narrow streets to headquarters, the deafening wail of their sirens echoed off the walls.

"Jost, I don't understand. What are you doing here? This is the Free French sector."

Krupp looked at Charlotte questioningly.

"I am here by the invitation of the mayor to help the police clear up these murdering terrorists. More to the point, I am so glad to see you here, looking as enchanting as ever. Why did you come to Auch?"

"This is where Ferdi used to live," Charlotte said – rather lamely, she thought. What was she going to say to Krupp? What was Ferdi going to say at his interrogation? What if their stories were too different?

In the cathedral square, the two Volkswagens suddenly went one way and the BMW started downhill towards the river, the siren silenced. Charlotte was about to say something, but Krupp put a gloved forefinger to his lips, without turning to look at her.

At the river, the car stopped in a small, pretty tree-lined square.

"Thank you, Langer," Krupp said to the driver, who jumped out of the car and walked away, lighting a cigarette. He was clearly used to his officer's orders for discretion.

Jost and Charlotte sat in the back seat of the car in silence. Charlotte stared at the river. All she could think of was the dead elderly woman in the priest's house, slumped forward, her hands tied behind her, preventing her from falling to the floor. Her chin resting on her chest, her salt-and-pepper hair covering her face. Her crumpled floral dress was ripped up one side, exposing a white petticoat. Did Jost kill her?

The tree-lined square, which had a grass island in the centre, was completely quiet except for the tinkle of water from the river and the odd loud quack from a duck. Three sides of the square were bordered by cream-coloured terraced houses with terracotta tiled roofs. They seemed to be deserted – the dark brown-red shutters were closed on all three levels. The fourth side was formed by the riverbank. Empty boat pontoons bobbed about in the slow-flowing river. The sun sent stabbing shafts of light through the leaves of the trees, casting fluttering shadows over the car. It was warm with a slight breeze, a perfect day for sitting in a quiet square. But Charlotte was uncomfortable.

Jost gazed up at the trees with a relaxed grin. He lit a cigarette and turned his attention to Charlotte's rigid face. She was staring at the pontoons, outwardly seething with anger but inwardly worried and scared.

"I thought we could talk alone, *liebling*. I have not seen this pretty face for such a long time." He had removed his black leather gloves and stroked her flushed cheek with the back of his fingers.

"Jost, I do not think it is very nice of you. You have interrupted my wedding and —"

"Shush, shush, shush, I don't want to hear about any wedding. You are mine, not some limp-wristed painter's," Jost said.

"I am certainly not yours. Why do you think I would want to belong to you? You are a—" She caught herself just in time; she was about to say that he was a gratuitous murderer, a killer of old, defenceless women, and a torturer.

"A what?" Jost said, slightly alarmed.

"A swine!" Charlotte said lamely instead. He mellowed.

"Why did the baron pick this priest to get married?"

"Why? What is wrong with that priest? And how do you know Ferdi is a painter?"

"I just do. I had information that he and this priest were up to something."

"Who gave you this information?" Charlotte was shocked. "You probably tortured it out of them!"

"No!" he said emphatically. "The informant works for us … and in any case, I would not torture anybody! I am hurt that you would think I could torture people." He was plainly lying, but she had to be careful of what she said to this man. She must not lose her composure or get riled. Stay calm, Charlotte, she said to herself.

"No, I don't think you could torture innocent people," she lied, thinking of poor Clarice. "But what is happening to Ferdi and the priest?"

"All priests are corrupt. All French priests help the enemies of Germany. Catholics cannot be trusted."

"You cannot arrest people because of their religion!"

"Why not? Anybody who is celibate, and can't make love to a beautiful woman, has got to be pretty strange. Why would you care anyway? You are Swedish. You are not even catholic. Or was that nasty little man Hueber right about you being English? I will have to ask him when I go back to Paris."

"He's dead," said Charlotte with satisfaction. But Jost did not seem to take any notice or appear to care. He smiled and put his arm around her, drew her close and rested his chin on the top of her head. Charlotte felt herself cringe. "He must have died in the bombing," Charlotte said breathlessly. "He was there that last night."

"Ah – poor Hueber. He had quite a soft spot for you." He laughed. "Have you seen Colonel Deller lately?" Charlotte was surprised, and pushed herself away from him.

"No! Why would I?"

"Just wondered. He has disappeared with quite a lot of things that do not belong to him."

"Like what?" Charlotte wondered if he meant the collection. Should she ask? Perhaps not.

"Just articles that belong to the Reich that he had collected. And more importantly, something he promised me." Jost took her chin in his hand and turned her face up to look straight into his face. "I remember promises," he said gently with a little smile, his hazel eyes and long eyelashes momentarily captivating Charlotte. "It was Deller who put me onto your baron."

"What do you mean, put him onto Ferdi?" Charlotte asked.

"They knew each other. Bed pals, probably."

"Colonel Deller is certainly not …" Charlotte went quiet.

"Not what?" he smirked. Charlotte said nothing. She turned away from him and gazed ahead at the square, thinking, worried about what she had said. "So, it was Deller who gave you this information? I did not think—"

"No, someone else gave me that, not Deller. I have not seen Deller for well over a year. The last time I saw him was the morning after you and I spent our first night together. A night I will never forget."

Their eyes met; neither spoke for a while. The man in front of her was not the cruel man she had recently discovered; he was Jost, the sensitive man she fell in love with. Charlotte desperately wanted to kiss him. She felt such a surge of lust it worried her. She attempted to turn her head away and tried to stifle a sigh, without success. Her hand went up to her lips, then she stroked her cheek to conceal her blushes. She took a surreptitious glance at Jost. To her relief, he was bathing his face in the sunshine with his eyes closed.

She was worried that Jost was looking for Deller, and that Deller knew the baron and possibly Father Reynders. There was a short silence. Jost relaxed his embrace.

"What is going to happen with Ferdi, Jost?" Charlotte asked softly, changing the subject. She felt calmer. She was still in his arms, but not in such a tight hold. It felt good. This bothered her. She reminded herself what this man was: a Nazi murderer who tortured people like Bertrand and who killed Jews, and also Bo and probably Clarice, an old woman, tortured until she died of fright.

"He will be interrogated back at headquarters. Don't worry, we will be gentle." He laughed again and cuddled her. "Come on, Freya, loosen up, this is not like you. I tell you what, you marry me. I will win the war and we will go back to my estate in Aschersleben together, live in my big house and have lots of lovely children. Hitler is a friend of mine, you know."

"What are you talking about? I am not marrying you. You are a Nazi murderer!" A bubble of temper rose in her chest.

"That's not very nice of you." Jost looked perplexed. "What has been said about me?"

"Oh, that you have been killing people – Jews mostly, not enemy soldiers like you are meant to in war!"

"Oh that." He lightened. "Jews are mostly blood-sucking animals anyway."

"Jost, they are human beings like you and me."

"No, they are not, Freya," he said light-heartedly. "They are parasites, vermin, and must be eradicated. Anyway, why are you so worried about the Jews all of a sudden? Don't tell me the baron is a Jew?" He laughed again at the absurdity.

"No, but he is a very nice, honourable man, unlike you. I hate you, Jost. You broke my heart and you need to be punished!"

"Freya, Freya, what am I to do with you? Look at you." He held her face in his hands. One hand went to the knot of hair on top of her head. He found the hairpin, pulled it out, and her hair fell onto her shoulders. It was dirty, and Charlotte felt a little uncomfortable at Jost seeing it. But then she realised she was being quite ridiculous; he would not notice things like that.

He gently held her face and kissed her lightly on the lips. She tried to draw away.

"You are so beautiful, a terrible waste on the baron, who looks like he could not blow down a dandelion. He is certainly not as good-looking as me." He let go of her and slipped away, stretching to show off his physique, hand on hip, the other sweeping over his body as though presenting himself in a circus ring. His medals twinkled against his black uniform. He removed his pistol from his holster and held it across his chest, turning his head for Charlotte to see him in profile. "What do you think? Magnificent, don't you agree?" He then looked critically at her. "And what are you wearing? You look like some kind of farm labourer. Not exactly wedding clothes. Theodora would not approve …" He stopped, suddenly serious. He put the pistol on his lap and held Charlotte by the shoulders at arm's length.

"How is Theodora? She was not involved in the bombing?"

"She died too," Charlotte said simply, casting her eyes down. Charlotte noticed a ceremonial dagger in a decorative sheath attached to Jost's belt.

"I am sorry. She was such a good friend." Jost did not seem that sincere. He leant back against the folded-down car roof, his face tilted up at the trees, the sunbeams dancing over his handsome face, his eyes closed. "When this war is over, you and I will have such fun," he said.

"Possibly, Jost," she said as gently as she could.

There was a long pause, a thoughtful silence. Charlotte moved closer to him, which seemed to delight him. A smile formed over his lips, and he slowly opened his eyes. His face turned to a picture of horror. Charlotte was on her knees on the seat, holding Jost's SS dagger, which she had quietly inched out of its scabbard. It was now half a metre above his right eye. With both hands on the handle, she raised the blade up and aimed at his eye. He instantly deflected her thrust with his left hand, grabbing her wrists. Charlotte's knee pinned his right arm against the seat. She had repositioned herself to put as much weight as possible behind the thrust of the knife. But instead of going into his eye, the blade of the dagger dragged down the side of his face, slicing a long jagged cut into his right cheek. Charlotte pushed down as hard as she could.

"Ahhh, Freya, for Christ's sake!" The pain of the knife slicing into his cheek must have been enormous. He tried to push Charlotte off. His arm buckled and in that moment the knife sank into his left thigh, up to the hilt. Charlotte could feel the blade scrape over the femur as it sank into his flesh. Blood gushed out of the wounds. Jost's mouth gaped open, about to cry out in pain. Charlotte quickly pushed his leather gloves into his mouth to stifle any noise. He turned bright red, mucus streaming from his nose as he exhaled noisily. Charlotte, alert and in control, looked over at the driver who was more than a hundred metres away and clearly had not heard anything. She felt Jost trying to release his right arm from beneath her knee. She still had hold of the knife, but his other hand was now on top of hers.

"Let go of my hands, Jost," she said coolly. She started to twist the knife and heard a crunch as the blade scrapped the bone. He emitted a stifled scream, and tears of pain began to roll down his bloody cheek as he looked at Charlotte in alarm. Charlotte felt his grip loosen. She pulled her hands free, which created more pain. She picked up Jost's Luger from his lap, stood, and pulled the trigger – nothing happened.

Jost was concentrating on the dagger in his leg. Charlotte remembered to cock the pistol, and found the safety catch. She aimed at the largest part of his body and fired. A bullet went in with a thud. He looked up in shock at her. She then remembered the driver. He was running over to the car – he must have heard the shot. She dropped down behind the seat, aimed the pistol, and as soon as the driver's head came into her sights, she fired. His head jerked back and he fell onto the road, dead.

Charlotte inched herself away from Jost. His right hand had grabbed a handful of her coat and skirt in a desperate attempt to keep her from escaping, but he weakened, and she prised his grip off her clothes. She opened the door of the car, then looked back at Jost. She felt a mixture of huge satisfaction and sorrow to see his beautiful face marred by an ugly ten-centimetre gash, and in such terrible pain – all caused by her. He looked like he was pleading for her help. She momentarily felt a pang of sadness for him. His bulging brown eyes were wide in agony, and she could not work out if he was dying. He tried to remove the gloves from his mouth. Charlotte levelled the Luger to his forehead and said, quietly, "Don't."

He put his hand down, his eyelids growing heavier. "Goodbye, Jost. We will never meet again."

With that, Charlotte slipped away. She stuffed the Luger into her pocket. Jost had slithered down and lay dying on the back seat of the car. She half thought she would drive the car back to the hiding place, but she could not drive. She would never be able to move Krupp's body out of the back seat, and she would get terribly lost. The dead driver had fallen in front of the car, and Charlotte had to look away when she saw he was bleeding profusely from the back of his head, all over the cobbled street.

Charlotte walked towards the river, a little shocked as to what she had done, and then trotted along the bank to get back to Ferdi's car. She had to get Theodora to help her rescue Ferdi and the priest.

18

Charlotte walked quickly along a busy road that ran alongside the river, and crossed the next bridge. A lot of traffic and people were on the bridge; it was five o'clock and everybody had finished work. Charlotte kept an eye over her shoulder, but there was no sign of anyone in pursuit. She went to push her hair out of her eyes only to see her hands were covered in Krupp's blood. She quickly stuffed them in her coat pockets. She wondered if she had any blood on her face, because she got some strange looks. She hurried on as though she was late for an appointment.

An hour later she saw the hedge and the dilapidated roof of the boathouse. She went towards it, calling out softly to Theodora. To Charlotte's dismay, and some alarm, nobody was in the car. It was covered in old planks of wood and bulrushes. She crawled inside and lay on the back seat, Krupp's Luger clasped in her bloody hand, resting on her chest with the safety off. As she lay there, she saw on the ceiling of the car, in Theodora's lipstick: "*Back soon – T*".

Charlotte burst into tears.

She waited and waited, it seemed for hours. She was considering whether she should try and make for the Spanish border on her own when she heard a rustle outside the car. She could not see out of the back window as the planks had blocked her view. She cursed herself for not leaving a gap to spy through at anybody approaching. Charlotte held the Luger in both hands and pointed it at the sound.

There was a hissed shout of "It's us." Theodora's voice was a huge relief.

"Where the bloody hell have you been?" Charlotte cried in frustration.

"The pain in Bertrand's leg was getting too bad. I said he needed a hospital. *He* said there was one just under a kilometre up the pathway, this side of the river. So, I carried him there. But it turned out to be more like two kilometres away! Where is the baron?" Theodora said in alarm when she had eventually got Bertrand into the passenger seat.

"Captured, along with the priest in the house you sent us to."

"Bloody hell!" said Bertrand. "I don't know what we can do now. We must get some fuel and some food."

"We must rescue Ferdi," said Charlotte.

"That, my dear, is nigh on impossible. How did he get captured?"

"Jost Krupp was waiting for us."

"Krupp?" exclaimed Theodora

"The bastard who did this, you mean?" Bertrand said tapping his leg, now in plaster.

"Yes, but he is now dead."

"What?" Theodora exclaimed again. "My God, Freya, don't tell me you killed him as well?"

"As well as who?" asked Bertrand.

"As well as my stepfather and a Gestapo man," Charlotte said with difficulty. There was a pause as Bertrand eyed Charlotte with a look of a mixture of alarm and respect.

"Freya, tell us exactly what happened," Theodora said, settling herself into the driver's seat.

Charlotte told them about all that had occurred – the capture, killing Krupp in the back of the car, coming back to an empty rendezvous. Charlotte turned on Theodora. "Tell me again: why did you leave the car?" She knew she sounded peevish.

"The leg was getting more and more painful, and Theodora thought it could be infected. I knew a hospital was somewhere nearby—"

"Nearby? It was bloody miles away!" Theodora protested.

"So, she virtually carried me there. Luckily, the doctor who saw us was Turkish and fell in love with Theodora and was able to wash out the wound. He gave me some penicillin – God knows where he managed to find that – and patched me up, all for a pair of Theodora's diamond earrings and one of her lovely smiles."

"Could he help us with some fuel?" Charlotte asked.

"No. He may have fallen for Theodora, but he was pretty suspicious of me. He could not work out my accent. I said it was southern German. I don't think that washed, frankly."

"But what are we going to do about Ferdi?"

"Nothing!" a voice said as the door of the car swung open. There stood the baron, unhurt, wearing a long leather coat with military captain's epaulettes, which was a little disconcerting.

"For Christ's sake, what are you doing here? How did you escape?" Charlotte squeaked.

"My dear fellow," said Bertrand, "we – I – thought you'd had it, by what Freya was saying." Bertrand looked Ferdi up and down. "You like the Nazi look then, eh?"

"What does 'had it' mean?" Theodora asked.

"Killed, he means," Ferdi said back in French. Charlotte and Theodora both looked appalled at Bertrand.

"Long story, but I managed to escape. But Père Reynders, I'm afraid, was not so lucky. Clarice too, I think."

"Really?" Bertrand said. "Thank God you made it. We have got to get out of here somehow." Bertrand was assuming command again.

They sat in the car, Charlotte and Ferdi in the back, Theodora in the driver's seat, and Bertrand in the passenger seat with his plastered right leg stretched out the door.

Charlotte was bewildered by the speed of events, the lack of concern for the death of the old woman and the priest. She repeated the story about Krupp to Ferdi, who was terribly impressed. All the time she was looking at Ferdi curiously. He was completely unscathed and still looked relatively neat ... as always. Charlotte was also a little upset that he had not displayed any kind of relief on seeing that she was safe.

"There are no German troops about," Ferdi said. "I wonder where they all are?"

"They've probably been hauled off to the Italian front, or to Russia, poor buggers," said Bertrand.

"Poor buggers?" Charlotte shouted. "Why poor buggers?"

"They will undoubtedly get killed, if not by the Red Army, then by the coming winter." Charlotte's incredulous expression plainly annoyed Bertrand. "They are not all like the SS. They are just ordinary soldiers, doing their duty. You have only met Nazis, I imagine – your average German is a nice chap ... some of them."

Theodora and Charlotte looked at Bertrand with a mixture of disbelief and confusion.

"How did you escape?" Charlotte asked Ferdi when they had all stopped talking. She was suspicious.

"Yes, how did the priest get killed and not you?" Theodora asked. Ferdi seemed surprised at Theodora's accusatory question. He sighed, paused, and took a deep breath.

"I was rescued by a pigeon."

There was a stunned silence. Ferdi looked around at the faces in the darkening interior of the car with a slight smile.

"A pigeon?" Bertrand broke the silence. "A bird-type pigeon – *un pigeon, eine* … what is it in German?"

"*Eine Taube*?" Theodora said.

*

Ferdi told the bewildered assembly about how he and Père Reynders were taken, their hands bound in front of them and tethered to a bar in the car. They were driven to a large house on the cathedral square, marked with a small brass plaque outside the house announcing "*Consul à l'Empire Allemand*". No vast red flags with swastikas cascading down from the roof or draped across the front of the building like most Nazi-occupied establishments. No wonder they never noticed the building when they had walked into the square an hour before.

He was concerned and extremely worried when he saw Charlotte drive off in another direction with Krupp. The priest and he were bundled out of the car. Père Reynders did not look scared and appeared resigned to what was about to happen to him.

Père Reynders was a stooped man, his thinness accentuated by being dressed entirely in black, with no white clerical collar, or his customary cassock or jacket. He had very short stubbly grey hair, his white face looked old and yet he was possibly only forty according to Bertrand. As he was pushed up the steps by a guardsman to the front door of the house, he looked across at Ferdi and gave him a sad smile. Ferdi was alarmed. Was this meant to be a smile of encouragement?

Their hands were still tied in front of them with leather thongs. They were shoved up the stairs of the house, up three floors to a large fourth-floor attic room with a straw mattress at one end. There was a single dormer window with four dirty panes of glass. At the bottom of each pane of wobbly glass was a growth of green moss; the view over the roofs of Auch was like looking through river water.

A helmeted guard brought in two wooden chairs and slammed them down in the middle of the room. He pointed to the men to sit on the chairs. The two prisoners sat facing the window, both appearing unafraid. One of the guards was an older, thick-set German with a scar under his chin, the mark of an old soldier and wearing a helmet chinstrap for many years. As Ferdi looked into the German's face, the German guard sniggered and winked. Ferdi winked back, with a suggestive little smile. The guard pushed Ferdi onto the chair, hard. The chair rocked backwards and nearly tipped over. He was about to push the priest onto his chair when he pulled himself up abruptly and looked back at Ferdi. He grabbed him by the collar and growled: "*Sind Sie ein Schwuler – ein Homosexueller?*"

"*Je ne vous comprends pas.*" Ferdi pretended not to understand, unmoved by the German's aggression. He tried to look stern and keep his features as calm as possible. He was, however, slightly taken aback that the guard should have picked up any indication of Ferdi's homosexuality. It was something he was sure he was able to hide. But then maybe the guard himself was also a homosexual.

The door of the attic room flung open and a tall, bare-headed SS officer ducked under the low entrance and strode over to the two prisoners, his head to one side to avoid hitting it on a beam. However, his head was in no danger of hitting anything, so it made him look quite comical and did not have the desired effect of intimidating the prisoners.

"My name is Captain Weichselberger," the man said in heavily accented French. He wore his leather coat over his shoulders and shrugged it off, handing it to the thick-set guard who was now properly at attention.

"Why are these swine not tied to their chairs yet?" he shouted at the guards. The guards both busily holstered their pistols. They took a prisoner each and started to untie their hands.

Ferdi was looking out of the window, going through various scenarios for some kind of escape. He was unconsciously watching a bird of prey chasing a pigeon over the rooftops. He realised that the pigeon was being chased towards the attic room window. Both guards had their prisoner's hands untied and were about to tie them onto the chairs when the pigeon smashed into the window behind the officer with a fantastic crash. All but Ferdi were startled by the pigeon's noisy arrival. It fell at the feet of Captain Weichselberger, who jumped back in alarm and knocked his head on a beam. Ferdi took advantage of the distraction. He whirled around and thumped his boot into the nearest guard's midriff. With fists bunched, he punched the guard as he bent, winded, as hard as he could across his jaw. He heard a painful crack. All his work at the SOE training base at Box Hill Road was proving very useful. He quickly lunged at the other guard, who had seen him strike his colleague and was pulling out his pistol. Ferdi grabbed the guard's pistol arm, brought up his knee and forced the guard's straightened elbow down over his knee. The arm cracked, the pistol flew out of his hand, the guard howled in pain.

Captain Weichselberger was still woozy from hitting his head and also preoccupied by the pigeon that was now flapping frantically around the floor with one wing. Feathers were everywhere. He became aware that Ferdi had taken control. He raced over to the priest to stop him getting hold of the pistol on the floor, but the priest got to it first and pointed it at Captain Weichselberger.

"Shoot him!" cried Ferdi, but the priest hesitated. The captain grabbed Reynders's hand and tried to stop him taking a shot. Ferdi was still struggling with the other guard, who was defending himself as best he could with his remaining good arm. Somehow Ferdi was knocked to the floor by the priest struggling with Captain Weichselberger. He turned onto his back quickly, and saw the guard take a swing at his head with his boot. Ferdi managed to catch the boot and twisted the foot violently. The guard shouted in pain and crashed to the floor, his helmet falling off his head.

Captain Weichselberger and Père Reynders were still wrestling with the pistol face to face. The pistol was compressed between them, the captain's hand clamped over the barrel, twisting it, trying to get it off the priest. Ferdi could see this was not going to end well. Suddenly there was a muffled bang. The priest and the German captain looked at each other, trying to work out if either of them had been hit. The priest pulled the trigger again, then crumpled onto the floor.

As the priest hit the floor in a heap, Ferdi retrieved the second guard's helmet and, holding it by the chinstrap, swung it at the pistol, spinning it out of the captain's hand. He swung the helmet at the German's head. It connected with a bone-crunching, hollow thud. The German captain fell to the floor like a chopped down tree, a large, bloody dent just above his ear. He landed on the other guard, who was moving, regaining consciousness.

Ferdi went to the priest's body and picked up his hand to test for a pulse. There was no pulse to be found. He spotted that the first guard was coming round and kicked him in the head, picked up the officer's leather coat, and made for the door. He saw the poor pigeon huddled quietly in the corner of the room, panting, a flash of red blood on its wing, a little black eye watching his every move.

Just as he got to the door, he saw the handle turn. Ferdi put his back to the wall. The door opened quickly and he hid behind it. Three men, all in German uniform, piled into the attic room, pistols drawn. As they ran over to the wounded Germans, Ferdi swiftly crept out, shutting the door quietly behind him and locking it. He moved out the way just before shots were fired. They must have seen the door close.

"That was how I was rescued by a pigeon!" Ferdi said proudly.

"Poor Père Reynders," Charlotte said.

"Poor pigeon." The others turned to look at Bertrand. "Oh, I apologise! I am sorry about Père Reynders as well, but it was inevitable. All of us ran a high risk of getting caught. I'm only surprised that, so far, out of the five of my old team, Père Reynders is the only casualty this year."

"What about Clarice? She's dead." Charlotte was angry. "Where's the rest of your team, Bertrand? How do you know they are not all in a prison somewhere, waiting to be rescued?"

"They probably are, my love, they probably are," he said reflectively, then he cheered up. "Or we will see them in Spain tomorrow with the escapers I was meant to pick up today. But we are not going to get far in this car without fuel."

"I've got some," said Ferdi. "I stole a twenty-litre can of petrol as I left the courtyard of the German headquarters. I don't know how much there is in the can, but it was quite heavy!"

"Good show, Baron, bloody splendid show!" Bertrand said.

"With the captain's coat and a borrowed SS cap, I got a few salutes as well." Ferdi turned to Charlotte. "Freya, can I talk to you outside. We'll put the fuel into the tank."

"Yes, all right. But take that awful coat off." They got out of the car. Ferdi held out his hand for Charlotte to take, which she did, hesitantly. They walked out of the boathouse into the hazy evening sun.

"I was so frightened when I saw you get into that staff car with Krupp. I am so sorry. I should have protected you better."

"Oh, that's all right." Charlotte looked into Ferdi's eyes, elated by his concern; she never thought she was that important to him. He seemed to be so cold and uncaring about everybody except Ulrich Fuhrman, and, perhaps,

Bertrand. They walked down to the river, looking around to see if there was anybody on the path on the other side of the wall or across the river. There was nobody to be seen.

The day was coming to a close. It was still quite warm; a thin layer of cloud covered the sky, drawing in the light like a large net curtain. The river trickled by and a light breeze hissed in the willow trees, their branches draped in the river like women washing their hair along the riverbank. It was only an hour away from getting dark.

"When I saw you drive off with that man and I was being hauled off with the priest, I thought that that was it – the end! You were going to be killed, and we were certainly finished. Thank God for that pigeon!"

"You're not going to be able to tell anyone at home, you realise," Charlotte said with a smirk. "It's a memoir story for when you are old and reminiscing. Nobody will believe it anyway."

"No, they probably won't. The priest died pretty quickly; he was not tortured or anything."

"Good," said Charlotte. "A shame he did not have time to marry us."

Seeing Ferdi's shock, she quickly added, "Don't get me wrong, Ferdi, I would be honoured to marry you, be a baroness, but I don't think I'm your type."

Ferdi looked bashfully down to his shoes. "Perhaps I should get married," he said, kicking a stick into the river and watching it slowly float downstream. "It would solve a few of my problems."

He took hold of her hands. Charlotte was quite surprised. He noticed the brown stains of old blood on them and took out a handkerchief from his pocket, went down to the riverbank and dunked the handkerchief in the water. On his return he gathered up her bloody hands and wiped them clean. It was like a love ritual, gentle, solemn and caring. She saw his eyes glisten with tears. He quickly brushed them away.

"Ferdi?"

"I'm sorry," he said, shaking his head. "I did this once for Ulrich after he got a beating one evening in Berlin, before the war." He looked back up at Charlotte. "I'm just being stupid."

"Why did he get beaten?"

"He was from Sudetenland, Bohemia. He was trying to get into the SS, and his fellow recruits thought he was some kind of infiltrator."

"Why was he trying to join the SS?"

"I asked him to. For part of my network of informants. He was, thankfully, successful in getting into SS, with the help of Admiral Canaris. Ulrich's father is the admiral's cousin, a prominent Nazi in Friedland – a German – and a bully to Ulrich. He was pleased that Ulrich was going to make a—" Ferdi turned his face away. "Sorry."

"Thank you, Ferdi," Charlotte said, more for finding he could confide something so personal with her than for cleaning her hands. Ferdi threw the soiled handkerchief into the river, took Charlotte's hand in his again, and walked towards the boathouse.

"You were brave to finish that Nazi off. Very brave indeed. How do you feel about it?"

"You know, I loved him once. He was everything I thought a man should be. I thought he was so handsome." Charlotte put her hand up to her chest where she could feel the cross under her blouse. She looked up at the dull, darkening sky, with a slight orange glow to the west, her eyes blinking quickly, trying not to cry. Ferdi put an arm around her shoulders. "I have not so much grown up in the last few days," she said, "I feel as though I have aged."

"Krupp will not be the only man you will love. You are young, very beautiful, and courageous."

"I have killed four men! And not with a gun from afar. They were all up close to me. I could smell them, feel their breath on me—"

"This is war, Freya. This would never happen if there was not a war on. Remember that. And we are at war with a particularly nasty enemy."

"I know. I suppose my stepfather was my enemy at the time I killed him. But I killed him because of what he did to me, what he did to my aunt Stella – making her miserable. She wasn't particularly loving towards me, but she was the only mother I had, and he drove her into madness."

She stopped walking unexpectedly as a thought came to her. "I forgot that you knew Colonel Deller," she said abruptly. "I think Jost said it was Deller who knew where we would be – and where to find Bertrand."

"Really? I don't think it would be Deller. He doesn't know Bertrand, or anything about him. Bertrand thinks it is a German-Canadian posing as an RAF pilot called Schenker who was responsible for his group being betrayed. A Spanish girl, who escaped from a prison camp, was very suspicious of him and told Bertrand. She confronted Schenker, who denied that he was a spy. That evening Schenker unsuccessfully tried to kill the girl and ran off."

"How did Bertrand know that she was not the spy?"

"She was badly mutilated." Ferdi coughed nervously and looked over towards the car. "A Star of David was cut into her chest with a knife by a Nazi holding her captive."

"Good God! What is wrong with these people?" Charlotte felt lost. Shaking her head in despair, she said, "I had a treacherous stepfather, and I've a drunk traitor for a father who is an SS colonel. Aunt Stella will turn out to be Hitler's mistress next!"

"Actually, I think Franz-Joseph's mother, your paternal grandmother, was Hitler's mistress for a while," Ferdi said seriously. Charlotte eyed him, hoping it was a comment in jest. It seemed not.

"For Heaven's sake, how on earth was he your friend?" Charlotte threw up her hands. Ferdi looked rather embarrassed and ignored her question.

"I think that's how he got to be a colonel in the SS and a job looking after the art in Paris."

"Stealing it, you mean." She wagged her index finger. "Deller said a strange thing to me, in Le Palais, a few years ago. He said that the collection – the Barrett Collection – belonged to my uncle Jason." She waited for a reaction. "What do you make of that?"

"I really don't know, Freya. I have little knowledge of—"

"And then Jost said that Deller had promised him something … items … that Deller had disappeared with."

"Like what?" Ferdi said, concerned.

"I don't know, I wanted to ask but I was not brave enough." She was annoyed with herself. Now she would never know.

Ferdi had always known Charlotte as a cheerful person, but these past few days had taken the joyfulness and youth out of her. Her usual optimism had gone, her natural beauty was fading slightly. He felt he must do something to help her but didn't know what. Unfortunately, he felt he was not the person to cheer her up. That would be down to Theodora. Ferdi was far too serious, and he wished Bertrand was fitter as he would be just the character to distract Charlotte from the past couple of grim days.

It was decided that after they put the petrol into the car, they would sleep for two or three hours until it was totally dark. Everybody should have been very tired, but nobody could sleep. They would drive to Spain at night. Hopefully the clouds wouldn't block the moonlight too much and they could drive without lights.

19

On arriving in Madrid, after a day and night travelling from Esterri d'Àneu in the Pyrenees mountains, Bertrand had to be admitted into hospital. His leg was not in good shape and was nearly removed to save his life. He pleaded that it should not be cut off. The hospital had huge stocks of penicillin, which stopped the infection in Bertrand's leg, and all talk of its amputation subsided.

Bertrand's leg healed but it would never be completely straight, as Theodora had warned when they first met. Theodora's jewellery yielded a sizeable amount of cash, Charlotte's jewellery only a modest few Spanish pesetas.

They settled in a small house owned by the British Embassy. It was a three-storey terraced house with sand-coloured walls, situated in a narrow, noisy street. At the back of the house was a courtyard garden that managed to get some sunlight. There were no other people in the house apart from a quiet cook and maid called Marta, who hardly talked and bustled around *los ingleses* – the English, as she called them – with a shy smile and a giggle each time Ferdi said "Gracias" to her. They all felt safe. A huge weight had been lifted from their shoulders – the war did not exist here.

The house was much smaller than Le Palais and had only Marta busying about as opposed to a brigade of SS servants. The four of them seem to rattle around, sleeping, reading and relaxing. Bertrand, once his leg was better, spent a lot of time with members of his Comet Line team. He was quite mysterious about where he went most days. Charlotte gathered that one of his team, like him, was injured whilst escaping.

Bertrand had fallen in love with Theodora, and they had a wonderful few months in Madrid getting to know each other. Theodora liked Bertrand but was not in love with him. She did, however, enjoy his company. He was funny, gallant, cheery, and full of scintillating stories of his pre-war life.

The greatest surprise to all – including Charlotte – was, after a lot of talking and soul-searching, Charlotte *did* marry Ferdi, after all. He was worried – without foundation, according to Bertrand – of his sexuality being exposed. And Charlotte had no wish to fall in love again and was getting a little fed up with being pursued by lots of elderly, mostly Spanish, Lotharios. She rather enjoyed the thought of being a baroness, Lady Saumures – Baroness Freya Saumures. The marriage was never consummated, and the honeymoon was two nights in Cádiz, accompanied by a howling winter storm. Ferdi wanted to paint the orange groves and the staggered white houses of the town of Vejer de la Frontera, but that never happened as the weather was so bad.

Their marriage, however unconventional, conformed in some respects. Charlotte was extremely fond of Ferdi, especially after his great concern about being captured by Jost Krupp. Ever since that evening in Auch he had been attentive towards her – protective, charming and, to some extent, loving. He did not want to allow any further danger to come to her, fussing if she went out on her own in Madrid.

Ferdi was a serious man, the opposite to Bertrand. He was intelligent – both Theodora and Charlotte respected his perception and wisdom. He had a dry sense of humour and Charlotte would find herself chuckling at something he had said, several minutes after he had said it. He enjoyed solitude, and every now and then would disappear for a couple of days on a mysterious errand, ensuring Bertrand took on the task of minding his new wife.

Ferdi loved Charlotte platonically. She was so glamorous and beautiful. The extraordinary experience of being envied by other men for being married to Charlotte was exhilarating. Their relationship was strong and happy. Their happiness, however, was tempered when Charlotte discovered a lot more about Ferdi's role in the war.

She was shocked, as was Bertrand, to hear that Ferdi was recruited by the *Abwehr* in 1938 when he was in Berlin. This was *after* he was enlisted by Sir Sussex Tremayne into MI6 in 1925.

"You bastard, what do you mean, recruited by the Kraut secret service?" Bertrand grabbed Ferdi by the lapels of his jacket, pulling him over a dining table with surprising strength for someone so slight.

"Bertrand, you are going to have to release me and calm down."

"Bertrand, do be careful, we have only just got your leg mended," Theodora said tenderly, stroking the fist that held Ferdi's lapel.

Bertrand released Ferdi. "Carry on then," he said challengingly. "What is this about you being *Abwehr*?"

"It is just that. I have been a double agent for the German Secret Service for the past five years. Admiral Canaris is head of *Abwehr* and recruited me in 1938."

"How on earth did you manage to get recruited in the first place?" Charlotte asked.

"Through Ulrich. He is the son of Canaris's cousin. Ulrich was already working with me and MI6 and said Canaris was looking for agents with useful backgrounds."

"But what secrets did you give *Abwehr*, Baron?" Bertrand scowled at Ferdi.

"None really. He wanted information about various people in the Nazi Party in Paris. Canaris would give me names to check as well. He is not a fan of Hitler."

"What is this rubbish, Baron?" Bertrand shouted. "He is one of the top Nazis in—"

"He *was*, but he is not happy about elements of the war."

"How do you know all this?" Bertrand asked.

"I know Canaris quite well. He is a good man. I can't go into much more." Ferdi glared at Bertrand. "Everything I do is for the good of my mother's country, Great Britain."

"So – you *are* on our side, but the Germans think you are on their side?" Charlotte asked.

"At this moment, I am 'Baron'. I am indeed working for the German Secret Service, *Abwehr*, as a secret agent, on my way to England to spy on troop movements, posing as an escaping British agent for MI6. However, Himmler is trying to oust Admiral Canaris as he does not trust him. He could be removed from office at any time and he is the only member of the current German government that knows of my role."

"What is your role, Baron?" Bertrand looked rather stern.

"To gather information – evidence – on Nazis for future war-crime trials. Canaris recruited me as he thought I was a German baron, by the way."

Ferdi took out a *Reisepass* – a German passport – with a photograph of himself, and countersigned by Admiral Wilhelm Canaris. Ferdi handed it to Bertrand, who leafed through the buff-coloured booklet and said, "That's how we sailed through the border seamlessly. This is like gold, Baron! I wish I could have one. I could go anywhere. Why didn't you produce this when you and Père Reynders got captured? It would have probably saved his life!"

"I didn't have it on me. I left it in the car with my pistol."

"That was a terrible shame," Bertrand said, slightly less aggressively. "And endorsed by Canaris himself! How did you fake it? *Who* faked it?"

"It has been very useful, especially travelling into Germany after war was declared. But it is not a fake."

"What is Canaris like?" Bertrand asked.

"He is a highly intelligent man. He hates what Hitler is doing to the Jews. He tried to protest about the mass murder of Jews in Poland by the *Einsatzgruppen* – an SS execution squad – but got told off by Field Marshal Keitel." Ferdi cast his eyes down at his hands, embarrassed. "I had arranged a meeting with him in Paris—"

"When?" Charlotte demanded.

"Last March."

"Just you and him? What did you talk about?"

"No, I arranged it with London. The head of British Intelligence and he met up in a convent, just outside of Paris. I was basically his driver."

All went quiet until Charlotte said, "So, you are a triple agent? They – the Germans – think you are a German agent who has become a British agent, and that you are a double agent for them, when in fact you are really a British agent, spying on the Germans."

"Yes … in essence," Ferdi said.

"Why was Hueber giving you a hard time?" Theodora asked. "He must have known you were working for the Germans – supposedly."

"I don't know why he was so suspicious. I showed him that passport. Gestapo, I suppose, work in different ways. He was something of a megalomaniac – a little man with a lot of self-importance. No searches were done, it was just Hueber throwing his weight around."

"I suppose that's why the gallery was not searched on the day I came," said Charlotte.

"You know, you are worrying me a lot, Baron." Bertrand sighed.

"Yes, I know I am probably worrying you. I'm pretty anxious myself."

"So why are you telling us all this?" Bertrand asked. "Surely this is top-top, kill-you-if-I-tell-you secret?"

"Yes, it is, but I needed to reassure you that I am on your side. You must keep all of what has happened in France to yourselves – all of you. When we get back to England, you will be questioned about your experiences in France during the war by the authorities. I would keep your answers as simple as possible. Say nothing about me, the gallery, or the files. Leave that to me."

"*If* we get back to England, you mean," Theodora pointed out.

Another thoughtful silence followed. Bertrand was plainly brooding about what he had heard.

"Baron, just assure me you are not a quadruple agent, will you? If I find you are, after all, a bloody German spy, I will rip your balls off before I kill you!"

"Oh my God, Bertrand!" Charlotte squeaked. "That is horrid!"

"Sorry, Freya. Forgot you are a baroness now," Bertrand said. Charlotte punched his arm.

"I assure you I am one of you, Bertrand. The trouble is," Ferdi carried on, "I am a marked man. The *Abwehr* may not exist much longer, and Himmler may want me dead, because they think I have been turned and that I am in league with Canaris – which I am not. Luckily, I don't think I am that important. This is one of the reasons why I have escaped out of Paris."

"Are you going to stay in Spain?" Charlotte looked confused and worried. "Because the jewellery and our money is not going to last much longer."

"No, I am going back to England. I must go back."

"Why?" Bertrand asked, still with some suspicion.

"I have to organise the retrieval of the Wasp Trap files … from Paris." Ferdi was tentative. "They are files on Nazi personnel, mostly in France – information gathered by a group of secret service agents, run by me and Ulrich Fuhrman. There were some women as well. Theodora is all that is left," he said sadly. Theodora nodded in agreement.

"Christ, Baron, you are a complicated chap. You are too hot for me." Bertrand flapped his hand as though trying to keep cool. "Where are these files?"

"Bricked up in the gallery cellar."

"We can wait until the war is over and pop over then." Bertrand sounded blasé.

"Unfortunately," Ferdi went on, "there is a file on a group of people that go under the name of WASP. It was the last piece of information I got from Canaris." He sighed. "These are people who are very powerful, very dangerous, and will do anything to ensure their identity is kept secret. That is why we will have to get the files sooner rather than wait for the war to be won."

"WASP?" Charlotte said. "What does it mean? Is that why they are called the Wasp Trap files?"

"Partly, yes. WASP stands for War Against Socialist Parties."

"Who is in this group, Ferdi? Do we know any of them?" Theodora asked.

"I cannot say, I'm afraid, except Admiral Canaris was a member. He – with the help of the *Abwehr* – has helped supplement and contribute to the Wasp Trap files. He has also supplied a lot of other intelligence, including information on WASP. He has a healthy dislike for communism."

"Any British people? Moseley?"

"It's run by an Englishman, we think, but unfortunately we cannot prove it."

"What?" the three said in unison.

"Bollocks to being proved," Bertrand said, looking fascinated. "Give us the scoop. Who is this man—?"

"Let's wait until we get home, Bertrand," Ferdi said. "Why I am telling you this is if I should die, I have left instructions as to how to get the files back to Sir Sussex Tremayne, head of War Intelligence in London. When it is safe to do so, I will go and get these files, which are in three large metal boxes, from under the galley."

"But you are not going to die now, Ferdi. You are safe in Spain, back in England soon. If we get torpedoed on the way back, we will all go as well! Have you told anyone else?" Charlotte asked pointedly.

"No. Sir Sussex Tremayne is the only one."

"Really?" Bertrand eyed Ferdi, still a little sceptical. "How did you get so involved in all this, and how did it get so complicated?"

Ferdi scanned the three people at the kitchen table, gauging how much he should say to them.

"Sir Sussex Tremayne – my boss in MI6 – is my godfather."

"Nice to have as a godfather!" said Bertrand.

"He enlisted me in 1925, mainly to recruit Franz-Joseph Deller – whose parents worked closely to Hitler – to gather information about Hitler and the Nazi Party members. No one imagined the Nazi Party would become what it is now." Charlotte stood, about to say something, but Ferdi took her hand and carried on. "Deller's mother was close to Hitler, very close."

"And you trusted this fellow?" Bertrand asked.

"I did."

"But he's a drunk, Ferdi!" Charlotte exclaimed, sitting again.

"He wasn't to start with. He was a very useful contact. He fed information from Hitler's headquarters, all be it sporadically."

"And an SS colonel!" Charlotte exclaimed.

"Yes, he managed to go through the ranks thanks to his mother's help. He was put in charge of art and culture."

"And stole all my paintings … the Barrett Collection. You have got to find him when this is all over. I want my paintings back," Charlotte said crossly. "How dare he steal them. Lots of very valuable paintings that—"

"I will try my best, Freya. But I cannot promise anything," Ferdi said, slight annoyance in his tone.

"I've heard of the Barrett Collection," Bertrand said, "in Avenue Foch. Don't tell me that you are something to do with it?"

"She owns it, darling!" Theodora said. "And Deller is her father."

"What? Bloody hell!"

There was a long pause. Ferdi saw that everybody was confused. There was a lot to take in, he supposed. "But the Wasp Trap files take priority. We must get them back as soon as possible."

"How did you get so involved with all this, Ferdi?" Charlotte asked. "I thought you were just a gallery owner from Luxembourg."

"My godfather recruited me, and my role has expanded ever since. I had no idea there would be a war. When war was declared, Sir Sussex asked for more information and more intelligence." Ferdi leant forward conspiratorially. "My duties in Paris included starting an operation to collect information on the Paris SS and the Nazis. Also, French traitors who worked for the Nazis. This was headed by me with four *Sudetenlanders* – men from Bohemia – who managed to get into the SS. They all became SS officers just after Germany took over the Sudetenland. One of these men was killed by Czechoslovakians within two years of working for me. He was shunned by fellow Sudetenlanders, who hated these men for being members of the Nazi Party, unaware that he was, in fact, working for us – the Allies. The second man was Ulrich Fuhrman, who was murdered by Hueber." Ferdi's voice cracked and he paused. "The third member of the group was captured by the Gestapo, tortured to death, and—"

"By Krupp?" Bertrand said.

"No, by one of Hueber's men, just before our escape."

"Did he give anything away?" Charlotte asked nervously. Ferdi looked at Charlotte, and then slowly at the other two.

"The existence of these files was kept secret until this third man in my team – he was called Harold Rimm – talked. He worked at Gestapo headquarters as a clerk. He was accidently discovered with some sensitive files on him while he was enjoying himself at a Paris brothel. Rimm's wife had asked one of his colleagues to follow him as she suspected him of having an affair. When his colleague burst into the room, he not only found Rimm with a young woman, but also that his briefcase was full of copied files on two SS officers, which were on their way to me. The colleague gleefully reported this traitorous information to his superiors – and Rimm's wife.

"Rimm was tortured, and died telling his torturers of the Wasp Trap files. He managed not to mention my name, but he did mention the first gallery I had in Alsace. It took Rimm eight days to die in horrendous agony. His wife was arrested, as was the young woman found in the brothel, and both were interrogated and then shot."

"What is wrong with these people?" Charlotte looked pale. "And the fourth man?"

"Dead, I suppose. He disappeared last year. I was not able to find out anything."

She stared at her new husband. "Ferdi, I am wondering if your life is far too complicated for me. No wonder you are so serious. You've got so many secrets, so much responsibility."

20

Val-André in Brittany was chilly for October in 1943. Franz-Joseph Deller had never enjoyed solitude when he was a younger man, but recently, he relished being alone. He had newly discovered that solitary pursuits – drinking and painting – were to be his aspiration in life.

He had been happily resting – as he thought of it – in Alston House, being waited on by Claude, with his daughters, Claudette and Claudine, for nearly a year. The collection of paintings he had acquired from Le Palais were safely crated up in the garage to the side of the house. He thought he would live out the war here, as there were no Germans around and the war seemed to have missed this part of Brittany. Every port and major town was occupied by the Germans, mainly by the German Navy and U-Boat pens. Val-André was not only empty of Germans, but also of tourists. It was nearly a ghost town.

He had spent almost six miserable months at Alston House, looking after Alice Barrett, Charlotte's mother, whilst she was pregnant with Charlotte in 1925. It was a lovely house, owned by Alice's brother, Sir Jason Barrett. It was unlikely Jason would turn up whilst the war raged on.

The house was perched on top of a high headland, overlooking the long bay of Val-André. Every day, Joseph would go to the top of the steps that zig-zagged down the side of the cliff to the sandy beach below. These were the very steps where Alice plummeted to her death, days after Charlotte was born. Alice and Joseph were having a terrible argument about Charlotte and her upbringing. There was a howling gale, rain lashed against the cliffs, and the argument got very overheated. Alice took a swing at Joseph's head with a rock. Joseph was drunk and angry. Alice lost her footing and tipped over the handrail, crashing onto the rocks thirty metres below. It was a horrid and tragic accident, and Joseph's heart ached with regret and sadness every time he remembered the vision of Alice's body smashed on the rocks, blood pouring out of her head and the rain washing it away.

It took him a month before he had the courage to descend the steep steps again, to walk into town at the other end of the kilometre-long bay for a drink like he used to almost exactly eighteen years ago. He thought of Alice every day he was at Alston House. He thought of Charlotte – what would she look like? Pretty? Plain? Fat? Thin? And where was she?

His idleness was curtailed when there was a knock on the front door. A young Wehrmacht lieutenant was standing there when Claudette answered it. She gave a little squeak of alarm and ran into the sitting room where Franz-Joseph was snoozing off a long lunch.

"Monsieur – the Boche– he is at the door!"

Joseph had hoped to give the impression that he was an Englishman hiding from the war. When the lieutenant walked into the sitting room, unannounced, Claudette looked astounded when Joseph conducted a rapid and animated conversation in German.

"Heil Hitler! Colonel Deller?" Claudette hid behind Joseph and looked at the German lieutenant over Joseph's shoulder.

"Yes?" Joseph stood, bewildered, and answered the lieutenant's salute weakly. Claudette scurried out of the room and hid in the kitchen.

"We have been trying to locate you, sir."

"Why?" Joseph bristled with anger. "They know I am on sick retreat," he said, knowing there was no such thing – but this young, bookish-looking lieutenant would not know that.

"I see, sir. I have your new orders for you, sir." He presented an envelope marked with a Nazi headquarters stamp. Joseph swiped it out of the lad's hand, still eyeing the young officer with disgust.

"How did they know I was here? I had not told anybody."

"I do not know, sir. I think one of your colleagues was on leave here in Val-André, sir."

"You are dismissed, lieutenant."

"You do not seem to have a car or a driver, sir."

"No, I have my truck. I have some valuable items that . . ." Joseph stopped to think, he might be offering too much information. "That is not the issue here," he said angrily. "Who are you again?"

"Sir, do you require a driver for your truck?" The lieutenant seemed not at all nervous about what he was saying to a high-ranking officer, which annoyed Joseph intensely. Joseph was about to shout at him to get out when he thought it would be useful to have a driver to help move the collection.

"Yes, send one up tomorrow. That will be all."

"I have a driver here now, sir. My instructions were to ask you to take your new post today."

Joseph was appalled. He ripped open the envelope and looked at the orders.

"Bordeaux?" Deller exclaimed. "But it will take days to drive to ..." He looked at the orders again and saw it said St-Émilion – he was to oversee a vineyard. He weakened and continued in a less forthright manner. "It will take a long time to drive to Bordeaux. I think I will start off first thing tomorrow."

"I am sorry, sir, my orders were to drive you there as soon as possible."

"Whose orders are these, may I ask?" Joseph tried to sound as superior as possible, but nothing was shaking this lad.

"Lieutenant General Otto Dietrich, sir, the minister—"

"Yes, yes, I know who he is." Joseph had completely forgotten that he had put in an application, a year ago, to run a vineyard for German trade. Joseph had no idea how to run a vineyard, how to make wine, or even how to bottle it. Only how to empty a bottle, which was the attraction of the situation. He thought there was nothing to do but pick the grapes once a year and send them off to someone to press them. Simple. His new instructions were to supervise the 1944 vendange the following September – nearly a year away – make the wine, bottle it, and sell it in two or three years' time. He had lied to some extent to Otto Dietrich, the minister of culture, when he said he was a wine expert – as well as an art expert – meaning he certainly enjoyed drinking wine.

"Why has he ordered me to take on this ... this task?" Joseph asked.

"Lieutenant General Dietrich," the young officer peevishly started saying, "was meant to be sending Captain Holter to the vineyard, but Captain Holter was killed in Bordeaux by the Free French. So you, sir, got the assignment instead."

"Killed, you say?"

"Yes, sir. That is why you have an armed detachment of the Wehrmacht waiting to protect you, waiting for you outside."

Joseph was astonished. He sat down and thought. He knew he was only going to be there for a couple of months as he had a new mission after Christmas. So he prepared to go to his new assignment with an element of glee.

"Then I will get packed. Wait for me outside!"

*

Joseph and his entourage arrived in the evening after a long drive. He had slept most of the way. The young lieutenant and Joseph rode in a small staff car, a talkative sergeant driving, and two elderly soldiers drove Joseph's truck behind them. Joseph wondered how two men, a sergeant and a lieutenant constituted an armed detachment. None of them knew about the collection they had loaded up into the back of the truck.

Joseph seemed to remember the sergeant saying the château was a well-established vineyard and had produced some of the best red wines sold throughout the world, that the wine commanded a high price. The sergeant enthusiastically informed Joseph – when he was awake – that Château du Pevillon was a Premier Cru, and that the past two years had proved to be potentially wonderful years; 1944, he thought, would surpass them. Joseph, however, got bored of the sergeant's ramblings and fell asleep again.

*

Joseph rose the next morning, disorientated and hung-over. He hardly remembered the journey the day before, only that it was interminable and the chatter from the sergeant kept interrupting his sleep.

After a very late breakfast of coffee and a cognac to take away his headache, Joseph settled in front of the fire in the study of his new assignment: Château du Pevillon, a domaine within St-Émilion, fifty kilometres from the city of Bordeaux. Château du Pevillon was a ramshackle, once elegant, seventeenth-century château, untended, and part of the house had fallen down. The eastern wing was still intact and was where Joseph established his headquarters. He thought about the collection of paintings in the truck parked in the courtyard buildings, just outside the study window. He must move them somewhere less damp very soon. He had hessian bags of salt and baking soda littered about the crates to stop any winter dampness.

The lieutenant knocked on the study door.

"Good morning, sir."

"Morning," Joseph growled, his hand holding the side of his head. "What is it?"

"We have been recalled to duties, guarding the U-Boat pens in Bordeaux, sir."

"Have you?" Joseph stood, delighted. "Before you go, instruct your men that they will have to bring the crates on the lorry, into the house and put them in the entrance hall. You will leave my lorry behind."

"The sergeant will remain here to assist you."

"I don't want any help."

"But sir—"

"I do not need any help." He had a thought. "I cannot do anything this time of year. I am sure the know-it-all sergeant understands this."

"Very well, sir. I will get the crates into the house."

At midday, the lieutenant knocked on Joseph's door. He had with him an elderly peasant woman, wearing a tight brown headscarf and swathed in colourless dark clothes.

"This woman will come to clean at midday, five days of the week, sir. I don't know her name." The woman held a blank expression,

"Is she able to, lieutenant? She looks as though she will crumble into dust."

"She's the baker's mother. She will bring bread and supplies. She has been paid, so if she does not turn up, she will be found and shot. She has been told this."

"Hence her sullen countenance, I presume?"

"Yes, sir. I have lit the range in the kitchen for her."

"She's not living here, is she?"

"No, sir, in the village at the end of the lane. She will cook a meal—"

"Do you cook, madame?" Joseph yelled in French, which startled both the lieutenant and the woman.

"A bit, monsieur. My boy will make stews and—"

"Very good, but you may not touch the boxes in the hall. You can go." He turned to the young lieutenant. "I am in safe hands, lieutenant. You are dismissed."

The officer saluted Joseph and said that he would return after Christmas. He had left some supplies in the kitchen.

Joseph looked out of the study window at the chilly courtyard. He watched with satisfaction as the staff car drove out of the muddy yard. A tall gate off its hinges was drunkenly propped up on the brick gateposts. Joseph made a mental note to repair the gate, mainly to deter visitors.

He decided that now the men had all gone back to Bordeaux – including that very rude young Wehrmacht lieutenant and the know-it-all sergeant – he would have a look at the paintings in the crates. He wondered what had happened to the old woman. Did she go with the others?

"Hello, old woman?" he shouted. No answer.

After shouting a few times more around the house, with no response, he poured himself another glass of red wine and staggered out into the hallway.

Now that he was alone, he removed his uniform jacket and put on a heavy cardigan. He undid his necktie and his top shirt button.

He pulled the blanket off one of the larger crates, which stood even taller than him. The wooden crate had swastika emblems burned into the wood. His heart was beating with excitement; he had not seen the contents for well over two years. He looked around for a screwdriver or some kind of tool to lever off a side panel. He opened all the drawers in the hall table but found nothing suitable. He tried a cupboard; it contained brooms, mop buckets and a thing with feathers on a long pole … but no tools. He slammed the cupboard door shut and looked around again. He was getting frustrated, distressed and angry. He had trouble focussing his eyes. He had drunk too much. Walking aimlessly in circles, he could not think. He put his glass of wine down, put both hands on a hallstand, looked down at the dirty wood floor and tried to calm himself. "Think, Franz-Joseph! Just stop and think," he said to himself out loud. He swayed a little – he must sober up. "Coffee!" he said. "I shall find some coffee in the kitchen. I might even find a tool of some kind."

The kitchen was down the end of a short narrow passageway lined with storage cupboards on one side. Joseph bounced from cupboard door to wall as he staggered down the passage into the cavernous kitchen. There was a large black wrought-iron range at the end of the room. Joseph seemed to remember the lieutenant saying he had lit the stove. It looked like he hadn't. He cursed the young officer for his incompetence.

In the middle of the room was a wooden table with four wooden chairs. A box of tinned food – army rations, it looked like – sat in the middle of the table, along with some black bread on a chopping board. The kitchen had a high ceiling with a single bright light bulb. The window above the deep square sink was also very high and took up most of the wall. It was getting dark outside so there was nothing to see beyond the small courtyard illuminated by the kitchen light. Joseph saw a threadbare sofa, which once was a dark blue but now had patches of black on the shiny arms, beside the stove along the wall opposite the window.

"I will rest my head for a while, just to clear my brain." He lay down on the sofa, placed a cushion onto the arm. There was a distinct smell of damp dog in the upholstery. He lay down his head and instantly went into a fitful sleep.

He dreamt of huge mice squeaking loudly at him, then they transformed into Alsatian dogs that barked furiously and terrifyingly at him and then ran off, frightened by huge paintings falling onto him from a bright, sunny blue sky. Then, large bottles started emptying torrents of red wine into his mouth. He tried to keep up with the flow of wine, drinking as fast as he could, but it was too great a flow. He turned away from the deluge and spun in the air, never stopping, turning and turning, over and over, getting faster until he abruptly woke, only to find himself lying on the floor of the kitchen on his front, a blanket tangled around his legs. He stood, rubbed his eyes to try and get them to focus, struggling to recollect what had happened. Where did he find a blanket?

He remembered where he was. He must try and find a tool to open the crates. Joseph rummaged in the drawers either side of the sink but found only cutlery, cloths and soap. He took a good look at a table knife. He bent it to see how strong it was, but it was plainly not going to work as a crowbar.

Coffee. He would try and make some coffee. He put a kettle onto the range. The range was only just warm, and Joseph could see there was a tiny glimmer in the grate. He went to open the grate door to put in some wood. There was a sharp hiss as he burned his finger. "Ahhh, Christ!" he cried in pain, and kicked the grate door in anger. It flew open. Joseph looked at it in surprise, then at the burn on his forefinger. "You damned stupid door! You hurt me!"

He saw some neatly cut bits of wood beside the cooking range and picked up a few thin pieces of kindling, put them onto the embers, and watched to see if anything happened. There was quite a lot of smoke but no flames. He gingerly lowered himself down on his knees, not wanting to fall onto the old wrought-iron oven range. He sat on the floor and moved his head level with the grate and started blowing at the embers. A few small, lacklustre flames sprung up around the wood. Joseph's head started to swim. He got up onto his knees and clasped his hands together in fervent prayer: "Dear God, please help me light this fire, and dear Lord, help me stop drinking. Oh Jesus Christ," he cried, "help me, please, to do the right thing!" Tears started to form in the corner of his eyes.

"Why is that, Franz-Joseph?" said a voice.

"I am hearing things now!" Joseph said in anger.

"No, you are not. Turn around, Colonel," said the voice. Joseph swung around on his knees, and standing there, legs astride, a hand on his hip, proud and arrogant, was an SS officer. His fur-lined black leather coat was slung over his shoulders, his black SS uniform sharp and bedecked with medals. Everything seemed to shine on him, from his knee-high jack boots to the peak of his cap, set at an angle on his head, and his black cane in his hand. He looked huge from where Joseph was kneeling.

"Off your knees, sir. You will get your uniform dirty. Or" – he slowly cast a judging look over Joseph's clothes, a whimsical smile on his lips – "should I say, dirtier. Is that a cardigan, Colonel?"

"Who are you?"

"My dear Colonel Deller, don't you recognise me? Your old friend Jost Krupp."

Joseph blinked. He recognised the name but not the man he could see before him. He had an ugly scar running down his right cheek.

"What are you doing here?" Joseph barked in anger.

"Looking for you, my friend." Krupp walked with a heavy limp, helped by the black polished walking stick, towards Joseph and offered his hand to help him up. The vivid scar on Krupp's cheek resembled a huge fencing scar.

As he got to his feet, Joseph recognised Krupp. How he had changed. He pulled his arm out of Krupp's helpful hand. "I can manage, thank you. How did you get wounded?" There was a self-conscious smile on Krupp's once handsome, now disfigured face.

"That little bitch Freya Jorgensen, you know, the pretty one at—"

"But why? What did you do to her?" Joseph yelled, regretting his outburst as a shot of pain hit his forehead. Krupp looked at him curiously.

"I was not doing anything. I was questioning her about why she was running away from Paris with a man … a known British spy."

"Who did she run away with?"

"That man … you told me about him, the spy from the gallery, Saumures."

"No I didn't! What do I know about spies? Anyway, Freya is not a spy, she's Swedish."

"She is possibly not who she says she is," Krupp said. Joseph was not listening; he was brushing dust off his uniform trousers. "Your friend Baron Saumures is the infiltrator. I got information about his network and the name of his contacts in the south of France. He walked straight into my hands!" Krupp said joyously. "He was with Freya – getting married, would you believe!"

Joseph sat at the small wooden dining table, a look of bewilderment on his face. Krupp strolled over to the stove, shut the grate door with his stick, flipped a lever on the base of the stove, and the whole thing sprung to life. Joseph was fascinated. How did people just do things like that? Krupp shrugged his leather coat off his shoulders and threw it on the sofa. He turned to warm his back against the growing heat from the stove and smiled contentedly.

Joseph was trying to take in what Krupp was saying but he was confused. He tried but failed to remember the reason why Krupp had said he was here, in Château du Pevillon.

"Why are you here, Krupp?"

"As I said, to find you. I did not want to be taken off permanent duties after I came out of hospital, and I found this soft job for you, looking after a vineyard. So, I said I would come and pay you a visit. Where are all your men, by the way?"

"They were needed to guard something ... somewhere ... can't remember. Anyway, I don't need your help, so you can sod off!" Joseph was angry at Krupp's presumption and frustrated at not being able to think properly.

"Have you got any wine from this lovely vineyard I could taste, Colonel?" Krupp sat down on the chair opposite Joseph. He still wore his cap, the peek casting a sinister shadow over his face. The whites of his eyes could just be seen through the shadow, making him appear like some kind of spirit. He was smiling slightly, amused, possibly at Joseph's anxiety. Joseph's shoulders dropped in despair; he was not strong enough to argue. He stomped off to the study to get his unwanted guest some wine.

In the hallway he saw with dismay that the end of one of the large crates had been prised open and the canvas of Caravaggio's *Portrait of a Courtesan* was halfway out.

Joseph's blood started to boil. How dare Krupp mess with his paintings! How long had he been asleep for? He saw the crowbar Krupp must have used to open the crates. Where did he find that? He picked it up and shouted, "Captain Krupp – come here immediately!" He straightened himself up and held the crowbar, ready to strike Krupp about the head as soon as he came down the passage from the kitchen. He was surprised to hear a light cough from the shadows to his right and saw with alarm two helmeted SS troopers. Joseph was aghast. He dropped the crowbar onto the floor with a clang.

"It's Major now, sir. What can I do for you, Colonel?" Krupp limped from the kitchen passage. "Ah, yes. You should meet my men. They brought me here. Do you have anywhere for them to lodge?" Joseph whirled around to see to Krupp standing close beside him.

"Yes, well ... What is the meaning of this?" Joseph waved his hand at the open crates.

"Just wondered what they were, Colonel." Krupp went over to the Caravaggio and stroked the ornate frame. "That's beautiful. Mine, I believe. The Barrett Collection's – what is it? A Caravaggio?"

"Yes, they belong to me now." Joseph realised his mistake and rapidly corrected himself. "I mean, the Reich."

"Really?" said Krupp, eyeing Joseph with a disparaging smile. "Does the Reich know you have got it … the collection, that is? And I trust you have remembered our arrangement?" Krupp tapped the portrait with his stick. Joseph could not believe Krupp knew what he had planned for the paintings, and yet he was being regarded with suspicion. Krupp must be guessing. "Now my men, Colonel, they need a place to rest their heads. They have been on the road since dawn, and it is now nine in the evening. They have rations – I haven't."

"Yes, well, they will have to …" Joseph turned to the two stony-faced soldiers and tried to sound superior, which was becoming difficult as his head ached and he was feeling sick. "Your quarters are above the garages outside. It is where the pickers are billeted in the summer."

"Thank you, Colonel," said Krupp. "I am sure that will suffice. However, it is pretty cold out there, and damp. They will find some rooms upstairs."

"Oh, do what you please. Just don't get in my way!"

Krupp removed his cap and hung it on the hallstand. "Shall we try that wine, Colonel?" He limped slowly towards the study, looking into the open doors on the way. The two soldiers threw out a Nazi salute and a jarring "Heil Hitler" that rang through Joseph's tender brain. He answered them with a vague salute and went after Krupp.

Joseph found Krupp had settled in his easy chair. He had poured himself a glass of red wine from Joseph's open bottle and was gazing into the fire through the wine glass, appreciating the colour.

"Took the liberty. This is a delicious wine, Colonel. I put a couple of logs on the fire, it had nearly died. Perhaps a bottle for my men?" Joseph glanced at the fire that was now a roaring blaze, and then at Krupp, then at the glass of wine in Krupp's hand. He did not know what to do: lose his temper and demand Krupp to leave, or just give in? Giving in was easier. Joseph sighed miserably and went to a box of wine behind the easy chair, and selected a bottle amongst the packing straw.

"You there! Bottle of wine by the door!" he shouted, placing the bottle by the study door.

"Glasses? A corkscrew, perhaps, for my hard-working men, Colonel? They are crack SS troops, not Wehrmacht peasants like the youth and his elderly soldiers who brought you here," said Krupp, putting his bad leg onto a footstool.

"They will have to fend for themselves." One of the soldiers picked up the bottle, clicked his heels as a thank-you gesture, and went off back to his colleague.

"Have you got any more men with you?" Joseph asked nervously.

"No, no, don't worry, you are safe."

Joseph did a double take.

Krupp continued. "Had you forgotten, Colonel, you are here because the last German agent at this vineyard, Captain Holter, was murdered last month?"

"No, I had not realised." Deller looked out the window at the darkness. He quickly drew the curtains and sat in submission in the chair beside the desk beneath the window. He turned the chair to confront Krupp. "The thing is, Krupp, I do not want any help. I would rather deal with this on my own. The grapes are picked and they have been made into wine, and there is nothing to do until next spring."

"Don't you want some help with the Barrett Collection, Colonel Deller?"

"No! … Thank you. I think you would be best served to go to Bordeaux and find new orders from—" He had forgotten the officer's name.

"From Otto Dietrich? He sent me here," Krupp said, clearly enjoying watching Joseph's frustration.

Unable to control his temper, Joseph blurted out, "I don't want you here! I just want to be left alone. Anyway, the paintings are being taken to Berlin next spring, but it is top secret. That is when I could use your help, Krupp."

"All right, Deller," Krupp said condescendingly. Joseph glared at him. "I mean, my colonel. I will sort something out within the next couple of days. My leg needs less wet and cold, anyway."

"How were you wounded?" Joseph asked again.

"I was questioning a prisoner, your friend Freya from Le Palais. She stabbed me in the leg with my SS honour dagger and then shot me with my pistol. She managed to miss my spine by millimetres – missed all vital organs, but took a chunk out of my rib and a bit of a vertebra. The bitch has made me lame for life, nearly lost the leg! And look at my face; what woman is going to look at me now?"

"You know Le Palais was bombed a few months ago and everybody killed? I thought that Swedish girl was killed too – what was her name?" Joseph said quietly, his eyes half-closed with tiredness. He found a glass in the corner cabinet, poured the rest of the bottle into his glass and drank it like water. He then walked gingerly to behind the chair where Krupp sat, to the wine box, and rummaged through the straw again for another bottle. He opened the bottle and replenished their glasses.

Deller was now almost totally inebriated. He staggered from his chair to the cabinet to the bottles behind the chair, always on the brink of falling. Krupp watched the performance with a frown. This man was addled; he would not last a minute out here. Krupp decided to return to the château in two months' time, in January, when he expected he would find Deller in a drunken heap, probably dead, and load up the collection. It would look fine in his mansion in Aschersleben.

"Sit here, my colonel," Krupp said kindly. "I will put some more logs on the fire, find a bed and sleep. I will take my men and get out of the way tomorrow."

"Very kind of you, Krupp."

Krupp stood and raised his glass.

"Heil Hitler!"

"Whoever," toasted Deller. Had he said this to any other SS officer, he would be regarded as treasonable. A frown then came over Deller's face. "What do you mean, they were getting married? Who were?"

"Baron Saumures and Freya."

Deller spluttered. "That's preposterous!" He looked confused. "Where was this?"

"Auch, South-West France."

A sudden realisation came over Deller's face. "I know Auch, it's where— Did they marry?"

"No. As I said, I was talking to Freya when she shot me. They both escaped."

"Really? Too bad," Deller said dozily. He slumped back into the easy chair, his cardigan unbuttoned, his white shirt spattered with red wine. He gazed hopelessly up at Krupp's scarred face smiling down at him.

"You are a good fellow, Krupp." And then he passed out.

Krupp went to the kitchen. He found some cheese in the cheese-safe and some black bread in the larder. As he ate, he thought about Freya, her gorgeous face and hair, her eyes, her lips. Perhaps, one day he would find her – and then what?

21

The smoky conference room was cold and poorly lit. The meeting was called by Sir Sussex Tremayne, SIS Head of Allied War Intelligence, part of MI6. Around the table were six men.

"Thank you for coming to this meeting," Sir Sussex said, still seated, a cigarette in the crook of his fingers, his other hand stroking his white naval beard. "I hope it was not too difficult for you to … eh." He coughed lightly, distracted by the papers in front of him. He gestured at the man in naval uniform to his right. "Commander Stanley here will be taking notes of this meeting. This meeting is classified, and all minutes will remain in my office safe." He indicated towards a desk behind him. "I would like to ask Dr Steven Sykes to start us off. Sykes, gentlemen, is part of a specialist unit code-named 'Boniface' – highly classified, dedicated to breaking coded messages from the enemy. Dr Sykes."

"Thank you, Sir Sussex." A pale middle-aged man in a grey suit rose from the table. "With our success at our department in intercepts of enemy communications, thanks to the capture of a German encoding machine, we have recently found that the enemy are using this kind of machine to transmit from Britain." Sykes looked down at his notes, pushed his spectacles back up his nose and carried on. "Our American agent, code name 'Intrepid', has intercepted some messages via Spain to a high-level American Secret Service person. The messages originated in London." All eyes turned to Sykes, waiting for the punchline. "These messages – three of them – were encrypted, we believe, by a German encryption machine and were sent to someone in Washington a month ago."

"Do we know the content of the messages, Dr Sykes?" one of the men asked.

"No, Mr Northey, we do not, yet. The reason is we will have to wait for the messages to be sent from America for decoding here, in my department. The Americans have been sitting on these messages for two months, trying to decode them themselves. They are not aware that we have one of these new decryption bombe machines and are able to decipher German encrypted messages."

There was a moment of thought around the table.

"What is this encryption machine called, do you know?"

"That is highly classified, Sir Jason."

"What is the identity of Intrepid and can we trust him or her?"

"We don't know who Intrepid is, Sir Jason," said Sir Sussex, leaning forward. "Only Mr Menzies, head of the service, knows him or her." Sir Sussex drew on his cigarette, regarding Sir Jason Barrett sternly. "Why do you question the value of this intelligence, Sir Jason?"

"It just sounds rather unlikely that the Germans would have such a sophisticated machine and it would be used from these shores. Surely a straightforward wireless signal, with code books." Sir Jason cast his eyes around the table to see if there was any agreement.

"One of the things we have gleaned from these messages," Sykes carried on, "is that they are all signed off with WASP in plain letters, not encrypted, for some reason."

"Or it was encoded, and WASP means something else?" Northey said.

"We do have some evidence," said Sir Sussex, "that there is an organisation, or secret political espionage group, called WASP. An American contact had heard from various sources of its existence."

"What is this secret group? How do we know it is an enemy group?" another man asked.

"We don't know, Mr Morris," said Sykes. "However, they were transmitting on an enemy machine. We do not use German encoding machines."

"Do we know the American contact who knows about WASP?" Morris asked.

"The contact was involved in a fatal accident on his way back from Germany to America," Sir Sussex said, standing. "Gentlemen, we need to find the person or persons who are transmitting from here. That is the purpose of this meeting. We want all your British agents in London to concentrate on locating this dangerous enemy spy. The equipment needed to transmit to Spain will be enormous, so they must be using established equipment covertly, such as the BBC transmitter at Bush House or somewhere else, capable of transmitting on a very high wavelength."

"Do you know when you'll get the American encrypted message, Dr Sykes?" Sir Jason Barrett asked.

"We hope within the next few days, sir."

"May we see the content of the messages?" Morris asked. "It may help us with where it was transmitted from."

"That will be up to Dr Sykes and his department, and the prime minister," Sir Sussex Tremayne said gravely, "if it is judged to be helpful in finding the author of the messages. Otherwise it will be up to the War Office as to who gets to see the messages." Sir Sussex sighed. "We seem to be down the pecking order in this … this … for some reason. However, I will remain in contact with the chief and keep your departments informed." Sir Sussex walked to his desk, followed by Stanley. He said over his shoulder, "Thank you, gentlemen." The men all stood.

Sir Jason strode up to Sir Sussex. "May I have a moment of your time, Sir Sussex?"

"Yes, Sir Jason, take a seat. I regret I have not got long as I must prepare for my weekly briefing with the prime minister." Sir Sussex indicated a chair for Sir Jason to sit in, drumming his fingers impatiently as he waited. "How may I help you, sir?"

"I believe I may have a name for the person that we seek regarding this … situation, Sir Sussex."

"Really? This is good news. How sure are you of this?"

"Quite sure. He is called Franz-Joseph Deller. My team have information from my people in France that he is in England."

Sir Sussex could not conceal his surprise. "How do you know about this man Deller?"

"He is an Austrian, an artist and a colonel in the SS."

"Sir Jason, I asked how you know Franz-Joseph Deller?"

"He was our Paris gardener."

Sir Sussex raised an eyebrow. "Well, leave it with me, Sir Jason. Deller is already known to us and will be picked up if he is in England." It was Sir Jason Barrett's turn to be surprised. "After your wonderful work capturing Hess, you may, yet again, have helped your country invaluably." Sir Sussex stood and put out his hand to be shaken. The interview was over. He pressed a button on his desk. Stanley appeared. "Sir Jason is leaving, Stanley. Thank you so much, Sir Jason."

*

The prime minister sat opposite Sir Sussex Tremayne, giving him a lazy glare, surrounded by a fog of cigar smoke. They sat in the Cabinet Room, having come to the end of the weekly War Intelligence briefing, which took place between just Sir Sussex and Winston Churchill.

As Sir Sussex got up to leave, the prime minister remained seated and asked, "What is this WASP business that is being talked about, Sir Sussex?" Sir Sussex was taken by surprise. He particularly wanted to keep anything about WASP to himself until he knew more about it.

"I did not know you knew about WASP, sir." Sir Sussex sat again.

"Then what is the fuss?"

"Is there a fuss, sir?"

"According to your man Commander Stanley, there's a fuss."

"I see." Sir Sussex was perplexed. Why would Stanley divulge such a thing? "Well, you will get a message soon from Dr Sykes at Boniface, for your attention."

"Boniface?" Churchill asked. "Remind me."

"Code name for the team at Bletchley Park, sir."

"Oh yes. When will this message arrive back from America?"

"Possibly at some point this week. It was sent via an Enigma machine, a German encoding device."

"But nobody knows about Enigma, Sir Sussex!"

"That's the mystery, Prime Minister. Only you, me and the team at Boniface know we have a captured an Enigma machine."

"How do we know it was coded by such a device?

"From what the CIA agent described, the way the message was sent – in blocks of five capital letters in columns – was just like an Enigma encoded message. The Americans sent part of a message to us, but not all. They thought they would have a go at decoding the messages but failed." Churchill smiled slightly. "The section we received asked for estimates of American troops being sent to the UK. And it was signed by WASP."

"Who was it sent to?"

"A chap called Rushton in the American secret service. He escaped to South America just before he was about to be arrested."

"Well, what do we expect from America?" the prime minister scoffed. "What do we know about WASP, Sir Sussex?"

"It is a political espionage organisation that, as far as we know, is against communism and socialist politics. WASP stands for 'War Against Socialist Parties'. More worrying is that it may be linked to a German organisation called the KGK, standing for *Krieg Gegen den Kommunismus* – War against

Communism – run by, we think, Admiral Canaris." Sir Sussex removed a cigarette from his silver cigarette case and tapped the end on the box, then lit it with a match.

"I know about the KGK."

"Really, sir?" Sir Sussex was astonished. Churchill pushed an ashtray across the desk for Sir Sussex's spent match. "Thank you, sir." Sir Sussex thought for a moment. Churchill was plainly not going to say any more about the KGK.

Sir Sussex tried to remember what he was saying. "We do not know much about WASP. One of our operatives has some idea about its existence, but not about whether it is a dangerous organisation, or a threat to our security. However, there is some evidence, a very small amount of … how can I put it? … tittle-tattle, that WASP may be involved with the enemy, namely gathering Allied intelligence for use by the enemy. Now this message about estimated Allied troop movements has made it a little more serious."

"Too bloody right. It has gone beyond tittle-tattle, as you call it, Sir Sussex. I am grieved that you have not alerted me sooner about this. How big is this organisation, do we think?" Churchill asked crossly, glancing at his fob watch.

"I don't really know, sir. It may be just one person, as opposed to an organised group. The source is not very reliable, hence why I had not brought it to your attention. I am surprised Stanley has."

"But the encoded message came from here, Sir Sussex, and was sent to America. Is it an American-based organisation, do we think? It sounds like an American thing."

"Again, we are not certain."

"Has this got anything to do with Operation Wasp Trap?"

"It is a coincidence that the word 'wasp' seems to be used. However, it is Baron Saumures, my godson, who entitled the operation, and it is his contact that brought the information about WASP in the first place, back in 1937, I think it was. He claims he was recruited by the head of WASP."

"Do we know about this head of WASP?"

"No, sir."

The prime minister sat back in his chair and took a large suck of his cigar. The end glowed red-hot, illuminating Churchill's face in an orangey glow. He blew out a huge cloud of smoke.

"Sir Sussex, I do not want your current work distracted by WASP." Sir Sussex raised an eyebrow. "Any organisation that is against communism is worthy of our support."

"Really, sir? I must say I am very surprised—"

"Keep an eye on it, though. Keep me informed. I will want to meet your godson when he returns from his duties."

"Yes, sir." Sir Sussex was troubled by the last statement.

He was about to voice his concerns, when Churchill said stridently, "I have grave views on two things, Sir Sussex."

"Yes, sir?"

"I would prefer we keep *our* intelligence to ourselves. I am resolved not to share too much with the Americans. Do I make myself clear?"

"Yes, sir."

"Also, Sir Sussex, I am sure you are aware of my contempt for communism." Mr Churchill stood and started walking towards the Cabinet Office door. "These bloody Soviets are getting too arrogant. Stalin is clever, and I don't think Roosevelt realises this; he is too sick. I had hoped that together with Germany and the United States, we could rout out Stalin and his communist government. But Herr Hitler is worse than Stalin!" Churchill stopped dead and swung around to look at Sir Sussex. "I met Hess, Sir Sussex," he said, a little irate, "at Whetstone in Barnet."

"Good God, did you, sir? I was not informed of this. Did anything come out of the meeting?"

"Regretfully not. He was a little upset with his government. He is convinced Hitler set him up. We didn't talk long – a couple of minutes. His eyebrows alarmed one a little. Huge ... met in the middle. Rather neanderthal."

The meeting was over. A wake of smoke followed the old man like a tugboat. He walked towards the Cabinet Office door with surprising speed for a man of his age and girth. He opened the door for Sir Sussex to step through. "A delight to see you again, Sir Sussex. Same time next week?"

"Yes, Prime Minister."

*

Sir Sussex put on his overcoat and placed his bowler hat angrily onto his head. Perhaps he should investigate WASP further, now the prime minister wanted to know about them too. Nobody, except his godson, seemed to think there was any merit in this ... this ... What was it? A movement? A bunch of terrorists?

He left Number Ten Downing Street via the Cabinet Office door onto Whitehall. He crossed the road to the entrance to the Ministry of Defence building.

As soon as he got to his office, he yelled, "Stanley, I need a word!" Commander Stanley bustled into Sir Sussex's office looking nervous. With him was Leading Wren Helen Willett, Sir Sussex's secretary, also looking flustered.

"Yes, Sir Sussex?"

"Not you, Helen!" Sir Sussex shouted. Seeing Wren Willett frown at his uncharacteristic rudeness, he added, "Sorry to be abrupt, Helen, government stuff." Wren Willett forced an unforgiving smile and left the office.

"Stanley, why did you brief the prime minister about WASP?"

"I'm sorry, sir, he forced it out of me."

"What? … Stanley, do you take me for a complete chump?"

"No, sir. The prime minister asked me about the Joint Intelligence meeting earlier and asked for the—"

"But that was meant to be kept confidential, Stanley. I said so at the start of the meeting!"

"He *is* the prime minister, Sir Sussex. And he asked me directly about the meeting."

"Why didn't you warn me before I went over to Number Ten?"

"I tried to, but you were preparing for the meeting and you told me to bugger off."

"Did I? Sorry about that. But how did he know about WASP?"

"He had been talking to Sir Jason Barrett."

Sir Sussex was surprised and concerned. He sat heavily at his desk. "I see, Stanley. How much did you tell him?"

"Only that there was a meeting and WASP was discussed. Apparently, Sir Jason asked if he could see the correspondence that Boniface was decoding, using the decoding bombes. The prime minister was going to ask you."

"Sir Jason wasn't mentioned at the meeting. Only Baron Saumures." Sir Sussex stroked his beard in thought. "The PM's only worry is that we don't share too much intelligence with the Americans."

"What do we do about WASP, sir? Is it a credible threat, do we think?"

"No, I do not believe it is, Stanley … at the moment. The PM has a theory that WASP is an American-based organisation, and now he is interested in knowing more about it. My new concern, however, is Sir Jason Barrett going behind my back."

"Shall I call him in, sir?"

"Leave it for now. Sir Jason has given us a name of a suspect."

"Really, Sir Sussex? Who?"

"Franz-Joseph Deller."

"But that's ..."

"Very strange, I agree. Even stranger, Deller was the Barrett's gardener in the nineteen twenties."

They stood in silence, contemplating the latest revelations.

"We need to get Ferdinand and his team back from Spain. He will know what has become of Deller."

22

Charlotte became very relaxed – and perhaps a bit bored – during the months they waited for transport back to England. She loved the social life of Madrid. She enjoyed the attention she constantly received from the city's fashionable set, all of whom seemed to be either German, elderly, fat Spanish men or young stringy Spanish youths. She was invited to all the social events with the baron and was in constant demand at the winter balls, concerts and operas. Baron and Baroness Saumures raced up the out-of-season social ladder of Madrid society. Charlotte's Spanish was becoming very good and she found it easy to learn, unlike Ferdi who struggled.

The cut over the baroness's eye had healed. She was happy and it showed. The warm autumn days in Madrid turned into cool winter nights. Dinner parties with dignitaries each weekend became the norm. Charlotte had only experienced this kind of social life when she was stuck at Le Palais. She had never been to so many wonderful houses as an adult. She was also feeling most liberated after three years cooped up in Le Palais with little, if any, freedom of movement in Paris.

"You would never know there was a war on, would you, Baroness?" *Generalissimo* Francisco Franco y Bahamonde said to Charlotte as they ate quail at a banquet to celebrate the Spanish dictator's birthday on the fourth of December.

"We have enjoyed our time here in Spain, Excellency. It has been a great relief to escape from the war for a while." Charlotte placed her hand on the general's arm.

The general's wife, Carmen, was watching the way her husband was captivated by the young baroness and said to Ferdi, sat to her left, "Your wife must be the loveliest woman in all Europe, Baron."

"You are kind, madame. She is indeed enchanting, but she seldom regards herself as beautiful."

"The gentlemen at this table are all very envious of the *generalissimo*, I see."

"I think it is I they are envious of, *mi señora*," Ferdi said gallantly. The general's wife paused, and then burst into laughter at Ferdi's ludicrous graciousness. She must have been beautiful when she was young, and she had enjoyed the attention of many a handsome young army officer. She now looked dowdy, grey, sunken-eyed and awfully thin. Ferdi looked dashing and handsome in his borrowed white tie and tails.

The ball, after the dinner, was held in the large ballroom at the palace of El Pardo, where General Franco and his wife lived. Charlotte was honoured to partner the *generalissimo* for a few dances. She was dazzling in her evening dress of pale silver-grey silk. Her gold hair swept down her back, to the envy of all the raven-haired Spanish women in the room and the admiration of every man. Ferdi danced with the First Lady, María del Carmen Polo de Franco.

As the rest of the guests joined the dance, Charlotte spied Theodora with a dashing, tall gentleman. "Who's the handsome gentleman, Theodora?" Charlotte later asked, with a crafty smile. They were in the lady's powder room, on their own.

Theodora looked deadly serious. "His name is Colonel Hans-Jürgen Stoltz. He murdered all those Jews in the Drancy jail a few years ago. He's a nasty piece of work. Bertrand asked me to keep an eye out for him. He wants to know what he is up to."

Charlotte shot her hand up to her mouth. "How on earth did you come upon that information?"

"Bertrand told me."

Bertrand had been invited to the ball but he decided that it would be unwise to attend. "I can't dance with my gammy leg. Anyway, it will be full of Nazis, and I will want to kill the bastards!" he said. He'd decided instead that he would be their chauffeur for the night. He had even washed and given the rather rickety Peugeot a cursory polish.

"Bertrand knew Stoltz was coming to Madrid. He is here, according to Bertrand, trying to find someone."

"Who, Theodora?"

"I don't know … I don't think Bertrand knows. It's all rather mysterious, don't you think?"

"How does Bertrand know so much about Stoltz?"

"He said one of his escaper guides – a Spanish girl – told him about Stoltz. He says he is going to kill him."

Charlotte was mystified. "Bertrand is a dark horse, isn't he? Do you know him … Stoltz?"

"Yes, we met in Berlin before the war. He used to come to the club. He was always with a young, pretty girl – looked quite like you, come to think of it, with shorter hair. He wants me to introduce you to him!"

"Why, for heaven's sake?"

"I think it is something to do with how you look, don't you think?" Theodora was wary. "He's a bit old for you, isn't he? What am I going to do, Freya?"

"Introduce me!"

"What? Are you mad? He's a dangerous Nazi."

"What can he do to me here, at the *Generalissimo's* Ball, in neutral Spain, with as many Allied guests as German?"

"Just be careful, Freya." They headed for the door. Theodora turned and faced Charlotte, concern on her dark features. "You're not going to do anything stupid with him, are you?"

"Like what?"

"Seduce him."

"No, Theodora, I am a married woman!" Charlotte charged past Theodora and as she went through the door of the powder room, she said over her shoulder, "I am going to kill him myself."

*

Charlotte sat in a large, high-backed dark-red sofa in a library, next to the ballroom. She stood out against the dark-coloured sofa as though a spotlight shone on her. Theodora approached with the tall, sandy-haired German, in full evening dress with a white bow tie. He was thin, handsome, with sharp angular features and bright light-grey eyes behind frameless glasses.

"Colonel Stoltz, may I present Baroness Freya Saumures."

"Delighted, Baroness." With a slow bow, he gathered up Charlotte's proffered gloved right hand as though to kiss it. "You are, if I am permitted to say, enchanting. I should congratulate the baron. I am mortified that we cannot be closer acquainted." His eyes roamed up Charlotte's arm to her bare shoulders, down to her bosom, and then slowly up to her eyes. She regarded him with interest, her head at a slight tilt, an enigmatic smile on her lips. He was charming, dashing, and perhaps something of a rogue. Charlotte felt a fluttering thrill in her chest. "May I sit with you?" he asked. Before Charlotte could utter a word, he sat with a flourish of his tails so he did not sit on them. He perched on the edge of the sofa and gazed, enthralled, at Charlotte. Theodora was left standing. On seeing this, the German leapt to his feet, offered a chair for Theodora to sit on, and then resumed his perch beside Charlotte.

"What are you a colonel of, Herr Stoltz?" Charlotte asked.

"The SS, my lady."

"I do so love the SS uniform, Colonel. Why are you not in uniform?" Charlotte stroked Stoltz's arm as she said this. He could not conceal his delight.

"I-I left it in Munich, I'm afraid."

"With all your medals?"

"Uh … yes, my lady, with all my—"

"Have you got lots of medals, Colonel Stoltz?" She gazed at him through her long eyelashes, a mischievous smile on her lips.

"Well … uh … a few, you know." He was embarrassed. All the bravado that he initially showed had melted away as Charlotte hoped. She was enjoying her power. It was like being at Le Palais again. She had not forgotten how to use it, and she intended to use every bit of it to get this murderer.

They chatted for half an hour about Spain, the Spanish, a bit about Paris. Theodora looked a little panicked when the colonel asked whereabouts Charlotte lived in Paris, and went into a coughing fit.

Then Charlotte abruptly said, "What brings you to Madrid, Colonel?"

"I am on the trail of a group of Jews. A group of terrorists are transporting these enemies of the Reich over the Pyrenees mountains."

Charlotte kept her composure. "How exciting!" she said enthusiastically. "But are we not quite a long way from the Pyrenees?"

"Well, yes, but we think the ringleaders are here in Madrid."

"How very brave of you, Colonel," Charlotte enthused. Whilst Stoltz's head was bowed in modesty, she flashed a worried look at Theodora.

"Have you caught anyone yet?" Theodora asked with as much enthusiasm in her voice as possible.

"No, they seem to have found another route. That is why I have come to this side of the border, to see if I can get them at this end."

"How clever of you, Colonel Stoltz," Theodora said. "I am sure you will track down these awful people. They have little intelligence anyway, these Jews." Charlotte's eyes widened at Theodora's shocking performance.

"Thank you, madame. They will indeed be caught. They think they are safe in Spain." The conversation went into a lull.

"Colonel Stoltz" – Charlotte stood, as did the colonel, as though to end the interview – "my husband is not able to take me to see the artist Joaquín Sorolla y Bastida at the Sorolla Art Gallery."

"Then permit me to escort you … and Madame Theodora." Stoltz jumped at the opportunity.

"It is a little out of the way, however. It is in Paseo del General Martínez Campos, I believe." Charlotte knew this as she and Ferdi had been to the exhibition the day before.

"I will be at your service wherever you may care to go. Perhaps some lunch after?"

"How lovely. Will it not be lovely, Theodora?" Charlotte was beginning to sound like a Jane Austen novel and smiled to herself. Concern slowly grew over Stoltz's face.

"Yes, darling," Theodora said.

"Can I say eleven o'clock at your hotel?" he asked. Charlotte was stumped. She had forgotten they all lived in a rather run-down town house belonging to the British Embassy.

"No, I have to do some shopping first. We will meet in the beautiful gardens behind the gallery at eleven." Charlotte leant in close to the colonel and gave him her most warming smile. "I must go now. You are so kind to help us tomorrow."

Stoltz held Charlotte's hand and bowed over it, and similarly saluted Theodora.

"May I get your coats and wraps, and see you to your car?"

*

Bertrand was sitting in the car, watching the Nazi salute the ladies. He had to be a bloody Kraut with that hair, thought Bertrand. His nerves bristled. He drove the car up to the entrance as the women swept elegantly down the steps, escorted by the tall German. Bertrand leapt out of the car. He was about to shout at Theodora for keeping him waiting, when Charlotte put up her finger to shush him, and told him to open the back doors as though a chauffeur.

"What is going on?" he whispered as they got into the car.

"We are trying to look like respectable ladies – a baroness and her companion," hissed Theodora. Bertrand limped back into the driving seat and they drove off.

"Where's Ferdi?" Bertrand asked.

"He went back earlier. Took a taxi. We had a row." Charlotte said sadly.

"Well, come on, who's the Kraut?"

"You should have seen her, Bertrand. I can do nothing else but admire the rapidity with which Freya was able to reduce a self-assured SS officer to something resembling a babbling youth!"

"But who is he?"

"*That* is Colonel Hans-Jürgen Stoltz. And we have got him to take Charlotte to a gallery."

"Good God! This is very exciting. Well done!"

"Thanks," said Charlotte. "Bertrand, how do you know so much about this man?" Bertrand made no comment. "I can kill him for you, if you like."

"Christ, Theodora, what have you been putting into Freya's head?"

*

Ferdi sat at the end of the kitchen table the morning after the ball, his elbows on the table, the heels of his hands rubbing his eyes. Charlotte was standing beside him, Theodora was sitting drinking her coffee, both women apprehensive.

"This is madness, Freya, and dangerous." Ferdi sounded anxious.

"He is a Nazi criminal," Charlotte argued. "He dedicates his life to killing Jews … all Jews! Now he is tracking down Bertrand and his escape line. We should kill him."

"Well, you can't just murder Stoltz."

"Why not? He has murdered hundreds of people!" Charlotte threw her hands up and sat down beside her husband. A mixture of anger and concern coursed through her. Ferdi's reaction was not what she expected. She had always respected Ferdi's opinion and thought she knew him.

"My dear, it is murder. We are in a neutral country, under Spanish law. Stoltz has not been tried … How do you know he killed all these people, all these Jews?"

"You will have records on him in your files. You will see how bad he is!"

"Yes, and we will use those files to try him after the war."

"That will be too late." Charlotte was emphatic. "By then he will have tortured and killed more people, including maybe Bertrand. He is here spying on us and killing Jews." Charlotte sighed, slumped into a chair and looked up at the ceiling.

"Ferdi, this man is a monster," Theodora said. "I knew him before Paris. You only knew about him at Drancy. I knew him in Germany."

Ferdi was quiet for a moment. Charlotte was still staring at the ceiling, in a sulk.

"I am uncomfortable that you are going to summarily execute a man who has not been tried, in a neutral country—"

"I killed Krupp, so I can kill—"

"You killed Krupp – your enemy – in self-defence, within a country at war! What has happened to you, Freya? I—"

"In the neutral zone," Charlotte interrupted loudly, her temper rising, "whilst you and the priest were being tortured at their headquarters!"

Ferdi eyed Charlotte and then Theodora. "You are in favour of this, Theodora?"

"I am. I was not at first as there was no plan and it could be dangerous, but now there is a plan."

"There is a plan?" Charlotte said.

"Bertrand has planned it. He's been planning it for a while now," Theodora said. "He will be in in a moment, and we will see what you think, Ferdi. Freya, I really hoped there could be a way for you not to be involved."

"What? But Theodora, I want to be involved!"

"I'm sorry," Ferdi said. He was angry, something they had not seen before. "I will not allow you to murder a man – or anybody, come to that – here."

"You can't just—"

"I can, and I will not allow you to kill this man. We have no hard evidence of any crime; we are in a neutral country, and we will be as bad as the Nazis if we kill a person because he is alleged to have tortured or killed people. Do I make myself clear?"

At that point, Bertrand entered the kitchen. He looked at the women and then at Ferdi. "I thought you would have a reason to bugger this up, Baron," he said testily.

"I'm surprised at you, Bertrand," Ferdi said, upset. "This is apparently something you cooked up."

"I have a source who knows this Stoltz character. She was mutilated by him and he killed some of her family. He is not a nice Nazi – but then there are very few that are."

"Then she should do her own dirty work. Why should we get involved?" Ferdi said.

"*We* are not getting involved – just me." Bertrand looked at Theodora. "My source can't do it as she is very ill. She has an injury that has become infected. An injury inflicted on her by Colonel Hans-Jürgen Stoltz! Theodora said she would help."

Ferdi rose loudly from his chair, the chair legs scraping on the slate floor, and left the kitchen. Theodora and Charlotte's eyes met. Theodora cocked her head in submission, Bertrand shrugged his shoulders. Charlotte threw up her hands and sat heavily back into the chair.

"I shall go to the gallery," said Theodora, "and send your apologies, Freya."

"Thank you, Theodora," Charlotte said sadly.

*

Bertrand sat in the driving seat of the Peugeot looking as stoical and serious as possible. He was parked outside the entrance gate of the gardens of the Sorolla Art Gallery. In front of the Peugeot was Stoltz's Mercedes; to Bertrand's and Theodora's relief, no driver was present.

Theodora had gone into the gardens to collect Colonel Stoltz. The story she was to tell him was that the baroness had been held up by her dressmaker and would be grateful if Herr Stoltz would meet her at the Lago Casa de Campo, the lake at the centre of Madrid, noted for its gardens and magnificent fountain.

"Why there, Madame Theodora? It is cold, and there is nobody around." He looked irritated.

"It is also very pretty for sitting and looking at the lake. She would like to see the marvellous fountain in the centre of the lake, Colonel." Theodora winked. "I think the lack of people is the reason."

"Oh, I see!" A delighted smile came over his face. "Whereabouts shall I meet her? Which part of the lake?"

"Follow my driver; I will show you. If I may, I will travel with you, and my driver will take me home. I trust your driver will take the baroness back to her hotel?"

"Would be delighted; however, I am driving myself."

"Even better," Theodora said. They walked out of the art gallery gardens and up to the huge Mercedes car with a Nazi flag on each wing. Theodora waved at Bertrand to show them the way to the lake.

All the way to the Lago Casa de Campo, Colonel Stoltz asked questions about Freya, about her marriage, her likes and dislikes. He even flirted with Theodora, which irritated her. They approached the lake at the northern end, under some trees. A light mist surrounded the edge of the lake. Theodora instructed Stoltz to drive up to the edge.

He was unsure of the whole arrangement as he drove around the deserted lake. "Is this some kind of set-up, Theodora?" He was getting agitated. "When will she arrive?" he asked with some trepidation.

"There she is now, coming through the mist." Theodora pointed out the side window. As soon as Stoltz turned his head, she lifted her handbag to the back of his head and pulled the trigger of the pistol concealed within. The side window was instantly splattered with blood, and shattered when Stoltz's head crashed into it.

Bertrand suddenly appeared. "Well done, my girl!"

"Who are you calling a girl?" Theodora said. "Anybody about?"

"No – deserted. Let's get his clothes off. I have a bag here."

The two of them tied a canvas bag over his head so as not to get covered in blood, and stripped Stoltz down to his underwear. The bullet exiting his head had obliterated most of his face, but they removed anything that could identify him. The car number plates were taken off, as were the Nazi flags.

Bertrand took out a pair of binoculars and scanned the edge of the lake. The far side was still misty so no one would see as they pushed the Mercedes into the lake. The car sank quickly. Bertrand happened to know that the place selected was six metres deep and sloped down to eight metres.

*

The small house in Madrid was quiet and joyless the day after the assassination. Charlotte was upset, as was Ferdi, that Theodora and Bertrand had killed Stoltz. Charlotte wanted to know everything that had happened. Ferdi was out most of that morning, and when he returned, he hid himself in the garden, chain-smoking and not wanting to know any of the details.

Charlotte took out a coat for him to wear as it had turned very cold for Spain.

"I am sorry, Ferdi," she said quietly, taking his hand in hers. "I really had no idea Theodora and Bertrand were going to do that. I had asked her just to tell him I was not coming."

"They had to kill him. He would have pursued you and discovered me and Bertrand." He paused, his eyes cast to the ground in front of him. "But it is still murder." He turned to look at Charlotte. "And you should not have encouraged him, Freya!"

"But I—"

"I blame you for this," he continued. Charlotte was shocked. "I just hope we leave Madrid before the body is discovered."

"Ferdi!" Charlotte burst into tears. "How can you blame me for that man being killed? He was a murdering Nazi." She swiped her tears away angrily.

"I have told you my thoughts on this matter. None of you will leave this house, not until we leave Spain. I have organised our travel for, hopefully two months' time. It is not ideal – we are going by boat to England."

"But that is perfect, at last we—"

"It is far from perfect! We will be in a fishing boat, leaving Bilbao. It will be dangerous this time of year."

"But we will be in England, Ferdi. Safe."

"Possibly, Freya, possibly," Ferdi said sadly. "From now on, you will all do as you are told, or I will leave you here to get back on your own." Ferdi stormed back into the house. Charlotte heard him saying the same thing to Bertrand and Theodora in the kitchen.

Ferdi spent the final two days in his room, not eating. Charlotte left food and water outside his door, but it was left untouched. At one stage she wondered if he was still in his room and knocked, only to get a sharp response saying he did not want to be disturbed.

"It's not like the baron to sulk like this," Bertrand said.

"I think he is making a bit of a drama of it all, personally." Theodora stretched out on the sofa, reading a book and tapping her cigarette into a full ashtray on the floor.

"Well, I am worried," Charlotte said. "I think we may have gone too far with Stoltz. What if Ferdi says something to the authorities in England?"

Bertrand laughed. "He will not say anything to the law. He is not that type."

"I am worried if he goes off without me. I have no one back in England, except a dotty aunt and my uncle Jason, who is not a nice man. And Theodora, what about her? She has never been to England, have you, Theodora?"

"No, but I will survive. I don't need anybody."

"What do you mean?" Bertrand said, affronted. "If the baron wants to go off in a huff, I will sort you both out. You stick with me, ladies." Both women looked at Bertrand dubiously. He threw his arms up in protest. "Well, I will!"

23

Just before Christmas, Franz-Joseph Deller presented a letter to the British Ambassador in Madrid.

"Your Excellency, may I thank you for this interview," Joseph said. He was in rather scruffy clothes. But then, most escaping people looked scruffy. "I trust my credentials will explain that I need to be transported home, to England, as soon as possible."

"It will indeed be a challenge, Mr Dent, especially with your cargo." The ambassador turned to a man standing behind him. "This is Chippenham, Mr Dent. He will take charge of your case. I regret you may be here some time before we can do the checks on you and your cargo."

The difficulty that Mr Chippenham had was the instruction to get not only Joseph back to England but also to ship five very large crates with him. Mr Chippenham was additionally told that this man, Joseph Dent, was not to be allowed out of the embassy until he was moved for transport, and that he was not to allowed to meet any other escaping British subjects. The directive came from one of the highest authorities in the War Office, Sir Jason Barrett.

*

Jost Krupp returned to Château du Pevillon in January. He rode resplendently in his Mercedes staff car. So convinced was he that he would find the mortal remains of the colonel, he had the foresight to bring a field coffin with him in the truck following up the frozen drive to the house. The day was crisp and cold with bright, clear sunshine. Small fluffy clouds scudded across the sky in the biting wind, and the snow, that fell unusually on New Years' Day, had nearly all thawed. A lovely way to start 1944.

As the convoy approached the château, Krupp saw that the gates had not only been closed but also renovated. The driver hopped out of the staff car and went to open the gate, but found a heavy chain and padlock had been placed around it.

"Break down the gate with the truck. I'm not having this!" Krupp was furious. It looked like Deller knew he was coming and had decided to lock him out.

The truck pushed the gate open, tearing one gate off its hinges. Krupp strutted – as best as he could with a limp – up to the front door of the château. He saw that Deller's truck was still parked in the sheds. As he was about to open the door without knocking, a big man, nearly two metres tall with wide shoulders, black shaggy hair and beard, and eyebrows that met at the bridge of his nose, tore open the door. He grabbed Krupp's leather holster belt and jammed a shotgun under Jost's chin. The man was completely unafraid, not at all fearful of the SS uniform as most people were. The two soldiers in the trucks piled out, armed with rifles.

"Why did you do that to my gate?" the huge man rumbled in French. He hoisted Krupp up onto his toes.

Krupp was terrified. He had never been in this kind of danger. He spluttered, trying to control his voice. "Put me down or my men will shoot you."

"Not with you in the way, they won't. Why did you do that to my gate? I had just made them good, you Nazi trash!"

"We believe there is a German officer here. He is under arrest. I am here to take him into custody," Krupp said steadily, only just managing to keep an expression of official business. The giant looked at him, relaxed his grip on Krupp's belt and lowered his shotgun.

"He went last year," said the giant.

Krupp was confused, the initial fear and anger subsiding on both sides. "Monsieur, may I come in and we will sort out this ... situation?" He could see the man was not a complete fool, unlike most men of his size. The man released Krupp's belt and stepped into the house. Krupp motioned to his sergeant driver that he was going to be a few minutes.

The inside of the house had changed completely since he was last there. The main difference was that the hall seemed larger, completely empty of bulky crates.

"Tell me, monsieur, what happened to the crates that were here?"

"We helped the German gentleman take them away the day we moved in," said a cultured French voice. A woman in her late fifties, tall, elegant, with grey hair tied up in a chic bun, emerged from the study.

"My name is Valérie Félix de Valois, major, and this is my cellar man, Gaston, and his wife." She indicated to a petite woman coming from the kitchen: "Ella is my cook. We acquired this vineyard from Monsieur and Madame Bénézet, through the German gentleman, Herr Deller. I did not know he was an army officer. He said he was a civilian."

"Was he not in uniform?" Krupp limped up and down the hall, looking around suspiciously.

"No, monsieur, he spoke very good French, like you." Madame Félix de Valois then remembered, "He had bought a large lorry to take all the crates. His lorry is still in the barn, broken. I regret I do not know where he has gone. Or what to do with his lorry."

"How did he pay for a lorry?" asked Krupp, more to himself than madame. He was full of disappointment and despair.

"The vineyard cost nearly two hundred thousand francs. We paid the deposit last year." The woman looked concerned. "We have all the documentation. He was very thorough. It was good value for this great vineyard. We had been looking at this—"

"Yes, yes, yes … I'm sure it is all correct. But you have no idea where he is now?"

"I think he mentioned Spain," the giant man said, and they nodded to each other, agreeing with his recollection.

"Well, thank you, and good day." Krupp limped out of the house.

"Oi! What about our new gate?" the large man said, raising his shotgun again.

"You will have to take it up with the Wehrmacht in Bordeaux. We are on military duty and, as an occupying force, have rights to search private premises for criminals. You should not have chained the gate. Good day."

Krupp got into his staff car and turned to his sergeant. He was seething with anger.

"We will come back tomorrow – early morning – and wipe that lot out," he fumed. "Communist swine! I will put a bullet into that giant moron's head myself."

A thought suddenly occurred to him. "I fancy spending the rest of the war here. I've got this gorgeous girl in Bordeaux …" Krupp started to snigger, quickly joined by his sergeant.

*

There were many ways of getting back to England from Spain – all dangerous. Sometimes by boat via Gibraltar or Barcelona, sometimes from one of the heavily guarded ports on the west coast. The best and quickest was to fly from Madrid but with great risk of being shot down. There were too many spies working for the Germans living in Madrid. Small networks of spies were being handsomely rewarded by Germany to report all Allied movements, whether at sea or by air. Air strips nearer the west coast were being sabotaged by the Spanish, loyal to the Nazis, or simply being paid by the Germans to stop the Allies escaping.

A little over five months after Charlotte, Theodora, Bertrand and Ferdi arrived in Madrid, Ferdi managed to get them passage back to England. He had preferred to go by aeroplane from an airfield just outside of Burgos, northern Spain, but there would be no flights until March when the weather was better and repairs to the runway had been made.

On a cold, wet February morning in 1944, Ferdi and Charlotte's little band, along with an escaped American pilot called Chuck, stepped onto a Spanish fishing boat in Bilbao on the north coast of Spain. After three choppy days and nights on a turbulent sea, they stepped onto British soil at Falmouth in Cornwall. Everybody except Bertrand was seasick the entire time. It was a very rough sea, but it meant U-Boat action would be low. Charlotte and Theodora could not hold any food down, even after Bertrand's theory of curing seasickness: to eat as much bread as possible, even after throwing it up, washed down with lots of water laced with rum. Charlotte could not work out if she was drunk half the time or just ill. Her stomach ached, her head swam, the whole journey was a nightmare. Theodora tried to get her to start smoking as this helped her, but Charlotte thought it would make her even more sick. However, it seemed Bertrand's cure did start to work just as they came into Falmouth harbour.

From Falmouth they travelled by train to London and then down to Ferdi's house in Petworth, Sussex, via Clapham Junction.

Charlotte felt she was returning to normal as she hung her head out of the train window. Early clumps of daffodils grew out of the grass as they drew slowly out of Falmouth. Cornwall was warm for this time of year.

Her first view of her mother's native country was not what she had expected. It was so beautiful, even on a cloudy day. At times the train ran along beside the sea, and then through lush downland, woods, and green fields of grazing black and white cows and fluffy sheep. As they approached Reading, Charlotte fell asleep on Theodora's shoulder. They were safe.

24

Only the buzzing insects could be heard in the deathly quiet of a hot summer afternoon at Château du Pevillon, until the stillness was shattered. Krupp heard a shout at the front of the house. "Jost!" the voice shouted through the door. "Major Krupp!"

"My dear Adolf." Jost appeared from around the back of the château. Adolf Diekmann was a major in *Das Reich* of the Waffen SS. He was tall, blond, with a long, pointed nose, charming smile, and only twenty-nine years old. Krupp limped up to Diekmann, his hand outstretched. "What brings you to St-Émilion?"

"We are on the march, Krupp! We have just come up from the town of Agen, south of here." Diekmann eyed him with concern. "What happened to you?" He looked alarmed at the scar on Krupp's face and his limp.

"Got into a bit of tangle with partisan terrorists in the south. Got stabbed in the leg and shot in the back. There is still a bullet in my spine. You are still fit, I see." Krupp exaggerated his injuries, which was not hard.

"Bad luck."

"It's nothing – got this cushy job though! What are you up to?"

"We are on our way to wipe out some French militants who kidnapped one of my officers."

"Who got kidnapped?" Krupp was astonished. "Who would be so rash as to capture a German SS soldier?"

"They got Helmut Kämpfe."

"Christ! Come in, Adolf, come in. Where are all your men?" Krupp envied Diekmann's battledress. He looked menacing in his camouflage jacket, jodhpurs and black jackboots. He held his forage cap in his hand.

"They are resting up on the main road, in the village up there. I heard you were here, thought you could help." Diekmann removed his jacket, revealing a light-green vest and skinny but muscular arms. A dark-blue "O+" was tattooed on the inside of his right forearm, denoting his blood group.

They entered the kitchen. All four quarters of the huge windows were open, and a cool breeze was welcomed. "We are on our way to Normandy. The enemy have landed there, you know."

"Yes, a bit of a surprise for us all. It's a shame I cannot come with you to Normandy. This leg, you know, and the bullet in my back."

"Don't worry, Krupp, we will win the war for you!" To Krupp's relief he was not being asked to go to war with Diekmann to Normandy.

They sat at the bare wood kitchen table, a bottle of red wine and some glasses in the centre. A young jacketless SS soldier came in, clicked his heels and was about to shout Heil Hitler, only to be rewarded by Krupp shouting, "Get out! Wait until I call you." The boy scuttled off.

Although it was only ten thirty in the morning, Krupp offered, "Some of my wine, Adolf?"

"Have you a beer? I long for a beer. The bloody French only drink wine and brandy."

"Halstenberg!" Krupp barked. The boy returned, clicked his heels again.

"Sir?"

"Do we have any beer?"

"Yes, sir. I will—"

"Is it cold, lad?" asked Diekmann.

"It is in the cellar, sir." Diekmann waved approval and the young soldier opened a door to one side of the kitchen entrance and disappeared down some steps. He returned with a crate of Excelsior beer bottles.

Diekmann looked dubiously at the bottles. "French beer?" He plucked one from a crate, took a knife out from a sheath on his belt and prized off the cap. "Glass!" he demanded. Halstenberg hurriedly placed one in front of each man and then left with a slight bow.

"What happened to Helmut Kämpfe?" Krupp asked.

"The militants killed him after kidnapping him and some other men."

"Why?"

"We had started executing partisans and Resistance, I suppose. Not many, a few dozen, that's all. They managed to catch Kämpfe in a bar, with a woman, I think."

"What do you need my help for, Adolf?"

"There is a village near here." Diekmann took out a small map from the top pocket of his jacket that was draped over the back of his chair. He took a deep draught of beer whilst scrutinising the map. "It is called Oradour-sur-Glane. Fancy giving us a hand? You speak French like a native, and I don't."

"I have nothing else to do," Krupp said. He had not done much in the way of fighting in this war – he left that to the Waffen SS. "What do you want me to do, apart from translate?"

"We will encircle the village and kill anything that moves. Those bastards kidnapped, tortured and killed one of our own. It is about time we finished these terrorists off. They have killed many German soldiers and they just leave the bodies on the street!" Diekmann drained his beer and slammed the glass down on the table. "You can take command of a machine gun section, to cover the crowd. It keeps them in order, having that threat. I will ask the mayor for thirty hostages, and then search the town for weapons. Shoot the hostages if they don't hand them over. We will probably shoot the lot anyway. They are all pigs!" Diekmann looked around the tidy kitchen. "Got a woman around, Krupp?"

Krupp smiled. "Yes, a stunner. But she is working for someone in Bordeaux at the moment."

"Doing what?"

"No idea. She is in with the secret lot, so I don't really know. Don't care, really. She's great in bed." He sniggered. Diekmann appeared unimpressed.

"Well, don't tell her about what we are doing. Women are … well, you know."

He didn't know, but Diekmann was young and was not probably very experienced in life. "How did you find out about Kämpfe?"

"I got some information from a man in the Milice."

"A French man?" Krupp was dubious.

"The Milice have been trying to coral the partisans and fanatics around Tulle, in between here and Agen. The Milice Française hate these communists and Jews as much as we do." He drained his beer and opened another bottle. "I need some help, Krupp. I've got this Wehrmacht officer … he is absolutely useless, timid, if you know what I mean. A captain called Günther Wolff."

"Not a good SS officer?"

"No, he was sent to replace Kämpfe. He is a poor excuse for a German."

"You must have other officers?"

"All my other officers are taking most of the regiment north. Captain Gance, a good man, is in command. I could not leave it to Wolff." Diekmann sighed. "I have a few very good sergeants, thank God. But I need another officer, one with some guts, to come with me."

"What are you going to do with him – Wolff, I mean?"

"I will probably end up killing him, putting it down to terrorists."

Krupp drank his beer. "When do we go?"

"Got some battledress, Krupp?" Diekmann stood, put on his jacket and his holster belt. "Let's have a little lunch with the men."

"Be with you in a minute, Diekmann. Halstenberg!"

"Don't take too long putting on the make-up, Krupp, or I will go to the party without you."

*

Oradour-sur-Glane lay beside the river Glane. The quiet village consisted of a main street with a few lanes running off it. There was a pretty church, a tree-lined small market square, schools – boys' and girls' – a bakery, *salon de coiffure*, a blacksmith, a *pension* hotel, a *bar-tabac*, houses and barns. It was a sunny late afternoon, not much wind and only a few people around. The neatly pollarded plain trees that lined the main street had sprung into new leaf. The sandstone walls of the houses echoed birdsong and children at play.

The few people who were out and about became aware of soldiers appearing all around their town. There was shouting, and men went out onto the main street to see what all the commotion was. People slammed and locked their doors.

The local doctor, Dr Jacques Desourteaux – who also served as the mayor of Oradour-sur-Glane – had just finished seeing a pregnant woman in her little apartment above a workshop, in the centre of the town, beside the *pension*. He got into his car. He noticed confused men and women running about further up the street. He started his motor and was pulling out when his windscreen shattered and the tip of his left shoulder exploded in a mist of blood. Alarmingly, a tuft of material on his jacket started oozing red. He tried desperately to see where the shot had come from.

He saw four huge half-track battle transporters, painted in mottled greens and sandy-yellow camouflage, drive slowly and menacingly into the street from the direction of the bridge. Troops poured out of the back of each vehicle. They all started to shout in German at everybody in the street. The door of the doctor's car was torn open and a soldier, who came out of nowhere, grabbed the doctor by his injured shoulder. "*Geh raus!*" he shouted.

"Everybody must gather in the square," an SS officer said loudly in French, standing on top of a troop carrier. "Who is the mayor?" demanded the officer.

"I am," said the doctor, "but my—"

"Instruct your town crier to gather all townspeople, including children, in this square for identity checks. Immediately! Those trying to escape inspection will be shot."

Dr Desourteaux looked around for the town crier, Jean Depierrefiche, the village blacksmith. He saw the blacksmith running towards him from his workshop.

"What is going on, Doctor?" the stocky man asked. He gasped when he saw the mayor's bloody tuft on his jacket shoulder.

"The Boche want to do identity checks of the whole town. Go and summon everybody to gather here, in the fairground square. They are shooting anyone trying to escape the checks, Jean," the doctor impressed on the smith.

"What about the Jews?" the smith hissed. The village were hiding two Jewish families.

"They will just have to take their chances, but the Germans are not asking if there are any Jews, for some reason." The doctor was becoming distraught, his injured shoulder more painful. He did his jacket button up and placed his left arm into the jacket as if a sling.

Dr Desourteaux was bundled into the fairground square. He looked back at his car; the motor was still running and he felt he should get his bag. He turned to the sergeant ushering people in the street to the square.

"I must turn the motor off, and—" The sergeant pointed a machine gun at the doctor, who stood stock-still, an expression of utter horror on his face. The sergeant swung his machine gun, aimed it at the doctor's car and shot a whole magazine into the engine. Steam rose up and the motor stopped. The sergeant looked back at the doctor and said, with a wry smirk, "It stops." The doctor turned to see all the people being ushered into the square had stopped and were looking at the sergeant with a mixture of shock and disgust.

"*Los geht's!*" the sergeant shouted and waved his machine gun at the stunned crowd.

The crier's drum could be heard thumping around the small town and the smith's cries summoning the village to meet in the fairground square. The square was filling up with people. Women, children and men, huddled in family groups, looking worriedly at the huge machine guns on the half-tracks that were trained on them. Standing on one of the half-tracks was the imposing SS major, an ugly scar running down his cheek. He was perched high, overlooking the crowd, like a carrion crow waiting for his quarry to die.

Every now and then, a military truck would drive to the edge of the square and more terrified people would pile out of the back. The doctor recognised them as people who lived on the outskirts of the town.

Eventually the square was full. There were well over five hundred people crammed into it. Every now and then, the doctor could hear shots around the edge of the village. He was extremely worried about what this meant. His wife and ten-year-old daughter were nowhere to be seen, but the square was so crowded, they could be anywhere.

"Women and children under sixteen to assemble in the church," the SS officer shouted. He barked orders to the troopers in German and then turned to Desourteaux. "Monsieur le mayor, who is the village doctor?" the SS officer asked pleasantly.

"I am," Desourteaux said, panic fluttering in his chest. "I am the doctor as well."

"Are there any people too ill to travel?"

"Travel where?" Aware that he might have sounded angry, he quickly changed tone. "I mean, from their beds or on a train?"

"Do you have anybody who is bedridden? They will be shot if they do not get into this square within the next fifteen minutes." The doctor took in a breath of shock. His mind was in turmoil, desperately trying to think if any of his patients were immobile. He could not think of any. "I don't believe there is anybody who is bedridden. There is a pregnant woman above the workshop. Being summer it—"

"Thank you, Herr Doctor," the SS major interrupted. "Ask all the men to sit and face the north side of the square. My men will assist you."

The doctor did as he was told. The troopers then started shouting orders and shoving the men into lines.

"There will be silence!" the SS officer shouted. He held his Luger to his side, his finger on the trigger. He was menacing and yet charming at the same time. It was very unsettling. He did not seem volatile or mad, like most Nazis. He was calm, precise, impenetrable – difficult to read. The men all fell silent. As the hubbub went down, the doctor, to his astonishment, could hear singing. The women and children were singing "Un Petit Cochon" as they walked to the church.

The officer in command, it seemed, was not the SS officer who spoke French, but a tall, thin Waffen SS major who looked far too young to hold such a rank. He addressed the men in German and the SS officer translated:

"We are here to search for weapons used by the Resistance and terrorists. We will take thirty hostages." As he spoke, thirty men in the front row were being told by the soldiers to stand with their backs against the wall. "We would be grateful if you could tell us where the arms, ammunition and other prohibited items are hidden in the village, to save time. We will search the village and if we find no arms, we will release the hostages."

Dr Desourteaux was somewhat relieved. He thought there were far more sinister motives for this invasion. He knew there were no caches of arms in the village. But the doctor was still confused as to why they still had not asked to see identity papers. At no point had anyone been made to show their documents.

The German major now asked that the men be split up into six groups. The troopers started shouting and sectioning off the men and shepherding them to various buildings. The doctor's group was driven into the Laudy Barn on the other side of the fairground square.

A line of SS troopers, heavily armed, formed a guarded passage for the men to be herded into the large empty barn. The barns were used for animals during the winter or for storing straw bales; now, in the summer, they were empty, waiting to be filled with straw after the harvest.

The doctor was about to protest, when he saw the baker's son say something to, he presumed, an officer, and a rifle butt was slammed into his side. The doctor began to feel dread well up in his chest from his stomach. He wondered what had become of his wife or daughter. Hopefully they were safe in the church.

Then he heard lots of shouting in German. He swung around to see four men on bicycles, powering down the street, out of the village. There was a loud volley of shots and all four men fell. Aided by a walking stick, the SS officer with the scarred face limped up to the men and shot each one in the head. The doctor felt sick.

"What is going on, Doctor?" the baker asked, terror on his face. He saw the doctor's injured shoulder and asked, incredulously, "Have you been shot?"

"Yes, but it is not too bad." He diagnosed that the bullet had grazed the flesh above his clavicle but had not broken it. If he nursed it and didn't use the arm, he should mend within six weeks. Luckily his skills were in less demand in the summer.

As the doctor and the other men approached the barn door, two Waffen SS soldiers barged past them carrying a heavy machine gun. As he entered the barn, the soldiers had already set up the large machine gun on a tripod on the floor, near the entrance. An army officer – not in SS black but dressed in army grey – stood nervously beside the machine gun.

"Can you tell us what is going on, Herr Captain? Nobody has been asked for their papers yet," the doctor shouted in his rough German. The captain looked up, anguish on his face. A rifle was butted in the doctor's back, and he fell heavily on the dirt floor.

As he lay, he saw the SS major with the walking stick enter the barn, his cap set at an angle on his head. The captain stood stiffly to attention. The men with the machine gun remained on one knee beside their weapon.

The noise of chatter got louder as more men came into the barn. The major watched them assemble. He drew out his pistol, fired a shot in the air that shattered a tile way above his head.

"You will remain quiet," the major said. "If one more man talks, he will be shot."

"But sir—" A local farmer came forward and stood beside where the doctor was being helped up by the baker. The major took aim and shot the farmer in the head. The farmer dropped like a felled tree. Dr Desourteaux instinctively went to his aid.

"Leave him! Or you will be shot as well, Monsieur le mayor," said the major.

The captain was plainly upset by the actions of the SS major, thought the doctor. But there was nothing the young officer could do. The soldiers crammed all the men in one end of the barn. Not a sound was made other than a quiet whimper from someone. One man was violently sick. All looked very worried. The doctor, along with the baker, stood to one side of the barn, three or four lines of men in front of them. Being a tall man, the doctor could see over the heads of those in front. He estimated more than fifty or sixty men were standing close together in the barn.

The major whispered something to the captain, who looked aghast and walked out of the barn. As he left, the two heavy barn doors were pushed shut. The major then took his stick, pulled two halves of the handle apart to reveal a shooting stick seat, and sat behind the machine gun. The doctor was astounded to see that not only did the major put his hands up to his ears, but he also saw a machine gun soldier pull back on the action-return to put the first bullet into the weapon. He flipped up the safety catch.

From outside there was a loud explosion. The major smiled and shouted, "*Schießen!*"

The machine gun roared. The noise was intense. The bullets tore into the men's legs and thighs, and by the time the doctor could see what was happening, two bullets had shattered his right femur, and then his left fibula. His ankle destroyed, he fell heavily onto the man in front of him, who had already had most of his leg shot away.

The doctor writhed in pain. He looked at the other men being systematically scythed down like long grass. Blood splashed everywhere. Men thrashed in agony, and the ones at the back of the barn tried to climb the walls to the window three metres up, anything to get away from the inevitable bullets. The doctor wondered if he was in a dream, but the pain was real. He was beginning to feel faint, light-headed.

As suddenly as it started, the firing stopped. The doctor was lying on his chest, on top of a man's back and bloody legs. He tried to look up to see what was happening. He thanked God that he was still alive. But then he saw that although quite a few of the men were alive, they were badly wounded. Terrible cries of pain, shouts for help, all unheeded. The doctor could not feel his legs or his hips. A searing pain ran around his midriff and lower back. He concluded his back must be broken.

Then, a dreadful smell of petrol. The doctor tried to raise his head over the sea of writhing bodies, but his right arm did not seem to work; his elbow had been shot away and he could see a bone sticking out where his forearm should be. He felt no pain in his arm, only in his legs and back. He saw four soldiers, all carrying large petrol cans and straw, walking over the backs of the wounded men. At the edge of the writhing bodies stood the Wehrmacht captain, holding a burning torch, an expression of devastation on his face. The SS major stood just behind him, whispering something in his ear.

As a soldier came towards him, the doctor shouted in German, "What are you doing? You cannot mean to kill us all?" The answer was a boot in the face. He momentarily blacked out. He awoke with the pain in his back and the man behind him lying on top of him. He spat out some blood and teeth. He could not see out of his left eye; his face felt as though it was burning with acid.

Then, all the soldiers had gone. The pungent smell of petrol was getting stronger. Men were coughing and gasping, some shouted hysterically, some just prayed. The doctor looked for the SS officer. He saw him and was about to shout something when the scarred major shot the army captain in the head. The doctor thought he must be dreaming, hallucinating with the pain and the petrol fumes. He looked up again only to see the major rifling through the captain's pockets, removing the dead man's jacket, before flames erupted in front of him.

The heat came over the doctor very quickly. The last thing he heard before he died was the agonising screams and the crackle of burning bodies. He prayed his wife was safe and that his ten-year-old girl was not too frightened. He saw the women and children being driven into the church, so they would at least be spared the awful vision of him and his friends, patients and townsmen dying in agony.

*

"What happened to Captain Wolff, Major Krupp?" Diekmann asked Krupp. The majors both stood in the back of a half-track, travelling slowly out of the burning town.

"He decided to become a traitor, Major Diekmann. He tried to help a wounded terrorist and got killed for his trouble." The sergeant driving the half-track laughed out loud.

"He was pretty useless. I am glad he has gone. He would never have made a good SS officer!"

"Certainly not." Krupp looked serious. "Why did you have him in your regiment?"

"He was a Wehrmacht captain who guarded something ... somewhere. His aunt – a friend of mine – wanted him to grow some balls – he grew tits instead!" More sniggering from the sergeant.

"I see. Has he got family?"

"Why are you so interested in Günther Wolff, Krupp?"

"No particular reason. Does he have family?"

"No – just his elderly aunt in Hamburg."

Diekmann had his arm up. Soldiers were lined up, in ranks, behind the half-tracks. Diekmann drew down his arm and the church instantly went up in explosive flames. The screams were drowned out by the fires that raged throughout the town. Every now and then, a shot could be heard when an escapee was caught.

"Not one French terrorist is alive, no witnesses. The plan went well, don't you think, Krupp?" Diekmann said with satisfaction. He smiled at Krupp and slapped him on the back. "And I am rid of that nancy Wolff, thanks to you, my dear Krupp!" He shook Jost by the hand. "I will take you back to your vineyard. You have done well. I will see that you get a commendation."

"I would rather you didn't, Diekmann. They may think I should do more fighting and take me away from my vineyard."

"Really? I doubt you will be there for long. The invasion started four days ago – had you not heard?"

"They are not likely to strike this far into France."

"That is why we have been called, Krupp. They are moving rapidly. All the Panzers were in the wrong place – they still are, I am informed."

Krupp was in deep thought as they drove out of Oradour-sur-Glane. Every building was ablaze.

"Adolf," he said seriously, "I think I am going to disappear."

"What do you mean?" Diekmann looked worried.

"Oh, nothing serious. With my French, I may assume the guise of a winemaker in St-Émilion. Spend the rest of the war with my bad leg up, screwing my lovely girl from Bordeaux."

"OK, Krupp. I hope to see you again soon, where we can have a good German beer and some schnapps!"

25

Krupp knew Brunhilda Baumgartner worked for the German Secret Service, the *Sicherheitsdienst* – the SD – but what she actually did in the SD was rather mysterious. He met Hilde – as he liked to call her, for she did not look like a Brunhilda – in Bordeaux after she was smuggled back from England, where she had spent two years – as far as he gathered – working for an English businessman. That was all she told him.

She was a pale, handsome woman, with short, bobbed black hair. She was much older than Freya, and certainly not as beautiful, but she was good fun and company for him during his time at the vineyard. She was also amusing, and highly experienced in matters about the bed. All qualities he enjoyed in a woman. His only slight reservation about Hilde was that she was very secretive and was highly intelligent.

"Jost, I am going to have to go to Paris," said Hilde. "The enemy invasion is gathering pace and apparently the Americans are racing through Italy." The sound of the dispatch rider's motorbike could be heard puttering away up the drive from the château. She read the contents of a brown envelope with *Streng Geheim* – Top Secret – on a red tape wrapped around the envelope, the red wax seal with a swastika indent broken.

She was wearing a wide-brimmed black straw hat, black silk short culottes and a tight black revealing top that looked like a man's vest. She had a preference of wearing black clothes, which pronounced her wonderful figure and pale complexion. They sat outside the château on a terrace of old cobbles, in a suntrap, she under a parasol, he stretched out on a steamer chair. "They will be in Paris by the end of the month, I think. It's a mess!" Hilde sighed.

"That soon … in Paris! Do you really think?" Krupp said, annoyed. "I don't care really. I am just annoyed that I may have to leave my vineyard." He rose from his steamer chair, went up to Hilde, and stroked her left breast with a rakish smile. Hilde put her arms around his neck and gazed up at him. "Are you coming with me? Might as well. The Americans will be here any day now."

"Who is going to look after my vineyard when I am gone? You can't go to Paris! Stay here and run the place."

"I am certainly not staying here to run a vineyard!" Hilde spluttered, amused at his presumption. "I am an important spy, my darling!"

"Cosying up to an English 'milord', pretending to be a secretary, isn't spying!"

"And I suppose swanning around a Bordeaux vineyard, drinking and eating, is soldiering?"

"I helped clear up some insurgence, and anyway, I am an injured soldier," he said, hurt.

"And how did you get injured? In battle?" Hilde had a knowing smile on her face. "You don't have to answer, my love, you forget you've told me all about the Swedish girl." She patted his chest condescendingly. "But we are going to have to find you a different identity."

"I have already got an alternative identity." Krupp stood back from her, and with his hands on his hips, raised his chin and announced: "May I present to you, Captain Günther Wolff of the Wehrmacht 325. *Sicherungs-Division*."

"How did you do that? Who is Wolff?"

"He was killed at that French terrorist village we destroyed, so I decided to die and live on as Günther Wolff."

"So, you swapped your identity for someone else? Did he look like you?" Hilde looked dubiously at Krupp.

"Thinner – same black hair, but I have the scar." He gazed into Hilde's eyes. "I am, however, travelling to Berlin in my SS major's uniform so we will travel in first class on the train."

"I am not going to Berlin, I'm going to Paris," Hilde said sadly, stroking his arm. "We can go together as far as there. You can go on to Berlin and take over from that moron Hitler."

Krupp was furious. "It's not Hitler, he is surrounded by idiots, cowards—"

"It was Hitler who decided to fight on two fronts. It was Hitler who sent my brothers to fight in snow with no winter clothing, food or ammunition." Her hands gripped hold of the lapels of his white linen jacket.

"How would you know that?" Krupp said, pushing her away.

"Because they are both dead! Klaus died in my arms with an untreated wound to his foot." She stared down at her shoes.

"Shot it himself, I should think," he said, limping towards the French windows to go into the house. Hilde ran to stand in front of him, her face puce with rage. He continued: "You cannot talk about the Führer like … WOW!" Hilde slapped him across his face with the back of her hand and he staggered backwards. She kicked his stick away. He fell, hard on the cobbles. She stormed off, into the house.

Krupp took some time to struggle to his feet. He started pacing around the terrace. He picked up Hilde's letter. It was from Ernst Kaltenbrunner's office – head of the SD. Jost winced as a shaft of pain shot through his injured leg and right buttock where he had landed on the hard cobbles.

Hilde reappeared, looking like thunder. He tried to stop himself from putting up a defensive hand, but all she did was swipe the letter from him and go back into the house. Krupp yelled after her, "I am sorry, my sweet," in a lame attempt to get back in her favour.

Krupp felt inadequate. Now he was crippled he felt vulnerable, unable to fully defend himself, even from the anger of a slight woman like Hilde. He had lived with his infirmity for nearly a year, and this was the first time he had felt so helpless. He was undermined and emasculated. Life would have to change.

*

The following day, Krupp and Hilde were driven to Limoges, on their way to board a train to Paris, in the late afternoon.

In the car, Hilde was about to say something to him – she was pointing a finger, still boiling with temper – when he said to her, calmly, "I am sorry, my love, I should not have said those things about your brother."

"No, you should not have," Hilde said in a virtual whisper. She was surprised. Krupp was a dangerous man, ruthless and generally unforgiving; this was a total change of character. She seldom lost her temper – it would never do to become angry in her line of work, it led to mistakes. This had almost resulted in a big mistake: making an enemy of Jost Krupp.

The train ride to Paris was going to be an ordeal; they had discovered there was no first-class carriage. The journey would be over four hours in a third-class carriage, with hard leather seats and full of troops being mobilised to help defend Paris. They were all quite old men, tired and looking unmotivated. Krupp was in full black SS major's uniform. His Knight's Cross of the Iron Cross with Oak Leaves medal was displayed proudly on his chest, along with the Blood Order medal. Soldiers sprang to attention, clicked their heels in salute as he went past with Hilde following, dressed in a skirt, blouse and light jacket over her shoulders, all in black. Her every move was observed by the men in the carriage, especially her stockinged ankles and black high-heeled shoes, making her thin legs look enticing. Krupp felt so powerful in his uniform, watching these soldiers gawking at his Hilde, and then seeing a flash of fear in their eyes as they saw him. If he was able to strut, he would have.

"We will be sitting here, Sergeant," Krupp said to a middle-aged man in a well-worn uniform, in the last group of four seats. The sergeant had not heard or seen the SS major approach. He sat, his legs up on the bench opposite, his tunic unbuttoned, revealing a vest with holes covering a large belly. He was smoking and looking out the window, wiping sweat off his brow. His battered helmet was on his lap, his rifle perched up on the window frame.

Krupp poked him with his stick. The sergeant grabbed it. "Hey, who the hell …" he snarled, then saw the major. His face became a picture of horror. He stood quickly, his helmet and weapon crashing to the floor. "Very sorry, Major, I'm a bit deaf from the shelling." He brushed off the seat that his feet had been on, gathered up his helmet and rifle, and tried to button up his tunic, inching out of the booth of seats, at the same time bowing slightly. Hilde slipped in and sat.

"That is fine, Sergeant," Krupp said. "Put our cases up, would you?" He tapped the luggage rack above his head with his stick, then pointed to the other end of the carriage where their shiny leather suitcases sat in the doorway.

"Certainly, sir." He turned and barked at the closest soldier: "Get the major's cases from the end of the carriage and store them up in the racks. Be quick about it!"

"Where is your officer, sergeant?" Krupp sat stiffly on the leather seat, making out that his injuries were painful, hoping he was giving the impression that he was a serving and wounded soldier.

"Dead, I think, sir. Sorry, my lady." He turned to Hilde. He must have been in service before he joined the army; he had a servile stoop when talking to Krupp, who was sprawled out over the two seats like a monarch on his throne. Hilde sat opposite, erect, gazing uncomfortably out of the window. An amused smile played on her lips.

"There seems to be no first class on this train," Krupp observed – this would have been where the man's officer would be. The sergeant made no comment, his eyes flitting nervously from the major to the floor and then to the lady and then back to the floor, continually wiping sweat off his forehead with a spotted blue snuff handkerchief.

The suitcases arrived and were hauled up to the luggage racks. There were three heavy leather cases, only one of which belonged to Hilde. "Thank you, Sergeant, you may go," Krupp said. The sergeant left with a click of his heels and sat in the adjoining four-seated booth, ready to serve the officer in any way he could.

*

After five hours and thirty minutes of a noisy journey in a hot, stuffy carriage, they arrived early evening at Gare Montparnasse, not quite in the centre of Paris. As the train drew up to the platform, a crowd of army officers and sergeants were waiting. They started hammering on the windows to rouse the men on the train. The deaf sergeant opened the window and asked what was going on. An officer told him to rally his men immediately. Paris was under attack from the enemy.

Hilde Baumgartner and Captain Günther Wolff dismounted the train last. Hilde had decided it would be wise to change Krupp's identity, which he did in the deserted carriage, with Hilde keeping a lookout. Krupp was now in a dark suit, white shirt and thin black tie. A Nazi member's badge in his lapel and a trilby hat completed his non-military attire. He had left behind his beloved SS major's uniform with his precious medals attached. Hilde wisely dissuaded him from keeping them in case he was captured. He thought the likelihood of capture was quite absurd.

"My love," she said, stroking his cheek whilst he gazed upon the abandoned leather suitcase as though it was a coffin with an old friend lying in it, "it is for the best, believe me." They stepped out of the carriage and left the station. They waited for a taxi to take them to Gare du Nord so Krupp could go to Berlin.

"Günther," she said with a slight smile, whilst they waited in a lengthy queue of people for a taxi, "what is it like being a captain again?"

"It is not so different. I was a captain for a long time, once."

The queue consisted of mainly French people, all giving Krupp and Hilde nervous sideways glances.

Soldiers were pouring out of the station into trucks.

"It is a shame Adolf Diekmann is not here. He would have seen off the enemy," Krupp said.

"He certainly would have, my love. Do you know how he died?"

"In action, apparently. He was going to be tried for the mass killing of the terrorists in that French village. He decided to fight the enemy in Normandy instead of wasting his time at a trial."

"What was he being tried for?"

"'Exceeding his authority'. *Verfluchter* rubbish, if you ask me! Sorry." Krupp was not angry, just upset – he had admired Diekmann. "There should be a staff car for officers," he said, changing the subject, looking up and down the busy Boulevard de Vaugirard. As he said this, he saw an SS officer with a clipboard under his arm get out of a large, six-wheeled Daimler-Benz. He ran into the station through a different entrance, having left the car door open. It was a good fifteen metres up the road and Krupp wondered if he, Hilde and the porter could get to the car before it drove off again.

"*Suivez-moi* – follow me," he said loudly to the elderly porter, who was smoking a cigarette, leaning on his trolley. The procession marched off, with Krupp in the lead, his stick clicking along the pavement.

"What's happening?" Hilde hissed at him.

"There is a German staff car just up there. I need to get to it before it goes." The car was stationary, the door still open; it must, Krupp hoped, be waiting for the captain to return.

As they got to the car, he was relieved to see an SS colonel he knew in the back seat. He knocked on the window. The colonel turned to look at him angrily and waved him away. Krupp opened the door. "Alois Brunner, it's me, Jost Krupp." The colonel looked up at the scarred face with a squint, mouth open, trying to recognise his old friend from Drancy prison. A smile of recognition came over his face. "Krupp! We thought you were dead, killed by partisans in the south."

"An exaggeration, Alois, or should I say colonel? Congratulations. This is a friend: Fräulein Brunhilda Baumgartner, Hilde for—"

"But that is who we are looking for!" exclaimed Brunner.

Krupp swung round to look at Hilde, astonished, then back to Brunner. With a slight tone of suspicion he said, "How did you know we were coming up to Paris today?"

"My office sent the order. I was told she was with you in St-Émilion, but you had been killed in June by terrorists," Brunner said.

Krupp was still speaking through the open door of the Daimler-Benz and his leg and back were beginning to hurt.

"May I sit in the car, Alois? My injuries are getting a bit painful."

"Of course, Krupp. Would Fräulein Baumgartner care to join us?"

They both got in the huge vehicle and sat beside the SS colonel. Brunner tapped the driver on the shoulder. "Go and track down the captain, Sergeant. Say we have found who we are looking for."

Hilde looked worried. "Colonel, what are my orders? I am with the SD, not the SS!"

"I am to take you to the Hôtel Georges Cinq, where your assignment is staying."

"My assignment? Who's my employer?" Hilde looked intrigued.

"No idea, I have just those orders from *Obergruppenführer* von Choltitz's office," Brunner said plainly, looking out of the window towards the station entrance. "Where is that man?"

"Brunner, what should I do? Am I needed in Berlin?" Krupp was concerned.

"I don't know, Krupp." Brunner looked at him dubiously. "You are dead! So, you can stay with me and help us get out of Paris before the enemy arrive."

"They are not going to retake Paris, are they? I just travelled up with a whole company of men."

"They are on their way in, Krupp, believe me. And the Free French Army are out in strength in Paris and are making it very difficult, to say the least. There have been general strikes and the French are not cooperating with us at all!"

The driver had found the captain, and they set off to the centre of Paris. To avoid military traffic, they took the back roads. Which, it transpired, was a mistake.

*

Ten minutes later, in the middle of a street of partially destroyed houses, the Daimler-Benz staff car had to come to a sharp halt when a large truck drove into its path. The driver quickly put the car into reverse only to see a second truck appear from behind, and gently shunted the Daimler-Benz.

A wiry, dark man in a leather jacket ran out of the rubble, holding a submachine gun, and shouted, "Throw out all weapons and get out of the car!" He wore the armband of the FFI – the *Forces Françaises de l'Intérieur*. A second FFI fighter appeared half draped over the bonnet of the car, pointing an old light machine gun at the people in the car. They were only a kilometre from the safety of – they thought – the Hôtel Majestic, German headquarters.

Krupp looked around to see if these two men were the only terrorists. He was disappointed to see about ten more FFI fighters emerging from the trucks and surrounding houses, encircling the car. The road was narrow, deserted, and there was rubble everywhere.

Suddenly, Hilde flung open the car door and scrambled out.

"Help me, help me, please!" she yelled in English. Both Krupp and Brunner were astounded. "They have taken me prisoner!" One of the FFI fighters shouted to a female soldier to take the English woman and search her. Hilde was dragged away from the car and the FFI woman put her arm protectively around her. Hilde had managed to muster real tears; so much so, Krupp thought that she really was a frightened prisoner.

"Clever bitch!" he muttered.

The SS sergeant driver threw out his pistol and got out of the car, and was forced to lie on the ground, face down. Krupp and Brunner then got out. Krupp pulled out his papers. His stick was taken away and, with a Luger pistol pointed at his head, he was searched, along with Brunner and the SS captain. Because Brunner was in SS colonel's uniform, he was given more attention.

All this was done in eerie silence. The FFI fighters talked in rapid, hushed French, did everything quickly, and then bundled the men into the back of the truck that straddled the road, their hands tied in front of them. Krupp complained of pain. The FFI fighters then piled into the back of the truck after them, all pointing various elderly firearms at their prisoners. Hilde had disappeared.

As they drove off, Krupp saw some women fighters painting large "FFI"s, with white paint on the doors, and a V-shape emblem on the bonnet of Brunner's Daimler-Benz staff car. All Nazi emblems were painted over or removed.

*

Three hours later, the floor of the main dining room of the Hôtel Majestic was totally covered with German prisoners, mainly officers, sitting on the floor, huddled close together. All the chairs and tables had been moved elsewhere. The Hôtel Majestic used to be the headquarters of the German high command in France. Now it served as a prisoner-of-war camp, run by the FFI and the Allied Forces. Every prisoner was registered, and those who had been recorded as committing crimes were taken away to be put on trial. SS and Gestapo officers were the first to be processed. Krupp was thankful of his new identity as he watched Brunner being led away.

For hours Krupp sat hunched on the hard wood floor. He tried to shift his weight to stop the pain in his back. He lay down, which brought some relief.

"Günther Wolff?" he heard someone shout. He sat up. A man in a suit accompanied by an armed FFI soldier was standing at the restaurant door. He shouted again, "Günther Wolff!" Krupp put his hand up. The two men strode as best they could through the sea of seated men, across to where he sat.

"Yes?" Krupp said.

"Are you Captain Günther Wolff of Wehrmacht 325, *Sicherungs-Division*?" the suited man said, standing over Krupp, looking down his nose at him. Krupp had propped himself up on one elbow. He was surprised to be singled out like this.

"Yes."

"Do you speak French?"

"No," he lied.

"Get up, follow us."

"I can't get up. I am injured, serving the—"

"Be quiet!" the suited man shouted. "You – you" – he pointed at the two closest men sitting next to Krupp – "pick him up, smartly now!"

"Where is my stick, my cane?"

"You will have to walk without one." The FFI man slid behind Krupp and pushed him in the small of the back. "Get a move on, filth!"

"That will do, Maurice. These are prisoners of war."

Günther Wolff and the two Frenchmen walked slowly from the old dining room into what was the ballroom. Krupp was told to sit again on the hard floor, which he did with a lot of complaining.

At one end of the ballroom were German officers. The higher ranks could lean on the wall, but all the other ranks – which included Krupp – had to sit uncomfortably on the hard floor. If they needed to stand, they had to put up their hand and ask one of the two machine gunners covering the floor from a balcony, or the FFI officer on the stage at the other end of the ballroom.

On the stage sat a group of men, four being Paris police officers and three more men in civilian clothes. The spokesman of this committee was a young man in a suit with long black wavy hair and a full black beard.

"Your attention, please," he said politely in heavily accented German. "The committee for the Liberation of France are proud to announce that Paris is now fully liberated." There was a cheer from the stage. He carried on. "Please stand when you hear your name called."

Krupp sat uncomfortably on the uncarpeted ballroom floor, his bad leg jutting out and his back aching. He thought about losing his temper and getting shot – it would all be over, quickly and easily. But his attitude to self-preservation got the better of him. He was convinced this was all temporary and the Reich would rise up again, regroup and return to France. He wanted to be around for when that happened. Perhaps go back to his vineyard.

As the names were called, Krupp suddenly heard, "Günther Wolff, Captain Günther Wolff?" He tried to stand. He saw sixteen other men standing, each with a police officer tying their hands together. Wolff's name was the last to be read out. A police officer came up beside him when he waved his hands and said in French, "I am unable to stand. I have a wounded leg." The policeman grabbed his jacket by the shoulder and dragged him up onto his feet.

"May I have a cane?" he asked the policeman as nicely as he could.

The policeman just said, "Limp!"

The *commissaire de police* addressed the men standing before him and the committee. "You have all been found to have committed war crimes in France." The *commissaire* was sitting at a trestle table, a French police officer seated either side of him. The long-haired bearded man sat at the end of the table, glaring at the row of Germans. Two men in suits and ties were busy behind the *commissaire*, taking out sheets of paper from filing cabinets with Nazi emblems stencilled on them. There was a howl of protest from all seventeen Germans standing in line on the ballroom floor, looking up at the committee.

Krupp could not see Colonel Brunner anywhere. He must have gone before another court – or whatever this was.

"I will commit each one at a time. Judgement and sentencing will be immediate." Once this was translated, there was a lot of complaint from the prisoners. Krupp could not imagine what Wolff could have done to warrant being charged. He was such a mouse, a complete idiot. He also wondered where the board, or judges, or whatever these men were, got their information.

One by one the accused went before the board. Most were sentenced to twenty years and led out the room. As his new name began with *W* he went last.

"Captain Günther Wolff, you have been found guilty of being the guard commander in charge of a group of prisoners, mainly Jews, that constructed the labour camp at Schirmeck, in Alsace. You were in command between April 1941 and June 1941."

"What rubbish, I was not even in France in 1941," Krupp said in faultless French, taking everybody by surprise.

The *commissaire de police* looked at the paperwork on his desk. "Due to the efficiency of the German records, Captain, it states here you were not only in command of a construction party at the camp known as" – the *commissaire* looked down at his notes – "as *Natzweiler-Struthof*, but it documents how many civilians, men and women, were cruelly neglected by your guards and died of injuries sustained during the construction of the camp. Matters that contravened two main statutes in the Geneva Convention, that Germany is a signatory to." The *commissaire de police* looked up from the table, removed his glasses, and took a long draw of his cigarette, which made Krupp lick his lips. He had not smoked for three days. The whole board of men looked at him with contempt. He wondered how on earth these records were not destroyed ages ago.

"I was under orders, sir." Krupp's only defence. The *commissaire de police* sighed and looked at his colleagues either side. One of the suited men behind the commissaire stooped to consult with him. The *commissaire* nodded approval.

"How did you get your injuries, Captain Wolff?" said the suited man. He had an American accent.

"In the line of duty, fighting the enemy," Krupp said flatly.

"You were not fighting the enemy whilst being in command of a prison detail," the bearded Frenchman said. "How did you get injured? By attacking defenceless prisoners?"

"I was attacked by French policemen, who were meant to be allied to the German—"

"That's enough, Wolff!" the bearded man shouted. He shook his head and said something to the *commissaire*.

"Captain Wolff," the *commissaire* pronounced, "you are sentenced to twenty years for your crimes. When the war is over, you may be retried and sentenced to death."

"But …" Krupp protested.

"That is all, Wolff. You and your kind should be wiped out, but that will make us as bad as the Nazis."

26

"Baron Saumures, I presume?" Sir Jason stood as Ferdi entered the small meeting room in the old public house just off Fleet Street. "My name is Sir Jason Barrett. This is John Alderson, my" – he hesitated – "colleague." Sir Jason indicated a pale young man, who scowled at Ferdi.

"How do you do, sir," Ferdi said. "I met Mr Alderson at my hotel."

"So you did, so you did. Please sit." Jason gestured to a chair across the table from him. "Sherry?"

"No, thank you." Ferdi felt nervous.

"Cigarette?" Sir Jason offered a silver cigarette case.

"No, thank you, I prefer my own." Ferdi took out a small leather case and removed a long thin cheroot, put it into a short ebony and gold holder, and lit it.

"First of all, welcome home. As you see, we are meeting in a public place as stipulated by you."

"Thank you." Ferdi was abrupt. Sir Jason regarded him hesitantly. Ferdi was pleased to see Sir Jason was looking slightly nervous.

"Very well, let me start." Sir Jason took out a piece of paper from his briefcase and put it on the table in front of Ferdi. It was a list, Ferdi saw, headed by a government "Top Secret" stamp. "This is a list of files that we do *not* want you to submit to the War Department when you retrieve the Wasp Trap files. I presume you have not yet collected the files from Paris?"

Ferdi's heart thumped, his stomach clenched, he felt the blood drain out of his face. He was shocked and surprised that Sir Jason knew about the files. He tried to remain calm. Keep breathing naturally, he said to himself. He scanned the piece of paper with concern.

"I am not sure what you are referring to, sir."

"This is a report from my department in MI6 that says you have – or had – a team that have gathered evidence against Germans, mostly SS officers, under the code name 'Wasp Trap'. Am I correct?"

"I cannot say, sir." Ferdi looked at the men opposite him.

"This," Alderson said, whilst removing another piece of paper from an attaché case, "is Sir Jason's authorisation to ensure these files are delivered to Sir Jason's office, and not to the War Department or Sir Sussex Tremayne."

Ferdi looked at the document Alderson proffered. It was headed with another government Top Secret stamp and gave Sir Jason, as Alderson said, the authority to take certain files from the Wasp Trap files.

"I am sorry, gentlemen, but I am not able to help you with this. I will leave now. Good afternoon." Ferdi stood.

"Baron Saumures," Sir Jason said, "you will provide these files to us, or you will be arrested and we will retrieve the files ourselves. And none of the files will then be submitted."

"You have no authority to arrest me!"

Alderson produced a warrant card stating that he was a detective inspector in Special Branch.

"I thought you were Sir Jason's secretary?"

"I am Sir Jason's colleague, Baron Saumures. I am with Special Branch. I work alongside Sir Jason, within MI6."

"What could you possibly arrest me for?" Ferdi was incredulous.

"Lewd behaviour, being a homosexual, for a start," Sir Jason said. Ferdi was stunned. "Harbouring a known Nazi sympathiser – your so-called wife – who worked with the Nazis in Paris. And I believe you have a woman staying with you, calling herself Madame Theodora, who is a known Berlin prostitute, working with the SS at an SS-run brothel in Paris." Ferdi's stomach clenched again. He sat back into his seat and looked at the list in front of him. "If you approach Sir Sussex Tremayne about any of this, we will not only arrest him but also your wife, her friend Theodora, and Bernard Trent."

"You can't arrest the head of war intelligence! What for?"

"He is under suspicion for running double agents … like you."

"I'm not a … Who are *you* working for, Sir Jason?" Ferdi asked.

"The British government, MI6 section, of course. Who do you think we are working for?"

"Well, I am not sure. I see your name is at the top of these files that you want." Ferdi stabbed a finger on the document in front of him. He saw other people on the list that surprised him: Jean de Tournet, Admiral Canaris and WASP, and more worryingly, Jost Krupp … amongst others. How did Sir Jason know Jost Krupp? And in what context? How did he know there was a file on Krupp?

"How do you know there are files on these people?" Ferdi asked. "How would you know there is a file on you? Why would we keep a file on you?" Ferdi stood and walked over to a small window that was open. He took in a deep breath of fresh air to steady his nerves. He returned to his chair. "These records are on people who are regarded as enemies of the Allies. Some of these people in the files can give evidence of war crimes committed. Most have committed war crimes."

Sir Jason scowled at him. Ferdi thought he was about to be arrested then and there, when Alderson suddenly stood, his fists bunched. Sir Jason waved him back. "I have been informed that my name crops up due to my association with Jean de Tournet. He is, after all, my brother-in-law. I am not having spurious information about me, or my associates—"

"How do you know who is in these files, Sir Jason? How do you know your name is amongst them? Jean de Tournet, for example, and Helmut Wagner … how would you know these people are mentioned?" Ferdi waved the list in front of him.

Sir Jason paused, looked up at Alderson who was still eyeing Ferdi aggressively.

"Sit down, John." He patted Alderson on the arm. "De Tournet has disappeared, possibly dead." Sir Jason sighed. "These files, I believe, allege I was associated with de Tournet, or claim that I have had dealings with the enemy."

"Have you, sir?" Ferdi sat back into his chair.

Sir Jason seemed to be tempering his anger.

"The assertions within that file are unfounded, and I don't want the file to be put into the public domain. My work within the Intelligence Service and, indeed, the Diplomatic Service should not be questioned, especially by someone like you or our old gardener, Franz-Joseph Deller."

"It is not conjecture, Sir Jason. It is fact, gathered over the years from information—"

"It is unfounded, and if any of these files are released to anybody other than Mr Alderson or myself, we will have you arrested along with your friends on serious charges. Trumped up if necessary." Sir Jason leant forward over the table. "I hope you are not considering warning anybody about this meeting. We have just as much on you as you think you have on me. And I am a little more respected than you, Saumures. For instance, you are currently serving as an *Abwehr* operative, are you not?"

Ferdi's shoulders sagged, he was stunned. Where had Sir Jason got this information? How did he know about the Wasp Trap files? What was he to do?

Sir Jason nodded at Alderson, who produced a small bit of paper. "This, Baron Saumures, is the name of a South African smuggler we recommend you use to take you over to France to collect the files."

"Thank you, but I am leaving this to the Royal Navy to—"

"You will use this man," Sir Jason said, a warning in his eyes.

"Very well," Ferdi conceded with a sigh. "Is he reliable?"

"No. I would recommend you do not use your own names or reveal what your cargo is."

"So why should I use him and not someone trustworthy like the Royal Navy?"

"Because he is fast, he will not be noticed, and he is discreet."

"And works for you, I presume?" Ferdi added.

"Sometimes," Sir Jason said. "He can be contacted by telegram. You can use my name. He will cost around two hundred guineas in gold, or five hundred US dollars."

"Who is going to pay that?"

"You are, sir," said Alderson.

27

Ferdi and Bertrand trained down to Newhaven, then took a taxi to the Crab Pot public house on the edge of Newhaven harbour, on the south coast of England. It was late evening when they walked into the deserted pub, staffed only by a large landlord. They were both dressed as fishermen in dark-blue overalls and reefer jackets. They were to meet a smuggler there.

Albert Jaffery was the type of man most people would take an instant dislike to. He was fleshy, dirty and indolent, with no redeeming facial features. When he entered the pub, Ferdi stood from the table beside the door and asked the man if he was the "African Fisherman".

"What's it to you?" Jaffery said, eyeing Ferdi with suspicion.

"My name is Max Finch," said Ferdi, "and this is Barry Smith." Ferdi indicated to Bertrand, sitting at the table watching Jaffery's slovenly demeanour. Jaffery took out and read a telegram that was in his pocket.

"Yah, well, you're the bloke," Jaffery said with a South African accent. "You don't look like a marine. You look like a flash git. Got the cheese?"

"The cheese?"

"The money. The money is upfront." He stepped closer to Ferdi, right up to his ear. Jaffery smelt revolting. "Two hundred guineas – gold, or five hundred US dollars – cash." Jaffery put out his hand.

"Christ, that's steep!" Bertrand said.

"Is he coming too?" Jaffery asked.

"Yes," said Ferdi.

"Then he's going to be extra."

"That's not going to be possible," Ferdi said. He produced a small leather pouch from his reefer jacket pocket. "There are sixteen gold sovereigns. Take it, or we will leave it."

"I'll leave it. You bastards can find someone else to take you over to France. Good luck." He turned to leave.

"Up to you, Jaffery," Ferdi said.

Jaffery swung round in surprise. "You know my name?" Jaffery said, now looking worried.

"We know your name, and the farmhouse where you live," Bertrand said, "and where your boat is moored, come to that."

Jaffery thought hard. "How did you find me in the first place? I'm not exactly in the phone book."

"One of your clients told us about you, and how to get in touch with you." Ferdi was sitting down now and lazily picked up his beer.

"What client?"

"He wished to stay anonymous."

"Yah?" Jaffery seemed undecided. He hovered about the door, looking as though he wanted to bolt, but kept his eye on the pouch that jingled when Ferdi dropped it on the table. Bertrand was watching his every move. Ferdi was guarding the pouch of gold just in case Jaffery made a grab for it.

"Come on, then," Jaffery conceded, and went to take the pouch. Ferdi grabbed it and held up five coins. "You will get two now, two when we get to Le Havre, and the last one when we return with our cargo." Jaffery sighed and swiped the coins out of Ferdi's hand. He took a step back and checked the coins with his teeth. Bertrand stood up quickly, unnerving Jaffery who went for his pocket.

"Are you armed, Jaffery?" Bertrand asked.

"No." Jaffery looked guilty. "Just a natural reflex."

"Well, we are. So don't try to stitch us up," Ferdi said. Jaffery looked at him.

"Are you a German, Mr Finch?"

"No, from Belgium."

Jaffery slapped the telegram on the table. "It says here that you are a Royal Marine, travelling to get a fellow marine back from a French hospital." He looked Ferdi and Bertrand up and down. "You are not marines …"

"And you are not a fisherman, Jaffery, you are a South African smuggler," Ferdi said. Jaffery stood, quiet, with his mouth open, looking from Ferdi to Bertrand to the telegram to the coins in his other hand. His shoulders drooped and he turned to leave.

"Come on, then, if we are to catch the tide. Got a car?"

"No, came down by train," Ferdi said. "We will come with you." Jaffery tutted and spat on the floor and stormed out of the pub.

"Cheery type of fellow!" Bertrand said.

*

Ferdi and Bertrand were both rather surprised by Jaffery. For a start, his boat was a converted German motor torpedo S-boat, or E-boat as they were called in Britain. *E* was for enemy. The slick-looking boat was painted entirely in black and pristinely clean, not a rope uncoiled, and every bit of metal gleamed. Jaffery had also managed to rebuild the superstructure on the main deck to look like a pleasure cruiser, with a substantial cabin in the bows and a large cargo area at the stern. And because there were no torpedo tubes or gun emplacements, the whole craft looked much lighter, riding high in the water. Jaffery had the boat moored up in his boathouse, beside his farmhouse, on a creek that ran out into Seaford Bay. The boathouse and creek were entirely hidden by high reeds.

"This will do up to fifty knots and can outrun anything on the water," Jaffery boasted. "That's why I demanded the high fees."

"Well, quite a craft, Barry, don't you think?" Ferdi said to Bertrand with a sceptical smile.

"We should be in Paris and back in an instant, Max."

"I'm not taking you to Paris!" Jaffery shouted.

"No, you're not. You are dropping us off at an inlet off the Seine, at Berville-sur-Mer. We are meeting someone there. You will hide there until we return."

"How do I hide this?" Jaffery gestured towards his thirty-two-metre-long vessel.

"Don't worry, we have made arrangements. However, I was not expecting anything this big," Ferdi said, getting on board. Bertrand limped onto the boat.

"Where did you get this boat, Jaffery?" Bertrand asked.

"None of your business." Jaffery cast off the lines and gently pushed out the bows. He stepped expertly into the boat and up onto the capstan block, sat on the leather upholstered seat, and pressed two buttons. Two large diesel engines erupted beneath them, and the boat accelerated off.

"This creek is only navigable for two and a half to three hours, twice in twenty-four hours," Jaffery shouted over the engine noise as they sped out to the open sea. "I only travel at night, between dusk and dawn."

"With no running lights switched on? How do you not bump into anything?" Bertrand asked. Jaffery answered by flicking a switch and a long, bright beam of light shone out from a spotlight in the front of the windscreen.

*

When they got to Le Havre, after just over three hours at sea, they cruised gently up the Seine for four kilometres to a creek at Berville-sur-Mer. The sun was rising in front of them, and the river traders and cargo vessels were beginning to stir.

They found the small, narrow creek, only just wide enough for the S-boat to traverse. Jaffery complained at every stage of navigating up the creek. The creek ran into a small lake where they found a short mooring pontoon under some trees. A red oil lamp glowed at the end. Two people could be seen on the pontoon, waving in the low light.

Beatrice and Adam greeted Ferdi with enthusiastic hugs and smiles. They had not seen him since his escape from Paris. Bertrand was welcomed as a hero – Beatrice even kissed him enthusiastically. He was delighted by the welcome from such a bonny thing, with unruly brown hair and a pretty, round face which continuously smiled. Plainly, the excitement in seeing the baron again was infectious. Jaffery remained in the boat and scowled at the happy reunion.

He shouted at Ferdi, "Remember, Finch, you have eight hours maximum. Any more and I am off, back to Newhaven."

"You will wait until we return, Jaffery. Or no more money. Don't worry yourself!" Ferdi did not wait for a response; he turned and followed Adam and Beatrice.

"Is he going to bugger off without us, Baron?" Bertrand whispered.

"It's fifty-fifty, Bertrand. If he has a spare key somewhere, or knows how to hot-wire the engines" – Ferdi showed Bertrand a silver key on a piece of string – "then he may bugger off without us!" Ferdi smiled broadly. Bertrand guffawed with delight and slapped Ferdi on the back.

"You are a crafty old baron!"

*

Adam had acquired a small pickup truck, which sped towards Paris. They were stopped by police roadblocks at Rouen and each of the six bridges over the Seine, until they got to Rue St Anne and Ferdi's gallery. Ferdi and Bertrand both carried British government diplomatic passports and special travel orders to and from Paris. They sailed through each of the roadblocks with ease. Beatrice and Adam sat in the back of the truck and produced their special passes and French identity cards, supplied by the SOE.

The gallery was mercifully untouched by the bombing but ransacked of all art – mostly German art, so nothing valuable. They knocked down the false wall in the cellar and retrieved the Wasp Trap files: three metal bottle-green locked boxes, each with a leather carrying handle on the lid. Ferdi also retrieved four of his portraits, two of which were Charlotte's parents, Alice Barrett and Franz-Joseph Deller, a portrait of Ulrich Fuhrman and one of Ferdi's mother.

On the way back from the gallery with the file boxes safely wrapped in canvas, they drove past Le Palais. Ferdi took out a small camera and took a photo of the remains of the once magnificent mansion.

"Is this where Freya and Theodora were?" Bertrand asked in awe.

"Yes," Ferdi said sadly. "It was a lovely house. I never saw inside, but I am told it was a wonderful place."

"What did you use to bomb it?" Bertrand asked. "And how did you do it? It's a bit exposed out here on this road."

"Adam, Beatrice and I used rifle grenades, big ones, from the house behind. It took about eight grenades to do that. Two of them went through the window at the back and slid through into the main hall in the centre of the house, but none went off. So I sent in a fourth at a steeper angle and it set them all off, with devastating consequences." Ferdi took in a shaky breath. "It's such a shame. But it got rid of a lot of senior Nazis and allowed Theodora and Freya to escape." Ferdi was close to tears as he thought of Ulrich.

He turned away to see Adam and Beatrice hand in hand, looking at the ruin of the building with satisfied smiles on their faces. Being communists, Ferdi thought, they had fulfilled their destiny by destroying the bourgeoisie and the places they lived in.

"I am ashamed to say," Ferdi said wistfully, "I was totally responsible in destroying that beautiful house." He climbed into the truck and started it up. "But you must not tell Freya it was us."

"Why?"

"I don't know, but please don't. I have a feeling she will react badly." The others clambered aboard. "One more stop before we go home."

"Where now, Ferdi?" Bertrand asked.

"Drancy prison camp. I want to see if there are any records of Christina Jorgensen."

"The Nazis will have burned all the records, Baron," Adam pointed out.

Ferdi looked down Avenue Foch, deep in thought. "We could check if there are any records in Eighty-Four Avenue Foch, couldn't we? They may still have records."

"Come on, then," Bertrand said. "I wouldn't mind seeing where some of my colleagues were tortured. Pay my respects. They will more than likely have also burned all their records."

Eighty-Four Avenue Foch was an ordinary Paris town house, with a ground floor and five floors above. The main doorway was blocked by sandbags; there was no way in.

"If you want records, Baron," Adam shouted from the back of the truck, "you should try eighty-two. That's where they'll be."

Ferdi and Bertrand turned in astonishment. Ferdi said, "How do you know that, Adam?"

"We were here before the Americans."

"We?" Bertrand asked.

"The French Forces of the Interior," shouted Beatrice with pride, standing up and pumping her fist. Adam jumped down from the truck and marched up to the house next to number eighty-four. He opened the front door and went straight in. Ferdi and Bertrand swiftly caught him up as they entered the dark hallway, to find him being shouted at by a policeman and a man in brown suit. They stopped bellowing at Adam when they saw Ferdi.

"Who are you? You cannot be here. This is a restricted area," the brown-suited man said. Ferdi produced his government pass. "Those are British credentials, not French," the man said.

"We are here to see if we can find records of a person who went missing from Drancy internment camp," Ferdi said calmly.

"I don't like the way you are treating us, monsieur," Bertrand said. "This is Baron Ferdinand Saumures of—" Ferdi patted Bertrand's shoulder.

"Calm down, Bertrand." Ferdi could see the besuited man studying his passport and government pass, stroking his chin.

"Second floor, first room on the right," he said abruptly, taking Ferdi and Bertrand by surprise. "There are some Drancy records there, but not many. The Boche burned most of everything."

"Thank you, monsieur," Ferdi and Bertrand said together. Ferdi pulled Adam away from the gendarme; the policeman was plainly sporting for a fight. Adam was good at getting people in authority's backs up. They all climbed the stairs to the second floor and found the room.

After over two hours of trawling through various bits of paper, Beatrice appeared at the door. "You've been hours, Adam. I thought you had been arrested or something!"

"Why are you not guarding the truck?" Adam asked.

"I got bored. There's nobody about. It's deserted out there."

"Well, give us a hand. We are looking for any records that relate to extraditing prisoners from Drancy." Adam gestured hopelessly towards the rows of filing cabinets.

Ferdi was sitting on the floor, going through the bottom drawer of one of the filing cabinets. Bertrand was next to him, humming a tuneless tune, flicking through files.

"What is German for 'extradition'?" Beatrice asked, holding a file.

"Um ... *Auslieferung*, or *ausliefern* for 'to extradite'," said Ferdi,

"Here you are then," Beatrice said, holding up a file. "*Auslieferung von Gefangenen, Drancy 1940–1942* and *1942–1944*. There are only a very few names though."

Ferdi rushed over to her. "Why didn't you come up hours ago? Well done, Beatrice!" Ferdi flicked through a page of names. There was Christina Jorgensen; she had been shipped back to Sweden in 1941. Ferdi slipped the paper into his pocket.

The whole exercise of collecting the Wasp Trap files and visiting Avenue Foch took seven and a half hours.

*

Jaffery was waiting for them at the pontoon, seething with rage. He marched up to Ferdi aggressively and was taken by surprise when Ferdi dangled the key in front of him.

"What was the meaning of—" Jaffery spluttered.

"We did not want you to go off without us. Here is the rest of your money, Jaffery." Bertrand handed over the leather pouch of gold. Jaffery snatched it out of Bertrand's hand and then looked at the metal boxes.

"What are these? They are not a wounded marine!"

"We got these instead," Bertrand said. "Fair exchange for a Royal Marine, don't you think?" Jaffery looked bemused.

When the boxes were loaded into the cabin, Ferdi and Bertrand said an emotional farewell to Adam and Beatrice. Dusk was setting in, and Jaffery was eager to get going so he could see to navigate out of the lake into the river Seine.

In the cabin, Ferdi sat on a bunk beside the boxes, stroking the package that contained the portraits that lay on top. He was suddenly taken over by weariness with a tinge of sadness. He had at least eight years of work tied up in these boxes, and now they were about to be handed over to the War Office and intelligence chiefs. He was worried about who these files were going to, and whether he should have duplicated them somehow.

Altogether there had been twenty-two people in Ferdi's team who helped gather the information within the files. Some information came from the American CIA, and some from Admiral Canaris's staff within the *Abwehr*. There were, to Ferdi's knowledge, only three, and himself, left. The files had mostly been kept secret from enemy intelligence; however, the fact that Sir Jason Barrett knew about the files meant they were not that secret. Had Sir Sussex spoken about them to Barrett?

Ferdi now had to consider how he was going to remove the files Sir Jason wanted. In fact, Ferdi had to find a way so that no one would see the removed files unless, and until, Sir Jason was no longer a threat to Ferdi or his friends.

As soon as they were out at sea, Ferdi asked Bertrand to join him in the cabin.

"I need to have some privacy, Jaffery, and I would also be grateful if you could keep the boat on an even keel, so we can do some work."

"The less I see of you two, the better," said Jaffery, and expectorated a large gob of phlegm over the side of the boat.

Ferdi shut the cabin door on Jaffery and switched on the lights. They could feel the boat gather speed. Thankfully, the sea was relatively flat so there was a minimum of buffeting.

"What is this about, Ferdi?"

"Bertrand, as you know, these are the Wasp Trap files."

"So I gathered. What do you want us to do with them?"

"There are quite a few files. This one" – Ferdi opened the lid of the dark-green metal file box and removed the last file at the back – "and here it is – is the WASP file."

"The infamous WASP file! Let's have a look!" Bertrand was eager.

"Just hang on, Bertrand." Ferdi looked embarrassed. "It's too dangerous."

"Well why are you dangling it there, then?" Bertrand was disappointed that he could not see the file on this mysterious group.

"I just need you to listen. If I should die—"

"Oh God, here we go again … being dramatic!"

"*If* I should be killed, Bertrand," Ferdi continued vehemently, "I want you to go to Sir Sussex Tremayne and tell him what I am about to tell you."

"Why don't I just give him the file?"

"Because I cannot give certain files to the War Office, or Sir Sussex." Bertrand sat on a bunk bed, dumfounded. "And," Ferdi continued, just as Bertrand opened his mouth to ask why, "don't ask me why. It is for Freya's, Theodora's and your safety that you don't know." Bertrand shut his mouth. He slumped back against the bulkhead, a frown on his face. Ferdi pulled out a sheet of paper. "This file, the WASP file, shows the organisation is run by Sir Jason Barrett, along with some other notable people such as Sir Henry Channon, Lord Rathmore … and so on. All quite important people."

"What the devil!" Bertrand sat up.

"This is for your information only. I was approached by Sir Jason just two days ago, before we collected these files. He said if certain files – including this, the file on WASP – are not handed over to him, he will have you, Freya, Theodora and me arrested. He actually said we would be silenced."

"Silenced? What does he mean?"

"Killed, I imagine. He does not seem to have many scruples."

"No, he bloody doesn't." Bertrand was beginning to look doubtful.

"We have got to get these files – especially these six files Barrett wants – to London," Ferdi continued, "without them getting into the wrong hands. That is why we are going to make Jaffery land us in Arundel, not at his boathouse in Newhaven. Jaffery, I believe, works for people like Sir Jason, and I reckon we will have Sir Jason's representatives waiting for us when we get back to Jaffery's boatyard."

"So we are going to persuade Jaffery to park somewhere else? Why don't we just knock him out and take over the boat?"

"It would be easier if we just gave him more money. I'm not sure if we can navigate up the river Arun that easily at night."

"How difficult can it be to find the mouth of the river?"

"It's at Littlehampton, just along the coast, and there's a sand bar at the entrance. I am not sure we can do this without Jaffery. And I don't want this to get too messy as it will antagonise Sir Jason."

Bertrand stood and walked about. The boat hit a wave and he had to sit again. "I see." He gave Ferdi a sceptical gaze. "Here is the problem I have, Baron. I am a little worried about all this. You are on our side still, aren't you?"

Ferdi was surprised by the question. "I work for Britain and her Allies!" he said bluntly. "I have always worked for the British." He peered straight into Bertrand's eyes. "I am getting a little fed up with you doubting me, Bertrand. You did in Spain, and you are doing it now. If you are unsure about my motives and my allegiances, then this may have been a mistake." He put the file back into the box.

"I'm sorry, Baron. I am not very good at trusting people. It is in my nature. But surely you must understand, especially when you tell me you were recruited by the *Abwehr* and you are – so you told us in Spain – in the Germans' pay as a double agent. And we have to take your word that you are working only for the Allies." Bertrand tapped the boxes. "And now you want to withhold some of these files – these important files – from the War Office, and make me participate in this scam, without question? I am sure you can see why I am just a little unsure."

"Well, do you think I am working for the Germans, Bertrand?"

Bertrand hesitated for a few moments. "No, I don't believe you are."

"Do you trust me?"

"Mostly, Baron, of course, yes."

"Do you understand that I do what I do for honourable reasons?"

"Well, this is it. You must see how it looks to me when you say you are doing things that you really should not, like removing vital files, not handing them over to Sir Sussex – the head of war intelligence in MI6, for goodness' sake! And suggesting Sir Jason Barrett MP – a respected Englishman, part of the security services and working with the prime minister – is head of WASP. Can you see how it sounds a bit … you know … unlikely?"

"Sir Jason is not to be trusted!"

"So *you* say. You really suspect him of being a traitor? I don't know the man – never met him. None of us have, except you."

"He is actually Freya's uncle," Ferdi said, looking into Bertrand's eyes. Bertrand was astounded. "But again, that is another story and one I would rather keep to myself for now. I think Theodora knows, but Freya does not want her uncle to know she survived the war."

"But this is too fantastic, Ferdi. What a mess. If we cannot trust Sir Jason, can we trust Freya?" Bertrand stood, shaking his head. "Actually, I don't want to know. I am too confused. Just tell me what to do if you get killed." Bertrand smiled suddenly, surprising Ferdi. "Before I kill you myself!"

Ferdi pondered. "While I was in Paris, and compiling and organising the information in these files—"

"What information is in fact in these files? Am I allowed to know that? I thought it was stuff on some SS officers, war-crime evidence."

"Well … yes." Ferdi looked at the boxes. "There are about a hundred and thirty-eight files, some on Nazis working from the Hôtel Majestic, some from Eighty-Two to Eighty-Four Avenue Foch – all the SS and Gestapo places in Paris, including Nineteen Avenue Foch, where Freya and Theodora were – a few prison camps in and around Paris, and the officers and men who ran them."

"What, all of them?" Bertrand said, astonished.

"Most. Mainly ones that were thought to have committed war crimes."

"All of the bastards then. How do you know about Barrett?"

Ferdi sighed. He hoped Bertrand would just accept his word that Barrett was head of WASP. "Two separate informants. I met a German naval officer and secret service man called Kapitän Langer. My friend Ulrich Fuhrman introduced him to me as …" Ferdi stopped. He eyed Bertrand, feeling suddenly very nervous. He hesitated. He cast his eyes up to the light in the cabin. Bertrand kept quiet, watching Ferdi anxiously. "He said … Ulrich said … that he – Langer – enjoyed the company of men, like we do – Ulrich and I." Ferdi stopped to see if there was any judgement from Bertrand.

"Baron, we all know you are a homosexual. What happened?"

"Oh!" Ferdi said, slightly relieved. "Well … thank you. Anyhow, we got him drunk one night. We had a great party, just the three of us, and Ulrich told him to tell me about the organisation he had got involved with: WASP. And how it was highly secret."

"Not much of a secret service man, is he?"

"Indeed, but he knew I was part of *Abwehr*. He was one of Canaris's men. I asked him loads of questions, including who ran the organisation – to which he replied, an Englishman called Sir Jason Barrett."

"Traitorous bleeder!" Bertrand said.

"We got lots of details about WASP from him. Langer was high up in security in France. He rambled on and on, with great enthusiasm. We egged him on, more and more enthralled. Ulrich had to go to the lavatory a few times to take down notes."

"But Baron, we must hand this file over immediately!"

"We can't, Bertrand. Sir Jason is just too powerful. He's a friend of Churchill, he is in the cabinet, he has some of the British Intelligence Service and Special Branch working for him."

"Is Sir Sussex involved with him?"

"No, I don't think so; just soldiers, people to do his dirty work so he can keep clean and respectable." Ferdi thought for a moment. "I truly hope not Sir Sussex, otherwise, Bertrand, we are really buggered."

"Who was the other source?"

"In 1939, one of my informants said he was recruited into WASP by Barrett. The informant knew Sir Jason Barrett well."

"Is the informant reliable?" Bertrand asked.

Ferdi shook his head. "No, unfortunately." Ferdi decided not to tell Bertrand that the other informant was Franz-Joseph Deller.

"So, Sir Jason wants the file suppressed."

"Yes. Which is why there may be some credence in him being WASP. And he wants these five other files. This is just between us, Bertrand – Freya and Theodora must never know, unless—"

"You're bloody killed. I know, I know!" Bertrand and Ferdi's eyes met. Ferdi felt miserable. "Let us work out what we are going to do with Jaffery to get him to take us to Littlehampton."

"Yes, let's." Ferdi took another leather pouch out of his pocket. "If ten gold sovereigns don't work, Bertrand, you will have to persuade him. But I cannot see him turning *this* down."

28

As Ferdi predicted, Jaffery was persuaded to drop Ferdi and Bertrand off with their cargo in Arundel, twelve miles up the river Arun from Littlehampton in Sussex.

It was dark and cold, the river was at high tide, and the noise of the E-boat's engines shattered the peace and quiet as it raced up the river, the floodlight spotting the twists and turns. It took only twenty minutes to get to Arundel.

Just after they cruised under the road bridge, with merely half an inch clearance for the cabin roof, they came to a charming riverside pub, The Black Rabbit, shut and boarded up. There, waiting for Ferdi and Bertrand, were two almost identical men: huge, with short military haircuts and wearing dark reefer jackets. Ferdi was so pleased to see the two large men, he leapt out of the boat and shook both of the Tanner twins by the hand.

After the boxes of files were taken off the boat, Jaffery was paid and manoeuvred the boat to head back out to sea. Ferdi sat heavily on the bank of the river. He breathed out a huge sigh, sending a vapour trail into the cold air. He lit a cheroot, his first since leaving Newhaven.

"Bertrand, may I introduce you to Charlie and Bert Tanner. They have one of the estate farms."

"Good to see you, chaps." Bertrand shook each by the hand. "Would you put the boxes in the van?"

Bertrand sat beside Ferdi and looked at the river. It was the dead of night, a clear starry sky with no moon. Ferdi began to enjoy the safe sounds from the river, the lollop of the water, the hiss of the reeds in the light chilly breeze. He offered Bertrand a cheroot.

"Did you know this river is one of the fastest flowing rivers in the country?" Ferdi said, not expecting an answer.

"Shouldn't we get going, Ferdi?"

"Yes, I suppose so. I am just enjoying relaxing by the river." Ferdi stood. "I will drop you off at the house with the boys. I am going straight to London with the files before Sir Jason gets wind of our subterfuge."

"Oh!" Bertrand sounded surprised and plainly a little disappointed not to be going to London too. "OK then."

*

The Adolphe Hotel in Albemarle Street, just off Piccadilly, belonged to Ferdi's father. The old baron had owned most of Albemarle Street, and after his father's death, Ferdi became owner of one of the most prominent hotels in the West End and landlord to prestigious galleries and offices.

The metal file boxes were put into a secure meeting room. There was a tap on the locked door, which worried Ferdi. He hoped it was not Alderson or Sir Jason. Equally, he hoped it was not the War Office.

"Who is it?" Ferdi asked.

"Abbott, Baron Saumures," said the elderly night porter who had transported the files into the meeting room. "You ordered tea, sir, and I thought you might like some toast for breakfast."

Ferdi unlocked the door and the old man shuffled in. "There you go, sir, a lovely pot of rosie—"

"Thank you, Abbott." Ferdi took the tray. "I need to be left alone, please. On no account – no matter who – should I be interrupted. Clear?"

"Certainly, sir." The old man shuffled out the door again, shaking his head in confusion. Ferdi regretted having being a little abrupt, and hoped he would hear him add, "You are too kind, Abbott."

Ferdi took out every file within the boxes. He removed six of them and replaced the rest. He arranged the six files in a row in front of him. He removed his jacket and sat at the table. He took each file in turn and added notes. The edited files were placed into his briefcase. He went to the telephone on the sideboard and picked up the receiver.

"Number, please," said the operator.

"Whitehall 1218, please." There were a few clicks and then two ringtones.

"Sir James Grigg's office, can I help you?"

"Good morning. May I speak to the Secretary of State for War, please."

"Whom may I say is calling?" the woman asked.

"Baron Ferdinand Saumures. He is expecting my call."

"Certainly, Baron Saumures. I will put you through."

*

Burton Park Place was a magnificent and substantial red-brick Queen Anne house. Wooded hills surrounded the area behind the house, framing the stately home with a multitude of shades of greens. The late-afternoon sun in early May was warm as Ferdi's taxi drove up to the front door of the house over the gravel. Waiting on Ferdi's return from delivering the files to the Secretary of State for War were not only Charlotte, Bertrand and Theodora, but also the bearded, stout figure of Sir Sussex Tremayne. He stood on the gravel driveway in front of the house, chatting to Charlotte and Bertrand. Theodora was standing in the front door porch, away from the others.

As Ferdi got out of the taxi, Charlotte ran over to him and put her arms around him in a loving embrace.

"Welcome home, darling. I am so glad you are safe. Such great news: the war is nearly over!" Ferdi was quite taken aback. Charlotte had never shown that amount of affection towards him before. It felt like she was genuinely happy to see him. She released the embrace and took his arm, smiling fondly at him as they walked towards Sir Sussex.

"Well done, Ferdinand, my boy." The old man went up to Ferdi and patted both his shoulders. He was cheery for a moment, before adopting a serious tone. "Walk with me, my boy. Please excuse us, my dear," he said, turning to Charlotte. "Would you allow us chaps to have an important chat?" She smiled her consent. As the men took to the terrace, Ferdi looked over his godfather's shoulders to see Charlotte, Theodora and Bertrand looking concerned.

"Go in, everybody. We won't be long," Ferdi shouted.

They strolled to the wide red-brick terrace that ran around the house. Banks of blue lavender mixed with white campanulas in full bloom had bees and butterflies frolicking in the early spring sun. Ferdi unconsciously took in a lungful of air. The smell of home.

"This time of year is invigorating!" Sir Sussex said. "Autumn is somehow depressing, don't you find?"

Ferdi was a little taken aback. "I am not sure I agree, sir. Why?"

Sir Sussex stopped and stroked his beard in thought. "There is a day, in autumn, when you are suddenly aware that the swallows and swifts have flown off south to Africa – or wherever they fly off to. Marks the end of summer. The end of long, hot, balmy days and short nights. The approach of the season of rainbows, Ferdinand. Autumn. Like this bloody war, we gradually get nearer to the end – any day now, the end of the rainbow. Just the bloody Japs to sort out!"

"Yes, sir. But it is spring, and the war in Europe is nearly over." Ferdi regarded his godfather with some trepidation. He had not seen this poetic side of the old man. Sir Sussex and Ferdi stopped to look at the view of the Sussex Downs, smoking cigarettes.

"You have excelled yourself, Ferdinand. The war – your war at least – is over."

"Really, sir? Am I not required for any other mission? There is so much more to do, especially in the peace."

"No, you rest up with your beautiful wife." He turned to his godson. "I must say, Ferdinand …" Sir Sussex swiped the underside of his thick white moustaches, smiled and gazed back at the house. "I am mighty impressed. She is a wonderful-looking woman. Swedish, I gather."

"Yes, sir."

"Where did you find her?"

"We met in Paris, sir. I hoped to recruit her, but being a neutral—"

"Say no more, old boy." They walked on slowly along the terrace. "Anything else?" asked Sir Sussex. Ferdi wanted to tell his godfather about Charlotte's connection to Sir Jason Barrett but was aware that Charlotte had no desire to be identified. And in any case, it could be dangerous to disclose Charlotte's secret. "Anything you feel you need to get off your chest?" Sir Sussex persisted. "Do I need you to come to Box Hill for a thorough debrief? If there is anything else you need to say to me, you would tell me?"

"Yes, of course, sir." Ferdi was anxious Sir Sussex suspected him of hiding something. Which he was. The six files stored in his security box at his bank in Fleet Street.

"Did you get any further with this thing your friend found … WASP? It seemed you were on to something. You said at our last meeting that—"

"No, nothing really, sir. It was very difficult to find out anything more. I had no access to any further information, other than its existence."

"That is a shame. It sounded quite important to you. Mr Churchill wants to know more about WASP. I know a chap that may be useful, I will put him on it."

"But Sir Sussex …" Ferdi protested. He wanted to be able to control any revelations about WASP.

"I will see what this chap says when he returns from the Front. He's a journalist, unfortunately."

"Does this journalist know about me? My name?"

"No, that would not be appropriate. We do not give out names to anyone outside the service," Sir Sussex said authoritatively. "It's all very preliminary at the moment. If I do need to put him in touch with you, I will get you two together at my office. Anyway, I have only met him once."

"I would like to meet this journalist. Who is he?" Ferdi was getting agitated.

"Not now, Ferdinand. You rest up." Sir Sussex patted him on the shoulder. He then changed the subject. "I believe you stayed in London after you delivered the files. Any problems there, Ferdinand?"

"No, no problems," Ferdi said, feeling nervous but trying to not show it.

"Gather you had a meeting with Sir Jason Barrett," Sir Sussex said, in badly veiled suspicion.

"He wanted to see me."

"Why?"

"He wanted to know about the Wasp Trap files."

"Well I am jiggered." Sir Sussex was surprised. "You didn't tell him anything?"

"No, sir."

"How did he know you were in London?"

"He – or rather his colleague, Mr Alderson – found me at my hotel."

"When you had the files?"

"Yes, but they had been safely stowed away. He never saw them." Ferdi kept eye contact with the old man.

"You know Sir Jason is no longer MI6? He has been made special economic adviser to the prime minister."

"He said." Ferdi was abrupt. He licked his lips and confided, "I believe Sir Jason Barrett is not a man to be trusted, sir."

"Why do you say that, Ferdinand? I know you have reservations about the man."

"I believe he and Jean de Tournet were working together – to what end, I am not sure, but not, I believe, in the best interests of the country."

"But Sir Jason and his intelligence team gave us Hess! A fantastic bit of work for the Allies." There was a pause. They walked on, both heads staring down at the brick pathway in contemplation.

"What are Sir Jason's plans, do you think, sir?"

Sir Sussex hesitated. "He is a newspaper proprietor. And he has been put forward as MP for Tooting and Wimbledon at the next elections, for the Conservative party."

"I am very surprised, sir."

"Why are you surprised, Ferdinand? He has good credentials, he is a friend and adviser to the prime minister, and he is intelligent. More than can be said about some of the clowns in the government!"

"Was there no suspicion about him in MI6?"

Sir Sussex frowned. "There was a bit of a cloud, but one I can't really talk about. Nothing for you to worry about."

"Does he have any further access to war intelligence?"

Sir Sussex stopped abruptly. "What is this, Ferdinand? You are alarming me. Apart from his relationship with de Tournet, who, you tell me, was killed in the bombing, what other evidence have you to doubt Sir Jason's loyalties?"

Ferdi backtracked and said lightly, "How would he, for example, know about the Wasp Trap files?" There was a silence. They started walking again.

"He was in MI6." Sir Sussex sounded unsure. "He should not know, not his department. Unless Mr Churchill told him, which is likely."

"I see," Ferdi said quietly.

"Sir Jason gave us a name when we wanted to flush out a double agent. The name he gave was that of Franz-Joseph Deller, your friend."

Ferdi froze. "But he is—!"

"I know, dear boy. It was just rather peculiar that he had that name. Deller was his gardener, you know." Sir Sussex paused and stroked his beard. "Truth be known, I am rather glad Barrett left the department. He made quite a few people in the service uncomfortable, apparently. Threw his weight around to get information he should not have. He is now virtually in Mr Churchill's cabinet. I never really liked Barrett, but you must never tell anyone else about your, or my, misgivings. He has powerful friends."

Ferdi did not know what to do or say. If he said anything more about Sir Jason, Sir Sussex would become even more suspicious and try and find out what he was concealing.

They smoked in silence, gazing at the avenue of poplar trees, a haze of green on the branches as the new leaves started to sprout. Ferdi spoke first. "I knew I was being followed by MI6 in London, you know."

Sir Sussex smiled wryly. "MI5, actually. Just keeping an eye on you. Making sure you kept safe – out of trouble."

"Safe from whom, sir?"

"No threat in particular. You are very valuable to me, Ferdinand. How long was your meeting with Sir Jason?" Sir Sussex said, lighting another cigarette, trying to look unconcerned.

"We spent only a couple of minutes talking. We were in the Cheshire Cheese."

"I like that pub, good billiard table. What did you talk about?"

"He was asking about the Wasp Trap files, sir." Sir Sussex looked concerned as he surveyed the South Downs beyond.

"I think it must have been his friend the prime minister who told him about these files. The prime minister was the only person – other than my office – who knew about the files. What did Sir Jason want to know?"

"If they had been retrieved."

"Did you tell him?"

"No, sir. I would not confirm they existed. By the way, do you know anything about Sir Jason's Special Branch colleague? His name is Alderson, John Alderson." Ferdi wanted to know about Alderson. Was he really a Special Branch police officer?

"Alderson is his sidekick. He used to be Special Branch, I believe. He's not important. He does seem to stick around Sir Jason a lot, however." He frowned. "Have you heard from Deller?"

"He is in England somewhere, I think, sir. Not sure where, or how he got back."

"How do you know?"

"Just rumour. I got a letter from him not so long ago."

"Really? What did it say?"

"Just that he was on his way back to England. The letter came via the British Embassy in Madrid."

"How did the letter get back to England? Why have you not told me of this, Ferdinand?"

"There was nothing in the letter that would have been useful. It just said he was on his way to England. I picked it up when we were in Madrid. He must have travelled ahead of us."

Sir Sussex looked up to the blue, cloudless sky as if looking for inspiration. "Well, doesn't matter now. As soon as you know where Deller is, he has to come in. We need a debrief. His whereabouts must be kept strictly confidential,

Ferdinand. He is a loose end. He needs to be brought in, and not by Jason Barrett. Do I make myself clear?"

"Yes, sir," Ferdi said. "I am not sure how secure he is. He has taken to drink, and I lost control of him when I had to close up my gallery in Metz, in 1940."

"He was the person who started this WASP rumour in the first place. We need to sniff him out. Where did he go?"

"He arrived in Paris in 1940, the day of the occupation. He was an SS colonel in charge of arts and culture, apparently."

"Did he not contact you via Berlin?"

"No. When I lost the Metz gallery, my contact in Berlin was relocated by the Nazis to Paris. He was killed last year."

"But you think Deller is in England?"

"Yes, sir."

"Fine, we'll find him. What is the likelihood Deller has changed allegiances?" Sir Sussex asked. "Would he be working for WASP? Would he transmit messages to America?"

"To America? Not at all possible. He had enough problems with an ordinary wireless, let alone a transmitter!"

"So, he would not, for example, be capable of using an Enigma machine?"

Ferdi eyed his godfather in confusion before saying "No." And then as an afterthought, "What is an Enigma machine?"

"An encoding machine – highly secret. But Deller is Austrian, his parents are high-level Nazis. He could have turned, couldn't he?"

"I don't believe so, sir."

"Did he tell you any more about WASP? Or who the man in charge was?"

Ferdi decided he had to lie. "No more than it was an international organisation that was formed to combat communism."

"We know all that. Nothing else, Ferdinand?"

"No, sir."

The old man stopped to ponder. He turned his attention back to the view of the Downs.

"That is a lovely aspect, isn't it?" He patted Ferdi's back. "If that is all, I'd better get on. You should join your charming wife. Well, I will see you soon, I hope, my boy." He turned abruptly and marched back to his car. A driver leapt out and opened the rear door of Sir Sussex's dark-blue Daimler. Ferdi rushed to keep up. "I retire soon, you know, Ferdinand," he chuckled.

"Will you enjoy that, sir – retirement?" Ferdi asked. "You must come back here for some dinner, maybe."

"I would love to get to know your young wife. She is charming" – he got into the car – "simply charming. The Turkish woman, is she the one who told us about Jean de Tournet?"

"Yes, sir. I will tell you more about her soon. She was a fantastic asset to my team."

"Very well, keep it all under your hat. Goodbye, Ferdinand. Thank you again for all you have done, your contribution to the war and all that. Jolly good show. Your mother would have been terribly proud." Sir Sussex Tremayne closed the car door and was slowly driven away.

Charlotte emerged from the house and went up to her husband as he waved away Sir Sussex, concern over her face.

"What was that all about? Why did Sir Sussex want to talk to you?"

"He is my godfather … and head of war intelligence, part of MI6," said Ferdi in a quiet voice.

"Gosh," Charlotte said, taking Ferdi's hand as they walked back to the house. "Everything OK?"

"Yes, I think so. He just needed to know about the files, and whether they got to the War Office."

"Why didn't he want to talk to Bertrand as well?"

"Bertrand is part of the SOE, run by Stewart Menzies, Sir Sussex's superior. A different section of MI6." Ferdi hoped that would satisfy Charlotte's curiosity.

"He seems a nice chap, Sir Sussex, like a slightly thinner Father Christmas."

Ferdi smiled. "Anyway, I fancy a party," he said as Theodora and Bertrand joined them in the hallway of the house.

"What kind of party?" Charlotte squeaked with glee, clapping her hands.

"A 'We Survived the War' party, I should think, darling," Theodora said.

"That's about right, Theodora." Ferdi put his arms around Charlotte and Bertrand's shoulders and walked with them towards the drawing room. "My godfather says that is the end of our war."

"Oh, how wonderful!" Charlotte kissed Ferdi on the cheek. "Smoked salmon, caviar and trifle, lots of champagne and—"

"Well, there is quite a lot of champagne in the cellar, but I'm afraid we will be eating Spam – smoked Spam, Spam caviar and Spam trifle – for the foreseeable future," Ferdi said with regret.

"That sounds lovely, darling. What is Spam?" Theodora asked.

"It's ..." Ferdi started and then thought of something else. "I think we should all go to London and stay at our hotel."

"Our hotel?" the others all chorused together.

"Yes, the Adolphe Hotel in Albemarle Street, Mayfair. My father owned the whole block of Albemarle Street. It's mine now."

"Bit of a bloody unfortunate name for a hotel, old chap," Bertrand said, "the Adolphe – with Hitler and all!"

"Named after the Grand Duke of Luxembourg and my father's cousin."

"Is it still going?" Charlotte asked. "With the war and everything?"

"That's where I stayed last night. It has lost some of its glamour as it was used as an American Officer's club. American officers could gather and stay there." The others looked at Ferdi in wonder.

"A bit like Le Palais but for Americans," Theodora said, much to everybody's discomfort.

"Are you fabulously wealthy, Baron?" Bertrand asked with a huge grin.

"I would not say fabulously wealthy, not since the war has scuppered most of our income."

The four young people relaxed in the opulent drawing room of Burton Park Place with a mixture of excitement and anticipation. It was like the last day at school; no more exams to worry about, but unsure of what to do during the summer holidays.

"Ferdi, what do you own?" Charlotte asked, taking a sip of her pink gin and soda water. "Should not your wife know these things?"

"I suppose so, my dear." Ferdi pondered for a moment. "There is this house, three tenant farms" – he turned to his audience – "all around here: 2,200 acres. And properties in Albemarle Street in London, including the Adolphe Hotel, and then there is our family estate with a castle and vineyards in Fischbach, in the middle of Luxembourg. Sadly, ruined by fire just after the Great War, we think by Luxembourger republican socialists. The castle was empty anyway as my mother lived here."

"Christ, Baron!" Bertrand looked Ferdi up and down with new respect.

"I've never seen London," Charlotte said softly.

"Nor have I, darling," Theodora said. "Why don't we go and have our Spam party in London now?"

29

Two shafts from hooded headlights cut through the misty rain on a chilly, moist evening. A lorry drew up slowly outside a drab red-brick Victorian church in Battersea Park Road, south-west London. The mock-gothic church stood on its own amongst shadowy mounds of bricks and partially bomb-damaged terraced houses. When the headlights were switched off, it was pitch-black – the streetlights were still not being switched on.

An interior light came on inside the lorry cab. Three men, two large and broad-shouldered, one skinny, bearded and tall, dropped out of the lorry cab. The skinny man looked up and down Battersea Park Road. Once he was satisfied there was no traffic, he switched on a torch and shone it onto the canvas-covered trailer. The large men started to remove five hefty wooden crates, each crate taller than the men. A trolley rolled each crate to the church entrance. The skinny man unlocked the church door, and the crates were trundled inside.

After thirty minutes, all three men emerged from the church, and the thin man handed over a pile of notes to one of the large men. The two big men went off in the lorry, leaving the thin man behind.

He was alone on the pavement. He looked up to the sky; his vicars' dog collar could be seen in the beam of his torch. His eyes were closed, his hands gripped together in fervent prayer. He remained there, in prayer, for two minutes. His frizzy hair, beard, and his black jacket sparkled from the fine misty rain in the torchlight as he got wetter and wetter. His mouth was open as though drinking in the damp air. A car drove past and splashed through a puddle near to where the thin vicar stood. He awoke from his trance, turned, and went back into the church, his torch guiding him to the heavy church door. There was a flash of light as he stepped through a blackout curtain. The church door slammed shut and a heavy bolt slid over, locking him inside.

Jane Gardener stepped out of a doorway opposite the church and put up her umbrella. She switched on a small torch and slowly started to walk towards a car parked a hundred yards up the road.

*

"Dear God, Ferdi, have you seen this in *The Times*?" Charlotte strode into Ferdi's study, waving the newspaper. She was still in her dressing gown, a long white silk gown tied at her waist by a silk rope.

"No, I haven't seen the paper this morning." Ferdi had his head down writing a letter.

"Well, listen to this: '*Following the tragic death of Angus Matthews MP last month, the by-election, held yesterday, for Balham and Tooting, South London, was won by Sir Jason Barrett for the Conservative party.*'" Ferdi raised his head from the letter he was writing, astonishment over his face. "It goes on: '*Sir Jason Barrett is well used to government. He has, for the past year, been special advisor to Mr Churchill about the economy through these difficult war years. He is proprietor of the business newspaper,* The Sentinel, *and is also an advisor to the War Office on France, with his experience as* chargé d'affaires *in Paris before the war.*'"

"I am not surprised that your uncle Jason seeks more power, but I thought having a newspaper would suffice." Ferdi was thoughtful. "This is something else."

"What do you mean, Ferdi?"

"He is just not a person to be trusted in government," Ferdi said. Charlotte was surprised by his comment.

"He is perfectly qualified to be a Member of Parliament. I know I don't like him, he's not a nice man." She went up close to Ferdi. "But why don't you trust him? I didn't think you knew him." Charlotte wondered why this news had upset Ferdi so much. He was plainly agitated. Ferdi looked up from his desk at Charlotte standing next to him.

"You're right, I don't know him," he said quietly. "I'm sorry, he will more than likely do well." He sounded insincere and Charlotte frowned at him. She placed *The Times* in front of him.

"There's more. I will leave it with you. I must get dressed. Theodora and I want to go shopping, and then to the cinema in Petworth with Bertrand. Do you want to come?"

"He wants us all to call him Bernard, by the way, now we are all back in England."

"Oh! How am I going to remember that? I've got so used to calling him Bertrand."

"Bertrand was his code name. He feels unsafe using it, for some reason."

"OK, I will try to remember. I'll tell Theodora. See you for tea."

"Well, just be careful. Keep Bernard close." Ferdi looked worried.

"We will be okay, Ferdi, you know we use caution. The war is nearly over. Theodora just needs to get out once in a while or it gets a bit like Le Palais – being cooped up."

"I know, but I am still worried about you two, and Bernard, of course."

"So why not come with us?"

"No, thank you," Ferdi said, not looking up from the newspaper.

Ferdi kept his misgivings about Sir Jason becoming an MP to himself. With luck, his preoccupation with being an MP would mean he would probably not be pursuing Ferdi for the six files Ferdi had in a bank vault.

Ferdi wrote to Sir Jason to tell him the files he wanted were in safe-keeping, and that should anything happen to anyone, there were instructions for the files to be released to the press.

He was tempted to talk to Sir Sussex Tremayne of his fears about Sir Jason's pursuit of power, but the old man was about to retire, and anyway, his godfather did not seem to be all that worried about Sir Jason. Ferdi did not know who else to confide in. He regretted confiding in Bernard about the WASP file, it would put him in more danger, but there was no one else.

Charlotte had made it clear she did not want Sir Jason to know that she was still alive. Ferdi had only an inkling of why – just that she could not bear the man, and she knew that he, and her late stepfather, were involved in something together.

Ferdi wondered where Franz-Joseph was, what he was up to. Charlotte had pestered Ferdi often to track him down to return her collection of paintings. Where was Joseph? Where were these paintings? Was it possible Joseph brought them back to England somehow? He discounted this as improbable – it would be very difficult to smuggle fifteen canvases, some quite large, from the Continent in wartime.

30

After Paris was liberated on the twenty-fifth of August 1944, the Allies progressed to Germany and the Third Reich was crushed – eventually – on the eighth of May 1945. Charlotte, Theodora, Bernard and Ferdi all went to London to celebrate.

Charlotte's first encounter with London was not as she imagined. There was a lot of damage on the outskirts of the town and all around the river as they slowly rolled into a battered Victoria Station. Theodora seemed surprised at the amount of devastation around the station.

"I had not realised how badly London was hit by bombs." Theodora gazed at the buildings outside the entrance to the station.

"And this has all been cleared up. A Dornier crashed just over there, taking out a whole row of shops," Ferdi said with sadness. "Poor old London got very badly beaten up."

"What's a Dornier?" Charlotte asked.

"A Kraut bomber," Bernard said. He surveyed the devastation, tutting with his hands on his hips as they waited at a taxi stand. "I suppose there are taxis about?" Bernard asked a passing porter.

"There are a few, sir. You'll just have to wait, wontcha." Everybody looked at the elderly porter as he turned and limped off, muttering something about "bleedin' foreigners" as he went.

"I'm not a bleeding foreigner!" Bernard shouted after him. The porter turned around.

"You from round here?"

"No – Putney."

"You're a posh bleedin' foreigner then, aintcha." The porter wandered off with his trolley back into the station, leaving Bernard shaking his head, hands on hips, the others all looking at him with smiles on their faces.

A taxi eventually took them to the Adolphe Hotel. As promised, they had a party to celebrate surviving the war. Ferdi offered all staying at the hotel free drinks "until the cellar runs dry".

This was a side of Ferdi Charlotte had never seen: jovial, happy and carefree. He had been mostly morose since their return from Spain. He was bad at hiding his depression, not joining the others for meals for days at a time, forcing a smile at Bernard's jokes and hardly talking to Theodora.

Fortunately, the kitchens were able to find something better than Spam; the American army had left crates of meat and vegetable K-rations after they moved out of the hotel. The guests were delighted by the amount of nondescript meat in the stew.

"Ferdi?" Charlotte was sitting opposite him in their suite in the Adolphe Hotel, after the party. She was curled up on the sofa, still in her long black dress. "I want to go to Sweden and find Christina."

"When do you want to go?" Ferdi had untied his bow tie and undone his top button.

"Now."

"I see. I don't know where she was taken to in Sweden, Freya. We are going to have to ask the Swedish embassy to track her down."

"She will be in Gothenburg. She and Bo had friends who owned a bakery in the middle of Gothenburg in a street called Götabergsgatan, I think – or something like that. It is close to the university."

"How do you know this?"

"Christina always talked about Bo's huge hands. She joked that if he was not a soldier, he would be working with his best friend who owned a bakery. His large hands were perfect for kneading dough, making bread." Charlotte suddenly became tearful, remembering the laughter they had shared talking about Bo being a baker.

"What was the baker called?"

"I can't remember. But there cannot be that many bakers in Götabergsgatan, around the university."

"They may not be still there, Freya." She sighed, irritated by Ferdi's negativity. "I will not be able to come with you. Theodora doesn't have a passport yet, and in any case getting her back into the country will be difficult, and Bernard—"

"I'll go on my own, Ferdi. I don't need looking after! I just wondered if you knew how I could get to Gothenburg."

Ferdi dropped his head in submission. "I will find out tomorrow. We'll have to go to the Swedish embassy anyway, to get a visa. And then we will have to take advice as to how we can get Christina back here. Will she have papers?"

"I don't know. Thank you, darling." She smiled sweetly at her husband. "I'm off to bed. It was a lovely party." She turned at the door to her room. Ferdi was looking down at the ashtray on the floor, his cigarette in its holder, unlit, clamped between his teeth. "And I love your hotel," she added.

He did not look up. "Thanks" was all he said.

*

Charlotte's journey to Sweden was long, cramped, but uneventful. She left from Grimsby on a small Swedish cargo steamer bound for Gothenburg. It took thirty-eight hours; the sea was calm, thank God, the sun shone each day, and the sea air was like nectar. Charlotte was the only passenger, but not the only woman; the captain's delightful wife was also on board. Charlotte had a cabin just behind the wheelhouse, so it could be a little noisy at night. She suspected this might be the captain's cabin, relinquished to her. Each morning, Hector – well it sounded like "Hector" – brought her a pot of tea and sweet cardamon buns, warm and flaky.

"Do you make these yourself, Hector?" Charlotte asked. Hector blushed with a shy smile. He was young, blond, and broad-shouldered. He backed out of Charlotte's cabin without answering.

"He speaks no English, Baroness," the captain told Charlotte when she went into the wheelhouse with her tea. She had an open invitation to enter the wheelhouse whenever it pleased her.

"I just asked if he made the lovely rolls himself," Charlotte said.

"No, our cook makes them for us. He is a wonderful baker."

"Really, captain! Tell me, would he know a baker in Götabergsgatan, near the university?"

"I have no idea. I will ask him." The captain, who seemed quite young for a man in his position, went over to a telephone on the wall, dialled a number, and when it was answered, spoke Swedish to someone.

"He knows a place called Olofssons Bageri, near—"

"That's it!" Charlotte clapped in glee, surprising the captain. "Nils Olofsson was Bo's friend. Thank you so much, Captain."

When they arrived in Gothenburg, Charlotte was met at the bottom of the gangplank by a smart middle-aged man. He could not be anything else but British. He raised his bowler hat, hooked his umbrella over his arm, and came up to Charlotte with a huge beam of a smile, displaying discoloured teeth.

"Baroness Saumures, I presume?" he said in clipped diction. "I'm Mathew Beddows, from the British Consulate in Gothenburg. Welcome to Sweden."

"How do you do, Mr Beddows," Charlotte said. "How kind of you to make time to meet me here."

"I am a huge admirer of your mother-in-law, the Baroness Saumures, Lady Camilla. I went to school with her brother, the late Earl of Arun."

"I see." Charlotte realised she knew hardly anything about Ferdi's mother, or indeed that Ferdi had an uncle who was an earl. "Tell me, Mr Beddows, have you had any success in finding my friend Christina Jorgensen?"

"I regret not, Lady Saumures. The baron mentioned in his telegram that you may know more."

"I think I do. I believe she may be found near a bakery in Götabergsgatan: Olofssons Bageri."

Beddows looked surprised. "A bakery? We thought she was a relation of yours."

Charlotte smiled to herself. She thought the war may have drilled out British snobbishness – clearly not. "She is. However, she was unjustly taken prisoner by the Nazis in Paris. They murdered her husband, an ex-Swedish army officer." Charlotte hoped this would impress Beddows.

"What are your plans, Baroness?" Beddows asked as they got into a large Bentley with a Union Jack fluttering on the front bumper.

"I plan, if Christina wants to, to take her back with me and look after her. I have no idea what her current situation is. She may have started a new life, I don't know, but I need to find her and ensure she is okay."

"I see." Beddows seemed dubious.

"What are you worried about, Mr Beddows?"

"Well, we will have to sort out a visa for Mrs Jorgensen. As your relative, it should be quite simple." He still looked uncertain. Charlotte wondered if it was something to do with being a "relative". She hoped if she said Christina was a close relative, it would help smooth the way of getting her back to England.

Untouched by war, Gothenburg was a relief from the terrible destruction Charlotte had left behind in England. There were no damaged houses, and the streets were clean and tidy. Well-dressed men, and women in pretty dresses, strolled along the pavements in the sun.

Charlotte and Mr Beddows found the bakery, opposite a small park of grass and trees, thronged with young people going to and fro.

As it turned out, Christina was easy to find. When they drew up to the bakery in Götabergsgatan, there she was, wiping down the pavement tables. Charlotte watched her for a while. Tears started to form in her eyes. Christina looked so thin, and she had aged considerably since the last time Charlotte had seen her, what seemed a lifetime ago, at Le Palais.

Charlotte got out of the Bentley. Christina looked up from her work. She glanced at Charlotte and went back to her tasks. She looked contemplative and a little sad. Her hands suddenly stopped wiping the tables. She straightened herself up and looked back to Charlotte, who stood smiling, watching her old nanny.

"Charlotte?" Christina cried. "You are here?" Her hands went to her mouth. "But look at you, you are a woman!"

Charlotte ran to Christina and fell into her arms, her cheeks now awash in tears. Christina, her hair wrapped in a headscarf, only came up to Charlotte's chin; she seemed to have shrunk. She smelt of musty baking and detergent.

"How are you, Christina?"

"I am very well, my darling girl. But look at you! I can't believe it. Charlotte!"

"I'm still Freya. I'm married now."

"Married?"

"To a baron, no less. I'm Baroness Freya Saumures."

Charlotte could see a huge grin behind Christina's dimpled hands.

"A baroness," Christina said in wonderment. "Look at me in my old apron. I must be a sight." She took off her apron, revealing a serviceable dun-coloured dress, the only concession to femininity a thin cream ruffle around the collar.

A tall white-haired man in a white apron appeared out of the door of the bakery and frowned. Christina suddenly went quiet and carried on wiping down the tables.

"Who is this lady?" the man asked abruptly in Swedish. He leered at Charlotte, pulling his trousers up and flattening down his hair.

"Nils, this is Baroness Freya Saumures … my Charlotte."

"What do you mean, your Charlotte?" He turned on Christina and started a noisy rant in rapid Swedish. Christina kept quiet, answering yes or no every now and then. Nils's attention swung back to Charlotte, and Mathew Beddows, who had now joined her. With a shopkeeper's ingenuous smile, he bade them enter the shop and take one of the two empty tables.

"Sir" – Charlotte did not move – "I am here to take my mother back to England."

Everybody was stunned by Charlotte's comment. Charlotte hoped the lie would not be challenged. Christina just smiled with joy and made no comment. She slammed down her cloth and went over to stand beside Charlotte.

"Where do you live, Mamma?" Charlotte asked.

"Just above the shop, there."

"And she is very lucky to have such a nice room in the best part of Gothenburg," said Nils.

"Well …" Christina said, cocking her head to one side. "It is a nice part of Gothenburg, Nils. But I have hardly seen the rest of Gothenburg since coming home … and my Bo …" Her face crumpled, she gasped a shaky breath, then pulled herself together. She took Charlotte's hand and led her through the bakery to the kitchen, through the baking room with its large electric oven, and out to a yard at the back of the building. They ascended a metal staircase. At the top was a fire door that led onto a landing inside the house. Standing in the centre of the landing, carrying a bundle of laundry, was a tall blonde woman. Her eyebrows furrowed when she saw Christina and Charlotte.

"Christina?" She looked at them both with curiosity.

"Erica, this is my daughter, Baroness Freya Saumures. She has come to take me back to England," Christina said with pride.

"Who is going to iron these sheets and aprons then?" Erica looked shocked. She barged past Charlotte. Christina, with Charlotte in tow, followed her into a large room with a window overlooking the courtyard. Shelves were piled high with linen and blankets, and an ironing board stood in the centre of the worn pink and yellow carpet. A bed was pushed up against a wall, a basin at its foot. It was stiflingly warm.

"This is where I live, Freya, in the airing cupboard."

"You should be grateful, Christina," Erica said, turning to Charlotte with an ingratiating smile. "It's impossible to find anywhere to live in this area, with all the students."

Charlotte kept a steady expression. "Tell me, Mamma, were the Olofssons not your friends?"

"Nils and I took poor Christina in after she returned to Sweden." Erica Olofsson seemed flustered. "It was all we could do. She had no family or friends other than us. We had no idea she had a daughter, madame."

"Well …" Charlotte looked around the drab room, at Christina's meagre possessions on her pot-cupboard and the shelf above the basin. "After what she has been through, during the war, she deserves to be pampered by her daughter in England. Pack up, Mamma, we shall leave these friends of yours."

As Charlotte called Christina "mamma", she felt a stab of emotion in her throat. Christina was the closest she had ever had to a mother.

*

When Christina arrived with Charlotte at Burton Park Place, she was welcomed by Ferdi and Theodora. Charlotte tried to get Christina to rest and relax, but all Christina wanted to do was to look after the household like a motherly housekeeper.

Ferdi and Charlotte enjoyed each other's company. They listened to music and read, sometimes close together on the sofa, like a loving couple.

Every other month, Charlotte would invite a highly select few guests – no more than twelve – to dinner and entertainment. The entertainment consisted mainly of a virtuoso opera singer, or a pianist. Most of these performers were celebrities before the war but because of their nationality, and sometimes their religion, found they were unable to perform. Ferdi had a friend who was a former famous conductor, who found these performers.

At Burton Park Place, Charlotte and Theodora became quite an attraction to the local nobility. The rumours of two exotic, mysterious and attractive women living with a handsome but introverted baron in the middle of the Sussex countryside caused a stir in the staid environs of the Home Counties. Uninvited callers were actively discouraged. Ferdi had employed the services of bodyguards – the Tanner twins – to ensure their privacy and safety. Charlotte and Theodora were not sure what the threat was, or where it would come from.

The day after his retirement from British Intelligence, Sir Sussex Tremayne came to dinner.

"What are you going to do with yourself, Commodore?" Bernard asked.

"I am going to do nothing, Major Trent. I don't have a wife or children to worry about, just a garden and a pheasant shoot to keep me occupied." Sir Sussex turned to Ferdi. "I heard a strange story the other day, Ferdinand."

"Really, sir?"

"This should interest you as well, my dear." He spoke to Charlotte. "I heard that the house you were held in by the SS, in Avenue Foch, used to belong to Sir Jason Barrett's mother, Lady Joy Barrett. And that it was passed onto her granddaughter when she died, before the war." Charlotte felt her face redden, but luckily the lights were low.

Ferdi said, "I heard that as well, sir. And that Charlotte Barrett—"

"I believe she was called Charlotte de Tournet," Sir Sussex said.

"Well … Charlotte de Tournet, had disappeared."

Ferdi looked at Charlotte. She was feeling very uncomfortable. When he knew Sir Sussex was not looking, Ferdi tilted his head, questioningly, silently asking her to reveal her true identity.

"I believe, Ferdinand, she must be dead, or she would've come forward by now, now that the war is over." Sir Sussex looked directly at Charlotte. "What do you think, my dear?"

Charlotte's heart was pumping. Everybody at the table was watching her. Just as the table went quiet, Christina came through the dining room door, carrying a tray of apple pie and custard.

"Here we are, Freya, your pudding. I am afraid it is not real custard." She placed the tray in front of Charlotte. She was then aware of some tension in the room. "Oh, should I have called you Baroness?"

"No, no, Mamma. Come and join us. You should have got Rupert to serve this."

"He is too slow and gets in the way. He's a man." She went over to Sir Sussex, who stood with a broad smile over his bearded face. "I have some port, Sir Sussex. Would you care for some port with your apple pie? Sit, sit, sit."

"Sadly, I will have to refuse, madame. Port and I are no longer the friends we once were; it is now so bad for me. I can only have one glass of red wine a day, no brandy or whisky." He gallantly drew out a chair. "Will you not join us?"

"No, Sir Sussex. Thank you, but I am in the middle of a card game with your chauffeur and I'm winning." There was a ripple of laughter.

When they had eaten their pudding, Charlotte rose. "Theodora and I will go to the drawing room for our coffee, and leave you to your cigars, gentlemen." The men all stood as the ladies left the room.

"Tell me, Major Trent, about your war adventures. I believe you were part of the Comet Line. I hasten to add, I was head of war intelligence, so I do know about these things."

"Well, I am thankful I got through the war virtually in one piece, sir. Not many of us did."

"Indeed, Trent. I believe you were compromised?" Ferdi offered Sir Sussex a cigar from a humidor. "Oh, good show, Ferdinand! Where on earth do you get cigars from?"

"They are rather old. They have been here since well before the war, so they taste a little strange."

"Never mind. Well, Trent, did you ever gather who the traitor was?"

"We believe it was a Canadian airman called Frank Ruby. We had a Spanish girl who guided the escapers over into Spain. Once via San Sebastian to Bilbao, and once via a tiny village in the Pyrenees called Frontera del Portalet, as the San Sebastian route became highly dangerous. When she got to the village, Frank Ruby was waiting for her and the three airmen she was taking over. The three airmen were shot but Sara – the Spanish girl – got away with some injuries. She managed to get to Madrid – where she is from – and sent me a coded telegram warning me to get out of Le Tuko. The telegram was too late. It arrived minutes before the French police and the Gestapo appeared. I got my team away and I was clearing up when I got caught. The rest you know."

"What happened to the Spanish girl?"

"She died, I believe, of her wounds."

Sir Sussex puffed away on his cigar. "Shame," he said. He turned to Ferdi. "Madame Theodora is an interesting young woman. Do you know how she knows of the demise of Jean de Tournet?"

"She was there, with Freya, when the house was bombed. Nobody would have survived the explosion." Ferdi was finding these questions uncomfortable. He had already been officially debriefed by Sir Sussex. "But I told you all this last month, sir."

"Did you?" Sir Sussex had feigned poor memory before. "Getting old, Ferdinand. I won't talk any more about the war."

"I would be grateful for that." Ferdi stood and put his cigar in an ashtray. "Let's join the ladies."

Charlotte sat quietly in the drawing room, shoes off, legs curled up, hugging a pillow on her lap. She was watching Theodora and Bernard laughing at something Bernard had said. Sir Sussex and Ferdi were looking at photographs of Ferdi's mother and father. Charlotte was debating whether to confess to Sir Sussex who she really was.

Theodora thought Charlotte should confess to her true identity, mainly so she could claim back her entitlement to Nineteen Avenue Foch – no one would believe she had left the house to Theodora. And, as Ferdi had pointed out, Sir Jason could easily claim entitlement to the house, being a Barrett as opposed to, as Theodora put it, "a Turkish whore". But Charlotte was not particularly bothered about the house. It had been mostly destroyed by bombs in any case.

What was holding her back from revealing her true identity to Sir Sussex? Nothing. Except, she enjoyed being Freya, she felt safer somehow. Perhaps she would eventually come forward as being Charlotte. But not now. She would enjoy the peace and quiet being Baroness Freya Saumures. Her war adventures were over. She had no wish to do anything else but look forward to a peaceful, uneventful life with Ferdi, with Theodora as a companion, and Christina to look after her. Maybe one day she would even write a book about her war.

Epilogue

Sir Jason Barrett MP was pleased to be asked to be a junior minister in the Foreign Office. However, he was only in government for seven months. He then found himself in the Shadow Cabinet for nearly exactly seven years until Mr Churchill was made prime minister again in October 1951.

In 1951, Sir Jason became the Under-Secretary of State for the Home Department. This gave him access to the section responsible for reappraising German prisoners of war in Britain and the British territories, and sending them back to Germany. A selection of low-risk former German officers and other ranks were allowed to return to their homeland in 1946, where they would either complete their sentence at Landsberg Prison or be released early. The government wanted to send German POWs back to Germany as they were taking jobs from returning British servicemen.

During an inspection tour of Landsberg Prison in Lech, near Munich, Sir Jason took the opportunity to stage an emergency meeting of the WASP board, the first since the beginning of the war, at his castle, overlooking Lake Constance. Schloss Friedrich was an eighteen-century Baroque palace, small in comparison to the other castles littered around the vast lake, the banks of which were also shared with Austria and Switzerland. Importantly, the castle stood only a hundred and forty kilometres from Landsberg Prison, and a hundred and thirty kilometres from Zürich in Switzerland, from where most of the men gathered around the meeting table had travelled.

"Gentlemen, this is our first meeting since before the war. I am grateful for your attendance." Sir Jason addressed the group of distinguished-looking men. Beside him sat Jane Gardener, an attractive, pale-skinned young woman, dressed in black, busy organising pieces of paper.

"I am especially grateful to welcome Mr Donald Rushton, from America." Sir Jason nodded towards a man looking uneasy at the other end of the table of eight men. "Also, we have Tristan Langer, two men from the former Reich, and Boris Quint – he was our man in Moscow but was betrayed by a German communist. They are both former *Abwehr* agents. Quint had to fake his own death in Gibraltar." All eyes turned to the heavily bearded face of Boris Quint, who sat with his eyes cast down at the mahogany table, not acknowledging Sir Jason's introduction.

"May I say something, Sir Jason?" A man rose and took a lawyerly grasp of the lapels on his black jacket.

"Please do, Lord Rathmore."

"Gentlemen" – he turned to Jane Gardener – "Madame." She gave him a thin smile. "May I thank the director general, Sir Jason, for the work he has done for our cause."

"Hear, hear," echoed around the table.

"However, it pains me to say, WASP is no longer a force to be reckoned with. We have been gelded and let down badly by the Germans and the United States of America."

"Lord Rathmore." Langer stood. "I must object—"

"I agree with Lord Rathmore," said Rushton. "I also blame the United Kingdom, for not joining with Germany in attacking Russia!"

"And the United States" – Rathmore turned on Donald Rushton – "could have helped a lot more. Even Joseph McCarthy would not help us."

"That is because he was more interested in the rise of communism within America," Rushton conceded. "However, he did not trust the unwarranted secrecy surrounding WASP."

"Gentlemen" – Sir Jason put up his hands – "we cannot go this recriminatory route. It is done. The communists have most of Eastern Europe, and most, if not all, of our past work has been squandered." Jason sighed. "We now have some other issues to address. I have to confess, our organisation has been in danger of exposure since 1945. A Luxembourger, of all things, Baron Olivier Ferdinand Saumures, worked for the British Intelligence throughout the war, gathering information on Nazis and other like-minded people. In 1939, I recruited a man called Franz-Joseph Deller to keep an eye on Saumures. They were friends and fellow art students in the nineteen twenties."

"How did you manage this, Sir Jason? Isn't he the son of General Werner Deller?" Langer asked.

"He is. However, he killed my late sister, Alice." There was a collective intake of breath in astonishment around the table. "By accident, he claims. I threatened him with exposure to the French authorities if he did not keep me informed on what Saumures was up to. He turned out to be not particularly clever and an inebriate. Unfortunately, he also proved to be a poor informant."

Sir Jason sighed loudly. "I had unwisely, it transpired, told him I was the director general of WASP. Mainly because he had seen me at Hitler's headquarters in 1939, just as England – or should I say Great Britain and her Allies – went to war." A sense of uneasiness pervaded amongst the men gathered around the table. Jason left out that he had also instructed Deller to remove fifteen valuable paintings from Nineteen Avenue Foch, and to ensure they were brought back to England.

"Do you know, gentlemen?" Lord Rathmore looked peevish. "We have not achieved what we were set up to accomplish. We should disband this movement and regroup when there is more popular demand. Look at the world today." Lord Rathmore stood for emphasis. "We have Mao Zedong and communist China, the communists at war with the West in Korea, and the USSR taking over most of Eastern Europe. We have not really had any effect in subjugating communism, have we?" The men started talking together, some protesting at Lord Rathmore's comments, some supporting him.

"That's a little unfair!" said John Alderson, who was sitting to Sir Jason's left. "Lord Rathmore, we so nearly achieved our goals. We helped get Herr Hitler into power; General Franco still rules in Spain after WASP rescued him, with the help of Mr Quint and Captain Langer here, and placed him on the Spanish throne, as it were, where he is today. Sir Jason himself was able to guide the German army into France and take over Paris. He helped with advantageous negotiations at Vichy to ensure any partition would not include the Atlantic coastline, and we have agents that have infiltrated most every communist group in America and Europe."

"To what end, Mr Alderson, may I ask?" Lord Rathmore was on his feet again, looking about the table for support. "Hitler made bad mistakes: going after the Jews was a huge blunder, as was the non-aggression pact with Russia at the start of the war. Alienating America and Great Britain when, together with Japan, we could have removed communism from the world. Now Hitler's dead, Japan has been flattened and emasculated; our only hope of defeating communism in the East has gone up in a mushroom cloud. Because of this defeat in Europe and the East, we – all of us here – are at risk of being executed for treason!" Lord Rathmore turned to Sir Jason. "And now Sir Jason has revealed there is a file out there with our names on it, being used by someone as some kind of bargaining chip."

"What is the point of WASP today, Sir Jason?" Sir Henry Channing asked.

All eyes rested on Sir Jason, who sat at the end of the table, his hands linked behind his head.

"We are going to have to get rid of this Baron Saumures, Sir Jason," Rushton said eventually. "And I believe we are going to have to disband WASP."

"I am planning just that, Mr Rushton," said Sir Jason, feeling a little bruised by Lord Rathmore's rant. "I have plans to eliminate Saumures and to remove all evidence of WASP's existence. As Lord Rathmore concluded, we have not succeeded in our task to eradicate communism in Europe or the East, and we are highly unlikely to do so in the future."

"What about killing Saumures?" Rushton asked.

"I believe I have the man to do it," Sir Jason said quietly. "We have quite a few people to dispose of, to ensure our organisation is not compromised."

Jane Gardener slid over a buff file. Sir Jason opened it up.

"If we are disbanding WASP," Quint asked, "what is to become of the funds in the bank? Is there not a substantial balance in the bank in Zürich?"

"Gentlemen, Mr Quint has asked about our funding. The answer is that our finances, at present, are not exactly buoyant. Francesca Dioré has discontinued financing WASP, and, as far as I can gather from Tristan Langer, here, the *Krieg Gegen den Kommunismus* in Germany has ceased to exist. But DTS – my steel company – is still making money for WASP."

"There is still a substantial amount that was confiscated from Jews in Germany, Austria and Poland." Quint was looking critically at Sir Jason.

"Gentlemen, I anticipated this conversation. I have here the WASP accounts. The balance will be split equally amongst you. I will retain ten thousand pounds to fund the search and removal of the WASP files. Until these files on WASP and on me are made safe, and the protagonists neutralised, we must destroy all evidence in our possession as to the existence of WASP."

"How do you propose to neutralise, as you say, Saumures and Deller, Sir Jason?" asked Quint. "I can offer a man to assist you to rid us of these people."

"I am grateful, Mr Quint. However, I have a man in mind that will serve us well." Sir Jason picked up the buff file in front of him. "This man – I will not say his name – served in the Nazi Party and the SS since a young man. He has the Blood Order for his pivotal role in the assassination of General von Schleicher, Ernst Röhm and Gregor Strasser in 1934. He can pass himself off as a Frenchman – he speaks perfect French – and he speaks English."

"Where is this man?" Lord Rathmore asked, looking around the room.

"He is presently serving a twenty-year jail sentence for his so-called crimes during the war. Luckily, he had the foresight to adopt a separate identity, only to find his new identity had served as a guard commander of a Jewish work crew. In my current governmental position, I can get him released early."

"Sir Jason" – Lord Rathmore stood and gripped his lapels again – "assassins aside, is there any kind of future, do you envisage, for WASP?"

"What happens to our agents?" Sir Henry Channing asked. "Do we keep paying them?"

"Stop all operations," Sir Jason said. "These agents will have to go to sleep, as it were, as we are not going to be able to take any further action until we have more political clout and any intelligence on our organisation, or risk of exposure, has been eradicated. That means your agents will have to be brought back or disowned. I can help with any agents that cause problems."

There was a stunned silence.

"Thank you, Sir Jason, for this frank meeting," Lord Rathmore said after a good two minutes. "I think I can talk for the assembled here, we are somewhat surprised, and disappointed we are not able to do any more. As politicians, I trust you and Sir Henry, with me in the Lords, can urge Mr Churchill to counter any further demands on the autonomy of free countries. That we do everything possible to boot out the communists from Allied countries such as Poland."

"Hear, hear!"

"To conclude, Sir Jason, we are grateful for your leadership and trust. When it is right to do so, we should revive the cause, possibly with a younger leader but steered by you. I believe we should be more upfront and open. This secrecy, apart from anything else, is exhausting."

"Yes, yes, agreed." The men tapped the table in accord. Rathmore sat, and Sir Jason rose.

"Thank you, my lord. Now there is peace, to some degree, we must be cautious not to be caught. Some may say our role was traitorous. Passing on military strategies to Germany before and during the war, and accepting funding from the estates of executed Jews, may now be considered a crime."

"But we were only acting in the best interest of our countries!" Tristan Langer said.

"I should add, we must thank those who are no longer with us. Who helped valiantly throughout the war, against communism and socialist parties." Sir Jason sounded uncharacteristically emotional. Both Jane Gardener and

John Alderson looked on with concern. "Jean de Tournet for one; my fellow director in DTS – De Tournet Steel – is still missing. Admiral Canaris may have betrayed him. Our gratitude must go to Francesca Dioré, who contributed funds to WASP. Sadly, she was badly injured when confronted by the Free French Army during the invasion of Paris in 1945. She has become a recluse. And, of course, our friends in the Nazi Party, some killed at Nuremberg on trumped-up charges.

"I will leave you now. I will step down as director general of WASP. That concludes the meeting. I doubt we will meet again. Please remember to remove any and all evidence of your involvement with WASP for your own protection. You can contact me on this telephone number only." Jane Gardener handed everyone a sheet of paper. "Please do not use any names, just your code name, which you will find on the top of the page."

The whole table stood and applauded.

*

"Miss Gardener, have you managed to track down Jost Krupp's whereabouts yet?"

"Yes, Sir Jason. He is going under the name of Günther Wolff. He was not easy to find as he had escaped from a prison hospital bed in Rennes. He was eventually caught and sent to Britain. He is now in the hospital wing at Dancer's Hill POW camp in South Mimms, here in England."

"Is he going to be fit enough for what we want him for?"

"Yes, I believe so, sir. Here's a file I have compiled to put before the parole board for prisoner-of-war repatriation." Jane placed the buff file in front of Sir Jason. He opened it to reveal a photo of a dark man with a long scar under his left eye, running down over his cheek. "He was injured in 1944 by an escaping enemy agent. I believe he has exaggerated his injuries for a comfortable life in a hospital. He is ruthless and will be of great use to us."

Sir Jason paused. He scratched his chin whilst reading the file.

"He is only six years into his twenty-year sentence '*for being guard commander of a construction team of Jewish prisoners, building a labour camp at Schirmeck, in Alsace, between April 1941 and June 1941*,'" Sir Jason read. "How did he get his new identity?"

"Major Krupp had taken the identity of Captain Günther Wolff after executing him at the Oradour-sur-Glane massacre."

"He killed a fellow officer?"

"Wolff was underperforming – he objected to the treatment of Jews, according to his then commanding officer, *SS-Sturmbannführer* Adolf Diekmann. He asked Krupp to get rid of him … apparently."

"We need an assassin, Miss Gardener. He seems to be a killer."

"Without doubt, sir."

"Why is there no more information about Krupp?"

"I presume his files are somewhere in Germany. He is technically dead after being killed at Oradour-sur-Glane. He told me he swapped his identity tags with Wolff's."

"You know Krupp?" Sir Jason was surprised.

"Yes, sir. I met him in February 1944, after leaving here to go back to France to see my dying brother. Krupp was captured, along with me and an SS colonel, by the French Army in Paris. Luckily, he had assumed his Wolff identity. I escaped to return here as Jane Gardener."

"Well … with your recommendation, I will try for an early release. I doubt I will get him out for at least a year. If I do obtain a release, will he abscond, do you think?"

"No, sir, he has nowhere to go. His family estate is in north-east Germany and in the communist Russian sector."

Sir Jason sat and stared at the image of the man he hoped would eliminate any WASP agents who could reveal Sir Jason's identity, and help to covertly retrieve the files that had been hidden by Baron Saumures. Jason's position in government was being continually threatened by the existence of these files. He was unable to retrieve them without opening up the dangerous possibility that they could be released to the security services, or worse, the press. There was nothing John Alderson and Special Branch could do, or the redoubtable Jane Gardener, without putting themselves in danger of getting caught. Bringing in Krupp, a qualified killer, would rid Jason of his enemies. And should Krupp get caught, there would be no link to Jason.

"Find Krupp or Herr Wolff, Miss Gardener, and get the process of early release going. Do not mention my name; do everything through the parole service. It is imperative that there is no link between me and Krupp."

"Yes, Sir Jason," Jane Gardener said happily.

Jane Gardener – Brunhilda Baumgartner – nearly danced out of Sir Jason's office. She ecstatically clasped the file to her chest.

She was going to see Jost Krupp and get him released.

Author's Notes

Some notes about some of the real characters, places and events in this book.

During the Second World War, **Avenue Foch** in Paris became known as the "Street of Horrors", mainly because of the tortures and executions metered out at Eighty-Four Avenue Foch, by the Gestapo, from June 1940 to August 1944. They also took over Eighty-Two Avenue Foch. On entering Paris in June 1940, the Germans commandeered many large properties, hotels and municipal buildings, including the **Hôtel Majestic** on Avenue Kléber, Paris. This hotel served as the headquarters of the German military high command in France during the German occupation of Paris. The hotel ballroom was used to house captured Germans as described towards the end of the book. After extensive and costly renovations, it reopened as The Peninsula, a magnificent five-star hotel. *Source: Historyhit.com, Wikipedia.*

Alois Brunner was commander of the Drancy internment camp outside Paris from June 1943 to August 1944, from which nearly 24,000 people were deported. It is estimated he was responsible for the death of over 128,000 Jews. His fate is unknown; it is thought he escaped justice and is said to have died of old age – about 97 – in Syria. *Source: Wikipedia and The Jewish Virtual Library.*

Violette Szabo was a British–French Special Operations Executive (SOE) agent, a posthumous recipient of the George Cross. On her second mission into occupied France, Szabo was captured by the German army, interrogated, tortured and deported to Ravensbrück concentration camp in Germany, where she was executed. She was not executed by Jost Krupp at Drancy. *Source: Wikipedia*

Admiral Wilhelm Canaris was head of the *Abwehr* – the German Secret Service. He was an ardent anti-communist and was a supporter of Hitler to begin with. However, he was increasingly upset by the persecution of the Jews and the mass killings of the Polish people. Despite being a high-ranking Nazi, he was responsible for saving the lives of a large number of Jews and conspired to assassinate Hitler. He was eventually arrested for treason by Heinrich Himmler and was executed:

"In the closing days of World War II, in the grey morning hours of April 9, 1945, gallows were erected hastily in the courtyard. Wilhelm Canaris, Dietrich Bonhoeffer, Major General Hans Oster, Judge Advocate General Carl Sack, Captain Ludwig Gehre – all were ordered to remove their clothing and were led down the steps under the trees to the secluded place of execution before hooting SS guards. Naked under the scaffold, they knelt for the last time to pray – they were hanged, their corpses left to rot." *Sources: The Holocaust: Crimes, Heroes and Villains.*

As referred to in this book, Canaris was taken to the Convent of the Nuns of the "Passion of Our Blessed Lord", 127 Rue de la Santé, Paris, where he met a member of the Jade Amicol Resistance network, run by the British Intelligence Service and MI6, thought to be the co-leader of Jade Amicol, code name Colonel Arnould or Colonel Olivier. Canaris wanted to know the terms for peace if Germany neutralised Hitler. Churchill's reply, sent to him two weeks later, was simple: "Unconditional surrender". *Source: Wikipedia, www.military-history.fandom.com/wiki/Wilhelm_Canaris*

Canaris became disillusioned, not only with Hitler and Himmler but also the entire Nazi system as a political phenomenon. *Source: Hans Bernd Gisevius, in his book from 1947,* To the Bitter End.

My father and stepmother have lived in the area of France called the Gers for nearly thirty years. Bertrand's house, Le Tuko, was inspired by their house near St Puy. When holidaying with our children there, we witnessed these little rodents – locally called *courbets* – scampering over the wall and sunbathing in the morning sun. Sadly, I was told by my father that all these little creatures were eaten by a pine marten the following year.

Most of the terrible things the Nazis did are well documented. My wife and I, whilst on holiday, stayed in St-Émilion, near Bordeaux, to visit the vineyard Château la Gaffeliere, where I had helped with *la vendange* when I was a student in 1972. Château du Pevillon is a fictional vineyard but is based on a neighbouring vineyard that was commandeered by the Germans during the war. It has been swallowed up by neighbouring vineyards since, apparently.

We then went on to the village of **Oradour-sur-Glane**. Early on the morning of 10 June 1944, *SS-Sturmbannführer* Adolf Diekmann, of *Der Führer* Regiment of the 2nd Waffen SS Panzer Division, *Das Reich*, was approached by two members of the Milice, a collaborating paramilitary force of the Vichy Regime. They claimed that a Waffen SS officer was being held prisoner by the Resistance in Oradour-sur-Vayres. The captured officer was alleged to be *SS-Sturmbannführer* Helmut Kämpfe. Due to a breakdown in communications, they attacked Oradour-sur-Glane, a nearby village. *Source: Wikipedia* and *www.oradour.info*.

I interpreted these awful events through the eyes of the village doctor and mayor, Dr Desourteaux. The doctor's description of his experiences during the massacre is taken from eyewitness accounts of the only six survivors. Krupp and Wolff are the only fictitious characters in the story. The original village has remained untouched since that awful June in 1944 as a monument to the Nazi atrocity. It left a lasting impression on us. A journey through the ruined village is the opening scene in the 1973 television series *The World at War*, dramatically narrated by Lawrence Olivier.

The village was destroyed and 642 civilians, including women and children, were cruelly massacred by the German Waffen SS. A new village was built nearby after the war. President Charles de Gaulle ordered that the ruins of the old village be maintained as a permanent memorial and museum.

Printed in Great Britain
by Amazon